Brad took a few steps over to the light switch.

The thief gasped when he flipped it on.

But Brad was ready. He quickly turned the young robber around so they could face each other.

"Oh." Brad had the boy in his grip. Rather, he had *her* in his grip, he corrected himself.

"You're a girl." Brad could see she was more like a woman, but he was only starting to sort things out.

The woman glared at him. She had wispy blond hair that settled in soft curls around her face. And her face—she looked solemn and scared at the same time.

The only muscles that moved were her eyelids. She kept blinking.

"I dropped my glasses," she finally said.

Brad looked back and saw where her glasses had fallen on the floor. He also spotted on one of the café's tables a brown paper bag. Through a tear in it, he saw money…

Janet Tronstad was raised on a small ranch in the middle of Montana. Even though she has spent much of her life in cities, she still calls Montana home and has set most of her forty books there. Her books have been printed in various countries and their sales have put her on the *New York Times*, *USA TODAY* and *Publishers Weekly* bestseller lists. Janet currently lives in central California.

Allie Pleiter, an award-winning author and RITA® Award finalist, writes both fiction and nonfiction. Her passion for knitting shows up in many of her books and all over her life. Entirely too fond of French macarons and lemon meringue pie, Allie spends her days writing books and avoiding housework. Allie grew up in Connecticut, holds a BS in speech from Northwestern University and lives near Chicago, Illinois.

Mistletoe Redemption

New York Times Bestselling Author

Janet Tronstad

&

Allie Pleiter

2 Uplifting Stories

A Dry Creek Christmas and *Bluegrass Christmas*

LOVE INSPIRED
INSPIRATIONAL ROMANCE

LOVE INSPIRED®
INSPIRATIONAL ROMANCE

Recycling programs for this product may not exist in your area.

ISBN-13: 978-1-335-42995-7

Mistletoe Redemption

Copyright © 2022 by Harlequin Enterprises ULC

A Dry Creek Christmas
First published in 2004. This edition published in 2022.
Copyright © 2004 by Janet Tronstad

Bluegrass Christmas
First published in 2009. This edition published in 2022.
Copyright © 2009 by Alyse Stanko Pleiter

For questions and comments about the quality of this book, please contact us at CustomerService@Harlequin.com.

Love Inspired
22 Adelaide St. West, 41st Floor
Toronto, Ontario M5H 4E3, Canada
www.LoveInspired.com

Printed in U.S.A.

CONTENTS

A DRY CREEK CHRISTMAS

Janet Tronstad

In memory of my dear friend
Judy Eslick

For every one that exalteth himself
shall be abased; and he that humbleth
himself shall be exalted.
—*Luke* 18:14

Chapter One

Millie Corwin squinted and pushed her eyeglasses back into place. The night was full of snow clouds and there were no stars to help her see along this long stretch of Highway 94. Millie was looking for the sign that marked the side road leading into Dry Creek, Montana. She could barely see with the snow flurries.

What had she been thinking? When she had told the chaplain at the prison that she would honor Forrest's request, she hadn't thought about the fact that Christmas was in the middle of winter and Dry Creek was in the middle of Montana so she would, of course, be in the middle of snow.

She hated snow. Not that it made much difference. Snow or no snow, she had to be here.

Millie saw a sign and peered down the dark road that led into Dry Creek. Only one set of car tracks disturbed the snow that was falling. Hopefully that meant most people were home and in bed at this time of night. She planned to arrive in Dry Creek, do what she had to do, and then leave without anyone seeing her.

Millie turned the wheel of her car and inched her way closer to the little town.

She wished, and not for the first time, that Forrest had made a different final request of her while he was dying.

She met Forrest three years ago. He'd come into Ruby's, the coffee shop where she worked near the Seattle waterfront, and sat down at one of her tables. Millie must have taken Forrest's order a dozen times before he looked her in the eyes and smiled. There was something sweet about Forrest. He seemed as quiet and nondescript as she felt inside. He was restful compared with all of the tall, boisterous, loud men she'd learned to ignore at Ruby's.

It wasn't until he had been arrested, however, that she knew the whole truth about Forrest. He'd been a criminal since he was a boy and had, over the years, gotten deeper and deeper into crime until he'd eventually become a hit man. His last contract had been for someone in Dry Creek.

When Millie got over the shock of what Forrest was, she decided he still needed a friend. She had visited him while he was in prison, especially this past year when he'd been diagnosed with cancer. The odd thing was the sicker he got the more cheerful he became. He told her he'd found God in prison.

Millie was glad enough that Forrest had found religion if it made him happy. She smiled politely and nodded when he explained what a miracle it was that God could love a man like him.

Personally, Millie thought it would be a miracle if God loved anyone, but that it had more to do with God than the people He was supposed to love. However, since

Forrest was sick, she supposed it was good if Forrest thought God loved him and so she nodded pleasantly.

But when Forrest added that God loved her as well, she stopped nodding.

Of course, she kept smiling. Millie didn't want to offend either Forrest or God.

Then Forrest added that he was going to pray for her so she would know God's love, too. Millie could no longer keep smiling; she could barely keep quiet. She'd always kept a low profile with God and she figured that was the smart thing to do.

If God was anything like the other domineering males she'd seen—and there was no reason to think otherwise—then He looked out for His own interests first. If He noticed a person like her at all, it would only be to ask her to fetch Him a glass of water or another piece of toast or something else to make Him more comfortable.

Millie had grown up in a foster home where she was the one assigned to do chores. Usually, the chores consisted of cooking, doing laundry and taking care of the five boys in the home.

Millie didn't know if it was because she was easier to order around than the boys or if her foster mother really believed males were privileged, but—whatever the reason—she soon realized she was doing all of the work for everyone in the house and, instead of being grateful, the boys only became more demanding.

By the time Millie left that home, she'd had enough of dealing with loud, demanding males.

And those boys were mere mortals. She figured God would be even more demanding. No, it was best if God didn't even know her name. She didn't want anyone mentioning her to Him. She had no desire to be God's waitress.

Still, Millie wasn't good at telling people what to do or not to do, and she certainly couldn't tell a dying friend to stop praying. So she changed the subject with Forrest and asked what kind of pudding he had had for lunch. She would just have to hope Forrest came to his senses on his own.

He didn't. Every letter he wrote after that said he was praying for her.

When Forrest died, the chaplain at the prison forwarded a final letter Forrest had asked him to mail.

In the letter, Forrest said he had tried to right some of the wrongs in his life. He hadn't done anything about Dry Creek, however, and he asked Millie to go to the place and try to restore the little town's innocence.

"I fear I've made them distrust strangers and I regret it," he wrote and then added, "Please go there, without telling them who sent you, and do something to restore their faith in strangers. And when you go, go at Christmas."

Millie winced when she read that line in the letter.

Even though Forrest had gone to Dry Creek at Christmas himself, Millie knew it was more than that that made him suggest the holiday. Forrest knew Christmas was a lonely time for her.

Not that she didn't like Christmas. It was just that she always felt like she was on the outside looking in when it came to the holidays. She'd made Forrest tell her several times about the little town with the Christmas pageant and the decorations. It all sounded like a picture on one of those nostalgic calendars.

In the foster home where Millie grew up, they had

never done much to celebrate Christmas. Her foster
mother always said she was too busy for that kind of
thing. Millie had tried to make a fake Christmas tree
one year out of metal clothes hangers and tin foil, but
the boys had laughed at it and knocked it down.

Millie had never had a Christmas like the one Forrest witnessed in Dry Creek and now, it appeared, he
wanted her to have one.

Even though the thought of spending Christmas in
Dry Creek held a kind of fatal attraction for Millie, she
would never have agreed to Forrest's request if he were
alive and she could tell him face-to-face why his idea
wouldn't work.

For one thing, Forrest was asking her to make the
little town trust strangers again, and she wasn't the kind
of person who could do something that would make a
whole town change its mind about anything. Forrest
knew that.

Even more important, Millie suspected that if the
people in Dry Creek knew who had sent her they
wouldn't trust her even if she did manage to sound persuasive. After all, Forrest had tried to kill a woman in
their town two years ago. The people certainly wouldn't
welcome a friend of Forrest's, let alone want to celebrate
Christmas with her.

But Millie couldn't tell Forrest any of those things
when she got the letter, because—well, he was dead. So
she did the next best thing. She called the chaplain who
had mailed the letter and tried to explain why she wasn't
the person to fulfill Forrest's last request. The chaplain
listened and then told her Forrest had said she might
call and that Forrest wanted her to know his request
was important or he wouldn't have asked her to do it.

All of which was why Millie was here in the dark. She couldn't let Forrest down.

Of course, she couldn't do exactly what he wanted, either. Therefore, she made her own plan. She decided she would do what she could to restore Dry Creek's trust in strangers and she would do it at Christmas, but she would do it without actually talking to a single person. In fact, she'd do it without even seeing another person's face.

Forrest would have to be content with that.

Hopefully, she'd be able to do what she needed to do tonight, Millie told herself as she saw a few house lights ahead of her. She had gone down the road that led into Dry Creek. It was Saturday, December 22. If she left her presents in the café tonight, the people of Dry Creek would discover them on Monday, Christmas Eve Day.

By Christmas, the people of Dry Creek should all be talking about the kindness of the stranger who'd come to town in the middle of the night to bring them a wonderful surprise and who then left without even waiting to be thanked.

Maybe they'd call her the Christmas Stranger. Millie rolled her tongue over that phrase. Christmas Stranger. She rather liked the sound of that, she decided.

Brad Parker shoved his Stetson further down on his head and squinted as he tried to read his watch in the dark. Snow was falling outside and the heat from his old diesel engine barely kept the ice from forming on the windshield of his pickup. It was a sad night in Dry Creek, Montana when a thirty-four-year-old man ended his Saturday evening hiding out in his pickup without even a woman beside him to make it look like he had a reason for being there.

The worst part was, he'd already been parked behind the closed café for the past half hour, well off the road so no one could see him, and wondering when it would be safe to go back to the bunkhouse at the Elkton Ranch.

The last time he'd gotten back to the bunkhouse before dawn on a Saturday night was because of a tooth that was so infected Dr. Norris had insisted on opening the clinic to fix it even though it was Sunday—and everyone in the whole county knew Dr. Norris never missed a Sunday church service if he could help it.

Brad had been in enough pain at the time that he'd said yes when the good doctor asked him to come to church some Sunday morning. And, Brad told himself, he meant to do just that—someday. No one would be able to say Brad Parker didn't keep his word, even if they could say he was a fool to make a promise like that in the first place when he didn't own a tie and would rather have the root canal all over again than actually go to church.

Brad ran his tongue around his teeth. They all felt fine to him. He did an internal check for other pain and found none. He appeared to be in fine health. Which was a pity, in a way, because the guys would understand him making a short evening of it if he had reason to suspect he was dying or something.

If he wasn't dying, though, they were sure to guess the truth, and that was why Brad was sitting here in the cold. It was bad enough that he knew he always got depressed around Christmas. He didn't want to have to hear about it from the other guys in the bunkhouse, as well.

He'd left the poker party early because he was heading out to another game on the other side of town. He got halfway to the game and decided he didn't want to play anymore. All he wanted was to go home. Since he was already on the road, he just kept driving until he pulled into Dry Creek.

That's when Brad realized he couldn't show up at the bunkhouse yet. If Charlie hadn't stopped going to Billings on Saturday nights, no one would even be in the bunkhouse to hear him slip in early. But Charlie fancied himself the grandfather of "his boys," and he was sure to make a big deal about Brad and Christmas.

Brad shook his head. He never should have told the guys that his parents had been killed in a car accident just before Christmas when he was small. It had been five years ago that he'd mentioned it, and every year he still caught one or two of them watching him with a certain look in their eyes just before Christmas. He didn't know why they made such a big deal about it.

It wasn't a crime to get depressed at Christmas anyway. Brad made it through the other fifty-one weeks of the year just fine. If he wanted to feel sorry for himself one week out of the year, the rest of the world should just let him.

Still, as long as he was going to bed early tonight, he might as well get up early tomorrow morning. Maybe, since his week was already shot because of Christmas, he should just keep his promise to Dr. Norris and show up in church.

Yeah, Brad thought to himself grimly as he tried to make himself comfortable on the old seat of his pickup, he'd just get all of the bad stuff out of the way and start the new year fresh. No point in wasting a good weekend next year by going to church.

That's what he'd do. Get rid of Christmas and church in one fell swoop. But first he'd give Charlie another half hour to go to bed just in case the old man might surprise Brad and actually be asleep when he got home.

It was sure going to be some Christmas, Brad said to himself as he leaned back against the seat of his pickup and closed his eyes. Yeah, it was going to be some Christmas.

Chapter Two

Millie held her breath as the shadows of Dry Creek came into view. The little town was just as she had pictured it when Forrest told her about it. The clouds had parted and the moon was shining even though a few flakes of snow were still falling. There was one street lamp, and it gave off enough light that the flakes looked like glitter floating over the darkened town. A lone pair of tire tracks had packed down a thin path of snow on the road into town, but elsewhere snow sat soft and fluffy alongside the dozen or so buildings.

Millie could see the church with its steeple. The house next to the church had lights in the second floor windows and filmy white curtains. That must be the parsonage where the woman whom Forrest had been sent to kill lived. At the time, the woman had just been passing through Dry Creek when two little boys decided she must be an angel, and therefore just what they needed for the town's Christmas pageant.

Forrest always shook his head when he told Millie about the little boys who thought they'd found their own personal angel. Forrest had never known that kind of innocence in his own life. Of course, he hadn't been sent to kill the woman because the boys thought she was an angel. The woman had witnessed a crime, and that made some big guys nervous enough to want her out of the way.

Forrest was particularly glad he hadn't succeeded in that job.

The woman, Glory Beckett, was now married to Matthew Curtis, the man who was pastor at the church. The pastor also worked at the hardware store down the street, and Millie wished she could see that building more clearly. Millie's favorite memory of Forrest's Dry Creek stories was the part about the old men who sat around the woodstove in that building. If she were coming into town like a regular person, she would like to sit with those old men some morning and listen to them argue about cattle prices. It all sounded so peaceful. She truly wished—

Millie shook her head. She couldn't afford to dwell on those kind of wishes. A life around a cozy wood stove in Dry Creek wasn't meant for someone like her. She had her tables at Ruby's. They might be filled with scruffy men who wanted more coffee, but that was what she had for the time being.

Millie dimmed her lights when she pulled close to the café. No one was around, but she didn't want her lights to shine into the windows of any of the houses farther down the road. She didn't pull in too close, because the snow wasn't packed down that far off the road and she didn't want to get stuck. She checked the mirror behind her as she turned off her lights. No one was coming.

Millie opened her car's door. Forrest had told her stories about the café, and so she knew the spare key was sitting under a certain rock on the porch. With any luck, she would be in the café and have her surprises delivered in less than ten minutes.

Brad wasn't sure what woke him up. It might have been the lights on the car that was driving into Dry Creek. Not that the lights themselves would have woken him up. It was when the driver dimmed the lights that something stirred his sleeping brain. When he heard the thud of a car door quietly shutting, he opened his eyes. Even then half of his brain was thinking that Linda was coming in early to open up and maybe he could get a cup of coffee.

He discarded that theory as soon as he thought it. Linda had closed the café for Christmas week so that she could go visit that boyfriend of hers in Los Angeles. Linda had said the town could use the café if anyone wanted to cook a Christmas Eve dinner like she had in the past, but so far no one had agreed to do the cooking. In any event, Linda wasn't even in the state of Montana.

Brad slid open his pickup door and woke up completely. The cold air pushing into the pickup was enough to get a man's attention. He wished he didn't have to go and investigate, but he saw little choice. Everyone knew Linda was gone, and if someone had mischief in mind, now was the time they would do it.

The snow softened Brad's footsteps as he walked along the side of the café. He looked in the corner of the window and saw a figure moving around inside. Whoever it was had thought to bring a flashlight, and the beam of the light was flickering around inside. The flashlight sealed the argument for Brad. No one who had any business being in there would bother with a flashlight when the light switch was right next to the door.

It must be some kid, Brad thought to himself. He could see the boy's shadow and judged him to be around eleven or twelve. Brad figured a boy that young would be more nuisance than trouble. Brad looked over at the car parked in front of the café. He didn't recognize it, but it was a kid's car all right—a beat-up old thing the color of crusty mustard. It looked like it was held together with rubber bands and bubble gum—but it was still a car. Which meant the boy was probably at least sixteen.

With any luck, Brad could deliver the boy back to his parents and that would be the end of it.

Millie's fingers were so cold she had a hard time keeping the flashlight steady. She had set the bag of flannel Santa socks at her feet and the other bag, the one with the hundred-dollar bills, on the table in front of her.

It was the perfect thing to do with the money Forrest had given her before he left for Dry Creek two years ago. Millie had tried to give the seventy-five hundred dollar bills to the police, but they didn't want them because they couldn't prove they were connected to a crime. She didn't want them because she couldn't prove they *weren't* connected to a crime. She had been poor all her life, but she'd never knowingly profited from the misery of others.

Millie had fretted about what to do with those bills until she'd realized they were the solution to her problem in Dry Creek. She'd give a bill to each person in Dry Creek along with a note saying the money was from a stranger. That would make them all trust strangers more, wouldn't it? A hundred dollars would do that to most people in Millie's opinion. It sure would have caused a stir with those boys in her old foster family.

Besides, she'd be able to get rid of the money and fulfill Forrest's request at the same time. It was brilliant. And the best part of all was, she wouldn't have to actually open her mouth and talk to anyone.

Millie supposed she should have pre-stuffed the socks and written her notes, but she had decided she would do that in the café. She wanted to think about how excited each person would be when they opened their socks and saw the money.

It had not been easy, but Millie had remembered the names of most of the people who lived in Dry Creek. Forrest had sprinkled his stories with a surprising number of names and, fortunately, they had stayed in her head. She'd written names on most of the socks. In her opinion, a present wasn't really a present unless it had a person's name on it.

Some of the names might be misspelled, but she was sure each stocking would find its owner. She even had a few labeled "Anyone," for those she might have missed. Most nights last month, after she finished at the coffee shop, she'd pick up the glue gun and personalize the Christmas socks. Before the glue dried, she sprinkled glitter on the writing.

She was proud of the socks. The money might be from Forrest, but the socks were from her.

Millie didn't know what made her think something was wrong. Maybe it was the fact that the air inside the café was suddenly a couple of degrees colder. Or maybe it was the darkness inside had grown just a shade deeper, like someone was blocking the moonlight that had been coming through the open door behind her. Whatever it was, she didn't have enough time to turn around before she felt the arms close around her.

Woosh. Millie felt her breath leave her as panic rose in her throat.

"What the—?" Brad revised his opinion of the juvenile delinquent he was apprehending. The boy might be small, but he wasn't puny. He had stomped on Brad's foot with all his might. The kid was wearing some kind of wool coat that made grabbing him difficult, but Brad had roped calves for the last twenty years and knew a thing or two about handling uncooperative creatures.

Brad grabbed the boy around the middle and hoisted him up in the air where his feet could do less damage. The boy gasped in outrage, but Brad didn't let that stop him.

"If you want me to put you down, you have to stop kicking," Brad finally said as he shifted his arms so that the kid was hanging on Brad's hip like a bag of grain. Brad had his arm hooked around his captive's stomach, and the boy's head was facing toward the café door. He wore enough wool to clothe a small army, and it bunched up around his middle. Brad was having a hard time keeping the boy from wiggling out of his arm so he could walk back to the light switch.

The boy must be deaf, because he sure wasn't doing what Brad had politely suggested. Which was what Brad would expect, considering the whole night had gone from bad to worse. Well, Brad decided, he'd had enough.

He took his other hand and pushed the wool coat up high enough so he could get a firm grip on the boy's stomach. The boy's shirt had come untucked in the struggle, and Brad figured his hand was firmly anchored around the boy's stomach.

"That's better," Brad said. The boy had gone still in his arm.

Brad took a couple of steps over to the light switch even though something was beginning to make him think he'd got a few things wrong. The boy must be even younger than Brad had figured.

His stomach was softer than anything Brad imagined you'd find on a boy of fifteen who lived around these parts. Maybe that was the kid's problem. No one had taught him to ride horses or wrestle calves. Brad doubted the boy had even done any summer farm work. That belly had never been scratched by lifting a hay bale or sliding under a broken-down tractor.

The boy gasped again when Brad flipped the light switch, but Brad was ready for him. This time he tipped the kid upright so they could face each other.

"Oh." Brad still had the boy in his grip, or rather—he corrected himself—he still had her—*her*—in his grip.

"You're a girl!" Brad could see she was more like a woman, but he was only starting to sort things out, and "girl" would do for now. He never should have left those poker games tonight.

The girl-woman just glared at him. She had green eyes and wispy blond hair that settled in soft curls around her face. And her face—she looked solemn and scared all at the same time. The only muscles that moved on her face were her eyelids. She kept blinking.

"You dropped my glasses," she finally said.

Brad looked back and he saw where her glasses had fallen to the floor. He also saw a brown paper bag with a long tear in it on top of one of the tables. Through the tear he saw money.

Brad whistled. "I guess I don't need to ask what you're doing here."

The woman went even stiffer in his arms.

"I'm not one to judge people," Brad continued as he carried her over to the brown paper bag. He began to wonder if the woman had been getting enough to eat. She sure didn't weigh much. He could carry her around on his hip like this for hours without tiring. "I figure you're poor enough that stealing some money from a cash drawer is tempting, but you'd be much better off getting a job."

The woman relaxed some. "I have a job."

"Now, there's no need to lie to me," Brad continued patiently. "No one's blaming you for needing help. But in this town we ask for help, we don't steal from each other."

"I'm not stealing."

For such a little bit of a woman, she sure was stubborn. Brad looked at the bag more closely and frowned. Why had Linda kept that kind of money in the café? Even though break-ins were rare around here, there was no point in tempting folks.

"What's your name anyway?"

"You don't know me. I'm a stranger."

Something about the way the woman said that irked Brad. "I wasn't planning to sit down and socialize or anything—I just asked your name."

"Oh. My name's Millie."

"Millie what?"

"Just Millie."

Brad sat down in the chair next to the table. As he

folded all six foot four of himself onto the chair, he shifted Millie so she sat on his knee.

Brad almost sighed. No wonder he had thought she was a kid. Even with her sitting on his lap, he still didn't meet her eye to eye. Which was a pity, because he'd been wondering if her eyes weren't more blue than green, and he'd been hoping to have another look. Of course, it wasn't because he was personally interested. It was just so he could answer the questions if he had to describe her for a police report. Looking down, he saw the top of her head. "How short are you anyway?"

That statement at least made Millie look up at him. Her face was no longer pale and scared. It was more pink and angry now. Of course, that was probably just because he'd been carrying her sideways.

"I'm just under five feet *tall*, not *short*," Millie said. "And I don't see what business it is of yours anyway."

Brad grinned. He'd always liked green eyes that threw spit darts at him. "Lady, everything about you is my business. At least until I can get the deputy sheriff to come pick you up."

That seemed to take Millie's attention away from him. She twisted around on his lap and looked at the door.

"Don't even think about making a run for it," Brad said. Until he said that, he had half a mind to give her a few dollars out of his own pocket and send her on her way. But he figured he should at least wait until she said she was sorry and promised to stop stealing from people.

"I don't run away," Millie announced.

Brad believed her. She sat as still as a stone on his lap, as if she was resigned to the worst. He didn't want to scare her. "Well, it's not like they'll probably lock you up or anything—you didn't even make a getaway."

Brad reached down and picked up Millie's glasses off of the floor, then gave them to her.

Millie took the glasses from him and settled them on her nose.

Brad frowned. Those glasses not only hid the golden tones in Millie's green eyes, they hid her face, as well. Without them, she was pretty in a quiet sort of a way. Her face was pale with freckles scattered across it. With her wispy blond hair and those solemn green eyes, she looked like pictures he'd seen of young girls living on the sun-bleached prairie a hundred years ago.

She didn't look like his ideal woman, of course. Her hair might be blond, but it didn't have any of the brazen look he preferred. He liked women with red lipstick and sexy laughs who knew how to flirt.

But still, for a quiet kind of a woman, she was pretty enough. Until she put those glasses on. The glasses made her look like a rabbit.

Of course, how the woman looked was not his problem. Brad stood up and wrapped Millie under his arm again. "Sorry I don't have any rope to tie you up with. So we'll just have to make do until I get the sheriff on the phone."

Brad sat down again once he reached the phone at the back of the café. He settled Millie back on his lap. This time it seemed more like she belonged there. Like he was getting used to her. "You don't really need those glasses, do you?"

"That's none of—"

"—my business," Brad finished for her. Well, she was right. She was too serious for the likes of him anyway. He needed a woman who liked a good time and would leave it at that. A woman like the one sitting on his lap would turn her green eyes on him and expect him to make a commitment to her. He didn't need any of that. Especially not when he was depressed anyway. He reached for the phone and dialed a number. The phone rang and rang. No one answered.

Brad sighed. It was time someone dragged Sheriff Carl Wall into the twenty-first century and got him a cell phone. What were law-abiding citizens supposed to do when they apprehended a thief in the middle of the night?

Brad looked back over at the bag of money on the table. The bag was small, more of a lunch bag than anything. Still, it was stuffed full. If she'd only been stealing twenty bucks to make it to the next town, he'd probably let her go.

But seeing that bag of money gave him pause. The side of the bag was split and he could see the bills. He wasn't close enough to see the denominations, but there were probably a few hundred dollars there. He wasn't doing anyone any favors if he let a thief like that loose in the night.

"I guess I'll just have to take you in," he said finally. The Elkton bunkhouse wasn't the fanciest place around, but it was built solid and all of the locks worked. He could just lock her in his room for the night, and get the sheriff to come out in the morning.

In the meantime, Brad would throw a tablecloth over that bag of money and lock the café door. It should be safe enough until morning when he and Sheriff Wall could come back and investigate. As he recalled, the sheriff was particular about the scene of the crime, and

Brad wanted to be able to tell him that he hadn't touched anything.

For the first time that evening, Brad had a happy thought. He might not need to go to church tomorrow morning after all, not when he had to clean up after a crime. Even God and Dr. Norris had to understand that keeping the law was important.

And, Brad decided, because he had fully intended to go to church, that should count as keeping his promise even if he didn't actually get there. He told himself it wasn't his fault someone had been stealing from the café.

Chapter Three

"Get in," Brad said as he held the door of his pickup open. The passenger door had a tendency to stick, and he'd had to put Millie down so he could open it. He'd kept one arm hooked around her stomach while he'd swung the door open with his other hand. "Get in."

"I never ride with strangers," Millie said as she braced herself.

Brad sighed. He could feel the woman tense up. He never knew a thief could be so particular about the company she kept. "Don't worry. No one's a stranger for long in Dry Creek—"

Well, that made her relax, Brad thought.

"Really? So you're not worried about strangers around here?" she asked as she turned around to face him. "You trust them?"

The woman sounded downright cheerful. Brad wondered why for a moment before he remembered. "We're not so trusting that we don't lock our doors, of course."

Brad lifted the woman up into his pickup and settled her on the seat. He knew he was lying a little, but he figured it was allowed under the circumstances. Some people did lock their doors when they went away for a trip—if they could find their keys, of course.

Brad figured he should drive his point home just so she knew she wasn't in some nostalgic Rockwell painting where everyone was easy pickings for any thief who might come driving by. "We've had our share of crime here. Why, we had a hit man come to town two years ago at Christmas. He tried to kill the pastor's wife."

"Oh." The woman was looking straight ahead as if there was something to see out the windshield of his pickup.

"Of course, we took care of him. Had him arrested and sent to prison." Brad congratulated himself as he shut the door on his pickup. That should let her know that the people of Dry Creek knew how to handle bad guys.

Brad walked around to the driver's side and got in.

"I'm sure he must have been sorry," Millie said.

"Who?" Brad put the key in the ignition.

"The man who tried to kill your pastor's wife. I'm sure he was sorry."

The woman's voice sounded a little hurt. Brad looked over at her. That's just what he needed—a sensitive thief. Ah, well. "You don't need to worry. The people of Dry Creek are big on forgiveness once you say you're sorry. If you just explain that you tried to take the money because you were hungry—"

"I wasn't hungry." Millie lifted her chin and continued to stare straight ahead.

Brad gave up. "Fine. Have it your way."

"I wouldn't steal even if I *was* hungry," Millie added quietly.

"Fine." Brad looked in the rearview mirror as he put

his foot on the gas and eased the truck forward. He really shouldn't feel sorry for a woman that determined to be unreasonable. "But if you were hungry, say real hungry, that might explain why you had broken into the café in the middle of the night."

There, Brad told himself, he'd given the woman an excuse for being at the scene of the crime. She could say the money was just sitting on the table and she'd only been looking for a piece of bread. He wasn't sure she was smart enough to use the story, but he'd done what he could for her.

Brad turned his pickup onto the road going through Dry Creek. The town sure was quiet at midnight.

After a few minutes of silence the woman said, "I'm not a thief."

Brad figured it was going to be a long night and an even longer morning with the sheriff. He was beginning to think maybe he wouldn't be getting such a good deal by skipping out on church to revisit the scene of the crime. What a night. He'd never imagined the day would come in the life of Brad Parker when church sounded like the better of two possibilities.

Millie's hands were cold. Ordinarily, she would put them in the pockets of her coat and they would be warm enough. But the man beside her made her nervous, and she wanted to keep her hands free. She didn't know exactly why, but it just seemed like a good idea. She'd never really liked big men, and this one had to be at least six feet tall. She could hardly see his face, not with the darkness and that Stetson he wore. Mostly, she could just see his chin. He needed a shave, but outside of that, his chin looked all right.

"I would think the jail would be back that way." Millie was trying to remember the map she'd studied before starting the drive from Seattle. The bigger towns were all west of Dry Creek. Going east, there weren't any towns of any size until you got to Minot, North Dakota. Leave it to a big man like that to have no sense of direction. Maybe he couldn't see very well with that hat on. If that was the case, she wouldn't criticize. She knew what it was like when a person couldn't see too well.

"I'm not going to the jail. I'm going home to the ranch."

"What?" Millie forgot all about being understanding. She knew she shouldn't have gotten into the man's pickup. That was a basic rule of survival. Never get into a car with a strange man. "You have to stop and let me out. Now!"

The man looked at her. "I told you I was holding you until I could get the sheriff."

Millie tried not to panic. The man was big, but he didn't look malicious. Still, what did she know? The only part of him that she'd gotten a good look at was his chin. "Usually, suspects are taken to a jail to be held for the sheriff."

"We don't have a jail in Dry Creek."

Of course, Millie thought, she knew that. "There's one in Miles City."

The man grunted. "You'd freeze to death in there this time of year."

"I have a coat." Millie put her hands in her pockets. She did have a good warm coat, and she was glad she'd brought it with her. "I'd really prefer the jail."

The man just kept driving. "I'm not driving back that direction tonight. The sheriff can take you there tomorrow if he wants. He's the one that has to okay turning the heat on anyway."

"They don't heat it?"

The man shrugged. "Budget cutbacks. They only heat it when they have someone locked up, so the sheriff tries to keep it clear this time of year."

Millie looked out the window. The night was black. It was even too cloudy to see any stars. She didn't see lights ahead that might have signaled a ranch house, either. Not that she was anxious to get to this man's ranch. "Is your wife home?"

Millie told herself to breathe. The man must be a local rancher. That meant he had to have a wife. If there was a woman around, she'd be all right. She trusted women.

The man grunted. "I'm single."

"Oh."

"Not single in the sense that I'm looking for a wife." The man reached up and crunched his hat farther down on his head. "Of course, I enjoy a date just like the next man. I'm all in favor of dating. You know, casual dating."

"Oh." Millie was trying to count the fence posts outside. How was she going to find her way back to Dry Creek when he stopped this pickup? She really wished the man had a wife. "Do you have a sister?"

"Why do you want to know about a sister?" The man's voice sounded confused. "Are you into double-dating or something? If you are, I could set up a date with one of the other guys—Randy is seeing someone pretty regular."

"Will she be there?" Millie felt her hands tense up.

"Where?"

"At your ranch."

"My ranch? Oh, ah, yeah. My ranch. I think so."

Millie relaxed. "Good."

Brad told himself he hadn't been this stupid since he was sixteen. He'd just lied to a woman to impress her. Why had he allowed her to think he owned a ranch? Hadn't she seen his pickup? It was an old diesel one. Did he look like he owned a ranch? He should have corrected her and said he worked on a ranch. Worked, not owned. Of course, he dreamed of having his own ranch, and he hoped to make that dream come true before long, but still—

And, to make it worse, the woman was a thief. It stood to reason she would only date a man with property. Of course, it wasn't like she was a bad criminal. Maybe he should tell her he was close to owning his own ranch. His ranch wouldn't be as big and fancy as the Elkton Ranch, but it would do.

Brad shook his head. Was he nuts? The last thing he needed was to fantasize about dating a woman who was a criminal.

He usually didn't fall into the trap of lying about what he had in life. Of course, he usually didn't need to—women wanted to date him because he was fun to be with. There were lots of women who would like to date him—women, by the way, who didn't have a rap sheet.

Brad shook his head again. He didn't know what was wrong with him. He shouldn't even be having this conversation with himself. Maybe he was running a fever or something.

He looked at the woman out of the corner of his eye.

She sat so close to the other door, Brad could have put two other women between them. Women, he might add, who would want to sit next to him. Millie, if that was her real name, sure wasn't the friendly type.

Besides, she had that little frown. He doubted she would recognize a good time if it came up and bit her on the backside. He shouldn't even care what she thought about him.

Brad turned the wheel of his pickup. The mailbox for the Elkton Ranch stood at the gravel road that led back to the ranch house. Fortunately, the boss was off spending Christmas with his wife's family in Seattle, so no one was home in the big house. The bunkhouse was just past the ranch house.

"I live here," Brad said as he eased the truck to a stop in front of the bunkhouse. Anyone with any sense would figure out from that that he didn't own any part of this ranch.

Brad expected some question about why he lived in the small house instead of the big house, but Millie didn't seem to notice.

"Someone's home inside," Millie said. The relief in her voice made her sound happier than if they had stopped at the big house.

Brad looked at the windows and, sure enough, Charlie stood in the window looking out to see who had driven up to the bunkhouse at midnight. It wasn't until Brad saw Charlie that he realized his plan had a small problem. The bunkhouse didn't have many rules. Actually, there were only two. No wet socks by the woodstove, because no one wanted to burn the place down. And no women allowed past the main living room of the bunkhouse.

Sometimes the rule on the socks was bent. But the one about women? Never.

Charlie would insist Brad turn around and go find Sheriff Wall and deliver the suspect to him. He wouldn't care that it was twenty degrees below zero outside and Brad didn't even know where the sheriff was right now, or that the suspect in question was unfriendly and uncooperative and looked at Brad, when she had those glasses of hers on, like he was the one who had committed a crime.

Brad decided he had had enough for one day.

"Here, you might want to wear my hat," Brad turned around and set his hat square on the woman's head. The woman's glasses were the only thing that kept the hat from falling halfway down her face. "And there's no need for the glasses."

"What?"

Brad plucked the glasses off the woman's nose and hooked the top button on her black wool coat. There, she looked like a juvenile delinquent again. "Just give me a minute of quiet and I'll have you safe inside."

"Safe inside from what?" The woman's voice was rising in panic.

"Ah." Brad thought. "Spiders. The man inside keeps pet spiders."

Brad congratulated himself. All women were afraid of spiders. But just in case. "He might have some snakes, too."

Brad could feel her stiffen up, and he felt a little bad. He pulled her across the seat to his side. "You don't need to worry, though. I'm going to carry you through to a safe place. You just need to be quiet for a little bit."

"Why?"

"Ah, the spiders go crazy when they hear any noise." Brad opened the door. The wind almost froze his ears now that he didn't have his hat.

Brad stepped out of the pickup and picked up Millie again. It didn't seem right to carry her like a bag of grain now that he knew she was a woman, but he didn't want to make Charlie any more suspicious than he'd naturally be. The truth was, those glasses of Millie's had reminded Brad that Charlie couldn't see so well at night anymore, and Brad figured there was a good chance he could slip Millie into his room without Charlie even seeing them. And he could do it, too, if he used the side door to the bunkhouse.

The door squeaked, and Brad tried to be as quiet as he could. The rooms for the ranch hands were all lined up in a row, and each had a door going off of this long hallway. At the end of the hallway was the main room where Charlie was standing by the window.

Brad held his breath. His room was only two doors down from the side door, and it would take only a little luck to reach it before Charlie figured out that he wasn't coming in the main door.

Brad put his hand on the doorknob leading into his room at the same time that he heard Charlie cough. Brad pushed the door open anyway and put Millie inside. "Stay there a minute."

Brad only waited long enough to be sure Millie was standing upright before he stepped out of the room and closed the door.

"That you, Brad? What's that you have?" Charlie asked as he peered down the long hallway.

Brad put on his best smile. "Nothing."

"Nothing?" The old man frowned.

Brad kept his smile going. "Well, Christmas is coming, you know."

"That's right." The old man relaxed and smiled as he walked down the hall toward Brad. "I forgot it's the time of year when a person shouldn't be too nosy."

"That's right. All those Christmas presents." Brad figured by now Charlie would be expecting more than the new pair of leather gloves Brad had tucked away in his drawer for the occasion. Brad figured he'd need to get Charlie a shovel or something big. Maybe a ladder would do.

"I'm glad to see you're in the Christmas spirit," the old man said slowly.

"It's a joy to give." Brad kept smiling. He wondered when lockjaw set in on a man's mouth. He figured it'd be coming any minute now.

"That's good to hear." Charlie was talking the same, but Brad noticed the old man wasn't looking at him anymore. Instead, he was looking over Brad's shoulder.

Brad turned around. Millie stood in the doorway of his room, and she wasn't wearing his hat or her glasses. She was wearing the coat buttoned up to her neck, which, with her blond curls and timid face, made her look like she was about twelve.

"I see we have company," the old man said gently.

"I thought you were going to stay in the room," Brad said.

"I'm not afraid of spiders," Millie said to no one in particular. Her face went white when she said it. "Unless they're black widows, and then anyone would be afraid."

Millie couldn't see much without her glasses. Mostly it just looked like a long tunnel with a white light at the end of it and several large rocks along the way. The clos-est large rock was the man Brad.

"If you have spiders, you really should make them stay out in the barn," Millie suggested. She'd taken off the hat he put on her head and looked for her glasses. "You forgot to leave me my glasses."

"Oh."

Millie didn't know why he needed to sound so an-noyed. She hadn't made any fuss about the spiders. "I would imagine they'll have spiders in the jail."

"No, they won't. Too cold," Brad said as he held out her glasses.

Millie could see the arm outstretched, and she reached for the open palm. Ah, there were her glasses.

She blinked when she put them back on. Usually, she didn't blink so much. At first, she thought it was be-cause of the light in the hallway. But that didn't make sense. Even though she couldn't see, her eyes had al-ready adjusted to the brightness.

No, what was startling her eyes was the man. She hadn't had a good look at him until now. My goodness, he was handsome. Not that she was interested herself. The closest thing to a boyfriend she'd had in the last five years was Forrest, and he'd turned out to be a hit man. She didn't exactly have reliable sense when it came to men. But still, she'd have to remember what the man looked like so she could tell the other waitresses at Ru-by's. They'd enjoy a story about a good-looking rancher who lived in a house full of spiders.

She took another good look at him so she'd remem-ber. Brad's hair was dark as coal, she decided, and he kept it just long enough to curl a little at the ends. The hair alone made him look like a movie star. But it didn't stop there. He had the blue eyes of the Irish. No wonder his chin was strong. The Irish always had strong chins. They also generally talked a lot, and that was what the man was doing right now.

Brad had stepped closer to the old man and was whispering something to him. The inside of the room was made out of oak logs. There were beige curtains on the window and long leather couches around the room. The old man nodded several times while Brad spoke.

Then both men looked up. Millie heard the noise, too. Even with all of the snow outside, it sounded like a dozen pickups had screeched to a stop out in front of the bunkhouse.

Brad didn't bother to leave the shadows of the hallway. He wondered what had made the other guys rush home from Billings. He looked at the clock on the opposite wall. It was only twelve-thirty. "There must have been a fight. There'll be a broken bone or two."

The door opened and eight other ranch hands stomped into the bunkhouse.

"Okay, who's hurt?" Charlie demanded as he stepped into the main room from the hallway.

All eight of the men who had entered the bunkhouse stopped. "We're worried about Brad."

Brad stepped from the hall into the main room. "Why? I'm right here."

"Oh." The men flashed each other guilty looks and then stared at the floor.

Finally, Howard, one of the older men, cleared his throat and rubbed the beard on his chin. "We thought we'd check on you, that's all. Heard you hadn't made it over to the other game."

"Since when is it a crime to go to bed early on a

Saturday night?" Brad was getting tired of apologizing for not spending his night gambling. Just because he didn't want to sit down with a bunch of smelly men and bet his week's salary against theirs, it didn't mean anything was wrong.

"It's just not like you," another of the men, Jeff, mumbled. Jeff was the only one who had taken his hat off when he came in the bunkhouse, and Brad could still see the snow melting on the man's shoulders.

"Whoa," Randy, the youngest ranch hand, said and then he whistled. "We take that back—it *is* like you. Going to bed early when you have company is an altogether different thing."

It took Brad a full ten seconds to realize what Randy was saying—or rather what he was seeing.

Brad turned around, but he already knew what he would see. Millie had left the hallway and was standing behind him. She was holding the neckline on her coat tight around her throat, and it made her look nervous and young. At least she had her glasses on so she didn't look as pretty as Brad knew she could.

"It's not what you think," Brad started.

"You don't need to say another word," Randy said as he grinned and backed up toward the door.

"Yes, he does," one of the other hands, William, spoke up. William had been an accountant before he became a ranch hand, and with his thinning blond hair and long face, he still looked like he was always trying to balance the books. William had known Brad for the past ten years. He was looking at Brad now like he'd never really known him, though. "Isn't she too young?"

"Of course she's too young," Brad snapped back.

"I'm twenty-three," Millie spoke up.

Brad groaned. How could the woman be twenty-three and be so dumb? "She's young for her age."

William nodded, no longer upset. "Still, it's the age that counts. Sorry we bothered you."

"You didn't bother me. Nothing's going on."

Brad could see the speculation in Randy's eyes. Randy was only twenty-two or so himself, and he looked like he was realizing Millie was more his age than Brad's.

Randy swallowed and spoke. "Well, if nothing's going on with the two of you, then maybe you wouldn't mind if I—"

Brad felt his arms tighten. It had been a while since he'd taken down any of the other guys with his fists, but he could still do it. "She's not in the market. Besides, you already have a girlfriend."

Charlie cleared his throat. "Now, there'll be none of that." He looked at Brad. "That's the reason why we have the rule—no women allowed."

"She's not here because she's a woman," Brad said. "She's here because she's a thief."

Brad expected his statement to bring some dignity to the situation. Instead, William looked at him like Brad was the one at fault.

"You don't need to lie. We're prepared to make some exceptions for you on account of—" William swallowed and stared at the floor "—on account of the time of year and all. If she eases the pain some, maybe we could let her stay with you for the night."

"What?" Brad was dumbfounded. Sometimes a man broke the bunkhouse rules, but never ever was anyone given *permission* to break them. How pathetic did they think he was?

"William's right," Charlie mumbled. "She could even stay with you through Christmas, since the boss isn't here. He'll never know. You've got your own bath and everything, so the two of you will be snug in your room. She'll make you happy."

Randy and the others just stared at the floor.

Brad snorted. "You're all hopeless. She doesn't make me happy. I caught her breaking into the café."

"Really?" William asked. He looked at Millie and smiled. "You're sure she wasn't just hungry? She's awfully small to be a thief."

"I'm not a thief," Millie said.

Brad looked over his shoulder. Millie stood in the hallway in that long wool coat of hers looking like a refugee. "Then what were you doing in the café with all that money?"

"I can't say."

Brad looked at the other men. "See?"

"Does anybody recognize her?" Charlie asked. He'd taken a step closer to Millie and was studying her. "Between all of you, I figure you know every woman over the age of sixteen in the whole county."

"Never seen her before," William said.

"I'd remember her if I had," Randy added.

"I'm a stranger," Millie said.

"A stranger who happens to be a thief," Brad added.

"Maybe," Charlie said thoughtfully. "She doesn't look like any thief I've ever seen, though."

"Well, we'll find out in the morning when I can get hold of the sheriff."

"The sheriff's not in his office tomorrow," William said. "It's Sunday—he'll be in church."

"Well, then," Brad said grimly, "that's where I'll need to go to talk to him."

There was silence in the room.

Finally Randy spoke. "You're going to church?"

Brad nodded. People went to church all the time around Dry Creek. What was the big deal?

There was more silence.

"Inside the building?" William finally asked. "Not just volunteering to shovel the steps like you sometimes do when it snows?"

Brad nodded. "Of course, inside the building—"

Randy whistled. "This'll be something to see."

"There's nothing to see. I'm going to just take Millie there to the sheriff and give her a chance to confess—"

"I didn't know they still did confessions in church," Randy said.

"I don't have anything to confess," Millie said. "Well, at least not about being a thief."

"Wow," Randy said. "This'll be something to see."

Brad was annoyed. "There's no reason to get all excited. There'll be nothing to see or hear in church tomorrow. I'm just going to tell the sheriff about the scene of the crime and—"

"You mean there's a crime scene?"

Brad shook his head. It was hopeless. "Anyone want to stay out here and chew the fat? Millie needs to go to bed and get her sleep, but I'll be sleeping on the couch out here and I'm happy to have some company for an hour or so."

"No, thanks." Randy grinned. "I think I'll be getting up early in the morning."

"Me, too," William added. "I haven't been to church in a while."

"You've *never* been to church," Brad said as he sat down on a folding chair. "You're as much of a heathen as I am."

"I was baptized as a baby," William protested as he turned to walk toward the hall. "That makes me a member."

Brad shook his head. "No, it doesn't."

"I think you need to pay dues to be a member," Randy added as he turned to the hallway, too.

"Just go to bed," Brad said.

Charlie nodded. "We all need our sleep."

Brad didn't know if it was sleep he needed. Maybe an aspirin would do him more good. He had a feeling he wasn't going to sleep at all tonight, and it wouldn't be because of the lumps in the sofa.

Chapter Four

Millie had been to church once when she was a child. Her foster mother had taken her to an Easter service because the child welfare representative was going to come the next day and there was always a question on the form the man filled out about church or other religious activity.

They had gone to an old church that had big stained-glass windows that showed pictures of Jesus in many different poses. Millie had been in awe. She liked the picture best of Jesus kneeling down beside a child. The child had been wearing a blue robe, and Millie had on a blue dress that day. She looked at the picture and pretended it was her that Jesus was smiling down at and talking to in such a friendly way.

When she left the church, Millie told her foster mother about pretending that she was in the picture with Jesus. Her foster mother said she was silly. She said those pictures of Jesus were from thousands of years ago and had nothing to do with today.

Millie still remembered the disappointment she felt. It was the first time she'd realized Jesus lived such a long time ago. Somehow she had the feeling he was supposed to still be alive today.

That was the last time Millie had been inside a church.

She was surprised that the church in Dry Creek didn't have any stained-glass windows. Of course, she remembered looking at the church last night in the dark and she hadn't seen any, but churches had always seemed mysterious places to her, and she expected to step into the church in Dry Creek and see something dramatic like a stained-glass window anyway.

Instead, the church was humble. The glass was frosted because of the cold outside, but not decorated in any other way.

There was a strip of brown carpet going down the middle of the church between the rows of wooden pews, but the flooring on both sides of the carpet was the kind of beige linoleum that she had seen frequently in coffee shops. The only problem with that kind of linoleum was that there was a special trick to getting off the black scuff marks. Millie looked down at the floor. Everything was scrubbed clean, but the black marks were still there. She could tell someone how to fix that.

Not that she was here to talk about the floor, Millie reminded herself. She was glad Brad didn't seem like he was in any hurry to actually go inside the church, either. They both just stood in the doorway.

There were quite a few people in the church already, but they weren't sitting down yet.

"Do I look all right?" Brad whispered down at her.

Millie looked up. She was getting used to Brad's face. Well, sort of.

Maybe it was because she'd spent the night on his

pillow and grown accustomed to the warm scent of him that lingered in his room even as he slept in the other room on the sofa. When you've been in someone's bed like that, she thought, handsome didn't seem to matter so much.

Besides, he didn't seem to care that he was handsome, so that helped some more. He was mostly worried about the tie he had around his neck. He'd had to borrow it from Charlie this morning, and Charlie only had two ties and said he needed one for himself. Charlie kept the black one, the one he called his funeral tie.

Brad had had to settle for a red tie with elves on it that Charlie had won in some bingo game at the senior center in Billings last year.

Millie nodded. The elf tie did go, in a way, with the green shirt Brad had borrowed from William.

"I feel stupid wearing dancing elves around my neck," Brad said.

Millie wasn't used to men admitting they felt stupid. "They look a little like drunken mushrooms."

"Really?" Brad seemed cheered by the idea.

Millie nodded. "At least I have my coat to wear."

Millie had bought the black wool coat years ago because it covered everything. She could have her waitress uniform on and no one would know. She didn't always like people to know she was a waitress when she rode the bus to work. Too many men felt they could flirt with any woman who was a waitress. Of course, the men were usually harmless. But still, she didn't want to be bothered.

Brad was frowning down at her. Millie wondered if maybe the coat wasn't too protective. She didn't want men to scowl at her, either.

"I could hold your glasses for you," Brad said finally.

What was his problem with her glasses? That was the second time this morning that he had suggested she not wear them. "My glasses are fine."

Brad nodded. "I thought they might fog up so you couldn't see. You might not know that. Glasses do that in the cold."

"I'm fine."

Brad nodded again. "Well, we might as well go in then."

There was a double door that led into the Dry Creek church, but only one half of it was open this morning.

Millie felt Brad take her elbow at the same time that they took a step into the church.

"Oh." Millie wished she had given her glasses to Brad. At least then she wouldn't see all the people who had turned around to look at them. There were tall people, old people, short people, and children. They all seemed like they were talking—until she and Brad walked into the church.

"Well, welcome!" A ripple of excitement went around the people standing in the church.

"Why, Brad Parker!" An older man stepped forward and held out his hand. The man was wearing a tweed jacket, and he smelled of old-fashioned aftershave.

Brad shook the man's hand. "Good morning, Dr. Norris."

"I'm glad you came." The older man wasn't content with a handshake. He slapped Brad on the shoulder, as well.

"I told you I'd come," Brad said.

Millie was glad Brad didn't move. She was also glad he was so big. She could almost hide behind him as long as he stood just where he was. Maybe no one would notice she was there.

"And welcome to you as well, young lady," the doctor said as he stopped looking at Brad and looked over at Millie. "We're glad you've come to worship with us."

"Oh." Millie gave a tight little smile. "I don't know if we'll be staying for—"

"Of course you have to stay for the service." An older woman stepped forward and beamed at Millie. "We're singing Christmas carols, and the Curtis twins are going to practice their donkey song—you know, the donkey who carried Mary to the Inn?"

"You mean the twins—Josh and Joey?"

"Why, yes," the woman said. The woman had her gray hair twisted into a mass of curls on the top of her head, and she was wearing a green gingham dress with a red bell pin. Millie knew who the older woman was before she held out her hand.

"My name's Mrs. Hargrove," the woman said.

Millie nodded and took the woman's hand. She never thought she'd get to meet Mrs. Hargrove. Mrs. Hargrove had written to Forrest several times while he was in jail. That's why Forrest knew so much about Dry Creek. And to think, Millie would hear the twins sing. Oh, she hoped Brad didn't want to meet with the sheriff before she could do that. "My name's Millie."

"How did you know about the twins?" Brad asked quietly.

Millie looked up at him and saw the suspicion in his eyes. She'd have to be more careful. "I thought you mentioned them last night."

"Me?"

"Well, maybe it was William—he brought me an

extra blanket in case I got cold and stayed to talk for a little bit. Did you know he used to do the books for a restaurant in Seattle?"

"William what? I thought you were going straight to bed. That's what everyone was going to do."

"Well, I couldn't go to sleep if I was cold, could I?"

Someone started to play the organ, and Millie was relieved to see everyone starting to sit down.

Brad was still scowling. But at least he'd stopped looking down at her, Millie thought.

"I don't see the sheriff here," Brad said.

"He'll be here any minute," the older man, Dr. Norris, said, as he gestured to the pews. "You're welcome to sit anywhere."

"I think we should sit at the back," Brad said. "In case Sheriff Wall gets here soon."

The doctor nodded.

Millie was glad that the sheriff wasn't there quite yet. She and Brad walked to the last pew and sat down. Brad seemed to relax. He even loosened his tie.

Now that Millie was getting a good look around, she noticed that someone had decorated the small church for Christmas. There was a short, stubby tree with tin-foil stars on it by the organ. Some of the stars were crooked, and they all looked like children had made them. Mixed in with the stars were some red lights that twinkled. Several poinsettia plants stood in front of the speaker's stand.

Some years at Ruby's they had poinsettia plants on the counter at Christmas. Once or twice the manager had given Millie one of the plants to take home after her shift ended on Christmas Day. They were hardy flowers and lasted almost till Easter.

"No one's wearing a tie, except for Pastor Curtis," Brad whispered in her ear. "I thought everyone wore a tie to church."

"This is sort of an informal church, I think," Millie whispered back.

Millie heard some sounds behind her and turned around. There stood all of the men from the Elkton Ranch bunkhouse, looking shy and out-of-place in the doorway.

"Welcome," the pastor said quietly from the front of the church. "Please take a seat anywhere."

The men filed into the back pew on the other side of the church, and the service started.

"I don't sing much," Brad whispered as everyone around them stood with a songbook in their hands.

"Me, neither," Millie said as she stood up. She figured it didn't matter if you sang or not as long as you stood up at the right time and were respectful.

Singing wasn't as hard as Millie had thought. Some of the songs were Christmas carols that she knew from the radio that played at Ruby's, and she joined in the singing of those—quietly, of course.

The church service reminded Millie of a roller coaster she'd ridden once. She was scared at every turn of the corner, but she found she enjoyed it if she sat back and didn't try to fight the experience. Being in church was kind of like that.

There was a light behind the wooden cross in the center of the church, and Millie decided she could stare at that. She wasn't sure she was supposed to be listening to the sermon since she was just here to wait for the sheriff, so she didn't want to keep her eyes on the preacher. Of course, she couldn't help but hear the sermon. It was something about grace.

Millie wasn't quite sure what it all meant. The pastor had said grace was when you got something for free, but the only time Millie had heard of grace was at Ruby's when sometimes a customer would pray before they ate. One of the other waitresses said the people were saying grace. Millie wondered now if the people had been hoping they would get their dinners for free and not have to pay. She was surprised Ruby hadn't put a stop to people saying grace if that was the case.

No one got a free meal at Ruby's unless they happened to be really down on their luck. Then Millie sometimes paid for their meal out of her tips for the evening. Millie wondered if grace was something like that. When she gave out a free meal because another person was hungry and couldn't buy the meal for themselves. She'd have to ask the pastor if that's what grace was.

Of course, she'd have to wait until Brad turned her over to the sheriff and the sheriff turned her loose. She didn't suppose the pastor would want to talk to a woman who was in the process of being arrested.

Millie's favorite part of the whole church service was when the Curtis twins put on their donkey faces and sang a song about taking Mary to the Inn. They walked up and down in front of the church like they were on a long journey. Once one of the twins brayed like a donkey and pretended to fly. That had to be Josh.

Millie hadn't thought about how difficult it must have been for Forrest to learn so much about the people of Dry Creek in the few days he was in the little town. Even with Mrs. Hargrove's letters, there was a lot he learned himself. He said he'd talked to people in the café and even stopped at a few houses to ask directions here or there and had stayed to chat.

"People will tell you anything if you get them talking," Forrest said to her once when she asked how he did it. "Everyone likes to talk."

Millie wished Forrest were here. He'd know what to do about the mess she was in. Of course, if he were here, he'd probably want her to continue on with her mission. She hoped Brad was right and that the people of Dry Creek did trust strangers. If they didn't, she sure didn't know how she'd get them to trust strangers now.

When the service was over, the pastor stood at the back door to shake hands. The men from the Elkton Ranch were the first ones in line. In fact, Millie suspected a few of them had tried to beat the pastor to the door so they could go through it before he even got there. But Charlie made them get in line.

Brad and Millie were right behind them.

"I'm glad you could join us this morning," Pastor Curtis said to Randy as he shook the younger man's hand.

Randy blushed and ran his finger around his necktie to loosen it. "We mostly came in to see the crime scene."

"What?" That was from Mrs. Hargrove. She was coming up to greet the men, too. "I know our singing isn't too good, but I'd hardly say it's a crime scene."

"No, ma'am." Randy turned even redder. "I mean the crime scene at the café."

A ripple of whispering went through the whole church until everything got silent.

"A crime! Has anyone seen a stranger?"

A gasp came from another corner. "Has anybody been shot this time?"

Millie looked around her. Forrest was right. He had taken away this little town's trust in strangers. She could see it in the faces around her. They were scared.

"It's nothing like that," Brad said gruffly. "Just a little bit of—well, maybe something was stolen."

"We have a thief?"

"I'm not a thief," Millie denied automatically. She wished she hadn't said anything when everyone turned to look at her.

"Well, of course you're not," Mrs. Hargrove agreed. "Anyone can see you're a nice young woman." The older woman smiled at Millie. "I was so pleased you were able to convince Brad to come to church with you."

Millie blushed. "Brad came to see the sheriff."

"Well, still—" Mrs. Hargrove kept smiling. "I can't believe you were stealing anything." The older woman looked up at Brad. "Are you sure she didn't just stop at the café thinking it was open and she could get something to eat? Maybe she was hoping to find a sandwich. Maybe she was hungry. Linda would have given her a sandwich if she had been there."

"That was a mighty green sandwich she was taking out of there. I was hoping to catch up with the sheriff so I could show him where I left everything." Brad looked around. "I thought he'd be in church this morning."

"He had something to do in Miles City," Pastor Curtis said. "But he's planning to be at our house for lunch, so he should be here any minute."

Millie looked around. She saw skepticism on a lot of faces. "I wasn't taking the money. I was trying to give it away."

Brad nodded. "Give it away? Where'd you get it from in the first place?"

"I can't tell you where."

Brad snorted. "You're going to have to think of a

better story than that if you expect Sheriff Wall to go easy on you."

"I think I hear the sheriff now," the pastor said. "Maybe we should go over to the café and get this settled."

Millie looked around. The faces that had been smiling weren't smiling at her anymore. They weren't exactly frowning, but she could see the caution in everyone's eyes. "I didn't do anything wrong."

"I'm sure you didn't," Mrs. Hargrove murmured as she patted Millie on the arm.

Millie noticed Mrs. Hargrove didn't look her in the eye when she said those words, however. Mrs. Hargrove had obviously reconsidered her confidence in Millie.

It wasn't the first time since Forrest died that Millie wished she could have a few words in private with him. If Forrest could see her now, he would have to agree that she wasn't the person to make everything better with the people of Dry Creek. She was going to make it worse. Even Mrs. Hargrove didn't believe her.

"He should have sent an angel," Millie muttered. Dead people could do that, she figured. There were supposed to be lots of angels up there.

"What?" Mrs. Hargrove looked startled.

"Who's 'he'?" Brad bent down and asked. "Do you have an accomplice?"

"How many of them are there?" someone else asked.

"It's me. Just me," Millie said. She had never felt more alone in her life.

"It's best if you tell the truth." Brad frowned down at her. "I should have figured you had someone else in this with you. He probably sent you in as bait and—" Brad whistled "—I left the money right there for him."

Brad took Millie's elbow. "Let's go."

Millie had to almost run to keep up with Brad's long steps. The air outside was cold, and she hadn't had time to put the collar up on her coat. She could feel the air all the way down as she breathed it in. "You don't need to hurry."

Brad only snorted and kept walking. A dozen other people were trailing after them. "Don't know why it took me so long to figure it out—of course, a woman like you has a man around. Even Randy figured *that* out. With those eyes of yours, of course there's a man around."

"I don't—" Millie started to protest and then decided to save her breath. He wouldn't believe her anyway. They'd soon be inside the café, and he would see for himself that the money was still there and there was no man in sight.

Millie wondered how she had made such a muddle of Forrest's request. The people of Dry Creek would be even more suspicious of strangers after she left. Millie looked up at the determined set of Brad's chin and corrected herself. She should have said if she left. If she was able to.

The rancher didn't look like he'd let her leave anytime soon. She almost wished she did have some man someplace who would come get her. Although, as she looked at the rancher again, she didn't know what man she'd ever known in her life that she would put up against the one in front of her.

She looked at Brad again. Had she heard right? Did he think her eyes were pretty?

Chapter Five

Brad turned the handle on the door to the café before he remembered he had pushed the button on the other side of the handle and locked the door when he left last night.

"The key's under the rock," Mrs. Hargrove offered as she stood at the bottom of the steps. "The third rock on the porch there by your foot."

"But I have—" Millie said softly.

Brad didn't listen to Millie. Instead, he let go of her arm and bent down to turn over the rock. It was a piece of granite from the hills in the area, and snow was lodged in its crevices. It looked like Linda had hauled half of the mountain down here to place around her café. Some of the rocks outlined a dormant flower bed, but the rest of the rocks were just scattered here and there on the wide porch.

Brad decided that, when this was all over, he was going to ask the sheriff to do a public service talk on how to lock a door and keep it locked. Someone needed to pull Dry Creek into the modern age. What was the point of locking a door when a person left the key under a rock a mere four feet away? Except— "There's no key here."

"—That's because I have it," Millie said as she put her hand in the pocket of her coat and pulled out the brass key.

"You have it." Of course, she had it, Brad told himself as he took the key she offered. He hadn't asked himself last night how Millie had gotten in. "I suppose you turned over every rock on this porch hoping to find a key."

Even as Brad said that, he looked at the other rocks. They were all covered with snow. No one had moved them in the last few days. Which meant Millie hadn't turned over every rock to find the key; she'd turned over only one. "How did you know which rock it was under?"

"Someone told me."

Brad didn't know how a voice as quiet as Millie's could give him such a splitting headache. He supposed he had begun to hope that she wasn't really the thief he had first thought her to be. That she was just going inside the café to get out of the cold and maybe to fix a sandwich for herself. He was even beginning to think that Linda might have left the money there in a brown paper bag and that Millie was just counting it.

The rock took away all of those comfortable illusions. "Someone must have scouted out the town. The whole thing was planned and premeditated."

Millie frowned. It wasn't much of a frown, but Brad noticed that the tiny lines in her forehead made her nose smaller, which made her glasses slip a little bit. When she spoke, her voice sounded hurt. "I wasn't going to do anything bad. 'Premeditated' makes it sound like murder or something."

Brad heard the gasp at the bottom of the stairs. He knew the whole congregation had followed him and Millie over to the café, so he wasn't surprised that everyone was listening. The gasp came from one of the Curtis twins. It was Josh. The boys were six years old and fascinated with the usual boy things. "Did she say murder?"

"Nobody is going to murder anyone," Brad said firmly, turning around. He didn't want the rest of the people to start thinking in that direction. "This is Dry Creek. We're not like Los Angeles, where they have murders on every street corner."

"We almost had a murder here," the Kelly girl reminded him as she twisted her ponytail. She stood off to the side of the porch in an old, worn parka.

Brad wished he could remember her first name. All he knew is that she had two older sisters that he sometimes saw in the bars in Miles City. He knew *their* names, not that it did him a lot of good with this girl. He'd just have to take a guess. "Now, Susie—"

"I'm Sarah," the girl corrected him. "Remember there was that hit man that came here? So you can't say it never happens." The girl turned her eyes from Brad and stared at Millie. "Maybe she's one, too."

Josh gasped again and turned his blue eyes up to Millie, as well. "Does she have a gun?"

"Of course she doesn't have a gun," Brad said automatically before he remembered that he hadn't really checked. "At least, I don't think she does—"

Brad was remembering that coat Millie wore. She could have a cannon tucked in the corner of that thing and the wool was so heavy it wouldn't even make a bulge. But she hadn't been wearing that coat the whole time, had she? Surely, he would have noticed if she was armed. She was too skinny to hide anything without the coat. Unless, of course, it was in the pocket of the coat.

Brad wished he'd just taken Millie to the jail last night. This was all getting out of hand. Where was the sheriff anyway? Brad ran his finger under his collar. It took him a minute to think of something to reassure the kids. "If she had a gun, she would have shot me by now."

"Some man came and tried to shoot my mom," Josh said to Millie. Josh was missing a front tooth, and he leaned toward Millie when he spoke. "That was before she was my mom."

"It happened at Christmas time, too," the Kelly girl insisted. "Right after the Christmas pageant. And we're having another pageant this year—I wonder if someone will be shot this year."

"I don't have a gun." Millie knelt down so she could look Josh in the eye. "You don't need to worry."

Brad snorted. He figured worrying was the only smart thing they *could* do, given the state of affairs. He took a side step closer to Millie and looked down at her. He really should find out if she had a gun. "I should frisk you."

"What?" Millie said as her eyes looked up to meet his.

Brad had a sudden vision of running his hands up and down Millie's coat. The problem was, the coat was so bulky he'd have to run his hands under her coat. He wasn't sure he should do that in full view of everyone. At least not with the kids around. Maybe if she wasn't wearing that coat, he could see if she was armed. "You should take your coat off."

"But it's cold."

Brad nodded. He'd tried. "We'll leave it to the sheriff. Where is he anyway?"

"I hear him," Mrs. Hargrove said. "He's using the siren."

Millie cleared her throat and turned so she faced the people waiting at the bottom of the porch. The air was cold, but most of the coats she saw were unbuttoned and unzipped. Everyone was looking at her so intently; they didn't even seem to notice the cold. Millie wasn't sure this was an ideal moment to try to explain, but sometimes a woman had to deliver her message any way she could. "Just because a man's a hit man, it doesn't mean he's a bad man."

"What?"

Millie figured the bellow behind her came from Brad. It was close enough to cause her ear damage, but she continued. She smiled at Josh and Sarah both. "Maybe the hit man was real sorry for the things he did and wished he could do something to make it all better."

Millie stopped there. She'd done her best. She hadn't gone against Forrest's wishes and said she knew him, but she'd come close. Surely, someone in the crowd would read between the lines and understand what she was trying to say. Mrs. Hargrove was puzzling something out. Surely, *she* would understand.

Millie figured she'd been understood when Mrs. Hargrove stepped up on the porch looking like she'd puzzled her way to some conclusion and was ready to speak.

"Are you a reporter?" the older woman demanded to know.

"Me?" Millie asked, aghast. "I could never be a reporter." Millie could think of a hundred reasons why she wasn't a reporter. "I don't even know how to type."

Mrs. Hargrove bent over slightly and looked at Millie's hands. "You've got a tiny ink stain on one finger. Maybe you write in longhand."

"Well, I write, but it's not the news," Millie protested. Didn't Mrs. Hargrove know that shy people never became reporters? They would have to talk to people. All kinds of people. The woman could just as well have asked if Millie was an astronaut who flew to the moon. "It's more like—well, I take orders for things."

Millie could tell by the faraway look in Mrs. Hargrove eyes that she wasn't listening anymore. She was, however, thoughtful. "Now that I think of it, I'm surprised we haven't had more reporters snooping around doing some kind of a sequel to the story they did back then—they were quite interested in our hit man and the angel. I must admit it was a good angle. And here it is Christmas again. People might be interested in seeing what had happened to the town where it all took place."

"I swear I'm not a reporter." Millie raised her hand. She'd place her hand on one of those Bibles people were holding if they wanted her to. "I don't even know any reporters."

"Well, let's hope you know a lawyer or two," a man's voice came from the back of the crowd.

Millie looked up. That must be the sheriff. He wore the uniform and—everything. She gulped. He had a gun.

Millie blinked and pulled the collar of her coat closer around her neck. "I don't know any lawyers, either."

The sheriff nodded. "I expect the county will have to get you one then. Not that they'll be happy about it. They don't even want to pay for heating the jail this time of year."

The sheriff stepped in closer and looked at Millie intently. She felt like a bug under a microscope.

"Unless, of course, you have money to pay for your own attorney," the sheriff added hopefully. "That would be good. My cousin over in Miles City works cheap. You might be able to hire him."

Millie thought of the remaining tip money she had in her purse and shook her head. "I used all my money driving here. I just have enough to get back."

"Where are you from?" the sheriff asked casually.

"Seattle."

"Lady, are you crazy?" Brad asked as he turned his back on everyone and jabbed the key into the lock on the door. "Driving all that way to rob us in Dry Creek? Let me tell you, the odds weren't great that you would find much money just lying around anywhere in town."

Brad shoved the door to the café open.

"I already told you. I didn't find the money here. I brought it with me."

Brad was tall enough that his shoulders filled out the doorway as he stood and turned on the light. "Yeah, and I'm the tooth fairy."

Millie took a deep breath. With a little bit of patience, she could explain everything to the sheriff. She could still keep Forrest's identity secret. She could just say that someone wanted to repay the people of Dry Creek, and she was the delivery person.

Millie heard Brad's low whistle before she stepped into the café, too.

"Don't touch the crime scene," the sheriff said as he stepped past Millie.

Brad had removed the tablecloth that he'd draped over the money last night.

"But look at these!" Brad had bent down and pulled one of the flannel Christmas stockings out of the sack on the floor. He had a look of horror on his face as he held it up. "I didn't get a good look at these last night."

Mrs. Hargrove and the pastor stepped ahead of Millie, too.

"Someone made them," Mrs. Hargrove said.

"I didn't have a pattern for the stockings," Millie said a little defensively. What did they expect? She'd relied on glue and hand-stitching to finish the stockings. Fortunately, she'd found several large remnants of red felt at a fabric store.

"It has Elmer's name on it," Mrs. Hargrove said, turning to tell everyone.

By now, half of the town of Dry Creek had come through the open door.

Mrs. Hargrove held another sock that Brad had pulled out of the sack. "This one says Jacob."

Millie could hear the murmur.

"I could see how a person might guess the name Jacob," someone in the back said. "But Elmer? I bet there's not fifty people left in the world with a name like Elmer."

"And here's Pastor Matthew and Glory." Mrs. Hargrove held up two more stockings.

The sheriff turned to Millie. "How do you know our names?"

Millie closed her eyes. "I was just doing a favor for a friend. He wanted to do something nice for Dry Creek, and he asked me to help him. That's all."

"We don't even have a phone directory anymore that lists everyone," Mrs. Hargrove said as she looked at all of the stockings on the table. "I'm not even sure I could sit down and write out everyone's name—not without a picture or something in front of me."

"My friend had a very good memory," Millie said. "He knew everyone's name."

"Is your friend Santa Claus?"

Millie looked down at the last question. Little Josh was looking up at her with hope in his eyes.

"I want a train," he said. "One that runs on the tracks and has a whistle. My dad says they're expensive, but I'm sure Santa Claus has one."

"My friend's not Santa Claus," Millie said softly as she knelt down to look the boy in the eyes. "But if he knew you wanted to have a train, he would have sent one to you. My friend's dead."

"Is he in heaven?"

"I—ah, well, I—" Millie didn't believe in heaven, but the little boy was looking at her with such innocence that she couldn't tell him that. And who knew? Maybe he was right. She certainly didn't know anything about it.

"My mother's in heaven," the boy said. "It's real nice there. I bet they have lots of trains. Maybe your friend could send one down from there—a super-duper flying train. Do you think they have flying trains in heaven?"

"I—ah—I wouldn't know," Millie finally managed to say.

"Me, neither," the boy agreed. "You have to die to go to heaven."

Millie nodded. "That's what I've been told."

"Looks like you've been told a lot of things," the sheriff said. His voice was not friendly like the young boy's. "Mind if I ask some questions?"

Millie rose to her feet. She supposed it was too much

to ask to be left alone so she could keep talking to Josh. "Go ahead."

"First, where are you from?"

"Seattle."

The sheriff wrote something in the black notebook he'd pulled out of his shirt pocket.

"That hit man was from Seattle," said an older man who had entered the café late.

"What brings you out this way?"

"I was doing a Christmas favor for a friend."

The sheriff looked a little interested in this, even though he didn't write anything in his notebook. "And who would that friend be?"

When Millie didn't answer, the sheriff looked over at Brad.

"Oh, no, it's not him," Millie protested. She didn't want anyone to suspect him of anything. "I don't even know him—not really. He was just doing his duty when he took me to his ranch last night—"

"His ranch?" The sheriff frowned. "You mean the Elkton place?"

"Is that your last name?" Millie turned to Brad. It was funny, she thought, that she hadn't heard his last name after all the time they had spent together. Of course, the time was hardly social, so she supposed it wasn't surprising. "I saw the name on the mailbox this morning."

The sheriff snorted and turned to Brad. "Did you tell her you owned the place?"

Millie saw the red creep up Brad's neck and said the only thing she could think of. "I think maybe I'm the one who assumed it was his place."

"But I didn't correct her," Brad said.

The sheriff shrugged. "Well, I suppose that doesn't matter. I guess it stands to reason you'd try to impress a pretty girl."

Millie pulled her coat a little tighter around her. She didn't much like it when Sheriff Wall said she was pretty. "We came to church this morning to see you."

The sheriff nodded. "Sorry I wasn't there. Now, answer me this—did you plan to take this money away from the café?"

Millie relaxed. "No."

The sheriff frowned. "So you're maintaining your innocence? You're saying you weren't in here last night planning to steal this money?"

"No, I was giving the money away."

Mrs. Hargrove gasped. "Don't tell me it's charity!"

Millie looked over at the older woman. She seemed more upset than she had been all morning.

"I bet it's that church in Miles City." Mrs. Hargrove was nodding emphatically as she turned to look at the rest of the townspeople. "Remember last year they wanted to give us food baskets? I told Pastor Hanks we didn't need their pity."

"Of course, we don't need any pity," the older man at the edge of the group said. "We can take care of each other."

"It's not charity," Millie said softly. "It's a gift from someone who cares about each of you."

"Maybe it's from Doris June," the old man said as he looked over at Mrs. Hargrove. "You told me she was doing pretty good at that job of hers in Alaska now that they gave her that big raise. Isn't she making another ten grand a year now?"

"Even if she is, my daughter knows better than to throw her money away like this."

"I wasn't throwing it away," Millie protested. "I was trying to do the right thing."

Sheriff Wall put up his hand. "No sense in anyone getting all stirred up until we find out where the money came from. Mrs. Hargrove, do you have that telephone number for Linda down in Los Angeles?"

The older woman nodded. "It's at home."

"Well, would you mind calling Linda and asking her how much money she had in the cash register when she left?"

"I'll be back in a minute." Mrs. Hargrove turned around and started toward the café door. "And while I'm there, I'm going to call that Pastor Hanks and give him a piece of my mind. Charity—we don't need charity. The people of Dry Creek are doing just fine."

She slammed the screen door on her way out.

"Now—" the sheriff looked around at everyone in the room "—I'm going to ask everyone to step outside. Until we know otherwise, this is a crime scene in here, and I intend to keep it pure."

Millie looked around. The day was warming up, and sun streamed in through the windows. Most people kept their coats open, so they must be comfortable in the café even though it wasn't heated. They were all standing around the tables.

Millie thought the old man who was at the side of the room, the one who had been talking earlier, might be Elmer. And the couple sitting down at a table were probably the Redferns. The woman looked pretty enough to have been a cocktail waitress in Vegas, and she was holding a baby who looked like he was a year old. Forrest hadn't met her when he was in Dry Creek, but he'd heard about her in a letter Mrs. Hargrove had sent to him.

The people started walking toward the door. Millie turned to join them.

"Not you," the sheriff said as he put his hand on Millie's arm. "You stay with me. I need to ask you some more questions."

Millie nodded. She supposed she'd have to expect questions. At least until Mrs. Hargrove was able to talk to Linda and find out that the money hadn't been left in the café when Linda went away.

"In the meantime, why don't you count that money?" The sheriff nodded toward Brad. "Give us some idea of what we're talking about here. Misdemeanor or felony."

Millie was glad that Brad wasn't leaving with the others. She didn't feel exactly comfortable with the sheriff, not when he was asking her all of those questions. She wasn't sure that Brad believed that she wasn't a thief, but she did feel safer with him around.

Brad looked up. "They'd give her a hard time if it was a felony."

The sheriff nodded.

"I don't think she intended that much harm," Brad said as he walked over to the table that held the bills. "She probably just wanted some traveling money. That car of hers looks like it'd fall apart if someone sneezed in it. She probably needs to repair it, and I'd guess that'd take a fortune."

"There's nothing wrong with my car," Millie said before she remembered the ping in the engine. And the hiccup in the carburetor.

"That car needs to be taken out and given a decent burial," Brad muttered.

Millie frowned. She was slowly figuring out that the reason she felt safe with Brad was because he saw her as a kid instead of as a woman. Not that she wanted him to look at her like he wanted to kiss her or anything. But it was annoying to be around him and realize he was so totally immune to her charms.

Of course, she wasn't exactly swooning over him, either. Granted, he was tall and powerful. She supposed most women would fall at his feet. Fortunately, he wasn't her kind of man at all.

She'd always thought that if she was going to be attracted to a man it would be a man who was quieter. Someone who didn't always require attention and service. Someone who would be content to blend into the background with her. A man like Brad didn't blend at all. He stood out and demanded attention.

No, she shook her head, Brad wasn't even close to her ideal man. She should be grateful he didn't notice her. And if he wanted to treat her like a kid, so much the better. She'd just treat him like a—a— Millie sighed. She couldn't treat him like anything but what he was. The most gorgeous man she'd ever seen, with or without her glasses on.

Chapter Six

"Well, how much money is there?" the sheriff asked.

Millie had sat down on one of the chairs and loosened her coat. The sun was shining in through the windows and had warmed up the café considerably. The red-and-white floor gave the place a cozy feel. There were a dozen small tables in the place. Millie wouldn't mind working in a small place like this if she ever left Ruby's.

Brad grunted in answer to the sheriff's question. He had sat down at a different table and counted the bills.

Millie didn't need to hear Brad's answer to know that there were seventy-five hundred-dollar bills in that sack. She supposed that was more than enough to be a felony. She wondered how far she should carry Forrest's request to not let anyone in Dry Creek know she was his friend. Surely, he wouldn't want her to actually be arrested.

"It's not as much money as it looks like," Brad said slowly. He didn't look at either Millie or the sheriff. "I didn't quite get it all counted, so I don't have an exact count. But I'd guess it's under a thousand."

Millie sat up straight at Brad's answer. "There's more than that."

Brad wanted to put his head down and bang it against the table. Here he was trying to keep Millie out of jail, and she was doing nothing to help him. He clenched his teeth. "I'm sure there's not enough here to warrant felony charges."

"Oh," Millie said.

Finally, the woman looked like she was coming to her senses. At least she didn't argue with him again about the amount of money on the table. What was Linda doing with all that money anyway? Business at the café hadn't been *that* good.

Brad wondered if Linda and that boyfriend of hers had managed to sell the farm they had just bought. Brad rather hoped not. He had his eye on that place himself, and almost had enough saved to put a good down payment on it if it came on the market again.

"Well, it's fine with me if it's not a felony," the sheriff said. He'd picked up a few pieces of paper with tweezers and placed them in a bag. "I'd just as soon not do the extra paperwork."

Brad nodded. "Looking for fingerprints?"

Sheriff Carl Wall nodded without much enthusiasm. He was a decent sort of guy. He wouldn't be any more comfortable than Brad would be if they had to send Millie away on felony charges.

Brad looked over at Millie. The woman should sit in sunlight more often. The light filtered through her short blond hair and made her look almost angelic. She just didn't look dishonest, and that fact made Brad hesitant.

Brad had always thought he was a pretty good judge of people. A thief should look like a thief—at least when he looked in her eyes. Brad had been looking in Millie's green eyes and not seeing anything that made him think she was lying.

"Not that it'll do much good even if I do find fingerprints," Sheriff Wall continued. "This is a public place. People can have their fingerprints all over here and it's not a crime. Besides, Millie didn't actually take the money off the premises. Don't know if I'd have enough to ever get it to trial. Plus, there weren't any witnesses."

Brad nodded. "I sure didn't see anything."

Brad decided he'd done more than his share of good deeds for the day. He'd gone to church and stayed through the sermon. He'd even sung a hymn or two. Then he'd had mercy on a poor woman who obviously needed someone to take care of her. "I guess it's sort of like grace."

Millie looked up at him and blinked.

Brad stood up and walked over to where the woman sat. "You know, the pastor in church talked about grace. That's how it is for you—not having to go to prison and all. We'll just call your sins forgiven."

Brad sat down in a chair across the table from Millie. He was pleased with himself. Maybe he should go to church more often. He seemed to have a flair for making moral points.

"I didn't ask for forgiveness," Millie protested softly, and then bit her lip. "I don't have anything to be forgiven for—at least, not with the money. The money is mine to give away."

Brad frowned. Well, maybe he wasn't so good at making those points after all. But then the woman looked tired. Not that she wavered in what she said. He had to admire the fact that she had stuck with her story. She was tenacious for such a little thing. He was kind of growing to like her. "Do you ever flirt?"

Millie looked startled.

"I was just wondering. You're always so serious." Brad had never been attracted to a serious woman until now. He supposed it must have something to do with the Christmas season. He was all out of whack around Christmas.

"Men don't respect you when you flirt with them."

Brad shrugged. "Sometimes it's just a way of being friendly."

Millie was quiet for a moment, and then she looked down at the top of the table. "That's what some of the other waitresses said. And then they told me I'd get more tips that way."

"You're a waitress?" Brad was surprised. Usually waitresses did know how to flirt. Millie's co-workers were right—they did get more tips that way. He knew he always gave a little extra to someone who had entertained him with a joke or two.

Millie looked up at him. "What's wrong with me being a waitress?"

Brad spread his hands. "Nothing. Some of my favorite people are waitresses."

It was odd, Brad thought. When Millie looked so serious, those glasses somehow suited her face. She was as solemn as a Madonna, but she looked good. Maybe it was just the sun in her hair and the defiant look in those eyes of hers.

"I can flirt," Millie lied. What was it about that man that made her want to prove him wrong on everything? It was a good thing he didn't ask her if she could fly.

Maybe it was the arrogant way he sat there and

seemed to assume someone should pay attention to him. He was the kind of man she usually didn't want sitting at one of her tables at Ruby's. Not that he'd probably be worried about that. He wouldn't starve. If he ever did get to Ruby's, the other waitresses would fight over bringing him his order.

"I just don't think it's honest to flirt with someone so they give you a bigger tip. A tip is for the service," Millie finished.

"And the smile," Brad said and paused. "I know a nice smile has cheered me up when I've been discouraged. I think that's worth something."

"Well, yes, of course. It's always good to be friendly."

Millie knew she sounded about as prim as a country schoolteacher. The truth was that she couldn't flirt with men because men, real men, scared her a little. Of course, she couldn't admit that to someone like Brad. "I flirt with short men."

Brad frowned at that. "How short?"

"Shorter than me."

"But you're not even five feet tall."

Millie nodded. "Short men need encouragement, too."

"I'm pretty short," Sheriff Wall offered. He had been quiet, and Millie had forgotten he was there, but he had obviously been listening. "Maybe a bit more'n five feet, but short enough to need encouragement."

"You're the sheriff. That's encouragement enough," Brad said.

The sheriff walked over to the table. "Maybe, but if the lady likes short men, I thought I should put my hat in the ring. She's not going to find any men around here who are shorter than me."

"She doesn't like short men."

Sheriff Wall smiled. "Just because you're six-four, there's no reason to be cross. Plenty of women like tall men. You should leave a few for the rest of us, especially if they like short men."

Millie figured the sheriff was right. Plenty of women did like men as tall as Brad. Somehow the thought wasn't as comforting as it should have been. She looked over at Brad. "I suppose you have someone special anyway."

Brad grinned. "I'm free as a bird."

Millie blinked. She couldn't believe she actually cared.

Brad heard the knock on the café door before it became a pounding. He was enjoying the pink that was covering Millie's face, though, and he didn't much want to get up and answer the door.

It was slowly occurring to Brad that Millie might have cured his Christmas blues. He hadn't had a discouraging thought since he'd met her. Of course, that might be because he'd been busy trying to figure out whether or not she was a thief.

Maybe he should do something like this every Christmas. He didn't suppose, though, that he could count on the café to provide him with a thief just before Christmas every year.

"Are you going to answer that?" Millie finally asked.

Brad looked at Sheriff Wall. "You're the public servant."

Sheriff Wall snorted. "That doesn't mean I get the door."

Still, the sheriff stood up and walked over to the door. Halfway there, he stopped and looked back at Millie. "Just remember, Brad's too tall for you."

Millie blushed a bright red.

Brad smiled. Now she looked like a Madonna with a sunburn.

Millie turned to look at the door. Maybe if she ignored Brad and his teasing, he would stop looking at her like that—like he knew something that she didn't, and it was causing him to smile like a simpleton.

"I'm not really six-four," Brad whispered to Millie. "If I take my boots off, I'm only six-three. I'm shorter than you think."

"I don't care how tall you are."

Millie turned all of her attention to the doorway. It wasn't difficult to do, because Mrs. Hargrove was waving something at the sheriff and trying to talk.

"Let me get my breath," she finally said.

Mrs. Hargrove was standing in the doorway and taking deep breaths. She looked like she'd been running or, at least, walking fast. Her gray hair was a little disheveled and her coat was unbuttoned.

"You should have taken it easy getting back," Sheriff Wall said as he helped Mrs. Hargrove to a chair. "We're not in any rush."

"But—the money's—not Linda's," Mrs. Hargrove said as she sat down.

Millie could see the sheriff frown.

"Did you say it's not Linda's?"

Mrs. Hargrove took a deep breath. "No one left any money in the café. I talked to Linda, and she cleaned out the cash drawer to buy her plane ticket. She also said she wished she hadn't, but that's a different matter."

"So that means…" the sheriff began thoughtfully.

Everyone was silent for a moment.

"How about that church?" Brad asked. "You know, the one with the Christmas baskets."

Mrs. Hargrove shook her head. "I called Pastor Hanks. He thought I was nuts. He said they don't have that kind of money to give away in Christmas baskets, especially this year. They're giving canned green beans and some of those fried onion rings, so people can make a Christmas casserole. Then he said it had been a hard year and asked *me* for a donation. I told him I'd send him five dollars."

Everyone was silent for another moment. Millie kind of liked the silence she found in Dry Creek. There wasn't any traffic noise. There were no airplanes flying overhead. There weren't even any barking dogs, although she supposed that was only for the moment.

"So the money was hers," Brad said finally as he looked at Millie.

Mrs. Hargrove beamed. "That means she's innocent."

"Still, something's funny," the sheriff said as he scratched his head. "For one thing, she made an unlawful entry here even if it was because she was hungry or something."

Millie swallowed. She'd forgotten about using the key to get inside the café. That had seemed like the least of her worries.

"Not that that's worth locking her up over," the sheriff continued. "Not with the heating problems over at the jail and all. It costs fifty bucks a day just to keep a prisoner in jail this time of year, and the café is open to everyone."

"I'm sorry about the breaking and entering," Millie offered.

"See, she's sorry," Brad added.

Millie looked at Brad. He was looking at her like she'd just passed some sort of test and he'd guided her through it. If she wasn't mistaken, the man actually looked proud of her. Millie couldn't remember the last time anyone except Forrest had been proud of her.

The sheriff nodded. "Still, we have to do something. We can't have strangers thinking they can come into town and break into a place of business and nothing happens."

"I could pay a fine," Millie offered. Now that the money was hers again, she could use one of the hundred-dollar bills to pay the fine. She could take it from one of the extra stockings. "If it's a small fine, that is. I don't have too much extra."

"How far are you planning on driving?" Brad asked incredulously. "That money in there would take you to either coast."

"The money's not for me." Millie realized the people of Dry Creek had not suspected she was going to put the money in their stockings. Which meant that she just might pull off a Christmas surprise after all.

The sheriff shook his head. "I'm not doing some kind of fancy fine. It'd be one thing if it was a traffic fine, but I'd have to drive into Miles City just to get a form for a special-circumstance fine."

"Well, you give parking fines all the time," Brad said. "Charge her with one of those."

Sheriff Wall looked at Millie. "Might be better to just give her some community service to do."

Mrs. Hargrove brightened. "We do have a lot of work left to get ready for Christmas."

"Christmas?" Brad frowned. "I was thinking community service would involve something like picking the litter off the roads or something. I could help her with that. But Christmas—"

"No one can do litter removal with all this snow unless they have a bulldozer," Mrs. Hargrove said. "Besides, we've always done a good job of celebrating Christmas in Dry Creek." Mrs. Hargrove looked at Brad. "Just because you don't like Christmas, it doesn't mean it's not a good community-service project. Besides, it's time you got over your problems with Christmas anyway. It'll do you good."

Brad stared at her. "Who told you I have problems with Christmas?"

"Everybody knows." Mrs. Hargrove shrugged. "Why do you think we let you park behind the café last night and didn't bother you?"

"You knew I was there?"

Mrs. Hargrove looked at Brad. "Christmas can be a hard time when you have memories you would rather forget. But as far as I know, the only remedy is to make new memories."

"I don't have any memories," Brad protested, and realized it was true. And that's what bothered him most about Christmas. Other people could talk about the happy times they had shared with their families at Christmas. But he couldn't recall any. He was five when his parents were killed in the car accident, but he didn't remember any Christmases before that. Surely, he should have some memories of Christmas.

"What would I do for Christmas?" Millie asked.

Brad thought she looked a little too eager for someone facing community service. Brad turned to the sheriff. "It's not supposed to be fun, you know. She can't just decorate a Christmas tree or something."

"She could help get ready for the church service," Mrs. Hargrove said.

"I could help you get those black streaks off the floor," Millie offered.

"You know how to do that?" Mrs. Hargrove asked.

Millie nodded.

"Then you're an answer to my prayers."

"Well, I can't just let her run around free, either," the sheriff said as he looked at Mrs. Hargrove. "I don't suppose you would—"

"I'll be happy to keep an eye on her."

Brad snorted. "She'd sweet-talk her way around you in no time."

Mrs. Hargrove's eyes started to twinkle, and she nodded to Brad. "Maybe you should join us then."

"What?" The sheriff frowned. "Oh, I don't think that will be necessary. I planned to keep an eye on her myself."

Brad grinned. Mrs. Hargrove might be old, but she understood a young man's heart. It didn't always need to be the short man who got a break with the new woman in town. Brad turned to the sheriff. "Don't you have to be on duty?"

Sheriff Wall grunted. "No more than you do."

"Things are slow at the Elkton Ranch this time of year. I'm sure they can spare me for a little civic duty."

Millie was bewildered. It sounded like both of the men actually wanted to spend time with her. And they'd have to watch her mop a floor to do it. That didn't sound like any fun. "You'll get your shirt dirty standing around."

"I have some old shirts," Brad said.

"And I have some extra scrub brushes just waiting

for a volunteer," Mrs. Hargrove said. "We've tried everything on those black streaks."

"I'll bring some coffee for a break when I come by in the morning," the sheriff said. "No point in anyone starting today. Besides, it's Sunday."

Brad turned to Millie. "I have some extra old shirts. You'll probably need one, too. I'll get you fixed up when we get back to the bunkhouse."

Sheriff Wall frowned. "I don't know if she should stay at the bunkhouse."

Millie agreed with the sheriff. "I don't mind the jail."

"Oh, you can't stay in the jail, dear," Mrs. Hargrove said. "It's cold this time of year. Besides, I think the bunkhouse might be just the place. Charlie will keep an eye on things."

"She can have my room. I don't mind sleeping on the couch."

"Well, it's all set then," Mrs. Hargrove said as she pointed to the money and then looked at Millie. "I guess that's all yours then. Keep it in a safe place."

"The bunkhouse is safe."

The sheriff nodded and looked at Millie. "Just don't go spending it too fast. I plan to make a couple of inquires just in case there've been any other thefts recently in the area. I should hear back today."

"Just as long as you know by Christmas," Millie said. She would want to have the stockings ready before Christmas Day. She was glad that things seemed to be working out. She didn't mind spending a couple of days in Dry Creek.

Millie looked at Brad. He was still smiling.

"Does everybody here drink the same water?" Millie asked. Maybe there was some kind of mineral in the water around here that made people smile a lot. She'd heard about places where the population was a little below average in intelligence because of a tainted water supply. She supposed a mineral that got into the water supply could have a similar effect on emotions.

"I guess we do," Mrs. Hargrove said. "We all have our own wells, but it comes from the same water table."

Millie nodded. "I was just curious."

Brad couldn't help but see the change that came over Sheriff Wall. The sheriff had been leaning against the wall by the door, and he straightened up. The smile left his face. His eyes narrowed like he was thinking.

"What kind of stuff do you figure you need to clean those black streaks off the floor?" he finally asked Millie.

Brad wondered why the sheriff was that interested in floor cleaners and then realized the man probably wasn't. Something else was going on here.

"I thought I'd get some baking soda," Millie said.

Mrs. Hargrove nodded. "That might work."

The sheriff was silent for a moment. "I've got baking soda at the office. I'll bring some out for you tomorrow. No point in buying any new."

"Oh, I don't mind," Millie said. "It won't take long to get some. And, if that doesn't work, I know another trick or two."

"Best to use county supplies since it is a public building."

"I wouldn't call the church a public building," Mrs. Hargrove protested. "I mean, it's open to the public, but we're independent."

"Still," the sheriff said, "I think it's best."

He turned toward the café door and motioned to

Brad. "Mind if I have a word with you before we head out? You know, to explain your duties and all."

"Sure." Brad got up. He wasn't sure what was making the sheriff look older than his years, but he expected he would soon find out. He was pretty sure it was related to this floor-cleaning project.

Brad had scarcely stepped out onto the porch and closed the café door behind Sheriff Wall than the sheriff started to talk.

"I don't like it," Sheriff Wall said. "All them chemicals and cleaners—who knows what she's up to? Especially when she's asking about our water supply."

"You're not worried she's planning to do something to our water?"

"Well, not the water. It'd be hard to hit all the wells. But I didn't like the fact that she was asking," the sheriff said. "The way I figure it, that money could be payment for doing something—maybe the something just hasn't happened yet."

"Oh, I don't think—" Brad began to protest, but then he remembered. Dry Creek wasn't the same place that it had been before the hit man had come two years ago. He could no longer just assume that the only crimes in town were kids being mischievous.

Sheriff Wall nodded. "All I'm saying is that we need to keep an eye on her until we know how she came by that money."

"Maybe she saved it," Brad suggested. He didn't like to picture Millie as a criminal.

The sheriff shrugged. "Even if she saved it, what's she doing carrying it around in a brown paper bag? Most anyone I know who saves that kind of money keeps it in a bank or gets a cashier's check or something."

Brad had to admit the sheriff had a point. What would a waitress be doing with that kind of cash on her? And all in hundred-dollar bills. It wasn't her tip money, that was for sure.

"I'll keep a close eye on her," Brad said. He felt another headache coming on. The only good thing was that he figured this Christmas would be one he'd always remember.

Mrs. Hargrove thought he needed memories. Well, it looked like he was going to have them whether he wanted them or not.

He couldn't help smiling a little. He guessed he did want them, especially if the memories included a little bit of a woman with green eyes.

Chapter Seven

Millie drove her car back to the bunkhouse at the Elkton Ranch thinking the rest of the day would be spent in Brad's little room. Not that that was bad. She supposed it was better than a jail cell. The room was warm, and he had lots of books that she could read. She wouldn't mind dipping into a mystery novel or taking a nap.

Brad had driven his pickup right behind her all the way to the bunkhouse. He said it was so he'd be sure she didn't get stuck in a snowdrift, but she knew he was also making sure she didn't drive off now that she had the money.

Millie smiled to herself. All in all, it hadn't gone so badly. She hadn't been forced to tell anyone that she was in Dry Creek because of Forrest. Now if she could just avoid any other questions, she would do fine. The more she thought about it, a quiet afternoon all alone in Brad's room sounded perfect.

Millie hadn't stepped all the way into the bunkhouse before Charlie came trotting over to the door.

"There you are!" Charlie said as he held out his hand for Millie's coat. "I was hoping you'd get back soon."

Millie looked up. Charlie was looking directly at her. "Me?"

Charlie nodded. "We need a woman's advice about the Christmas tree."

"Christmas tree?" Brad asked. He had followed right behind Millie through the bunkhouse door. "Since when do we put up a Christmas tree?"

"We decided this year should be different since we have company," Charlie said as he smiled at Millie. "Mrs. Hargrove called to tell you to dress in old clothes when you go down to clean the church tomorrow."

"Oh, I will." Millie slipped out of her coat and gave it to Charlie.

"Mrs. Hargrove is the one that said you'd be staying with us through Christmas," Charlie added as he turned to walk to the corner closet.

Brad decided the world had gone crazy. Charlie had shaved off his beard, and he usually didn't do that until spring. In addition, he was carrying Millie's coat to the corner closet as if they didn't always leave their coats in a pile on the one chair. And, unless Brad missed his guess, Charlie was also wearing his church shirt, and here it was the middle of the afternoon! Granted, it was still Sunday, but Charlie usually couldn't wait to change into his working clothes whenever he came back to the bunkhouse.

Plus, Brad took a tentative sniff, he could smell cinnamon.

Brad looked around. The smell was coming from the black woodstove that stood in the corner of the bunkhouse living area. He didn't have to walk over to see the tin can sitting on the stove. "Who's cooking cinnamon?"

Charlie was back from the closet and had the decency to blush. "I saw it on TV—you put a stick of cinnamon in some water and boil it. It makes the air fresh for holiday company."

Brad needed to sit down. He walked over to a straight-back chair that was sitting next to the stove. "I thought that's what coffee was for."

"I wasn't sure Millie liked coffee," Charlie said anxiously. "I didn't see her drink any at breakfast."

"Of course she likes coffee," Brad said. He had to move a bowl of popcorn so he could sit down. "She's a waitress."

Brad held the bowl of popcorn on his lap.

"Don't eat any of that!" Charlie ordered. "That's for the tree."

Brad looked down at the popcorn. "We're really having a tree? A live tree? Not just one of those tinfoil things that they sometimes give away at the diesel fuel place in Miles City?"

Charlie nodded emphatically. "Of course we're having a real tree. We've got to have a proper Christmas tree if we have company."

Millie blinked. She had never been someone's Christmas company. Charlie said it like it was an honor. A sliver of panic streaked through her. "I've never helped with a tree before."

Brad looked up from his popcorn and frowned. "Never?"

Millie shook her head. "I think they're pretty, of course. But I usually just got myself a poinsettia plant or something like that. A tinfoil thing would be just fine with me."

"Didn't your family celebrate Christmas?" Brad asked.

Millie blushed. "My foster mother was always too tired."

Brad gave a low sympathetic growl.

"Not that I minded," Millie said quickly. "I didn't need to have Christmas."

"Well, don't you worry about a thing, we're going to have just as much Christmas as we can right here," Charlie said. "And we're starting with a tree. How hard can it be to do a Christmas tree? That lady on television gave a few pointers. I'm sure we can figure it out."

"But there's a lot to having a tree. For one thing, you have to have decorations, and we don't have any," Brad said. "Everyone knows you need decorations."

"Well, Jeff's gone to Miles City to look for decorations," Charlie said. "All we need to do is get the stand ready for the tree, so that when he gets back we can go chop one down before it starts to snow again."

Brad frowned. "Where are you going to find pine trees this far down from the mountains?"

"We'll find something," Charlie said. "As I recall, there's a few pines on the north side of the ranch near that gully."

"But those trees are the windbreak for the north pasture," Brad protested. "The boss will have our hides if we chop them down. Besides, the cattle won't have any shelter then."

"Well, we wouldn't chop them all down. All we need is one little Christmas tree. The cows won't miss that. Then we'll get the popcorn strung and see what other decorations Jeff brings back."

Millie felt like she'd fallen down the rabbit hole and entered a whole new world. She was surprised she didn't have visions of sugarplums and reindeer danc-

ing in her head. Actually, come to think of it, she did
seem to have a little ringing in her ears. "Do you have
any aspirin?"

Charlie looked over at her and thought a minute.
"I think they'd be too small for decorations, but they
are white, so maybe we could glue them on to something red."

"The aspirin's not for the tree," Millie said. She was
beginning to feel the responsibility of being the Christmas company. No wonder so many people came to Ruby's for Christmas dinner. All they had to do then was
pay for dinner. They didn't need to provide inspiration.
"And—ah, speaking of the tree, I hope you're not doing
anything special just because I'm here. I don't mind
not having Christmas. Really. I usually don't do all the
Christmas things anyway."

"Don't you worry about Christmas," the old man
protested at the same time as he turned to scowl at
Brad. "And don't think that we're going to let you mope
around this Christmas, either. That's okay when it's just
us guys here. But it's not okay when you have company."

Millie decided she really needed that aspirin. Or she
would if she had to listen to Brad say one more time that
she wasn't his company, wasn't his girlfriend, wasn't
his date—wasn't his anything.

"You're right," Brad said simply. "I do need to cheer
up and stop thinking about myself."

Millie looked at him skeptically.

Brad smiled at her slightly.

Millie looked at him and frowned a little.

Brad grinned and just kept looking at her.

"No one said where there was an aspirin," Millie finally said.

"I've got some right here." Brad handed her a small tin.

"I never take aspirin," Millie said as she snapped the tin open. Half of the eight tablets were already gone. She took out two of the remaining ones and handed it back to Brad.

"Neither do I," Brad said as he picked out two tablets for himself. "Neither do I."

Brad decided he was going to do Christmas right if it killed him—which, in this case, it just might. If he had a brain in his head, he would drive Millie back to town and let the sheriff take over guarding her. Let the county pay a few bucks to heat the jail. He'd even bring her a tinfoil tree to set in the window.

Brad no sooner thought of it than the picture of Millie spending Christmas in jail passed by his mind and he knew he couldn't do it, not even if he went in and sat in the cell with her and the little tree.

No, he had to make Christmas special for her. He had thought he was the only one who had never done any of the usual Christmas things, but it seemed like Millie might have him beat. She seemed more clueless about Christmas than he did. And he would have to be blind not to see the wistful look on her face when someone mentioned the Christmas tree.

"Can't we just tie the tree to that pole lamp or something? You know, the cast-iron one with the bear?" Millie asked as she watched him carefully select two pieces of lumber to make a Christmas tree stand. They were out in the barn and the wind was blowing in the open door. Millie was sitting on a bale of hay. Brad had the light on even though it wasn't more than three o'clock in the afternoon.

"The tree would be all crooked that way," Brad said. Ever since he'd decided to celebrate Christmas, he was determined to not take any shortcuts. Not that the lamp idea was a bad one. Charlie had won that lamp at some senior bingo party, and it would bear the weight of a tree—it just wouldn't keep it straight.

Still, it was kind of sweet of Millie to sit there with that little frown on her forehead and worry about how to save him the time and effort of building a stand. "Besides, it's not a problem. I can make a tree stand in no time."

Brad had built line shacks and corrals. He knew a little about engineering and carpentry. A tree stand wasn't even a challenge, but he wasn't in any particular hurry to finish the task and head back inside where all the other guys were sitting around stringing popcorn.

"Well, I guess if it's a small tree, it'll work," Millie said as she stood and walked over to look down at the lumber. "It will be a small tree, won't it?"

"It'll have to be. A large one will be too big for the horses to drag."

"Horses?" Millie stepped back. "Aren't we going in the pickup?"

Brad shook his head. "Too much snow this time of year. The horses are a better way to get there."

"But I've never ridden a horse."

Brad looked up at her. She looked a little scared and nervous and he decided that her look must be growing on him, because he didn't consider all of the other options that they had. "Then you'll have to ride double with me."

Brad held his breath. He wasn't at all sure that she would want to ride double with him. She might not know it, but riding a horse double was almost a date in Montana. After all her talk about short men and flirting, he'd gotten the distinct impression that she didn't want to date anyone and, if he was honest, she especially seemed not to want to date him.

"I don't know…isn't it cold?" Millie asked.

"You can wear my parka. It's down-filled and good for twenty below zero."

Brad didn't add that the lining was some kind of special silk and he'd spent a month's salary on it.

"But what about you?" Millie looked up at him, and her green eyes were full of concern.

"Don't worry about me. I'll keep warm," Brad promised. He was slowly realizing he'd like nothing better than to have Millie lean into him as they rode his horse back to the ranch. He'd ride without a shirt or a coat if he had to, just to have her trust him like he was picturing in his mind.

Millie still had that little frown on her forehead.

"I can borrow one of the spare coats," Brad added, and watched as her frown lifted. He congratulated himself that she cared about him and his comfort.

"You wouldn't be able to drive the horse if you got too cold," Millie said.

"Oh." Brad decided maybe she didn't care as much as he'd hoped. Brad drove a nail into the lumber he had set for the tree stand. There was no need to prolong the task. He drove in another nail. "You don't need to worry. The horse knows the way back to the ranch anyway. Even if I couldn't ride him, he'd make it back to his stall."

Millie nodded.

Brad hammered the final nail into the lumber and stood up. "Here. We've got us a tree stand."

Brad opened the barn door for Millie and followed her out into the yard of the ranch. Snow covered most of the ground, although it had been pretty well stamped down from all the feet that had walked over it. The air was cold, and Brad saw Millie put her hands in the pockets of her long black coat. "I'll lend you some gloves, too."

"I can just put my hands in the pockets of your coat," Millie said.

"Not if you plan to stay on the horse."

Brad regretted his words the moment they were out of his mouth. He could tell Millie was worried, so he added, "Don't worry. I won't let you fall off."

Millie knew something was wrong the minute she and Brad stepped inside the main room of the bunk-house. There were two long strings of popcorn garland running between the bear lamp and green recliner. There were Christmas carols playing on a small CD player. What there wasn't any sign of was peace on earth and goodwill toward men.

All of the men in the room were hunched over something on the floor by the stove, and they were clearly arguing.

"I tell you it's wrong," Charlie said as he studied what looked like a large piece of white paper. "It doesn't look like any angel I've ever seen."

Millie walked over to the men. Someone had drawn a crayon picture of an angel—at least she thought it must be an angel. "Are those wings?"

"See, she can tell those are wings," Randy said triumphantly.

"She was *asking* if they were wings," Charlie protested. "That's a big difference."

Randy looked up at Millie. "It just didn't seem right putting wings on an angel like it was some big chicken or something. I mean, what's something like an angel doing with chicken wings? I think their wings should look more like a horse's mane. You know, rows and rows of curling hair. Now, hair is nice. It's got class. It's fitting for someone who lives in heaven."

"I notice the wings are blond," Brad said from behind Millie's shoulders. "You always were partial to blondes."

"That's an angel you're talking about," Charlie said. "Show some respect."

"Well, she's not an angel if she doesn't have wings," Brad said. "She's just a good-looking woman in a white nightgown with lots of blond hair. Lots and lots of hair."

"She kind of looks like that country-western singer with the big—" William began and then looked at Millie and blushed "—with the big hats."

Charlie cleared his throat. "I hope you're not planning on putting any—hats—on the angel. We run a respectable place here."

"We're a bunkhouse," Brad protested.

Charlie lifted his chin. "As long as we have Christmas company, we're a home, and a home has certain standards."

Brad was speechless.

"Wow, that's kind of nice," Randy said. "It's good to have a home at Christmas."

Brad looked over at Millie. How was it that one woman could make their bunkhouse a home for Christmas?

Come to think of it maybe that was why he got so depressed at Christmas. Christmas was a time for families, and every year when the holiday came around it reminded him that he was alone. All he had to do was listen to a song on the radio or pass by a display in a store to know that Christmas was for families. That must be it.

Brad was almost relieved. It was all because of decorations and ads that he was depressed. Everyone had to face the advertising world at some point and realize that just because someone in an ad had something it didn't mean he had to have it.

No, he just needed perspective. He certainly didn't need to change his being single. All he had to do was get through these few days each December.

He just needed to remember that Christmas was only one day. He still had the other 364 days left to enjoy his bachelorhood. The advertising world didn't make so much of families the other 364 days.

Yeah, he had the good life. Once he got past Christmas, his life would be normal again. He'd be worrying about a poker hand instead of popcorn garlands. It would all be fine. Christmas would be here and gone soon. Maybe even quicker if he could hurry it along. "We better go see about that tree."

"I rigged up a sled for the tree," Randy said as he stood up and brushed his hands off on his jeans. "My horse can pull that easy enough."

"I figured I could bring the ax," William offered.

"But you can't just leave the Christmas drawing," Millie protested.

"Oh, yeah," Randy said as he bent down and rolled the paper up. "I'll need to finish it after we get the tree up so we can put it on top."

Brad nodded numbly. It shouldn't surprise him that they were going to have an angel who looked like a Vegas dancer sitting on top of their Christmas tree.

"I'll have some cocoa waiting for when you get back," Charlie said as they all started to look for their coats. It took a minute for everyone to realize Charlie had hung the coats up in the closet. No one ever hung up the coats.

Brad almost shook his head. He wasn't the only one who was going crazy at Christmas. Randy was drawing angels and Charlie was turning into Little Miss Homemaker.

It was going to be a miracle if they all survived this Christmas without turning into city gentlemen with manicured nails who refused to change the oil in their car. Before long, they'd all be useless.

And it was all her fault, Brad thought as he looked at Millie.

How could one woman who looked so small make such a big difference in this old bunkhouse?

Chapter Eight

Millie felt like she was in a snow globe as she rode behind Brad's saddle. The sun was setting, but there was still enough light to see the snowflakes fall. The air was so cold it felt brittle, but Millie found the steady sway of Brad's horse comforting. The landscape dipped into a long gully and then rose to small hills all around.

Millie couldn't remember the last time she'd been in a landscape with such openness. She didn't see any houses or roads or telephone poles. All she could see were stretches of white snow and the hoofprints the horses had made on their way into the gully where the pine trees stood.

Charlie was right. The cows wouldn't miss the small tree they had cut and strapped onto the sled that Randy pulled behind his horse.

They had debated which tree to cut until they saw the little tree. The branches on the tree were crooked, and William, after studying the ground around it, said they were doing the poor thing a favor by cutting it down. It was surrounded by taller trees and wasn't getting enough sunlight to grow properly.

The tree reminded Millie of that tree she'd tried to make long ago out of tinfoil and metal hangers. The tree was spindly and deformed, but somehow it tugged at her heart.

Millie turned her head around. It was getting dark, but she could still see Randy and William following behind them. She quickly turned her head back. The gap between her and Brad's back when she turned let cold air between them. Millie shivered. She was glad she had Brad's back to block the wind that came with the snow flurries.

"Sorry," Millie whispered. She suspected the borrowed coat Brad was wearing wasn't nearly as warm as the parka he had lent her, so she leaned against him as closely as she could so that at least his back would be warm.

"No problem," Brad mumbled.

All of the horses kept their heads down as they walked into the wind, and Millie knew Brad kept his head down and had his wool scarf tied around his mouth. A bandanna kept his hat tied down and his ears warm.

Millie settled into her place on Brad's back. She rested her cheek against his one shoulder and wrapped her arms more securely around his waist. She had to lift the edge of his coat in order to hold tight to his waist, and she worried that in doing so she left room for a draft of cold air. She had offered earlier to put her hands on the outside of his coat, but he had declined, saying she'd freeze her fingers.

Millie could feel the snaps on Brad's shirt, and she kept her hands clasped around the snap just above his brass belt buckle. Her hands had made a warm spot against his stomach, and they were cozy there.

Millie wondered why she felt so comfortable pressed against Brad's back this way. Well, maybe "comfortable" was the wrong word. It was more a feeling of belonging than comfort. It must be because, with her hands clasped around his stomach, they had started breathing to the same rhythm. Or maybe it was because she could be so close to him and she didn't have to worry that he was going to turn around and want to talk or anything.

Millie sighed. It wasn't easy when you were a shy woman to spend any time around an outgoing man like Brad. She'd been a waitress long enough to know men like him weren't happy with simple conversation; they wanted witty remarks and flirtatious comments. The few times Millie had gone out with men like that she'd learned she wasn't what they were looking for in a date. Those dates had been disastrous, and she wouldn't care to repeat them.

It was too bad, she thought. There was something about Brad that she was growing to like, especially now as they rode through the darkening night. If only they could ride like this forever and not have to talk.

"You can see the lights of the bunkhouse," Brad said through his muffled scarf. "We're almost home."

Millie nodded and snuggled a little closer. Brad pulled on the horse's reins and she could feel his muscles ripple down his back. She thought for a second that she would have to remember to tell the other waitresses about this ride, but then she realized she never would. This night belonged only to her. Even though she could hear the hooves of the other horses behind them stepping on the snow, it felt like she and Brad were alone outside.

"I don't mind if you take it slow getting back," Millie whispered.

She felt Brad's muscles tense. He probably thought she was crazy.

"It'll be easier on the horses," she added. She didn't want to be pushy. "They must be cold."

"They're fine," Brad said.

Millie nodded.

Brad had never been so glad to see the shape of the Elkton Ranch barn come into view. And that was counting the time he'd almost frozen to death rounding up strays during the bad winter about ten years back. Brad needed to end this ride and he needed to end it soon.

If it didn't, he was going to go way over the deep end. He didn't know what was wrong. Millie wasn't the kind of woman he should be thinking about dating. Who was he kidding? He'd stopped thinking about dating a mile back there and had gone right on to thinking of the big time.

He needed to end the ride. For one thing, she deserved someone more permanent than him. He wasn't ready for the *big* time. He was the kind of guy women looked to if they wanted a *good* time. And that was the way he liked it. He steered clear of women like Millie who made a man think of settling down and having babies.

He didn't know what was wrong. Millie didn't even wear lipstick, and yet he'd been one breath away from starting to whistle the wedding march. He barely knew the wedding march and, besides that, his lips were near frozen from the cold.

Brad shook his head. It must be something about the way she laid her cheek against his back that made him want to take care of her.

Of course, he knew it was only the Christmas craziness, but if he started whistling some wedding song, he'd make a fool of himself for sure.

"Yeah, we're almost there," Brad repeated himself as his horse walked into the edge of the ranch yard.

Millie thought she must be frozen to the back of Brad's saddle. "I can't move."

Brad had ridden into the barn and swung out of the saddle easily enough himself. But Millie was stuck. Her legs felt like they were permanently glued to the saddle.

The air was warmer inside the barn and the horse was standing politely beside the feed trough waiting to be given some oats. Randy and William had ridden over to the bunkhouse so they could unload the tree from the sled, but Brad and Millie had gone straight to the barn to dismount.

Millie tried to move her toes, and she felt the muscles tighten in her boots. At least she didn't have frostbite.

Brad took the reins of his horse and led the animal over to a small pile of hay. "You're just sore from all that riding. I didn't know we'd be gone that long."

"I'm never going riding again," Millie said, and then gave an exaggerated groan for emphasis.

Brad chuckled.

Oh, my word, Millie thought, *I almost made a joke. And he laughed.* She couldn't remember the last time she'd joked with a handsome man. Usually she only felt relaxed enough to joke with her women friends and men like Forrest who were shy themselves.

"It might help if you take the coat off," Brad said. "That'll help you move easier."

Millie pulled her left arm out of the parka and then

finished pulling it off her right arm. She handed the coat down to Brad, and he set it on a hay bale. Millie shivered. It was cold, but she could move easier.

"Here," Brad said as he held his arms up to her. "Now let me swing you down, and you can sit on these bales."

Millie pushed against the back of Brad's saddle and tried to get her leg to properly swing itself over the horse. It didn't work. Finally, she just tilted her whole self over and let the leg come if it wanted.

Brad held his arms out to catch Millie. She fell into his arms and grabbed him around the neck. Usually when a woman had her arms around his neck, Brad recalled she also had a certain inviting look in her eyes.

Brad could only see one of Millie's eyes because he was actually facing her ear instead of her face, but he was pretty sure the look he hoped for wasn't there. Her eyes showed panic.

"Don't worry. I've got you," Brad whispered.

If it was possible, she looked even more alarmed.

"I can stand," Millie said.

Brad noted she didn't relax her grip on his neck, and her glasses were perched precariously on her nose.

"I think my leg just went to sleep, but it'll be fine when I put some weight on it," Millie added.

Since Millie wanted to stand, Brad shifted her, hoping to get her in a position where she could. He regretted it the minute he did it.

Instead of looking at her ear, Brad was now looking at those green eyes of hers. Both of them. Her glasses had fallen completely off, and he saw them resting on her shoulder. Without glasses, Millie's eyes went soft and dreamy. She relaxed in his arms.

Brad supposed Millie might have become calm because she couldn't see, but he told himself it was just possible that it was because she was caught up in the magic of the moment, as he was—and that she was thinking how close they were to kissing, and if he just moved an inch or two this way and she moved an inch or two that way, they would meet in a kiss.

Brad took a deep breath just like the one he took every time he climbed into the chute at the Billings rodeo. He was an amateur at bull riding, just like he was an amateur at kissing. He'd never realized before, though, that a kiss could take every bit as much courage as climbing on the back of a two-thousand-pound bull.

"Oh," Millie said softly as Brad moved a little closer.

"May I?" Brad asked. He looked carefully at Millie's eyes. He didn't expect her to give him a verbal okay, but he did expect to see in her eyes if she was okay with a kiss.

"Oh," Millie repeated even softer.

Brad didn't see any refusal in her eyes. He looked twice to be sure. Then he took a deep breath and kissed her.

Millie thought her heart was going to stop. Failing that, her brain was going to melt. And it was all because her glasses had fallen off and in all the surrounding blur Brad was kissing her like he thought she was a fragile china doll.

Millie had been kissed before, but never like she was precious.

"Oh," Millie said when he pulled away a little bit.

Brad was smiling and, for some reason, he didn't look nearly as tall as he had before. It must be because his face was a little blurry and fuzzy. Millie decided she should go without her glasses more often if it made men like Brad look so very nice.

Millie heard the barn door open even though she couldn't actually see the door open. She could, however, see the big blocks of gray color that moved inside, and then she heard the neighing of a horse.

"Hey, there."

Millie recognized Randy's voice.

"What's happening here?" That was William. He sounded suspicious—like he'd added up the columns and wasn't sure they matched.

"I need my glasses," Millie said. If she was going to answer questions, she needed to be able to see.

Brad handed her the glasses.

"I was just helping Millie get off the horse," Brad said. His arms were still around Millie's shoulders.

William snorted. "Looked to me like you were helping her with a whole lot more than that."

Millie put her glasses on, and everything became clear. She could see through the open barn door that the night was almost fully dark now. The light Brad had turned on inside the barn gave the walls a yellow glow. Hay bales were stacked in one corner of the barn and horse stalls lined another wall.

William and Randy were both sitting on top of their horses and leaning forward as they looked at her and Brad. Randy was grinning, but William was looking stern and worried.

"My leg went to sleep," Millie explained. "I couldn't get off the horse, and Brad was helping me."

William looked directly at Millie. "You just be careful of him. He's a heartbreaker, he is."

"Oh." Millie blinked. Of course. She knew Brad was a flirt even if she had forgotten it for a moment. Men like him kissed women all the time for no good reason.

To be fair, women probably kissed Brad all the time for no good reason, too. He was certainly worth kissing if all of his kisses were like the last one. It wasn't his fault that Millie was the kind of woman who liked a reason for a kiss. A reason being maybe she was becoming a little special to the man kissing her.

Brad looked up at the other two ranch hands in astonishment. "Since when am I a heartbreaker?"

Brad always made very sure the women he was dating had no illusions about him. No one's heart had ever been cracked as far as he knew. Certainly, none had been broken. He didn't date the kind of woman who would be serious. "Besides, last night you were willing to let her sleep in my room with me because I was feeling a little down about Christmas. And now I can't kiss her!"

"That was different," William said firmly. "We didn't know Millie back then. Now, well—anyone can see she's the kind of woman who deserves a guy who's going to make a commitment."

Brad wanted to argue with that, but he couldn't. He didn't know much about Millie. He didn't even know for sure that she wasn't a thief or that she wouldn't leave tomorrow without saying goodbye. But one thing he did know: she did deserve one of those husbands mothers always wanted for their daughters. She deserved a man who could give her a home and financial security. Brad might have that someday, but today he didn't. He had nothing to offer a woman like Millie except his diesel pickup, and he had a feeling that wouldn't do.

"Well, then, we'd best get to the bunkhouse," Brad said. William sure knew how to bring a man down to earth. "It's cold enough out here to spit ice."

William nodded and smiled. "Charlie wasn't kidding about the cocoa. That'll warm you up. We could smell it when we took the tree inside."

Brad nodded. He supposed he would have to be content with that.

"Does he have marshmallows?" Millie asked.

Brad looked down at her. Her short blond hair was sticking out in all directions because she'd pulled off the wool cap he'd given her earlier. Her glasses were still a little crooked on her face. Her cheeks were red from the cold, and her lips were warm from his kiss.

Brad would have promised Millie the moon—the least he could do was get her some marshmallows. "If he doesn't, I'll go get some."

"Where?" William stopped midway through stepping down off his horse and turned to stare at Brad. "Where would you get marshmallows way out here in the middle of the night? And it's Sunday. Even the stores in Miles City are closed by now."

From the expression on William's face, Brad would have thought he'd offered to bring Millie the moon after all. "I could borrow some marshmallows from Mrs. Hargrove. She always keeps things like that on hand."

William finished stepping to the ground before he gave Brad another peculiar look.

"She's a well-prepared woman—Mrs. Hargrove is," Brad said for no reason other than to try and stop the look that was growing and growing on William's face.

"You don't have a temperature, do you?" William finally asked as he took a step closer to Brad. "I hear the flu this season makes people a little light-headed."

"I don't have a fever," Brad said. He couldn't swear

that he wasn't light-headed, but he was pretty sure his temperature would log in at a normal 98.6 degrees.

"Well, we should get these horses taken care of and get inside anyway," William said. He gave Brad another curious look before he turned back to his horse. "No sense in hanging out here in the cold when we can be inside decorating the Christmas tree."

Brad nodded. He had forgotten about the Christmas tree. He had the whole Christmas thing yet to do. There would be the tree and more cinnamon on the stove. And that was only tonight. Tomorrow night would be Christmas Eve, and that would be even worse. He wondered if Charlie would want them all to go to the Christmas pageant at church. Brad had a feeling this was one holiday he would never forget.

At least when he thought of Christmas in the future, he could look back to this evening ride with Millie. If that wasn't Christmas magic, he didn't know what was.

Chapter Nine

The warm air in the bunkhouse made Millie's glasses
fog up.

She stepped to the side of the doorway so that she
wouldn't block the way as Brad and the other two men
came inside the bunkhouse. The air inside smelled of
chocolate and fresh pine. Empty cups ready for cocoa
were sitting on a small table by one wall. The ranch
hands were gathered around the small tree that was
lying on the floor next to the black stove.

Millie rubbed her hands. The wood burning in the
stove kept the large room heated. Her fingers had stung
a little from the cold when she first stepped inside the
room, but they were already starting to warm up. She
was grateful for the prickly feeling in her hands as the
heat reached them. That small tingling distracted her
from The Kiss.

Millie stole a look up at Brad. He might be accustomed to a kiss like the one they had just shared, but
she sure wasn't.

Brad was looking over at the group of men inside
the room so Millie took her time and studied him care-

fully. He was handsome as usual. He still wore his hat, but she could see his face beneath it and it all looked normal. He wasn't wearing any tiny smile or dreamy expression on his face.

Millie frowned. She knew William had said Brad was a heartbreaker and she supposed she shouldn't be surprised that he didn't look any different, but she had secretly hoped he would. Not that she'd expected him to be smiling like an idiot or anything, but shouldn't he have some sort of funny look on his face after a kiss like that? He didn't look like he was affected at all. He certainly didn't have the stunned look she knew she was wearing.

She watched as Brad said a quick hello to the guys in the bunkhouse and then as he wiped his boots lightly on the rug by the door. He took his hat off and brushed the snow off it before he put it on a rack next to the door. He still had a few snowflakes melting on his cheek and his face was a little red from the cold.

Outside of that, Millie couldn't detect anything different about him. There was no sign Brad's heart had been beating in an irregular rhythm or that he was remembering a particularly sweet moment. In fact, he had paid more attention to his hat than he had to her since they'd come inside.

If Millie had been wearing a hat, she wouldn't even have remembered she had it on after that kiss. She felt like her own heart had been dipping and fluttering as if it belonged to a crazy woman. She'd even been trying to remember all she'd ever heard about flirting so that she'd know what to say next.

But now, seeing Brad, she hoped the sputtering happiness she felt inside hadn't shown on the outside. She was grateful she hadn't tried to say anything on the walk back to the bunkhouse. She didn't want to embarrass Brad by gushing over him when the kiss seemed like it was just routine to him. He probably kissed every woman who couldn't manage to get off a horse by herself. Maybe he meant it to be kind, like kissing backward children on the forehead to console them for their clumsiness.

Millie blinked and told herself it wasn't a tear that she felt in the corner of her eye. It was just moisture from the sudden heat of the room.

"I'm a little tired," she said as she gave a small yawn and an apologetic shrug. That should get rid of any doubt that she was still excited about a kiss that had happened a full five minutes ago. She didn't want anyone to think she was gullible enough to think that kiss mattered.

"Here, let me look at you," Brad said as he turned his full attention toward her. He bent his head and peered at her critically.

"I'm fine, though," Millie hastened to add. She didn't want to overplay being tired. Charlie would insist she go lie down, and she didn't want to miss any of this time taking a nap. Even if the kiss was nothing to remember, she wanted to remember every minute about this evening.

"How tired?" Brad asked as he took hold of her wrist and began to raise her hand up.

Millie blinked. Was he going to kiss her hand?

Brad stopped raising her hand and put his thumb on her wrist to feel her pulse.

"Being tired can be a sign you got too cold out there," he said. His blue eyes had deepened with worry. Millie started to hope maybe he did care, until he added. "People usually go to sleep just before they freeze to death."

"I wasn't that cold—and I'm not really that tired." Millie decided Brad was looking at her now like she was a sick bug at the bottom of a microscope. That wasn't the kind of attention she wanted. "I'm just—fine."

There had been many times in her life when Millie wished she were clever, but during none of those times did she wish it as fiercely as she did now. She felt as if she only knew how to flirt and be bold, she would know how to capture Brad's interest. Even a bug that knew how to flirt could capture his attention when he was standing so close.

Well, Millie guessed that technically she had his attention, but it was only because he thought she might be overly cold and on the verge of death. Brad probably didn't want to deal with the sheriff, which he'd have to do if he let her die while he was supposed to be watching her.

Unfortunately, all of the advice on flirting from other waitresses that she had listened to at Ruby's hadn't left her with a clue on how to flirt with a man when he was standing right in front of her counting out her pulse to make sure her heart was beating normally so she'd be able to pay for any crime she might have committed.

Of course, Millie thought optimistically, a woman didn't need to know how to flirt to be friendly. And the first step in being friendly was to find out more about the other person.

"You know, I never did get your last name," Millie said as she looked up at Brad. She smiled a little to show she was friendly, but not so much that he would think she was *too* friendly. It was the best she could do.

Brad looked down at Millie. She was smiling politely at him like she was a cashier at the grocery store and was asking him whether he wanted a plastic bag or a paper bag to carry home his potatoes. He had just kissed the woman. Shouldn't she at least look a little moved by the experience? "It's Parker. Brad Parker."

Millie nodded at him.

Brad expected her to ask about the weather next, and he didn't think he could hold his temper if she did. It was downright humbling to a man to know his kiss could have so little effect on a woman.

If he wasn't a little off-center because of everything that was going on, he would be able to think of something to say to make Millie smile at him like a woman ought to smile at a man who had just kissed her.

He could tell her that her eyes looked like emeralds when she laughed or that her skin was as soft as velvet, but Millie didn't look like the kind of woman who would like any of those words. Even he knew they were clichés. Unfortunately, in her case they were also true. Not that that would matter. Women always liked something that they hadn't heard before. Brad couldn't think of one thing to say that didn't sound like it had been said a thousand times already.

How did a man describe a woman like Millie?

"I see Charlie has the tree all ready to go," Brad said finally as he finished taking her pulse. "Your heart rate seems healthy."

At least her heart seemed to be doing better than *his,* Brad said to himself as he turned to face the other men in the bunkhouse, who were all gathered around the little tree they had chopped down.

Brad was glad none of the men were paying any attention to him and Millie. He suspected that wasn't because of good manners but because they'd finally gotten a steady look at the tree. It had been half dark when Randy cut it down, and sometimes things looked different when they had some light on them.

"It's kind of small," William said as he tipped the tree upright. The tree barely made it to William's belt buckle. "And it's got a bald spot where it didn't get enough sun. At least, I think that's its problem."

William turned the tree around so everyone could see the place where there were no branches.

"It's beautiful," Millie declared as she reached out and tried to coax a nearby branch into covering the bare spot. "It just needs a little help, that's all."

Millie didn't get the branch to cooperate and she stepped back.

"I guess we could stick it in the corner behind the lamp—if we angle it just right no one will see the bald spot," Charlie said hesitantly as he measured the tree with his hand. "And then maybe if we put some extra lights on it right there—"

"I only got one string of lights," Jeff interrupted as he handed a plastic bag to Charlie. Jeff had been leaning against the wall, but he stood up straight to deliver his lights. "And I was lucky to get those—the stores in Miles City are all sold out. Vicki at the grocery store had to get that strand from the back room. I owe her dinner some night next week."

Charlie reached into the bag and pulled the strand of lights out. He looked at them for a moment. "But these are pink."

Jeff nodded. "Well, Vicki said they were Easter lights—they used them around the store windows in

April—but I figure lights are lights. There's no reason Christmas trees can't have pink lights."

There was silence for a moment.

"Maybe they'll turn sort of red when we get them on," Millie finally said. "Sometimes things look different when they're on a tree."

Brad didn't care if the lights were purple. Millie was looking at the tree the way he wanted her to look at him. "They'll look just fine. The thing is that they're lights."

Millie turned and looked at him gratefully. "That's right, and I've always liked lights."

Millie still wasn't looking at him with quite the adoration that she had for the tree, but Brad felt he was making progress. It was a sad day when he had to compete with a tree for the affection of a woman. Brad looked at the tree. To make it even worse that was one pathetic tree. He'd swear it had two bald spots instead of just one.

Brad reached up and patted his own hair just to reassure himself. It was damp, but all there. No bald spots for him.

"Did you get any ornaments?" Millie asked Jeff as she walked over to where the man stood.

Brad followed Millie over. He'd compete with the tree if he had to, but he wasn't about to compete with Jeff just because the man had a few fancy ornaments in his hand.

"Wait, let me get my camera," Charlie called out as he limped across the floor to the shelf on the wall. "I want to get pictures of the tree decorating from start to finish."

"Since when do you have a camera?" Brad asked.

Charlie never took pictures. Not even the time William rode the calf backward down the loading chute. Charlie always said a man should rely on his memory when it came to things he'd seen in his life.

"Jeff brought me back one of them box cameras— you know, they're made out of cardboard so if a cow steps on them or something you're not out a lot of money," Charlie explained as he picked up the dispos- able camera from the shelf. "I'm thinking of starting a Christmas memory scrapbook for the bunkhouse here."

Brad wasn't even stunned anymore. If the truth were told, he wasn't even listening. "That sounds nice."

Brad had stopped listening and just concentrated on looking. He wished he had a camera of his own, so he could take a picture of Millie. How did she manage to look twelve and twenty-three all at the same time? She had her head tilted to the side and was watching Jeff reach into the bag in front of him just like he was Santa Claus and the bag held the treasures of the world.

"Didn't your mother ever take you to see Santa?" Brad stepped a little closer so he could ask her the ques- tion and not risk it being heard by everyone in the room. He thought all mothers took their kids to see Santa Claus. He'd always imagined that, if his mother had lived, she would have taken him.

Millie looked up at him. Her eyes held on to the excitement of the tree as she shook her head. "I had a foster mother."

Somehow, Millie let him know all about her foster mother just by the flatness of her voice.

"I'm sorry." Brad was surprised by how much it dis- turbed him to know that someone had neglected Millie. She would have been the kind of little girl who should have had a mother who cared about her.

"It's all right," Millie said.

Brad scowled. No, it wasn't all right, but there was nothing he could do about it. Except perhaps get those ornaments for her. "If we need more things for the tree, I can drive to Billings tonight."

Charlie frowned and looked at his watch. "Even if the roads were good, the stores would be closed by the time you get there."

"They have that new place that's open twenty-four hours," Brad said. "What's it called—the something Mart?"

"Isn't that too far to drive?" Millie asked softly.

"It is when it's starting to snow like this." Charlie frowned again and shot Brad an incredulous look. "You've driven that road enough to know about that one place where it always drifts closed in a few hours after this kind of snow—now, I know you'd get to Billings, but you wouldn't get back before Christmas."

There was a moment of silence. Charlie stood holding his cardboard camera. He hadn't even taken one picture yet. William was still holding up the pathetic tree by its top branch. Jeff held the bag with whatever ornaments he'd found. Randy sat on the floor with a string of popcorn in front of him. They had all stopped what they were doing to look at Brad.

"Unless that's what you want," Charlie finally said quietly. "Not to be here for Christmas."

Brad was speechless. He had been ten kinds of a fool. Here he had spent years mourning the fact that he'd never had a family Christmas, and he'd had family who wanted to celebrate with him all that time. The guys in the bunkhouse weren't worried about his Christmas depression because it meant he wasn't his usual cheerful self. They were worried because they cared about him.

"There's no place I'd rather be for Christmas than right here with all of you," Brad said. His voice sounded heavy, so he gave a cough at the end of his speech. He wouldn't want anyone to think he was sentimental. It would be better if they thought he was coming down with something.

"Well, good then," Charlie said with a cough of his own. He set his camera down on a chair and pulled a big red handkerchief out of his jeans pocket to wipe at his eyes. "I think someone must have put some green wood in that stove—it's started to smoke a little and it's getting in my eyes."

"I don't see any—" Randy began, then stopped when William jabbed him in the ribs with an elbow. "Well, maybe a little smoke—"

Everyone was silent for a moment.

Finally, Millie spoke. "The tree doesn't really need decorations. It can still be a Christmas tree."

Brad could have hugged her for bringing them back to a safe topic.

"But I have some decorations," Jeff offered as he pulled a package of shiny red balls out of the plastic bag. There were six ornaments. "It might not be enough, but that's all they had left on the shelf."

"Well—" Charlie cleared his throat and put his handkerchief back in his pocket "—I don't want anyone worrying about decorations. I've been watching that television show, and that woman said you could make Christmas decorations out of anything you have around—old hair curlers or those cardboard things from toilet paper."

Randy frowned. "It doesn't seem right to have toilet paper on a Christmas tree."

"It's not the paper, it's the cardboard rolls."

"Oh." Randy still looked unconvinced. "I guess I just can't quite picture it."

"Well, do you have any old hair curlers lying around?" Charlie asked in exasperation.

Randy shook his head. "I guess toilet rolls are all right."

Everyone took a minute to look at the tree.

Brad was the first to hear the sound of a car—or maybe it was two cars—driving up to the bunkhouse. Charlie was the one who limped over to the window, however, and opened the curtains a little so he could see.

"Looks like we got company," Charlie announced. "Good thing I made lots of cocoa."

Millie walked over to the window, and Brad followed.

"Who'd be coming to see us?" Randy asked.

Brad had asked the same question. He knew every one of the men in the bunkhouse knew lots of people and went lots of places. But most of the places they went were bars, and the kind of people they met there weren't the type to come calling on a Sunday evening, especially when it was a long drive from the highway to the Elkton Ranch bunkhouse. When it was snowing, a person had to have a reason to come calling to the bunkhouse.

"Maybe it's Christmas carolers," Charlie said. "It looks like they've got a red light going—"

"It's the sheriff," Brad said. He doubted Sheriff Wall was coming to bring them a Christmas fruitcake.

Brad moved closer to Millie until he stood directly behind her as she looked out the window. The sheriff wouldn't be able to see Millie when he came in the door if Millie stayed right where she was. Brad knew he couldn't hide Millie from Sheriff Wall if she was wanted for a string of crimes, but that didn't stop him from wanting to try anyway. He told himself it was just because she was so little that he felt so protective of her. He didn't know why he had to get all mixed up with a woman who was probably a thief—and not a very good thief at that.

"What's the sheriff doing here?" Charlie said. Brad noticed the older man wasn't moving over to the door to open it.

"Maybe he found out something about Millie's money," William said with a frown. He wasn't moving toward the door, either.

No one was moving. Everyone just stood there worrying.

"Maybe it's not the sheriff," Jeff finally said. "Maybe he lent his car out to someone for the night and they got low on gas."

Brad snorted. "He wouldn't lend that car to his mother. No, he's here about the money."

"There's nothing he can say about the money," Millie protested softly. "It's just regular money."

Brad didn't even bother to answer her. There was nothing regular about a stack of hundred-dollar bills in this part of the country. He suspected there was nothing regular about it in Millie's life, either.

Chapter Ten

Millie had never seen so many silent men standing and looking at each other. Brad stood in front of her, and she wouldn't have even been able to see anything but his shirt if she hadn't moved to the side. She had no sooner moved than William stepped in front of her, and so all she saw was William's back.

Even Charlie, who had just opened the door, was still standing beside the open door like he was waiting for the sheriff to turn around and head back out of the bunkhouse. It took Charlie two minutes to close the door. By then the temperature inside the bunkhouse had fallen ten degrees.

Even when the door was closed, no one moved.

Finally, the sheriff spoke. "I thought I should check in."

He stood on the mat just inside the door, and the snow on his tennis shoes had not begun to melt. He hadn't smiled since he stepped inside. "Just doing my duty, you know."

No one answered.

"Well, you've checked in," Brad said finally.

Millie had never been a chatty waitress, but she knew that many fights had been avoided by a few friendly words, and sometimes it was as simple as finding a safe topic of conversation. She quietly stepped out from behind William and looked toward the sheriff. "Did you have an easy drive out from town?"

The sheriff turned to look at her. For her, he smiled. It was quick and humorless, but it was a smile. "Yes, I did."

Millie tried to smile back. "Good."

Brad shifted himself so he was in front of Millie again, but Millie didn't care. She had done what she could to start a regular conversation.

No one else offered any topics of conversation. Millie swore she could hear the frost growing on the windowpanes. Finally, she decided she needed to make one more attempt. She moved out from behind Brad again. "We've got a tree to decorate."

"I heard." The sheriff grunted. "That's why I'm here."

"You came to decorate our tree?" Brad asked in amazement.

Millie was glad she wasn't still standing behind Brad. She wouldn't have been able to see the astonishment on Brad's face if she had been. He was cute when he was dumbfounded.

"Not exactly," Sheriff Wall said. He finally took his cap off and held it in his hands. "I came to check out the story I heard that you rode horses back into the gullies to get the tree."

"Of course we rode horses," Brad said. "None of the pickups would have made it in all the snow back there."

The sheriff nodded. "I'm afraid I'll have to ask you to keep the barn locked then."

"What?"

Millie wasn't sure which of the men had asked that question. Maybe it didn't matter. They were all looking at the sheriff like he had forgotten where he was. Or maybe who he was.

"The barn doesn't have a lock," Charlie finally spoke.

"Oh," Sheriff Wall said as he looked at Millie and then studied the floor. "Well, then, I guess you'll just need to be sure that you keep a good eye on the—ah—the suspect so she doesn't steal a horse and ride out of here while she's under surveillance. I can keep an eye on the road through Dry Creek. But if she steals a horse and rides across the land, I'd miss her."

"Me?" Millie figured she was as astonished as the men now. "Steal a horse and ride it away? Across fields and everything?"

"She can't even get off a horse by herself," Randy said from the sidelines. "Probably can't get on one, either."

"She did just fine for a beginner," Brad said. "Nobody knows how to do anything the first time they try it."

"Me?" Millie still couldn't quite believe it. No one had ever accused her of doing something that adventurous before. "Do you really think I could do that?"

Brad figured he must have had a premonition about his life and that was why he never truly liked Christmas. People sure weren't themselves today, and the only thing that was different was that Christmas was the day after tomorrow. He couldn't believe Millie stood there looking at the sheriff like he had handed her a prize compliment.

"He's saying you would be running from the law,"

Brad said so she would understand there was nothing complimentary about it.

"Well, technically, it would be *riding* from the law," Sheriff Wall said. He'd stopped looking at the floor, and now, when he talked, he flashed a quick grin at Millie that made him look ten years younger.

Brad snorted. He could see the sheriff liked the look in Millie's eyes. She was looking at him like he had said something very clever. Brad would have been the first to congratulate Sheriff Wall if he had said something useful. But he hadn't. And it didn't matter how young he looked at the moment, the sheriff was too old for Millie.

"Could I learn how to ride a horse that quick?" Millie asked.

Brad started to feel uneasy. Millie looked a little too eager for his comfort.

"It's not about learning anything fast," Brad said. He looked at the sheriff. "You don't have to worry about Millie. Even if she knew how to ride a horse, she'd have more sense than to ride off by herself at this time of year across the fields. It's freezing out there."

"It's not so bad out," Sheriff Wall said as he started to take his jacket off. He still hadn't stopped grinning.

Brad frowned. He was finally getting a good look at the sheriff, and he was realizing what was wrong. He was wearing tennis shoes. That was part of the reason he looked so young. "What happened to your boots?"

"No sense in wearing them today in all the snow."

Brad snorted. "You've worn them in snowdrifts up to your hips. You're not wearing them now because they make you look taller—that's why. They add a good two inches to your height."

The sheriff shrugged. "There's nothing wrong with being short. I'm just being who I am."

Brad grunted. Who did Sheriff Wall think he was kidding? "I don't think many people are going to vote for a sheriff who doesn't wear boots."

"It's not election year for another two years."

"Time goes fast around here."

Millie figured Brad had that all wrong. Time didn't go fast at all. It fact it didn't even seem to crawl. It was frozen now that all the silence had come back.

"Maybe we should have some cocoa," Charlie finally said. He looked at the sheriff. "You're welcome to stay now that we know you've really come courting and not to make things difficult for Millie."

The sheriff looked like he was going to protest, but finally ducked his head in a nod. "Thanks."

"Courting!" Brad protested until Charlie cut in.

"A man's got a right to go courting," Charlie said firmly. "And the sheriff here is a good prospect for some woman. He's got a home—"

"He lives in the Collinses' basement," Brad said. "And that's only in the winter. I don't even know what he does in the summer when the water table rises and the basement's too damp."

"I'm looking around to buy a house," the sheriff said.

"And he's got a good public service job," Charlie continued, just as if Brad had not even spoken.

"A badge doesn't make a man any better," Brad said.

"I'm ready to get married," the sheriff said. "I'm not just looking for a good time, like some men."

Brad figured he was beat. Sheriff Wall was ready to make a commitment. Brad knew most mothers would look at a man like the sheriff and hope their daughters had sense enough to be interested.

Brad didn't like to be rushed. If he ever did get married, he wanted the marriage to be because he wanted to live with that particular woman and not because he had just arrived at some time in his life when he wanted a wife. But that kind of decision took time. The sheriff was as ready to marry as Brad was to date. Brad could never compete with Sheriff Wall if a woman was anxious to get married. And Millie, if she had any sense, would have to see that marriage to a man like the sheriff would solve all her problems.

Brad looked over at Millie. The smile on her face hadn't changed much since the sheriff started talking. Still, if she was smiling, that had to mean she was interested. Brad wondered if maybe he hadn't been too cautious about marriage in his life.

Millie didn't know why Brad had turned polite. He'd been arguing away with the best of them, and then he stopped and put a tight smile on his face and became quiet.

"Well, how many want cocoa?" Charlie said as he started walking to the small room off the back of the main room. That was Charlie's kitchen.

"I'd like some," Millie said. She turned toward Charlie. "And let me help you."

"No." Charlie shook his head. "You're our company, and the day I put company to work in the kitchen is the day that I retire as cook." Charlie looked around at the men in the room before looking back at Millie. "You sit and visit with the sheriff. Brad can help me."

Millie would have rather helped Charlie with the cocoa than sit and talk with a strange man. She didn't have anything in particular to say to the sheriff, especially since he had announced he was looking for a wife. He might be a little shorter than the other men in the room, but Millie couldn't picture herself being married to him all the same.

Of course, she still had to talk to him. The sheriff had walked over to the tree with her, and they were both looking at it.

"It's not always how big the tree is that counts," Millie remarked. That tree was looking shorter and shorter to her each time she saw it. She looked over at Randy. "You're not cutting more off the bottom, are you?"

"I'm not cutting anything off anywhere," Randy said.

"Maybe the branches are drooping when they thaw," William said as he walked over to look at the tree, too.

"Maybe we can set the stand on a box," Millie suggested. "I'm sure it'll look fine as long as it's up higher."

"And we don't have the decorations on it yet," Jeff chipped in as he carried his plastic bag over to the tree. He pulled out the string of lights again. "I tested these, and they're ready to go."

"But they're pink," the sheriff said as he looked at the lights. "Aren't you worried they'll make everything look a little strange?"

"The lights might look red when they're on the tree," Millie said. "You need to give them a chance."

Sheriff Wall looked at Millie. "You're right. That's the way we do it in Dry Creek. We always give everyone a chance."

Millie thought she might be turning a little pink herself. Not because she was embarrassed, but because she was annoyed. "You don't need to give me a chance. I didn't do anything wrong."

Brad held the mugs of cocoa a little higher. Good for Millie. She wasn't falling for the sheriff. She just stood there beside the tree looking a little fierce, like she was ready to defend something.

"Cocoa?" Brad offered one mug to Millie. "I put extra marshmallows in it for you."

Brad would have dumped the whole bag of miniature marshmallows in the cup if he could have. As it was, the melting tower of marshmallows only stood a half inch over the rim of the mug.

"Thanks." Millie took the cup and gave him a shy smile. "That's the way I like it."

Brad felt like he might be in the running after all. Just to make sure, he added, "That tree is looking pretty good."

"Do you really think so?" Millie looked up at him anxiously. "I'm hoping the decorations will make it look better."

"We've only got six ornaments," Jeff reminded everyone as he pulled one of the shiny red balls from the bag. "There won't be enough to cover the tree."

Everyone looked at the ornament Jeff held up. It had a scratch on one side of the ball, and silver showed through. The ornament was about two inches in diameter and hung a little lopsided from Jeff's fingers.

"I'll make some ornaments," Brad said. He regretted his words the minute they left his mouth. How was he going to make ornaments? Then he remembered a glimpse of a long-forgotten scene. He was with his father, and his father was showing him how to make cowboy ornaments for the Christmas tree. Brad must have been only four years old at the time.

"You will?" Millie's face was lit up. "You'll make ornaments?"

The look on Millie's face must have been what his own face looked like all those years ago, Brad thought.

"No one's getting me to make anything out of toilet-paper rolls," Jeff muttered. "I don't care what they call those ornaments."

"And this popcorn has too many kernels to string right," Randy added. "I keep poking myself with the needle."

Brad kept looking down at Millie. "All we need is a whole bunch of empty tin cans."

Brad thought he was looking at the prettiest Christmas ornament there was. Millie's smile lit up her whole face, and Brad stopped noticing her glasses altogether. She was beautiful.

"That's one thing we've got is tin cans," Charlie said. He was holding two more mugs of cocoa and gave one each to Randy and Jeff. "We can empty more if we need them."

"We have some old paint in the barn, too." Brad was reluctant to stop looking at Millie, but he figured he'd better. He knew she didn't like a lot of attention coming her way, and he didn't want to spook her off just when he was beginning to think the two of them might have a chance.

"I'm planning to buy a farm in the spring," Brad said, only half realizing he had spoken his words instead of just thinking them.

Everyone turned to Brad and looked puzzled.

Brad cleared his throat. "I had thought some of that old paint might come in handy when I buy my place, but it's better to use what we can now."

Brad was relieved that his explanation seemed to make enough sense to everyone that they didn't pester him anymore about what he had meant. He wasn't ready to answer questions about anything. He hardly knew himself what the tumble of emotions inside of him was about. He was forgetting who he was. He was Brad Parker. He liked women who liked a good time. He wasn't the kind of a man to make a commitment.

Brad stopped for a moment. He'd forgotten the most important thing: Millie. He didn't know much about her, but he did know that she hadn't had an easy life. She deserved a man who was better than Brad Parker and the sheriff combined. She deserved to marry a saint.

Brad looked at her. Everyone in the room had turned their attention back to the Christmas tree. Millie was frowning slightly at it.

"Maybe if we just move this branch," she finally said as she reached out and gently bent one of the branches.

Brad knew the tree was a hopeless cause. He also knew that it was a cause that was important to Millie. He might not be saint enough to marry her, but he sure could do his best with that tree of hers. "I've got some twine we can use if we need it."

Millie smiled gratefully up at him. "Do you think it will work?"

Brad nodded his head. He'd make it work even if he had to nail more branches on that tree. He was going to give Millie a good Christmas if he had to use every nail and tin can on the Elkton ranch.

Chapter Eleven

Millie let go of the sigh she was carrying. Randy had tied his picture angel to the top of the tree, and Charlie had turned off the last of the lamps in the bunkhouse. Everyone was standing in a circle around the tree. Millie decided there was no doubt the scraggly pine was a Christmas tree now that it was all dressed up.

Brad had used a hammer and a nail to pound holes into the sides of dozens of tin cans, and when he put a small candle in the middle of each tin, the candlelight shone through the holes and made hundreds of tiny twinkling stars. The cans themselves had been painted dark red, and some of them had white trim.

Jeff and William had tied the cans to the tree with haying twine before adding the decorations Jeff had bought. The strand of pink lights circled the tree a couple of times, and with the red of the tin cans, the lights actually looked like they belonged.

"It's beautiful," Millie said.

Brad let go of the sigh he was carrying. It had occurred to him when he was halfway through emptying out all of the soup cans in the kitchen that the tree would look homemade with the ornaments he was making. Tin cans couldn't really compete with ornaments a person could buy in the store. He didn't want Millie to be disappointed in the tree. If it wasn't too late to get to Billings and back, he would have dug his way past the drift that usually stopped people and gone out to buy more ornaments right then. Even now he wasn't sure. "You really like it?"

Brad wondered how it could be that, with five other men hovering around the tree, Millie smiled up at him like those tin cans were filled with diamonds instead of holes and it was all due to him.

"It's just like I've always pictured a Christmas tree should look," Millie said softly. "It reminds me of a starry night."

Brad swallowed. The light from the candles flickered over Millie's face in the darkness and then left her in shadow. "I'm glad you like it."

The other men were silent except for the sounds of swallowing or coughing or clearing their throats. Charlie was the only one brave enough to bring out his handkerchief and dab at his eyes.

"That smoke's still hanging around," Charlie muttered after he put his handkerchief back into the pocket of his overalls.

Each of the men had their faces turned toward the Christmas tree. The tree itself was standing on a wooden crate that Jeff had pulled in from the barn. Charlie had donated a few white dishtowels to cover the tree stand and the crate. Millie had arranged the towels so they looked almost like snowdrifts.

The clock was ticking in the corner of the room, and

the fire was crackling a little as it burned in the corner stove, but otherwise it was a silent night.

"It's too bad Mrs. Hargrove isn't here," William said finally. "She'd have us all singing a carol or two—"

Brad wished the older woman were here with them. She'd enjoy the tree.

"Oh, that reminds me," the sheriff said as his hand went to his shirt pocket. Sheriff Wall was wearing a white shirt with broad gray stripes and a black leather vest. "She asked me to give you something when she heard I was coming out here tonight."

The sheriff pulled several blue index cards with printing on them out of his shirt pocket. "These are the visitor forms for the church. In all the commotion, she forgot to have you fill them out this morning, and she felt bad about it."

Charlie frowned. "I didn't know you had to fill out a form to go to church. Is it like voter registration?"

"Nah," Sheriff Wall said as he fanned the cards out and held them out to everyone. "It's just a new program Mrs. Hargrove volunteered to do. I don't really know much about it—I've only gone to church the past month or so, and they didn't have them back then. I think it's just to give Mrs. Hargrove your address or something so she can send you another postcard."

"Mrs. Hargrove knows where we live," Charlie said, but he took one of the cards anyway. "Still, I guess it's only polite to thank the church for having us, so I guess I'll be filling one out."

After Charlie took a card, he gave a stern look to those around him. Finally, William took a card. Then Randy and Jeff each took one. Brad held his breath when he put his hand out and took one. Millie even took one.

Everyone just looked at his or her card.

"Mrs. Hargrove said something about handing them back to her when Millie comes to town tomorrow to do her community service," the sheriff said. He looked pleased with himself that he had delivered all of the cards. "I'll be happy to come by tomorrow and pick Millie up so she can get started."

"Millie and I will be in town at eight," Brad said. He put the card in his shirt pocket. He was perfectly able to see to Millie. "There's no need for you to drive all the way out here."

"I don't mind," the sheriff said before he shrugged his shoulders and looked at Brad. "Don't suppose it matters, though—I will see you and Millie at eight. I thought maybe we should meet in the café."

"I thought we were going to the church," Millie said. "To take care of the black marks on the floor."

"We'll start out at the café," the sheriff said as he walked toward the closet that held his coat. "We'll be wanting some coffee and the county runs a tab there. Linda showed me where everything was before she left—even her flavored creamers."

"Linda trusted you with the stuff in her café?" Charlie asked. The older man was frowning.

"Yeah," Sheriff Wall said as he opened the closet door and reached for his coat. "Of course she trusts me. I'm sworn to uphold the law."

"That wouldn't have made any difference to Linda a year or so ago," Charlie commented as he walked over to the door. "I guess she's finally growing up. She always struck me as someone who'd rather put poison in a lawman's coffee than creamer. I don't suppose she sits down with you while you drink it, though, does she?"

The sheriff grinned. "Now that you mention it, she does. I guess we all grow up sooner or later."

Sheriff Wall he put his coat on and walked toward the door before turning to the others in the room. "We'll see some of you tomorrow."

Millie smiled. "We'll be there."

"I'll wish the rest of you a Merry Christmas then," the sheriff said as he tipped his hat to the group. "Be sure and watch that tree of yours, or you'll burn the bunkhouse down."

"We'll be fine," Brad said. He had seen the flicker of worry in Millie's eyes. "There's enough snow outside to stop a forest fire anyway."

"That's true," Millie said.

Brad didn't bother to wave to the sheriff as the man opened the door and stepped into the night darkness. Sheriff Wall could find his way home all right. Brad was much more interested in Millie.

"I could bring some snow in if you're worried," he offered. He figured the candles would burn for another half hour or so. He wanted Millie relaxed while she watched it. "Just so it's handy if we need it for anything."

Millie was happy. She was having the kind of Norman Rockwell Christmas that she'd imagined. Granted, Christmas Eve wasn't until tomorrow, but she was sitting here with a group of people who had actually decorated a tree.

Millie had always known she could decorate a tree for herself when she was in Seattle. One year she'd even bought some tinsel and lights. But when it came time to get a tree, she didn't. Part of her Christmas dream was to decorate a tree with other people.

"We've got more cocoa," Charlie said as he sat down on one of the leather couches that Jeff had pulled closer to the tree. "It's self-serve in the kitchen."

Millie walked over and sat down on the couch next to Charlie. "You make great cocoa."

Charlie beamed as though she'd handed him a hundred-dollar bill. For the first time that night, Millie remembered what she was doing in Dry Creek. She had a mission, and it had nothing to do with tin-can lights and cocoa.

Millie looked around the room. She didn't feel like a stranger anymore. She wondered how she could fulfill Forrest's request or if it was really necessary.

"The community service won't be hard," Brad said as he sat down on the couch next to Millie. "No one really expects you to work."

Millie had to stop herself from scooting over to sit pressed against Brad.

"*I* expect me to work," Millie said. Her voice was a little sterner than she had intended. She didn't care what Sheriff Wall thought about her and her community service, but Millie hadn't been a slacker before she came to Dry Creek, so there was no reason to start now.

Brad smiled slightly. "I guess I'm not surprised at that."

"We can't all be prima donnas," Millie continued. She didn't want Brad to think she was boring, but she just couldn't summon up the effort to pretend to be carefree. She was a person who obeyed the rules in life, and that was just the way it was.

Brad smiled wider. "No chance of that happening. You won't even let me wait on you."

"You got me cocoa," Millie protested. She wasn't used to a man wanting to help her with her coat and that kind of thing. She was used to doing this for herself *and* a table of other people at the same time. "Besides, I don't need help with much."

Brad stopped smiling. "I scared you with all my talk of spiders before. I'm sorry I did that."

Millie didn't know who had moved, but she was sitting closer to Brad on the sofa than she had been before. She looked around the room. Charlie had gotten up from the sofa and was over by the table. Jeff and Randy had left the room, and she could hear them in the kitchen. William alone sat near the tree. If Brad only knew, it wasn't spiders she was scared of right now.

"It's okay," Millie said as she tried to move away from Brad without being obvious about it. She was afraid she had been the one to move closer in the first place, and she didn't want him to think she was—

"Oh." Millie realized that as she moved away, Brad moved closer. Maybe she wasn't the one who had moved on the sofa after all.

William got up and left his place beside the tree. Millie looked around. She and Brad were alone in the room. "Everyone's in the kitchen."

"Probably more cocoa." Brad doubted it was a sudden thirst for cocoa that had made the other men give them some privacy, but Brad was glad for the kindness they were showing him.

He wasn't sure if it was good news or bad news that Millie looked so nervous around him all of a sudden. He wished he had another month or two to get to know her before he kissed her again. But he didn't have a month. She would be gone by then for sure. He tried to slide down into the sofa cushions a little more. Maybe she really *didn't* like tall men.

Brad pulled the blue form out of his shirt pocket, more for something to do than because he even remembered what the form was for.

"I wonder what they send you," Millie said. She was looking down at her own form intently.

The Welcome Visitors form was as basic as they came, Brad figured, but he was grateful for it. Even with all of the lamps in the room off, there was enough light from the tree to see what was on the card. There was a graphic of a church on one corner and several printed questions in the middle of the card. One question asked if you would like someone from the church to visit you. The other asked if you had a prayer request. At the bottom, the church said they'd send a special gift to anyone who returned the card with his or her address. That must be what Millie had just read.

"It can't be much," Brad said. "The church doesn't have money to buy people anything. They've been raising money for the past year just to get a new organ for the place."

"Money's tight around here, isn't it?"

"Not so tight that we don't get by," Brad said. He didn't want Millie to think they were poor in Dry Creek. "And when money *is* tight—or someone has a health problem or something—we all chip in and help them over the hump."

Brad wished he'd paid more attention to the accountant he'd paid to do his taxes last year. Brad was so close to having enough to buy a place of his own that he had wanted to ask the man a few questions about buying property in addition to the usual questions about his taxes. "We're not rich by any means, but no one has lost their place or not had enough for some medical care— at least, no one that I've known of, and I've lived here for ten years."

"You mean you haven't always lived here?" Millie asked.

Brad could swear she was surprised. He tried real hard not to be offended. He knew some women put great stock in men who had traveled and been lots of places. Some of the waitresses he'd known thought travel was the measure of a man. Of course, that might be because they were used to truckers, and a trucker wasn't really a trucker until he'd been to both coasts a few times. But Brad had never had any desire to move around.

"I was born in Illinois," Brad said, "but I like Dry Creek. I don't expect I'll be moving from here."

"But surely you travel?" Millie insisted.

"Not if I don't have to," Brad said. He figured the woman might as well know him. He was a basic kind of a guy. No particular flash. He wasn't one to fly a woman over to Paris for her birthday. Now, he *might* drive her to the coast or up to Canada for a long weekend or something.

Millie didn't seem to have anything to say in response to him not traveling so Brad just sat there on the sofa. He figured his chances were about zero.

"Does anyone in Dry Creek travel?" Millie asked. She was suddenly realizing that she would need to leave in a couple of days. After she completed her community service, there would be no reason to stay in Dry Creek. And she couldn't stay. Once she gave out her Christmas presents, she would be broke. She'd have to go back to work. She accepted that, but she'd hoped that she might see some of the people in Dry Creek again. She'd hoped at least some of them occasionally went to Seattle.

"Mrs. Hargrove flew up to Alaska to see Doris June a couple of years ago," Brad said. "She liked the moose—they walked right down the streets in Anchorage just like they owned the place."

"Does anyone else go anywhere?"

Brad was silent a minute. "The sheriff goes to conventions every year—he gets around pretty good."

"Oh." Millie blinked and looked down at the card in her hand so that Brad wouldn't see the tears in her eyes. She supposed she was silly to have gotten so attached to the people in this town. Millie looked out of the corner of her eye at Brad. He was sitting a little awkwardly, like he was trying to push himself into the sofa cushions. He had a frown on his face, and he was staring straight ahead at the tree. But Millie wished he was the one who went to conventions. If he went to conventions, he was bound to come to Seattle once in a while.

"I went to a rodeo once," Brad offered.

"Really? Where?"

"Cheyenne."

"Oh." Millie realized that she had never heard of anyone having a rodeo in Seattle.

Brad swore he didn't know how to please a woman. He'd finally realized he could offer a wife some excitement, and Millie sat there looking like it was nothing to her. Of course, he supposed it didn't matter to her where he took any future wife. "Rodeos can be good entertainment."

Millie nodded. "Now that I know more about riding a horse, I can appreciate them more."

Her response certainly didn't ring with enthusiasm. Brad figured he could have suggested a trip to the dentist and gotten the same response. He told himself it was probably just as well. If excitement and travel were important to Millie, it was good that he knew it now.

"I should have gone and gotten some better decorations for the tree," Brad said. The poor thing looked a little forlorn to him just now, even though the candles were all still burning brightly and he had arranged branches so that he'd covered the bald spots on the tree. Why had he thought that tin-can ornaments could compete with the shiny new balls that people expected on their trees these days?

"I love that tree," Millie said fiercely.

"Really?"

Millie nodded firmly. "It's beautiful."

"Yes," Brad agreed, even though he'd stopped watching the tree and was watching Millie watch the tree. The candlelight reflected off her glasses and cast a golden glow all over her face. When had her face become the only one he wanted to look at? Her hair still didn't have any more brass in it, and she still didn't wear any of the makeup that he'd thought looked so good on most women. But she was beautiful.

Brad moved a little closer on the sofa. Millie didn't move away. He took that as a sign of encouragement and moved closer still. Millie did look up at him when he did that. But she didn't move away. Instead, she gave him a shy smile.

Brad moved all the way closer and put his arm on the sofa behind Millie.

Millie forgot about how much she would miss Brad when she left. She forgot about the fact that she was a cautious woman and not at all the kind of woman men like Brad wanted to date. All she could think about was the moment she was living.

Brad had his arm around her, and they were looking at the most beautiful Christmas tree she had ever seen. The light from the candles danced between the pine branches of the tree and reflected off the bottoms of the tin cans. The pink lights added a softness to the shadows the branches cast.

Millie was having her Christmas. The Norman Rockwell one Forrest had wanted her to have.

"I owe him an apology," Millie spoke without thinking.

"Who?" Brad said as he moved his arm from the back of the sofa to her shoulders.

Millie felt enclosed and happy. "Just a friend."

Millie took a good look around her. She wanted to remember this Christmas for the rest of her life. She hoped she'd remember the feel of Brad's arm around her as well as the flickering light of the candles on the Christmas tree. She'd never experienced anything like it yet in her life, and she wasn't hopeful enough to expect another one to come along. But she sure would be grateful if it ever did.

Chapter Twelve

Millie could smell the coffee the minute she stepped out of her car in front of the café in Dry Creek. It was only eight o'clock in the morning, but she felt like she had been up for hours already. She hadn't slept well and had to admit she was feeling annoyed with life in general. She didn't know what was wrong with her today.

Well, maybe she did know, she thought as she shut her car door. But there was nothing to be done about it. Last night had shown her what Christmas was all about, and the experience had made her feel more alone than she'd ever felt in her life.

No wonder her foster mother had never bothered with Christmas.

A sentimental Christmas wasn't worth it when a person had to go back to her real life. And for her, Millie thought, real life consisted of waiting on tables of complaining, demanding people at Ruby's cafe.

"I guess the sheriff is here."

Millie looked up at Brad when he spoke. He had driven behind her into Dry Creek after she had refused his offer to ride in his pickup with him. For some reason, she wanted to be alone in her old car. She certainly didn't want to be sitting next to Brad. The wind made his lips white and his face red, but he didn't seem in any hurry to step past her and go into the café.

The morning itself was dreary. The sun was hidden behind thick gray clouds, which probably meant snow was coming later today. The snow that had fallen yesterday was tramped down around the café and didn't look as clean as it had yesterday. A film of dirt had settled over everything.

"I hate snow," Millie announced.

Brad only grunted. "Everybody can't live at the beach."

"I don't live at the beach," Millie protested. She rented a small apartment so close to the docks that she perpetually smelled fish. She tried hard to convince herself the neighborhood was charming. "It's the waterfront, and that's altogether different."

Now that Millie thought about it, she didn't know what she had against snow. The weather on the docks in Seattle could be just as wet and almost as cold as Montana in winter. Maybe she had just always hated snow because it reminded her of all those days she'd spent with her foster family in Minnesota. She had moved to Seattle five years ago to start a new life. Some days, though, it felt like her new life was just a repeat of her old life. All that had changed were the people sitting around the tables that she waited on.

"It's all by the water," Brad said. His lips were pressed into a line that could not be mistaken for even the smallest of smiles. "I know there's fancy prices at the coast, but living by the water doesn't make a man a better man. There's nothing wrong with a bit of snow. Lots of good men live in the snow."

Millie didn't have a chance to answer because Brad started walking up the steps to the café. His boots stomped on each step, one at a time, until he reached the top.

Brad figured he had ruined any chance he'd ever had with Millie. But, he said to himself as he opened the door, it was probably just as well. There was no point in imagining how much fun he and Millie would have on a real date when he knew the price he'd have to pay when she left. The simple fact was, they had no future and he was wise to realize that.

Brad stood to the side and held the door for Millie.

He smelled cinnamon on her when she walked by. Millie had helped Charlie prepare an early breakfast this morning, and Brad couldn't help but notice she had been not only civil, but downright nice to Charlie. In fact, Millie had had a smile for all of the men in the bunkhouse...except for him.

Brad wondered when everything had changed with him and Millie. She'd seemed to like his arm around her last night. She had even snuggled up against him the little while they sat and looked at that tree.

It was the tree's fault, Brad decided. No good ever came from taking a pathetic little pine tree and dressing it up like it was something to stare at. It gave rise to all kinds of hopes in a man's chest that just simply weren't going to come true. Maybe there was a good reason he'd never liked Christmas, Brad told himself as he followed Millie into the café. Maybe he didn't like Christmas because he had the sense to be content with his lot in life and wasn't given to empty dreaming.

Christmas was nothing but a promise that hadn't come true in his life. Maybe it did for some people, but it hadn't for him.

"Good morning," the sheriff called out in greeting to Brad and Millie, just as if he were blind and not able to see they were miserable. "Looks like it'll be a good day."

"It's overcast," Brad said. "It'll probably snow later, unless it's too warm to snow—then it'll be some kind of icy slush."

Brad didn't know how any man could be optimistic with the thought of slush falling on him later in the day, though the sheriff seemed like he could be. At least he didn't flinch when Brad informed him of the prospect.

"I got the coffee ready for you, but I'm going to need to go into Miles City. I have some official work to get done," Sheriff Wall said as he started to put his coat back on.

Brad could see that several cups, napkins and spoons had been set out on one of the tables. Someone had even folded the napkins, and Brad was sure it hadn't been the café owner, Linda, because the corners were all crooked. When Linda bothered to fold napkins, she got them straight.

"Thanks," Brad said, even though he figured the sheriff wasn't listening to him since he was looking at Millie. Sheriff Wall was as pathetic as he was, Brad figured by looking at him. Maybe the sheriff was worse, Brad decided. At least Brad hadn't tried folding napkins to impress Millie.

"Did you sleep all right last night?" the sheriff asked Millie just as though he cared.

Millie nodded. Brad had to give her points for knowing to be cautious about the sheriff. Of course, he then took some points away when she smiled at Sheriff Wall as she said thank-you. A simple thank-you would have been enough. She didn't need to smile at the man. The lawman would be out folding more than napkins if Millie didn't tone down those smiles.

"I'll be back in a few hours," the sheriff continued. "Might even make it back for lunch. Mrs. Hargrove promised to make us her special meat loaf with black olives—it's her Christmas special."

Millie longed with all her heart to have a special Christmas recipe that people knew about. Since she usually worked on all of the holidays, her Christmas special was whatever the chef had made for the day. And the only reason people asked her for it was because she was their waitress. Most of them didn't even know her name.

"Maybe I'll ask for her recipe—unless it's a secret." Millie looked at Brad. "Do you think it's a secret?"

"I doubt it. It's hard to keep anything a secret in Dry Creek."

Millie didn't point out that *she* still had a secret. Maybe that's why she was feeling so cranky today. She had a secret and she didn't want to keep it a secret. She wanted to tell Brad what she was doing and why she was in Dry Creek.

"Well, I guess I better get going," the sheriff said as he nodded his head at Millie. "Besides, I see Mrs. Hargrove coming, so you guys will be getting down to work in no time."

Millie smiled goodbye to the sheriff. She guessed the spilling of secrets would have to wait until she got the floors in the church all scrubbed.

Thinking of the floors made Millie feel more cheerful. There was nothing like getting rid of black marks to make a person feel like they had accomplished something in a day. She might not have a special Christmas recipe, but she did have a special cleaning method.

"Aren't you worried about what she's going to put on those floors?" Brad asked the sheriff, just to remind the man that it hadn't been that long ago that he thought Millie was planning some kind of a crime. The sheriff had made that remark about the water supply and hadn't followed up. Brad wondered what kind of a lawman the sheriff was.

"Naw," the sheriff said as he waved goodbye. "I ran her through the system and got enough information on her to put my mind at ease. Besides, I have a buddy on the Seattle police force."

"Does that mean I don't have to do the floors?" Millie asked.

The sheriff stopped with his hand on the door. "Well, you still broke into the place…"

Brad held his breath. If Millie didn't have to do the floors, she didn't have to stay at all. He thought he at least had today to convince her to stay. He was glad she had the community service. If there was one thing he knew about Millie, it was that she didn't take the easy road anywhere.

Millie nodded. "I would do them anyway. I just wanted to know if anything was going on my official record."

The sheriff went a little pink at this.

"Don't worry," Brad said. "Unless I miss my guess, the sheriff didn't even file the report. He hates paperwork."

Sheriff Wall left the café as Mrs. Hargrove entered it, and they nodded to each other.

"Good, the coffee's on," the older woman said as she unwound a wool scarf that she'd worn around her head. "There's nothing like a cup of coffee to get me going in the morning."

Mrs. Hargrove drank her cup of coffee while she was standing on the welcome mat in the front of the café. "I got snow on my boots coming over here, and I don't want to track up this clean floor. We have enough to do with getting one floor clean. No point in adding another floor to the list."

Millie looked at Mrs. Hargrove. She was wearing a navy parka over a pink gingham dress. Forrest had told Millie that Mrs. Hargrove usually wore a gingham dress in some color or another.

"You don't want to get your dress dirty," Millie said. "Brad and I brought lots of old clothes if you'd like to borrow some."

When Millie left the bunkhouse, Charlie had insisted on giving her old flannel shirts to take with her and several pairs of men's overalls.

"They're full of holes," Charlie had said when he handed the two bags to Millie. "So you might want to wear a couple of the shirts at the same time—mostly the holes aren't in the same places."

Millie looked at the older woman. "I've got the old clothes in the trunk of my car. I thought I'd take them over to the church and put them on there."

"Makes sense, since the church is heated. Pastor Matthew said he went over and turned the heat on at seven this morning, so it should be comfortable by now. And don't you worry about these dresses of mine—they all wash up fine," Mrs. Hargrove said. "I haven't met the stain yet that I couldn't figure out—except for the black marks on the church's floor. I'm anxious to see how this baking soda idea of yours works."

"Oh," Millie remembered. "The sheriff didn't leave me the box of baking soda he said he had in his office."

"Don't worry," Mrs. Hargrove said as she patted the pocket of her parka. "I brought a small box that I had. It's brand-new—never been opened. Don't know if that makes a difference or not, but I'm not taking any chances. Those black marks have been bothering me for years now."

Millie knew how easily water splashed, and that was why she had worried about Mrs. Hargrove's clothing. She'd never once expected the woman to help her clean the floor. But it was clear when she, Brad and Mrs. Hargrove walked up the steps of the church ten minutes later that the older woman expected to scrub.

"Oh, no," Millie said as she took the final step up to the church. She had her purse strapped around her neck, and her hands were free. Her long wool coat kept her warm even though the air was cold. Millie stopped to take a breath. "You don't need to get down on your knees or anything. There's plenty of cleaning you can do without that."

"Maybe you could dust the rails of some of the pews," Brad suggested. He had carried up both bags of old clothes even though Millie had protested.

"You mean sit down while the real work is going on?" Mrs. Hargrove asked as she turned the doorknob on the church's outer door. "Nothing ever got cleaned by someone sitting down and taking a swipe at a little bit of dust. Besides, the pews will be cleaned later this morning. The twins do that when it's the Curtis family's turn at cleaning. I think they pretend the pews are dragons."

Millie knew the twins liked dragons. What she didn't know was that they cleaned the church. "Aren't they too young?"

"Too young. Too old," Mrs. Hargrove said as they stepped into the church. "Sometimes it seems that all of the work at the church is being done by the people you wouldn't expect."

Millie and Brad followed Mrs. Hargrove into the church.

"Of course, that's the beauty of it," Mrs. Hargrove said as she stood in the entryway to the church and unwound the scarf from her head again. "The Bible talks about the weak being made strong and the slave being made free. I figure that since the very beginning, the church has been surprised by what people can do and be."

"But that was a long time ago, wasn't it? The beginning, that is." Millie was remembering the time when she'd gone to church with her foster mother and the woman had told her that Jesus lived thousands of years ago and so had no meaning for today.

Mrs. Hargrove shrugged her shoulders. "God says a thousand years are but a day to Him. The way I see it, we're still in the early days with God and will be for a long time at that rate."

"You said there were scrub brushes around?" Brad asked. Just because God had all day didn't mean Brad did. He figured if he got the floor cleaned in the church before lunch, then maybe Millie would agree to go riding horseback again with him this afternoon. If he could get her leaning into him on the horse again, maybe he could talk to her and he could ask her to stay in Dry Creek for a little longer.

Brad decided he needed his head examined. Women didn't just stay in Dry Creek while they waited for some man to get to know them. No, he needed a better plan than that.

"Brad?" Millie asked for the second time. Brad was standing there, muttering to himself and frowning. He hadn't even heard her the first time she said his name.

"Huh?"

Brad focused on her, but she couldn't help but notice that his face turned a little pink at the same time.

"Mrs. Hargrove said the brushes are on the shelf above the sink in the kitchen. Do you know where that is?"

"Yeah, sure," Brad said as he started to walk toward the small room on the side of the church. "I was just going to get them."

When Brad stepped into the kitchen, Millie turned to Mrs. Hargrove. "I hope he's okay."

The older woman chuckled. "Oh, he's okay, all right."

"He seems a little distracted."

The older woman chuckled even harder. "I'd say that's a fair bet."

Millie frowned. She'd hoped to have another conversation with Brad like the one she'd had yesterday, and that didn't seem too likely if he was going to be distracted by something as simple as brushes.

"Is there a restroom where I can change?"

"Right through there, dear. The second door on your left."

Millie ended up wearing two flannel shirts and one of Charlie's old coveralls. She needed some twine to belt the overalls tight to her waist so they didn't flap around too much, but outside of that, everything had adjusted to her.

Millie decided it was a good thing she'd changed when she first got to the church. If she'd waited ten minutes, she never would have changed. That's when Pastor Matthew and his two boys came over to the church.

Millie had already started to scrub the first black mark. If she hadn't already been on her knees, the sight of Pastor Matthew would have put her there.

The minister wore an apron. Well, maybe it wasn't so much an apron as it was a dishtowel tied around his waist. But Millie could hardly believe what she was seeing. "He's going to start cleaning."

"I thought I told you it was the Curtis family's turn to clean the church this week," Mrs. Hargrove said. The older woman was sitting on one of the pews near Millie sorting through a box of crayons from one of the Sunday School classrooms. She had finally agreed to observe instead of scrub, since there were only two scrub brushes and Brad insisted he was going to take one and scrub beside Millie.

Millie had her scrub brush in one hand and water stains on her overalls. She'd clipped her hair back as best she could with the barrettes she had in her purse. She still couldn't believe it when she saw Pastor Matthew go into the kitchen with a mop. "But he's the minister!"

"I hope you're not saying that men can't scrub floors," Brad said. Millie looked over at him. He had speckles of black on his face and his forehead was damp. He had been working on some black marks about ten feet away from her, and Millie had to admit he was doing a good job.

"Well, ah, no, I wasn't saying that exactly." Millie wondered what she *had* been meaning to say. Of course, she knew that some men worked at cleaning. She'd seen janitors before. But, somehow, even with the janitors, she'd always assumed that they never cleaned or helped out at home.

"I'm just surprised that a minister would be doing the cleaning," Millie finally said. "Isn't he the boss?"

Mrs. Hargrove chuckled. "He'd be the first to tell you that he's not."

Millie couldn't figure it all out.

"When was the last time you did this?" Millie demanded as she sat back and looked straight at Brad. Even he must not clean regularly.

Brad stopped scrubbing. "Me?"

Millie nodded.

"I've never done this before," Brad said.

Ah, Millie thought to herself, she was right.

"At least not here," Brad continued. "But I do my share of cleaning up after other people. Just ask Charlie. We all take turns."

Millie frowned. This isn't what she expected. But even if Brad was willing to clean something on occasion, that didn't explain why the minister would.

"I thought ministers told people what to do," Millie said finally. She was puzzled. She had always thought that getting close to God would mean that she'd be run ragged doing errands for Him. He was powerful and He was male. That meant there would be no end to doing things for Him. "He should tell somebody to scrub the floor."

Mrs. Hargrove nodded. "I know it seems like that's

the way it would work. But God has turned everything upside down."

Millie felt like she was the one who'd been turned upside down. Why would someone who could order others around do anything? "And where's Glory?"

"I think she's painting a scene for the pageant," Mrs. Hargrove said as she put the blue crayons in a plastic bag and tied a knot in the bag. "Everyone decided to try a simpler pageant this year, but we still wanted it to be nice."

Millie wasn't so sure she wanted to talk about God, but she wanted to talk about the Christmas pageant even less. It seemed like every time anyone brought up the Christmas pageant, they also brought up Forrest. When Millie thought of Forrest, she remembered those Christmas stockings in her trunk and wondered if she'd ever be able to fulfill Forrest's final request.

"But who does all the praying if the minister scrubs the floor?" Millie asked. She remembered the blue card in her pocket and pulled it out. "It asks for things to pray about here—I thought the minister would do all that."

Millie figured the church must pull in lots of prayer requests each week. It would keep the minister busy praying for all of them.

"Well, he certainly does some of it. But we all pray," Mrs. Hargrove said as she looked at the blue card. "I'm glad to see the sheriff got the cards to you. Have you filled one out yet? I'm happy to take yours and put it with the others."

"I'll do it when I finish scrubbing." Millie put the card back in her pocket. She hadn't been going to fill one out. She had told herself there was no point. She thought God didn't care about her or the things that worried her. But now she was beginning to wonder if she had been wrong. Maybe He did care.

"Can I put down a secret request?" Millie asked. She didn't know how to name some of the longings she was starting to feel. But if God were as smart as everyone seemed to think, He would know what she meant.

"Of course." Mrs. Hargrove nodded. "That sounds fine."

Millie went back to scrubbing.

"The baking soda is working," Millie said as she rinsed off the piece of floor she'd just scrubbed. Millie leaned back on her heels and stretched her back.

Mrs. Hargrove stood up and walked over to where Millie had scrubbed. "Why—my goodness—it sure is! What a blessing!"

"I'm glad it's working."

Millie liked looking around the church when it was almost empty like this. Brad had moved over by the pulpit to scrub the floor there, and Mrs. Hargrove still stood next to where Millie was scrubbing. The Christmas tree Millie had noticed on Sunday looked even more humble as it stood beside the pulpit.

"We decorated a tree last night, too," Millie told Mrs. Hargrove. "It's a homemade one like the one here. It's beautiful."

Mrs. Hargrove nodded. "Sometimes they're the best ones. The Sunday school classes made the decorations for the tree here."

"Brad made our decorations."

Brad looked up from where he was scrubbing. His knees ached, and they felt stuck to the wet floor. But even with all that, his knees went weak when he saw the look on Millie's face as she talked about the decorations. She was describing their tree to Mrs. Hargrove, and it was apparent that any annoyance she might have felt toward him this morning was not felt toward the Christmas tree back at the bunkhouse.

Millie loved that old pathetic Christmas tree.

Brad was watching Millie and didn't pay any attention to the shadow that was passing beside him.

"So, that's the way it is," Pastor Matthew said quietly.

Brad looked up. "It's the tree she likes. She doesn't have much use for me."

Pastor Matthew smiled. "Well, we don't know that for sure, do we?"

Brad figured he did know, but he didn't want to contradict the man. Brad just waited for what he was sure was coming next. A minister was supposed to say something about faith and God and how everyone should reach for the impossible. But the minister didn't say anything, so finally Brad added, "I wouldn't think there's any point in praying about something like this."

Brad waited a minute for the pastor to disagree with him. Finally, Brad could no longer contain his feeling of hope. "Is there?"

Pastor Matthew smiled. "God cares about love, if that's what you're asking."

"I wasn't thinking that—" Brad swallowed and then stopped. "I mean it wouldn't be right to ask God something like this—I mean, He doesn't cast love spells or anything, does He? Something that would make Millie stay around awhile so she could get to know me."

Pastor Matthew smiled. "Maybe not love spells, but He can work miracles, and less than that seems to be required here. After we finish, stop by my house for a few minutes, and we'll pray about it. Glory's over painting the scenery for the pageant and we can have some privacy. That is, if you want it to be private."

Brad glanced at Millie. He sure did want it to be private. He didn't know what she would think if he said a prayer about her staying in Dry Creek. Come to think of it, he didn't know what he thought about it himself. He'd never prayed about anything before that he could remember.

"God might not know me." Brad thought he should mention the fact to the minister. "We don't exactly talk."

Pastor Matthew nodded. "I figured that might be the way it is."

Brad looked around the church. It wasn't just Millie who might find it odd if he decided to pray. The guys in the bunkhouse would never understand. Brad looked back at the minister. "This is confidential, right? I mean, seeing a minister is like seeing a lawyer, isn't it? You can't tell anyone, can you?"

Pastor Matthew smiled. "My lips are sealed."

Brad nodded. That was good. He didn't need a rumor going around that Brad Parker was in such deep trouble with his love life that he had to ask God to help him. Because, of course, he wasn't in deep trouble. Not really. Was he?

Chapter Thirteen

Millie had heard about the old barn that the town of Dry Creek had turned into a community center. There hadn't been cows in the barn for years, and someone had added heaters to the building when they had the Christmas pageant inside it a couple of years ago. The wood plank floor of the barn was scrubbed clean, and the unfinished wood had a weathered look to it.

The middle of the barn was the stage, and chairs had been set up all around the walls of the barn. High, tall windows let light into the area and several bales of hay were pushed against the far wall. The faint scent of paint thinner filled the cold, moist air inside the barn.

Millie looked up and saw the pulleys on the rafters that allowed the angel to swing down over the audience during the pageant. When Forrest had tried to kill the angel, he had waited until after she made her swing out and back. In fact, the pageant was over when he'd pulled out his gun. Forrest had been able to hide behind some tall screens that had been placed around and, at first, no one had seen that he had his gun pointed at the angel.

There were no screens anymore. In fact, as Millie

looked around, she saw a shiny new lock on the back door to the barn and there were no places to hide behind screens or curtains or large chairs. Even the hay was pushed firmly against the wall.

Forrest would have been saddened to see how his actions had made the people of Dry Creek feel unsafe. The lock on the barn wasn't the only new lock Millie had seen as she walked over to the barn from the church.

The day was still cold and Millie didn't have any snow boots to wear, so she had walked in the path of several tire tracks to avoid the loose snow that was lying on the ground. Brad had said he needed to discuss something with the minister and had gone off with him, telling Millie he would meet her later over at the barn.

Millie was glad to have a few minutes alone and lingered in the doorway to the barn for just a minute. The snow that was predicted for today was still not falling. The clouds had gotten grayer, though, and the air felt weighted. Something about the day matched her restlessness—like she was carrying around something cold and heavy inside of herself and she needed to let go of it just like the clouds needed to let go of their moisture.

It was those Christmas stockings, she said to herself. When she put the money in them and delivered them, she would have done all she could in memory of Forrest. She would be released from the guilt she felt on behalf of him.

When that was done, she would be able to leave Dry Creek, she told herself. The tie she felt holding her here would be gone. Her life would go back to the way it was, and she would have to try and be content.

Millie stepped all of the way inside the barn and quietly closed the door. The day was so overcast that someone had turned on the electrical lights that were attached to some of the rafters.

The pastor's wife, Glory, was kneeling in the middle of the stage area and painting what looked like a trellis. Old newspapers were spread around underneath wooden figures. Several open cans of paint sat around on the newspapers.

"May I take a look?" Millie asked.

Glory looked up from her paints and smiled. "You can take more than a look. You're welcome to pick up a brush and join me."

Millie walked over to where Glory was painting.

Large wooden cutout figures were lying on the floor beside Glory. Some of them had been painted and some of them were still raw wood. Millie counted three sheep.

"Is that a dog?" If the cutout had been any less like a dog, Millie would have assumed it was supposed to be a sheep.

Glory nodded. "I'm afraid that over the years, our pageant has picked up some additional characters that you won't find in the Biblical account of the Nativity. One of them is a dog named Chester. He's supposed to be a sheepdog, but everyone knows Chester just shows up anywhere in the pageant."

Millie knelt down and sat the same way Glory was sitting with her legs crossed. "I thought Chester was a real dog."

Millie remembered Forrest telling her about the dog that chased the chicken in the Christmas pageant he had seen two years ago.

Glory nodded. "He is. This is the committee's way of compromising. They decided not to have any live animals in the pageant this year, but they did ask that we make a cutout of Chester just like we have a cutout of the sheep. It's to keep the children happy. They all like having Chester in the pageant."

"It seems like in a barn you would have real animals," Millie said.

Glory nodded. "It was a difficult decision to cut back this year. But people just didn't seem to have the heart to put on a full-scale pageant. Usually we invite some of the area churches, but this year we're just doing it simple and for ourselves."

Millie didn't want to ask why the people of Dry Creek were having a difficult time. She was afraid she knew.

"It's the economy," Glory added. "Everybody just seems a little more worried this year than last."

"Oh, the economy," Millie said. That wasn't so bad. "It's tough all over."

Glory looked up from her painting and smiled. "Is that what happened to you? Did you lose your job?"

Glory was friendly and her questions didn't have any sting in them.

Millie shook her head. "I still have my job. I'm on a break. It might not be much of a job, but it's waiting there for me when I go back in a few days."

"Well, that's good," Glory said as she picked up a brush and dipped it into a small can of black paint. "It seems like around here everyone is looking for work. It's always worse at Christmas. My husband keeps thinking about adding another part-time person to the staff at the hardware store just to give someone a little help."

"That's nice of him," Millie said as she looked over the brushes. If she wasn't careful, she would be telling all of her worries to Glory, and she didn't want to do that. She would keep Forrest's secret until she could fulfill his request.

Millie nodded her head at the cutout animals. "Would you like me to paint one of the figures? If there's something simple, that is."

"Take any one of the sheep," Glory said. "Just paint it all white, and then we'll go back and paint on the hooves and the face."

Millie ran out of white paint after she painted two of the sheep.

"I think they had black sheep back then," Glory said as she passed the black can of paint. "At least it's a better color than the brown we're using for the donkey."

"There wouldn't be a black sheep at the Nativity scene, would there?" Millie asked dubiously.

Glory chuckled. "I don't know why not—the church always seems to specialize in black sheep."

Millie picked up a brush and dipped it into the black paint. She was beginning to think that the church was nothing like she had ever thought it would be.

The afternoon light had darkened by the time Millie finished all of the sheep.

"This one looks a little hungry," Millie said. Glory had given her suggestions on how to paint the sheep's faces, but then had left it up to Millie. "I hope the children don't mind."

Each of the cutout animals had straps on the back where a child was going to hold it during the pageant.

"The twins have already suffered their own disappointment. They wanted me to make some dragons, but I drew the line. I said I'd do Chester, but that was it. No dragons." Glory gave Millie a rueful look. "I think they wanted to surprise the angel when she comes out and says 'Behold, I bring you glad tidings.'"

Millie had never actually read the Bible. "There aren't...?"

Glory shook her head. "No. But the twins swear there should have been. I think they figure if Mary and Joseph had come in riding a dragon, the innkeeper would have given them better accommodations."

"That's kind of cute."

Glory sighed and stood up. "Yeah, they're hard to say no to. In fact—" Glory walked over to the bales and picked up two cutout figures that had been lying on top of them "—I made them these little ones for later—after the pageant."

Millie smiled at the two little dragon figures Glory had made. They were both still unpainted.

"Mrs. Hargrove is going to flunk us all in Sunday school if they use these in the pageant," Glory said.

Both Millie and Glory heard the voices of the men and looked toward the entrance of the barn. Pastor Matthew and Brad opened the door and stepped inside the barn.

"How's it coming?" Pastor Matthew asked.

"Good," Glory said.

Millie nodded and smiled.

Pastor Matthew walked over to Glory and gave her a kiss. Brad walked over to Millie, and she had a moment's panic that he meant to kiss her, as well.

"I painted a black sheep," Millie blurted out, and turned to walk back to where the animal cutouts were.

Well, Brad thought to himself, he guessed Pastor Matthew was right when he said God didn't hand out any love potions to people. Millie hadn't gazed up to him with anything near the look of adoration that Glory had on her face when she turned toward her husband.

Of course, Brad decided, it might be too soon for Millie to feel that settled, married love that Glory seemed to feel. Maybe a love potion would start out different—maybe there'd be a tingling sensation or something.

"Are you feeling okay?" Brad asked as Millie walked away from him. "Not dizzy or anything?"

"My one leg has a cramp in it," Millie said as she turned to him and then sat down. "It must be the way I was sitting. How did you know?"

"Oh, ah, there's a lot of paint fumes in here. I figured they might be affecting everyone."

"I don't think they'd give me a leg cramp," Millie said and stretched her leg out in front of her. "Unless it's some kind of slow-acting poison or something."

Brad had to congratulate himself. He'd just witnessed the opposite of a love potion. Millie wasn't even smiling at him now. In fact, she was frowning at him. He couldn't have done a worse job of it if he'd tried.

Brad sighed. He wasn't the kind of man who could be subtle. He'd just have to plough forward and hope that Pastor Matthew's God would have mercy on him.

"I wouldn't worry about it—the fumes aren't poisonous. I'm sure they haven't affected you at all. And that's good you're able to be around the paint fumes and not get sick," Brad said. He needed to get it out there before she started thinking she had the plague. "You know there's a job that's going to be opening up soon at the hardware store. Probably working with paint some. It might be a natural fit for you."

Brad decided Millie was looking at him like he'd

sprouted another ear. "Some people really enjoy working in the hardware store."

"I've always worked in restaurants."

"Well, maybe Linda needs someone to help her out in the café," Brad said. She wasn't making this easy for him.

"The café's closed."

"Well, now it is, sure—but it'll open again when Linda gets back from Los Angeles."

Brad didn't know how a man could break a sweat when the air in the barn was cold. Maybe he was the one getting sick from the fumes.

"Do you think she'd hire me?" Millie asked. Brad swore he saw a flare of hope in her eyes before it died. "After all this fuss about me breaking in and all. I mean, she might think I was planning to rob her."

"Oh."

"Of course I wasn't robbing her," Millie added. "It's just that—"

Brad nodded. He needed another prayer session with the pastor. After they'd talked and prayed, Brad had begun to have hope that Millie would stay in Dry Creek long enough for the two of them to have a proper courtship. He didn't think Millie was the kind of woman who would get engaged after knowing a man for only a day or two.

No, he needed some time to show her they would be good together. It didn't seem like it was such a big miracle for God to perform. It didn't require bringing someone back to life from the dead or parting a sea or anything. All Brad needed was a little time.

"How's your car doing?" Brad asked. That car might be his best hope. If the thing broke down, Millie would be around for at least a week while they sent away for parts.

"Fine," Millie said.

Brad nodded. He'd pray about that car of hers. He wasn't even sure you could call it a miracle if the car broke down before she left Dry Creek. In fact, it would probably be a miracle if it *didn't* break down. All he needed to do was have her drive it around until it died. He might not even need any prayer to pull this off. A full tank of gas might be all he needed.

Millie decided Brad was right about the paint fumes. They certainly seemed to be affecting him. One minute he was frowning, and the next minute he looked perfectly happy.

"I'll go open the door," Millie said as she stood up. The air outside was cold, but it was better to be a little cold than to be affected by those fumes.

When Millie opened the door, she saw that it was starting to snow. Tiny flakes were drifting to the ground. "It's snowing."

"We should get your car back to the ranch before the roads get slippery," Brad said as he walked over and stood behind her.

"I could ride back with you," Millie said.

"Really?" Brad looked happy and then he looked stern. "No, it's better if you drive your car back. Wouldn't want to leave it in Dry Creek. And your tank is almost full, isn't it?"

Millie nodded. She knew to fill her tank in Miles City. Brad was right. She did like to have her car close by just in case. Besides, she still had those stockings in the trunk.

"You might want to drive it out to the barn when you

get back to the ranch, too. Get some more practice driving in the snow. And then you'll want to drive it back tonight for the pageant."

Millie nodded again. She definitely needed her car tonight. It was nice of Brad to realize that, especially since he'd seemed so intent this morning on keeping her car off of the roads.

Chapter Fourteen

Mⁱⁱlie stood outside the bunkhouse of the Elkton Ranch and stared down at the contents of her car's trunk. The sun was setting and light snow was still falling. It had been snowing for several hours, but Charlie had said the roads were not in danger of being blocked.

Charlie seemed particularly pleased that there was no reason to worry about the roads. He'd already convinced all of the men in the bunkhouse to drive into Dry Creek tonight to see the Christmas pageant.

It was the Christmas pageant that was causing Millie's frown. She had just slipped a hundred-dollar bill into each of the red stockings she'd made, and she'd stacked the stockings alphabetically in two neat piles in the trunk of her car. She was all ready to deliver the stockings, but she didn't know how to do it now.

At first, she had thought she would go to the barn before the pageant and lay the stockings around the room on the chairs. But then she realized it would create a lot of fuss, and she didn't want to take anything away from the pageant.

No, she decided, she'd have to deliver the stockings

after the pageant. Maybe she could just leave them inside the barn door on the bench where people sat when they needed to take off their snow boots. Everyone would see them on their way out of the barn.

When Millie made her decision, she expected the heavy feeling inside of her to lift. She had almost completed her task. It hadn't gone as Forrest probably thought it would, but she would be able to deliver the hundred-dollar bills and finish what she had started. She should feel good, not sad.

After all, things were working out. Millie figured she was still a stranger to most people in Dry Creek— at least as much of a stranger as Forrest had been when he had been here. He'd only been in the little town a few days, as well. When she left, even the people she had met would eventually forget her name and what she looked like.

She would truly be a Christmas stranger.

And that, Millie finally admitted, was why she was sad. The people of Dry Creek might forget her, but she would never forget them. Not Glory, or Charlie, or Mrs. Hargrove. And especially not Brad.

Of course, Brad would forget her, Millie decided in a burst of irritation. The man couldn't wait for her to get in her car and drive off somewhere. He didn't even seem to care where she was going. She could have suggested she drive to the moon, and he would have encouraged her to do it. Just to please him, she'd already driven up and down the driveway into the Elkton ranch several times this afternoon.

Millie looked over toward the bunkhouse. The last time she'd parked her car this afternoon, she'd deliberately parked so she could see in the big window in the living room. Frost had edged the window, but she could still see the little Christmas tree on the opposite wall.

That tree would always be her favorite Christmas tree, even though Millie vowed she would decorate one for herself next Christmas. Something about this Christmas had changed the feeling she had inside that she needed to be on the outside looking in at Christmas.

Maybe it was going to church here and seeing the people all work together. Or being Christmas company at the bunkhouse. Or even riding out to get the Christmas tree with Brad.

Maybe it was all of it. She supposed it didn't matter. What mattered was that she no longer felt so alone. Not even, she swallowed, when she was leaving.

There, she thought to herself, she'd said it. She was leaving Dry Creek.

She really had no choice. She knew the job at the hardware store was a charity job and was meant for someone in Dry Creek. The pastor hadn't created the job to give it to someone who had just come into town. It might be an option to work at the café, but Linda was gone and there was no one to ask about working there.

It wasn't the stockings in the trunk that were bothering her, Millie finally admitted. It was her small suitcase that was sitting next to them. Millie had slipped the suitcase out of the bunkhouse earlier this afternoon without anyone seeing her.

She needed to be ready to leave Dry Creek. The longer she stayed, the harder it would be to leave.

Millie wondered if Forrest was looking down from heaven and seeing what a mess she'd made of her version of the plan. She knew now that Forrest had wanted her to meet the people of Dry Creek.

She had wanted to sneak into town and leave before anyone saw her. She would have succeeded, too, if Brad hadn't been parked behind the café.

For the first time it struck her just how odd that was. What had Brad been doing parked there? He couldn't have been having trouble with his pickup, because the old thing had started right up when he turned the ignition. And, if he'd had a flat tire, he wouldn't have been parked behind the café. Brad must have been sitting there for a long time, because she knew he hadn't driven back there while she was inside.

There was only one reason Millie could think of for Brad to be there, and she didn't like it.

Millie slammed the trunk of her car and headed back to the bunkhouse.

The main room of the bunkhouse was empty, but Millie heard someone in the kitchen.

Charlie stood at the stove stirring a big pot of something. Whatever it was, it smelled good, but Millie hardly noticed.

"I have a question for you," Millie said. She couldn't think of a subtle way to ask what she needed to know. "Around here, when you see a car that's pulled off the road at night, what do you think?"

Charlie looked up from his stirring. "Car trouble."

Millie shook her head. "There was no car trouble."

"Maybe it's late and no one's in the car," Charlie suggested.

Millie shook her head again. "Oh, someone was in the car all right."

Charlie smiled. "Well, if there's two someones in the car, then you have your answer. There's nothing quite as romantic as sitting together under the stars."

Millie nodded her head. She didn't know what had happened to the woman that had been in the pickup with Brad. "Do people around here ever drive into Dry Creek and leave their cars at the café before they go into Miles City?"

"Sure, if they're going to drive together most of the way." Charlie looked at her quizzically. "You worried about your car dying or something? If you are, anyone would be happy to give you a lift anywhere you need to go."

Millie shook her head. "No, my car is fine. Thanks."

Charlie shrugged. "Well, if you need anything, let me know."

Millie nodded. What she needed wasn't something Charlie could give her.

Millie walked back into the main room of the bunkhouse and sat down on a sofa. What she needed was to leave Dry Creek and Brad Parker before the cracks that were starting in her heart caused it to break in two.

Brad stopped and scraped his feet before he entered the bunkhouse. He'd been forced to drive back from Miles City all by himself. You'd think the other guys had never smelled women's perfume before. Brad had been determined to find the perfume that suited Millie best, and how was he supposed to tell what each one smelled like if he didn't have the sales clerk spray the air in front of him?

The other guys had gone together and bought Millie a wool scarf and some mittens, but Brad wanted a special gift, and that was a challenge in the small department store in Miles City.

Finally, Brad had settled on something called "Snow Angel" that the salesclerk swore was light and sounded, from everything he had told her, like it would be perfect for Millie.

Brad saw that Millie had been looking at the Christmas tree before he came in. When she heard him, she turned around.

"Sorry to let the cold air in," Brad said. When he had opened the door to the bunkhouse, a gust of wind had followed him in. "The wind's blowing out there."

"You must be cold," Millie said as she stood up. "I could start the coffeepot."

Brad shook his head. "I'll just warm up by the fire."

Brad had the bottle of perfume in his pocket. The clerk had wrapped the perfume for him, but he decided to wait until after the pageant to put the box under the tree. He didn't want Millie to think she needed to give him a present, so he didn't want her to know about the box.

Millie sniffed the air. The closer she walked to Brad, the more she could smell the perfume. It wasn't some kind of cologne for a man, either. No, the perfume was definitely the kind a woman would wear.

"I thought you were out with the other guys," Millie said.

"Oh, I was," Brad said. Millie thought he looked a little guilty, but he continued, "We had some business to take care of."

Millie wondered what the woman's name was. Not that it was any of her business, she reminded herself. "Well, that's good then, I guess."

Just then the rest of the ranch hands came into the bunkhouse. Millie noticed as each one filed through the door that none of them smelled of perfume. Which meant that, wherever Brad had been, he hadn't been with them.

Millie decided, as she blinked a few times, that it was just as well that she was leaving tonight after the pageant.

Chapter Fifteen

The pageant was scheduled to begin at seven o'clock, and by then the sky was completely dark. The snow flurries had stopped an hour earlier, and the clouds had parted enough to allow a few stars to shine through the blackness. The lights inside the barn showed through the high windows, and Millie could see into the barn each time someone opened the main door.

Millie parked her car as close to the barn as she could. She was surprised that Brad had offered to give her a ride to the pageant. She almost asked him why he wasn't giving a ride to Miss Perfume. But she didn't. She couldn't ride with him anyway, because she had the Christmas stockings. The Christmas stockings were supposed to be a surprise, and she no longer felt any desire to tell Brad all her secrets.

Brad would know soon enough anyway. Millie had decided the town of Dry Creek should know that Forrest was sorry, and so she'd enclosed a note in Mrs. Hargrove's stocking explaining everything.

The air was chilly when Millie opened the door to

her car, and she walked quickly to the barn. She'd come back later and get the stockings.

The light inside the barn was dim, and Millie could see the trellis in the middle of the floor that had a sign hanging from it saying Bethlehem Inn. From the sounds of the shuffling feet and giggles coming from behind a makeshift curtain at the end of the barn, the animals were getting ready to play their parts.

A stereo was set up in the barn and Millie could hear the muted sounds of Christmas carols. She also heard the sound of Brad's voice and saw him talking with a group of men gathered near a coffeepot in one corner of the barn. There was no one standing near him who might be Miss Perfume, but then, Millie reasoned, the woman might be one of the ones she saw helping the children get into their costumes.

Millie walked over to a place where there were several empty chairs. Walking through the people of Dry Creek wasn't as easy as it sounded. People smiled at her and greeted her every step of the way. She'd refused several offers of a chair by the time she reached the one she wanted.

Millie picked a chair that had empty chairs on both sides of it. She didn't want to get to know any more people in Dry Creek. She'd just be leaving soon anyway.

Someone turned the music up louder and flicked the light switches. That must be the signal that the pageant was ready to begin. The people who weren't already seated started to move to the sides of the barn where the chairs were positioned.

"May I?"

Millie heard Brad's low question as he sat down in the chair next to her.

Brad didn't know why Millie had such a surprised look on her face. He'd followed her car into Dry Creek to be sure she didn't have any mechanical trouble on the way. He'd even sat in his pickup for a little bit after they both parked until it became clear that she was not going to go inside right away. The only reason he'd gone in ahead of her was because he was beginning to feel like a stalker.

She should have figured out by now that he was planning to sit beside her.

"You're wearing perfume." Brad noticed the fact as everyone around them was sitting down. He hadn't thought she had been wearing perfume before. The scent she was wearing now was light and fruity. Maybe she wouldn't like the perfume he had bought for her. He should have asked if she had a preference. "What kind is it?"

"It's not perfume. It's peach soap."

"Ah, soap." Brad didn't know if that meant she would like perfume or not. Well, it was too late now anyway. He planned to give her the perfume tonight when they got back to the bunkhouse. He could only hope for the best.

The lights were dimmed almost completely for a minute.

Brad assumed by the sounds that the children were getting in place for the pageant.

The donkey was the first thing to come out from behind the curtain. The donkey was followed by nine-year-old Angie Loden wearing a blue tablecloth wrapped sari-style around her. A pillow made her look awkwardly pregnant, but the look in her eye made her look like a schoolteacher.

Millie smiled when she saw the little girl in blue. She wondered if girls playing at being Mary always wore blue because they had all seen the same stained glass picture of Jesus talking to the little girl in the blue robe.

Millie heard the choked-back laughter as the girl started her walk. She obviously wasn't as worried about talking to Jesus as she was about correcting the boy who was playing Joseph. Millie could almost hear the girl scolding him in a low whisper as the boy tried to keep up with the girl and the donkey. The boy was having a hard time not tripping on the hem of his robe, until finally Mary reached over and adjusted the belt around the robe so that material bunched up around the boy's waist, making the robe shorter.

One of the Curtis twins was carrying the cutout figure of the donkey, and he was leading the girl along the path toward the makeshift inn.

The Christmas music was turned almost completely off, and another voice came from the loudspeakers. Millie decided the voice was from a tape, because she didn't recognize it from the voices she'd heard in Dry Creek.

"At that time, Augustus Caesar sent an order that all people in the countries under Roman rule must list their names in the register," the voice said, as Mary, Joseph and the donkey slowly walked toward the inn.

Millie had not realized the whole Nativity scene started because someone wanted to collect everyone's name. She thought of the stockings in her trunk. They made a more appropriate Christmas gift than she had thought. She'd had to collect all the names of the people, as well. She knew how much trouble that could be. It gave her a certain empathy with Augustus Caesar.

Millie sat back and decided to enjoy the pageant.

She chuckled along with everyone else when the innkeeper looked uncertain about whether or not he had any rooms. Finally, Mary looked down some imaginary hall and said she could see his inn was filled with tourists, and so there were no rooms for those people who really needed a place to stay.

The angel didn't fly overhead like she had in other pageants, but a blond girl climbed a ladder and flapped her wings while shouting out "Behold!" with as much enthusiasm as the original angel must have had.

Chester, the real dog, chose this moment to run inside and shake the snow off of his coat.

Millie expected the adults to scold and ask who had let Chester into the barn, but they all just seemed to shrug their shoulders and turn their attention back to the unfolding pageant.

It must have been when the shepherds were coming in from their fields that Brad put his arm on the back of her chair. Millie could feel it on her shoulders. She'd been laughing at Chester's efforts to herd the wooden sheep, and she looked up at Brad.

Brad was happy. He'd moved his arm from the back of Millie's chair to her shoulders and she'd smiled up at him. Her face was still glowing from the laughter, and even though he wasn't the reason for her laughter, the delight she was feeling spilled over onto him.

Brad began to wonder if he was wrong about how long it took for a man to fall in love. He'd thought he needed to get to know Millie. But he was beginning to think he knew all he needed to know right now.

If the sheep hadn't arrived at the inn just then, Brad would have whispered something silly in Millie's ear. But she'd turned her gaze back to the pageant, and he wanted her to remember every single moment of this night. He'd wait and whisper in her ear tonight after he'd given her the perfume.

Millie sighed when the wise men started walking toward the inn. The littlest of the boys had trouble keeping his crown on his head and had to set his golden box of spices down on the floor so he could adjust his crown. Chester, of course, had to come over and sniff at the spices until he sneezed. Whatever it was that was supposed to be myrrh scattered across the floor.

All in all, Millie thought when the lights were dimmed for the last time, the pageant had been delightful. It had also gone much too fast.

Millie looked over at Brad. She'd have to say goodbye to him later. Maybe she wouldn't have to leave right after she delivered the stockings. But, for now, she should make her move while the children all came back on stage to sing "Silent Night."

The air outside the barn felt sharply cold to Millie after she had been inside. Brad had thought she was leaving to use the restroom, or he would have come with her. Setting the stockings out for everyone was something she had to do by herself. Forrest had been her friend, and she would help him do what he could to make his actions up to the people of Dry Creek. She had left Mrs. Hargrove's stocking on top of all the others, since it had the note inside it.

Millie could barely hold all of the stockings in her arms, but she didn't want to make two trips. She planned to leave them on the bench inside the door. Now that the pageant was almost over, it wouldn't be long before someone turned and saw the stockings.

Millie had left the door slightly open so that she could just push it completely open with her arms. She managed to come back inside the barn and stand by the door without anyone noticing her.

Everyone inside the barn was looking at the children singing in the middle of the floor, and Millie could see why. With their crooked angel wings and dragging shepherd robes, the children were charming. Even Chester was sitting calmly beside the wooden sheep while they sang.

Millie set the stack of stockings down on the bench. There were mittens and scarves on the shelf above the bench and some rubber boots under the bench. But the bench itself was clear until Millie set down her stockings.

When children finished their last notes of "Silent Night," Millie stepped back outside the door. She left the door cracked open so she could hear people's excitement. Within minutes, she heard the first exclamation.

"Look at these!" a woman's voice said.

"Don't touch them," a man's voice answered.

"Why, they're Millie's stockings," Mrs. Hargrove said.

Millie smiled. The older woman would convince everyone to trust that the stockings were okay.

"Look what's inside them!" That voice sounded like it came from a teenage boy. "It's hundred-dollar bills!"

"What's money like that doing here?" the man who had spoken earlier said.

"I wonder if the stores are still open. I'd love to get the kids real presents for Christmas and not just new mittens," a woman said.

"Maybe I'll get my train set," a little voice said.

Millie heard a chorus of excited whispers until the man spoke again.

"But what's the money doing here?" the man insisted loudly. "If we don't know what it's doing here, we shouldn't touch it."

"It's from Millie," Mrs. Hargrove said. "She left a note."

Millie could hear the people crowding next to Mrs. Hargrove.

"Is it counterfeit?" someone asked.

"No," Mrs. Hargrove said slowly. "It's money from Forrest."

"Who's Forrest?" someone else asked.

"That's the name of the hit man," someone else answered. "But what's that got to do with that woman?"

"Millie was his friend," Mrs. Hargrove said. "And she writes that Forrest wanted us to know he was sorry for what he did here."

There was almost total silence on the other side of the door.

Finally, Brad spoke. His voice was low, but Millie could hear it clearly.

"She was friends with a hit man?" Brad's voice contained a world of confusion and disbelief. "What kind of person is friends with a hit man?"

Millie turned to walk down the stairs. She'd heard enough. It was time to leave.

The air was just as cold when Millie walked back to her car, but she didn't notice a thing. The cold outside didn't begin to compare with the cold inside of her.

She opened the door to her car and was grateful that the car started right up when she turned the ignition. She backed the car away from the barn before she turned on the headlights. She didn't want her car lights to shine into the windows of the barn. She would leave Dry Creek as quietly as she had come.

Millie rolled down the window as she pulled away from the barn. She wanted to hear any last music that might be coming from the pageant. She thought they would turn the stereo on again with the Christmas carols, but she didn't hear anything.

Finally, she rolled her window back up. She'd have to listen to her radio instead.

Chapter Sixteen

Brad sat down on the steps outside the church. He wasn't planning to go to church this morning, but it had snowed last night, and he figured he'd shovel off the steps just to show God and Mrs. Hargrove that he didn't hold any hard feelings toward them. Well, not many hard feelings anyway. Which wasn't bad considering he had met the woman of his dreams and neither one of them had helped him to keep track of her.

Millie had slipped away from the barn on Christmas Eve, and Brad hadn't even known it for a full fifteen minutes. She'd said she was going to the restroom, and he'd believed her. By the time he realized she wasn't inside the barn, he'd gone racing outside only to see that her car was gone.

He'd gotten into his pickup and followed the road all of the way into Miles City thinking he would find her. When he didn't see her, he figured she had gone the other direction out of Dry Creek, and he came barreling back and drove all the way into North Dakota before he turned around.

That old car of hers went faster than he'd thought possible.

Brad stopped shoveling and leaned on his shovel. The days had been gloomy ever since Christmas. He'd always dreaded Christmas. But now he knew it wasn't Christmas that was his problem. It was all of the rest of the days that stretched out after Christmas was gone that were going to give him grief.

Even with all of the excitement in Dry Creek these days, Brad was miserable. Every time someone talked about what they had spent their hundred dollars on, Brad thought of Millie. He'd thought of her through conversations about toy dolls and new tennis shoes. Mrs. Hargrove even informed him about the new ice-crushing blender she'd bought with part of her money.

Brad still had his hundred-dollar bill in his shirt pocket next to his heart.

Brad had wished a million times since that night that he hadn't been shocked Millie had been friends with a hit man. He shouldn't have even been surprised. He knew Millie would be loyal to her friends, and that she took up with the underdogs. It only made sense that she would stand by her friends if they were arrested.

He wished he could tell her, though, that it was her note that made the difference to the people of Dry Creek, and not the money. Just hearing that the hit man had been deeply sorry allowed people to start trusting in strangers again.

Brad started moving his shovel again. The thing he really regretted, however, was that he'd never asked Millie for her address. He was sitting here with his heart full of things to tell her, and he didn't even know how to find her. All he really knew was that she lived somewhere around the waterfront in Seattle.

Brad had finished shoveling all of the steps when he saw the pastor come out of the parsonage and start walking toward the church.

"Good morning," Pastor Matthew called out. "You're joining us this morning for church, aren't you?"

Brad grimaced as the minister came closer. "I'm not fit for polite company these days."

Brad ran his hand over his face. He hadn't shaved for a couple of days, and he figured he looked pretty rough.

"Having a hard time?" the pastor asked as he came closer to Brad.

Brad nodded. "Not much I can do about it though."

The pastor looked at Brad for a minute. "If you want to come to my office with me, I think I have something that might cheer you up."

"No offense," Brad said as he leaned against his shovel, "but this is something prayer can't fix."

"God might surprise you," the pastor said as he started climbing the steps.

Brad figured God had already had His chance to work on Millie and had missed His opportunity completely.

"What you might not understand is that I need concrete help," Brad said as he started to follow the pastor. "I mean prayer is nice, but I need, well, real help."

The pastor had walked up the steps to the church and opened the main door. Brad still followed him as the minister crossed the back of the church and opened a door into a small room.

Pastor Matthew went to his desk, picked something up and turned around to face Brad.

"Is this concrete enough for you?" the pastor held out a blue card.

"Millie filled out a visitor's form?"

The tightness Brad had felt in his chest all week started to loosen.

The pastor nodded. "Of course, it wouldn't be right for me to give the information on this card to just anyone."

"Oh."

"However, I figure that a representative from the church should be allowed to call on Millie, since she did mark the box that asked for a visit from someone from the church."

"I've been to the church twice now—if the Christmas pageant counts."

Pastor Matthew grinned as he held the card out to Brad. "All you really need to do is invite Millie to next Sunday's service. I can even send a church bulletin along with you, so you have all the information."

Brad understood why people throughout the ages had kissed the feet of holy men when they got their prayers answered. "Thank you."

Ruby's café was on the Seattle waterfront, and most mornings in January the air was cold. The floor at Ruby's was made of thick wooden planks and the walls were filled with large paned glass windows. Ruby believed in natural light, plants and strong coffee. It was the coffee that brought the customers in, but Millie suspected it was the plants that made them want to linger over their meals.

Not that Millie was worried about customers who wouldn't leave.

She had just mixed up the order on table seven. Instead of bringing the man coffee with cream, she had brought him tea with sugar. In all of her years at Ruby's she'd never made a mistake on an order until after she got back from Dry Creek. Since she'd gotten back eight days ago, however, she'd made thirty-two mistakes. The reason she knew the exact number was because the other waitresses were trying to guess the limit of Ruby's patience and they were counting.

Of course, the waitresses all knew Millie's job was safe because they were running shorthanded. The dishwasher had quit, and Ruby had no sooner put the Help Wanted—Dishwasher sign in the window than one of the waitresses had quit, as well.

Not that the other waitresses weren't also sympathetic. They'd cooed and fussed over Millie that first day back until she thought she would have to take to her bed and have herself a good rest just to get some peace from people's good intentions.

Millie had distracted the other waitresses from their sympathy by telling them about the Christmas pageant at Dry Creek. When she left Montana, she fully intended to entertain them all with stories about Brad. But she found the stories she had thought were so funny when they happened now only made her feel sad. Even the story about the spiders would have made her cry if she tried to tell it.

Millie had slipped once when she was talking to Louise and had mentioned that she'd stayed in the bunkhouse in the room of a nice man.

The waitresses at Ruby's weren't usually impressed with someone who was just nice, but they seemed to know there was more to Millie's stories than she was telling.

The door to Ruby's buzzed whenever anyone opened it and came inside. Ruby said the buzzer allowed them to have good customer control. No customer was ever supposed to wait more than five minutes at Ruby's before he or she was seated and offered a cup of coffee.

So it was only natural that all of the waitresses looked up when the buzzer sounded.

Millie's mouth dropped open. In all of the days since she'd left Dry Creek, she never thought she'd look up at Ruby's and see Brad Parker walk into the café.

"What are you doing here?" Millie walked over to the man and asked.

For the hundredth time that day, Brad wondered if his plan was a good one. It was a long drive from Dry Creek to Seattle, and he'd thought of a million clever things to say to Millie when he saw her. But then he'd decided to just be himself and be honest. When he saw how white Millie's face was, however, he wished he had thought of something to tell her that didn't contain the words "I came because of you."

"I came for the job," Brad blurted out. He'd seen the sign in the window of the diner, and he was only beginning to see the advantages it offered.

"What job?" Millie frowned.

"Dishwasher," Brad guessed. He was almost sure that was what the sign said.

That seemed to leave Millie speechless. Finally, she swallowed. "Here?"

Brad nodded. "I think that's where the job is."

Millie just stared at him.

"I'm hoping they'll take me temporarily. For a few weeks," Brad added. "I could use a break from moving cattle."

Millie might be speechless, but Brad could hear the other waitresses start to chatter. Finally, one of them walked over to him.

Brad saw by the woman's badge that her name was Sherry. Ordinarily, she would be the kind of woman who would catch his eye. Her hair was all highlights and curls. Her fingernails were deep red and slightly pointed. Her smile was friendly and her uniform not buttoned up tight.

"I'm sure Ruby will hire you on the spot," the waitress said as she stepped closer to Brad. "I sure would."

"Back off, Sherry," an older waitress said. "This is a *nice* man."

Brad thought she said the word "nice" like it was a code.

"A *nice* man from Dry Creek, I believe," the older woman said as she gave Sherry a stern look.

Sherry shrugged her shoulders and turned away. "Can't blame a girl for trying."

Millie decided she better set down the coffeepot that she was holding. Come to think of it, she should just sit her whole self down.

Louise seemed to agree. She looked at Millie and said, "Now's a good time to take your break. We're not busy. There's no one on the patio."

Millie nodded as she turned toward the patio.

"Take your time. I'll send out some of those fresh donuts for you and your friend."

Millie walked out to the patio, and even though she heard his footsteps behind her, she was still surprised to see Brad himself behind her there when she came to the table and sat down.

"Mind if I join you?" Brad said.

Millie blinked. She hadn't noticed how nervous he seemed. She had always thought she was the only one who got nervous. "Please do."

Brad sat down at the small table across from Millie.

"What brings you to Seattle?" Millie finally asked.

"You."

Brad knew he'd been clumsy. He hadn't meant to rush Millie like that. "I mean, I came to see you because you asked for a visit from someone from the church."

Brad pulled out the blue visitor's card that Millie had filled out when she was in Dry Creek. The corners were bent because he'd kept it on the dash of his pickup all the way from Montana to Seattle.

"You came to invite me back to church?" Millie sounded incredulous.

"I came to invite you back to Dry Creek," Brad said quietly.

Millie didn't answer right away so he just kept on explaining. "I know it's too big of a decision to make right away. I know you've only known me for a couple of days. But you aren't going to get to know me better unless you're in Dry Creek or I'm here." Brad took a deep breath. "So I thought I'd stay here for a while so we can get to know each other."

Millie started to smile. She felt like someone had turned the sunshine on in the middle of an overcast day. "We're going to get to know each other?"

Brad nodded and started to smile himself.

"You're willing to wash dishes so you can get to know me better?" Millie still couldn't believe it. Most men she knew wouldn't wash dishes for any reason. "You know Ruby throws in the pots and pans, too. It's not just the easy stuff like glasses and silverware."

"I'd figured as much," Brad said as his smile turned into a full grin.

"You do get a share of the tips though," Millie added. "And meals—you get meals."

"I'd settle for a kiss or two from the right waitress," Brad said, and then he remembered something and reached in his pocket. "And I have a Christmas present for you."

Millie looked at the silver box with the red ribbon on it. No one had ever given her such a pretty gift.

Brad handed her the box.

"Go ahead, open it," Brad said.

Millie had half of the paper off when she started to smell the perfume. She recognized it from the fragrance that had surrounded Brad on the night of the Christmas pageant. *She* was the perfume woman in Brad's life! She had to blink a little to keep the tears away.

"You're not allergic, are you?" Brad asked.

Millie shook her head. She only had one problem at the moment. "I don't have a present for you."

Millie figured the hundred-dollar bill didn't count because that was really from Forrest. She hadn't expected to meet Brad when she went to Dry Creek, so she hadn't taken a present with her. And she hadn't expected to ever see him again when she left, so there was no reason to buy him one later.

There was only one gift she could think of that might please him, and she couldn't think about it too long or she'd decide it wasn't grand enough.

Millie stood up and leaned across the table. Then she bent down and kissed Brad square on the lips.

Millie had to swallow a chuckle, because she knew she had startled Brad for a second. But the man adapted quick. Before she knew it, the kiss was making her head spin and her knees buckle.

"Oh, my," Millie said when the kiss had ended. She was leaning into Brad and she was halfway into his arms. He moved around the table and settled her on his lap.

"You know, I have a feeling I'm not going to mind washing all those dishes at all," Brad said.

Millie just smiled. She had a feeling she wouldn't mind him washing all those dishes, either.

Epilogue

Four Months Later

Millie smiled as she looked at her bridal dress in the mirror. She had been staying at Mrs. Hargrove's for the past two weeks while she and Brad received marriage counseling from Pastor Matthew and made final plans for their wedding.

She and Brad had been going to a church in Seattle, but they both wanted to be married in the church in Dry Creek, especially after Millie started receiving the notes of thanks from the people in town. She was pleased that the notes were as likely to thank her for letting them know that the hit man was sorry as they were to thank her for the money.

The people in Dry Creek were good, solid people.

Millie and Brad intended to live their lives in Dry Creek and wanted to make the church their home. Since neither one of them had ideal childhoods, they knew that church would be their family.

Millie marveled at how much her understanding of God could change in just a few months. She and Brad had both asked God to help them understand more about Him, and they'd been astonished at what they were learning.

Millie fingered the lace on her veil. She had never thought she would know a man who wanted to take care of her as much as she wanted to take care of him. Brad had put a down payment on a ranch just outside of Dry Creek, and that would be where they would raise their family.

"Are you ready?" Mrs. Hargrove called up the stairs. "The carriage is here to pick you up."

When the ranch hands had heard that she and Brad were going to get married, they had rigged up one of the ranch wagons as a wedding carriage. Millie had seen the wagon this morning. It was covered with cascades of spring flowers. Pinks. Lavenders. And blues.

Millie refused to ride in the wagon without Brad, even for the short distance to the church, so everyone had decided to forget all the usual traditions, and she and Brad were riding to the church together. After the reception, they'd ride to their new home in the wagon, as well.

It would be a good start for them, Millie thought as she gave her face a final glance in the mirror and then headed down the stairs to her own true love.

* * * * *

BLUEGRASS CHRISTMAS

Allie Pleiter

For Christina
For who she was, who she is
and who she will be

Better is one day in your courts
than a thousand elsewhere;
I would rather be a doorkeeper
in the house of my God
than dwell in the tents of the wicked.
—*Psalms* 84:10

Chapter One

While "Mac" MacCarthy hadn't counted on peace and quiet when he returned to his office, he hadn't anticipated an opera-singing cockatoo, either.

December might not go as well as he planned.

Assuming the only logical explanation, Mac pushed his way through the connecting interior doors of the bakery adjacent to his engineering office. "All right, Dinah, what did you do to him?"

Dinah Rollings, owner of the Taste and See Bakery, looked up from her cash register. "To whom?"

Mac cocked his head toward the racket behind him. "I've got Luciano Pavarotti in feathers perched on my credenza. Very funny. Now tell me what you did to Curly so I can hush him up before cats start prowling the alley."

With both doors open, Dinah could evidently hear the bird. Her face was half surprised, half amused. "Not bad. That's from *The Marriage of Figaro,* I think. Didn't peg you for an opera fan."

Mac looked quizzically at his smirking neighbor. "You didn't do this?"

She raised an eyebrow. "No."

"Gil?" Mac named his best friend who, while no fan of opera, had been known to love a good joke.

"Haven't seen him."

"Cameron?" Dinah's new husband didn't seem the type, but as a former New York City native, Cameron might have opera in his background. And pranks.

Dinah shot him an incredulous look. "Not a chance. Look, Mac, I don't know who might have…"

At that moment, Pavarotti—the *real* one—belted out the aria in question from the stairway between their businesses' doors. And Curly, Mac's yellow-crested-cockatoo-recently-turned-tenor, joined in.

The second-floor apartment had been empty since Cameron and Dinah got married. Evidently, it wasn't unoccupied anymore. Opera music flooded the hallway when Mac opened the door that led upstairs.

Dinah came to the door. "Okay, maybe I do know who could be…"

Curly chose that moment to chase his avian muse, leaving his perch in Mac's office to bolt up the stairway in a squawking white streak of feathers and falsetto.

Mac took the stairs three at a time, ruing the fact that repairmen at his house necessitated that Curly spend this week at the office with him. Curly almost never bolted, but when he did, he went full out. Nothing good could come from this. Mac was a few steps from the top when he heard the shriek.

Taking the last risers in two strides, Mac looked in the apartment door to find a blond woman cowering behind a music stand, holding what looked like a conductor's baton as if it were a broadsword. The operatic waltz blared from a set of speakers on either side of the room, and Curly stood ducking and bobbing in time with the music from atop a bookcase to Mac's right.

"What is that thing?" she said over the loud music. Actually, shouted might have been more accurate. Shouted with great annoyance. Curly wasn't a small bird, and he looked like an invading white tornado when he flew anywhere. Mac could only imagine how frightening, at first sight, it was.

"That's Curly," Mac introduced, feeling ridiculous as he yelled above the orchestration. "He won't hurt you. He seems to get a kick out of your music."

Her eyes were wide. "It's not mutual. Get him out of here." She seemed to realize how harsh she sounded, for a split second later she nervously inched over to the stereo and turned down the volume before adding "Please."

"Aww," Curly moaned as the music quieted down. That was pretty tame considering all the smart-aleck replies Mac had taught the bird over the years.

Dinah burst through the doorway behind Mac. "Mary! Are you okay?" She went over to her, while Mac called Curly down off the furniture. "I'm sure that's not the welcome you were expecting."

She had every right to be annoyed. Mac's own ma could get spooked by Curly on occasion, and she knew what to expect from the feathered comedian. Curly had the good sense to look sorry for his actions, putting his head down and trying to hide under Mac's arm. "I'm okay, I think," Mary said shakily. She was a pale thing, with ice-blue eyes and hair only a shade sunnier than Curly's snow-white coat. "No damage done, unless you count my nerves."

Dinah took her arm. "Mary…it's Thorpe, isn't it?

Mary Thorpe, this great ferocious beast is Curly. And this is Mac MacCarthy. Sorry you had to meet under such goofy circumstances."

"I'm really sorry about this. Curly's usually more civilized, and he's hardly ever in my office. And he's never gone bananas over…um…whatever you were playing…before. I didn't even know you were up here."

"It's okay," she allowed, but it didn't sound like she meant it.

"Curly," Dinah addressed the guilty bird, "you just scared the pants off Middleburg Community Church's new drama director."

Serves Mac right for skipping church to go to a special service with Gil and the guys from Homestretch Farm last Sunday. Gil ran a unique reform program on his horse ranch, and occasionally "the guys"—as the juvenile offenders were known around town—visited churches in their old neighborhoods. Still, Mary didn't look like the kind of person Mac thought would be leading drama at MCC. Actually, he didn't even know MCC was planning a dramatic performance. Since his decision to run for mayor against "lifetime incumbent" Howard Epson, hadn't Middleburg seen enough drama without having to make more? Not that anyone could be judged by how they weathered a cockatoo air strike, but this Mary seemed a little small and frail for the job. Mac had seen herds of mustangs more compliant than the MCC congregation. "Brave soul. Sorry you had Curly here for a welcoming committee."

At the mention of his name, Curly poked his head up and gave Mary a wolf whistle. Dinah laughed. Mac rolled his eyes and thought about getting a dog.

"Are you an opera buff?" Mary asked Curly, putting the baton thing down.

"Not until today," Mac replied. "I've never seen him do that before. He usually just bobs around when I play Bill Monroe."

Mary gave him a blank look.

"Bluegrass music. Curly's more used to that than…"

"Mozart?" she offered. She shrugged. "I give him points for good taste."

"And bad manners," Mac added as he nodded at the bird. "Say goodbye, you rascal."

"Bye bye," Curly squawked, winking one large black eye.

"I'm really sorry again. Welcome to Middleburg. I'll keep Curly under tight surveillance for the rest of the week until the repairmen are gone at my house." Mac shifted Curly to his left hand and extended his right.

She shook it. Her fingers were small but very strong. "I'll turn down the volume so he isn't tempted again."

Mac glared at Curly. "Tonight we bring your other cage over here. No more free flying around the office for you, bud—repairmen at home don't buy you a license to make trouble here for the neighbors."

"Happy Birthday, by the way," Dinah announced as they made their way downstairs. "Park your bird and come on over for some mint chocolate chip biscotti. You need them."

No one ever really *needed* anything from Taste and See, but Dinah was very good at making people think they did. The woman's trademark enthusiasm had only doubled since she had married Cameron Rollings, who used to live in the apartment Mary now occupied.

"My birthday's not for another twenty-nine days, Dinah."

"It's December first, so it's the first day of your birthday month. Close enough."

Mac furrowed his eyebrows. "You're not going to say that every day from now until the thirtieth, are you?"

"Whassamatta?" Dinah teased, reviving her native New Jersey accent. "The passing decade getting to you?"

Sure it was, but that's not the kind of question he was going to get into with armchair therapist-baker Dinah Rollings.

"No," he said, applying a smirk. "Turning thirty is not fatal. Not yet."

Mac had barely settled at his desk when he saw his mother press her face against the glass window of his front office. She yanked open the door and stood in the entryway, one hand on each hip, a look of utter disgust on her face.

"I can't take much more of this nonsense," she said as Mac's father filed in behind her. "Land sakes. If one more person looks at me sideways just because you up and ran for mayor…"

Mac stood up. His mama was in the room, after all. He had manners, even if his bird didn't. "I sort of thought all the ruckus would die down when the holidays got here."

Pa walked over to sit in the guest chair of Mac's office. "If you ask me, it's just gotten worse." He shook his head in a combination of disbelief and amusement. "Y'all know what you got into?"

"Yep."

He did. God had hounded him for months. He had very good, very personal reasons for taking this unconventional step. He was no stranger to wild ideas like this, anyway. As a matter of fact, Mac preferred to shun the norm whenever possible.

Which often drove his mama nuts.

Ma waved her hands in the air. "As if this campaign weren't enough. Now there's this Christmas pageant. I thought they were just off their rockers thinking that hiring some Christmas drama director would help mend fences. You know Howard's already announced that he's gonna be in the play, don't you? You'll have to as well, to keep Howard from getting the upper hand." She blew out a breath and shook her head. "This won't be a distraction, it'll be a disaster."

As far as Mac was concerned, it already was.

Mary Thorpe stood in the empty sanctuary of Middleburg Community Church and whispered a prayer of praise. *I'm here. Oh, Lord, it's amazing, what You've done. I'm here.* The place was just what she'd envisioned; a steepled white church with a blue door on a rolling hillside with an old organ and wooden pews that had seen decades of worship. It even had a preschool attached—something she loved. This afternoon, she'd heard a tiny-voiced rendition of "Jesus Loves Me" that made her heart bubble up in happy relief. This is it. A real Christmas.

She inhaled. The place was infused with a wholesome, old-fashioned atmosphere. She ran her hand across a chipped, aged music stand and thought of the soprano soloist catfight she'd witnessed at her previous part-time job as the second chair violinist at a Chicago opera company. Not to mention the near nuclear-level war between coworkers at her other temporary job at an advertising agency, and thought "no more." She picked up a battered hymnal from a nearby pew. From now it'll all be "Peace in the Valley." It's perfect.

"Are you ready?" Pastor Dave Anderson's voice broke her reverie as he came up the aisle beside Mary. "Most folks were reluctant to do this drama at first, but Sandy Burnside, Howard and the other church elders convinced them." Anderson folded his arms across his chest and inclined his head toward Mary. "Still, y'all ought to be warned—they're an opinionated bunch, my feisty flock."

Mary tossed her blond ponytail over her shoulder and put her hands on her hips. "You haven't seen the Mid-American Orchestra String Section. *Opinionated* doesn't even begin to cover it. I'm ready to handle this."

"You know," the pastor amended, handing her a dozen copies of the nativity script they'd agreed upon, "I think maybe you are." He winked and crossed the sanctuary to his office.

Mary sat down on the pew and smoothed her hand over the stack of scripts. Middleburg was everything she'd prayed for. Her new address—Ballad Road—charmed her, dotted with shops and diners. And all the streets had musical names! Walking here, she had passed a quaint park with a sign that read "Tree Lighting, Wednesday, 7:00 p.m., Bake Sale to follow." Tree lighting. Bake sales.

God, in His wisdom, had led her to the middle of nowhere. The absolutely perfect place to disappear.

Chapter Two

This Sunday was just like his last Sunday at MCC; half the congregation avoided him in the church parlor after Sunday service. Dodging a sour look from Matt Lockwood, Mac focused his attention on Mary Thorpe. "Dinah told me you took cream and sugar," he explained, handing her a cup of coffee.

"She's nice. My apartment smells fabulous every morning, but I may put on ten pounds before New Year's." Mary smiled and waved to another member of the congregation. "They are an interesting bunch. Hey, I hear you're one of the reasons I'm here. Well, you and Howard Epson. The campaign and all. I thought I'd seen seriously dramatic local politics back in Chicago...."

Mac shrugged. "I'm not asking him to stop being mayor. I'm just asking to be a choice. We haven't had a choice for mayor since I was in high school. I think I'd do a great job, but if Howard wins, I'll actually be okay with it."

Mary took a sip of coffee and seemed to consider him.

Okay, it was sort of a cheesy speech, but that's really how he felt. He didn't want to start talking like a politician just because he ran for mayor, but lately stuff like that just jumped out of his mouth. "No really," he went on, not liking how she narrowed her eyes, "if people still want Howard, then that's what Middleburg should get. But they should *think* about whether they still want Howard."

"Speaking of what the people want, you do know you're both supposed to be in the production? Pastor Anderson told you, didn't he?"

"Oh, I've heard. I think I can manage something along the lines of third shepherd from the left."

She looked a bit tense. "Um, it's more involved than that. You've got a starring role. You're Joseph."

While Mac didn't like the idea of playing such a large role, he was sure Howard would be even less pleased. "And what about my worthy opponent?"

"Oh, we found the perfect part for him." She offered a weak smile. "He's God."

Mac stood in the barn at Homestretch Farm, having just finished a hearty Sunday dinner with Gil and his wife, Emily. After the meal, Gil had invited Mac to join him as he took care of a few things around the farm. That usually meant Gil had something on his mind, and Mac wasn't that surprised when Gil cleared his throat and sat down on a hay bale. "Emily said you got in another row with Howard at the diner."

Mac bristled. "You'd think I'd decided to do something life-threatening the way he and other folks talk. Everybody's always groaning about Howard, so why am I the first person willing to do something about it?" Mac had amazed even himself by how defensive he'd become on the subject. Running for Middleburg mayor did not qualify as a suicide mission. Still, when he announced his candidacy a few weeks back, people looked at him as if he'd just thrown himself on the end of a spear. They still did.

Gil fiddled with the large ring of keys he always carried. He had a habit of clanking them against his wedding ring. "You've showed me ads for four new cars in the last three months. New cars start catching your eye when you get antsy."

Mac rolled his eyes. "You've been reading Emily's magazines with all those quizzes or something. Wanting one new car does not constitute a midlife crisis. Pre-midlife crisis, rather," Mac corrected, as his grandfather was now in his late nineties and still remarkably sharp. He leaned back against a hay bale. "What are you getting at?"

"You like to stir up trouble, Mac. Always did. And a man with a weird bird and a fast sports car could just be scouting the next diversion." Gil looked serious.

"Meaning?" Mac knew lots of people who changed cars every two years.

"Are you running for mayor because it's what you want, or just because it'll get under everyone's skin?"

Mac was fully aware of his tendency toward shock value. He certainly could have thought he'd heard the Lord tell him to run for mayor when it might just be his appetite for ruffling feathers.

The truth was, actually, that Mac had been feeling restless. "Okay," he admitted to Gil, "I'm…how'd you put it? Antsy. But running for mayor isn't about that. I sat on this a long time. God's been after me for months, and yeah, I wasn't so sure it wasn't just me looking for a new thrill at first." It was something larger than that, something harder to explain. As Mac stared down the barrel of his thirtieth birthday, it felt as if life was sucking him into the expected routine. As if everyone else had figured out who he was supposed to be except him. He had no desire to "settle down" at the moment, but lots of folks—Ma chief among them—viewed him as simply staving off the inevitable. Predictability and inevitability chafed at Mac like he'd seen one of Gil's unbroken horses react to a bit in their mouths. If staying "unsettled" got under everyone's skin, they'd just have to get used to it.

"Only you," Gil said, "would think of running for mayor as 'a thrill.' Couldn't you just buy a horse or find a girl or something?"

Mac groaned.

"Relax, MacCarthy, I'm just pressing your buttons. I'm not out to trash your freewheeling, nonconformist lifestyle. Not that your mama hasn't asked me—repeatedly—to yak at you about the virtues of marriage. I just mostly want to know you're in the right place about this."

"That's just it. I'm not in the right place. I'm supposed to be someplace else."

Gil raised an eyebrow. Mac had been in Middleburg his whole life.

"Not *geographically*. Ever heard of a metaphor? I'm restless on the inside. Things don't feel comfortable any more. Or too comfortable, I don't know. I don't want to fade into the landscape here. Fall into some predictable rut. I really want this. I think I'm the guy, Gil. You know I've got a lot of ideas, and I think it's high time

Middleburg even remembered they *had* a choice when it comes to a mayor."

"Sounds like a campaign slogan to me."

Mac was growing irritated by the fact that every time he voiced a well-phrased or complex idea, someone said "sounds like a campaign issue" or "that could be your campaign slogan." Middleburg's mayoral race wasn't large enough to even warrant a slogan. He didn't want to be the kind of guy whose civic agenda could fit on a bumper sticker.

"There are lots of ways to stand out in the world that doesn't cause so much trouble." Gil folded his arms across his chest. "You've hashed this out? Seriously?"

By "hashing something out," Gil meant praying over it. Seriously. Gil Sorrent took his job and his faith very seriously. It's what had made him able to withstand the tremendous pressures and setbacks of the criminal re-habilitation farm he ran. It's what made him the kind of man who didn't mince words and never let down his friends. "Yes," Mac replied, and he had. He'd felt like he'd wrestled forever with this decision to run. His abil-ity to shake things up had led him down a few wrong turns over the years, and this seemed like a chance to finally channel that "talent" into something useful. To make his mark on the world before he slid into the bland predictability of…gasp…middle age. Shaking up was a far better choice than settling down, and this was a per-fect opportunity to shake up for the good of Middleburg.

Gil took his answer at face value. Their friendship had lasted long enough to put sugarcoating or lying out of the question. "And you're sure?"

"Yes, I'm sure."

Gil sat back in the hay. "Well, you've actually got

the personality to pull it off. Mostly. Emily'll burst out laughing the first time she has to say 'Your Honor'— I'm glad I don't have to." Emily and Gil had been on the city council before they'd married, and Gil had been the one to step down because spouses couldn't both re- main in office.

"Maybe my first official duty will be to change that silly protocol." Mac gave his friend a nudge. "It might be worth it just to hear you say 'Your Honor' to me. Who knew I'd have to run for office to get any respect from you?"

Gil stretched a foot out in front of him. "I haven't said I'd vote for you yet. Howard's a bit hard to take sometimes, but he does a halfway decent job."

"You complain about Howard all the time. We spent half your time on the council fighting Howard."

"That's just it. When you're mayor, who will I have to complain to?"

"Maybe you won't have to complain at all. Have you considered that possibility?"

Gil grinned. "Not in the slightest."

Mary waved back at yet another person as she made her way up Ballad Road toward her apartment, half spooked and half amazed by how quickly she'd come to feel at home. So many people believed in God here. And not just the Sunday kind of belief. These were day- in, day-out believers. It was the perfect place for her to grow her shaky new faith.

Almost from the time she had committed her life to Christ, Chicago had begun to vex her. Her earlier jobs—however enviable—felt hollow and unsatisfying. Her own parents had trouble understanding how anyone could leave an orchestral position *and* freelance ad agency work to lead a Christmas drama, but it was just too hard to be a new Christian in her other world. That verse about "rather be a gatekeeper in the house of my God" kept running through her head. A fresh, humble start felt so much easier.

She stopped at the window of an adorable shop called West of Paris. A charming blue glass vase caught her eye. A housewarming gift for myself, she thought, picturing it with a few sprigs of holly on her tiny dining room table. She couldn't pull off a decorated tree this Christmas, even if her mom and dad came as planned, but the vase seemed just enough of a luxury to suit her mood. As she entered, a wave of wonderful scents and music-box Christmas carols washed over her.

"Merry Christmas," greeted the woman behind the counter. "I'm Emily Sorrent, we met at church. You're Mary, right?"

Mary was still adjusting to strangers calling her by name. "That's me."

"Must be hard to be in such a new place for the holidays. Away from home and family and all. Are you settling in okay?"

Mary imagined such a new start might be a challenge around Christmas—for other people. For her, it was the best present of all. "Just fine. It's so peaceful here."

Emily smiled. "Peaceful? Are you sure you're in Middleburg? I haven't seen our little town so worked up in years. No, Ma'am, 'peaceful' is not a word I'd use to describe Middleburg these days."

"That's okay. People used to think the big city orchestra where I worked was glamorous, but I wouldn't ever describe it that way, either."

Emily got a funny look on her face and turned away for a moment under the guise of arranging some holiday ornaments. Mary couldn't figure out what she'd said wrong. Maybe being new in town wasn't all fresh starts and clean slates. "I saw that blue vase in the window," she offered, changing the subject. "I think it would be perfect for my dining-room table."

"It's made by an artisan in Berea," Emily described, brightening. "That color is his trademark. Look, here's an ornament he made in the same style." She held out a brilliant blue sphere with a sparkling gold center. "For your tree."

"Oh," Mary interjected, brushing her off. "I don't think I'll get a tree up this year."

Emily looked surprised. "No Christmas tree? You can't be serious?"

Mary took in the store, and realized there must be six fully decorated trees in Emily's shop alone. The woman took her holiday decorating very seriously. Even for a retailer.

"There's just me. I'd never be able to lug a tree up all the stairs to my apartment, and I own about three ornaments, besides. Christmas was my busy season in past years, and I never really had time to do all the trimmings. I'll just take the vase, thanks."

Emily crossed her arms over her chest. "No, you won't."

"What?"

"I don't know where you came from, but if you've never had a real Christmas, Mary Thorpe, it's high time you got one. And I am going to start you off. You can buy the vase, but it just so happens I'm running a special today. Every vase purchase comes with a free Christmas ornament. And I happen to know a whole bunch of big burly guys who will gladly lug your tree anywhere you want it. MCC's new drama director will not be too busy to have her own Christmas if I have anything to say about it. And I'm on the church board and the town council, so you can bet I have something to say about it."

Mary could only smile. "Okay, I'll think about it." She'd just effectively been commanded to have a happy holiday, and she couldn't be more pleased. She took the ornament and spun it in the sunlight, enjoying the blue and gold beams it cast around the room. "Dinah warned me about you."

Emily winked. "Oh, honey, you ain't seen nothing yet."

Chapter Three

Curly was singing.

This was a bit hard to take, especially because the bird insisted on singing the same piece of music he'd learned from Mary Thorpe's stereo earlier. Even an extra dose of sunflower seeds had failed to quiet the cockatoo. Mac looked up from the drafting table a third time, then let his forehead fall into his hand. "Enough, bird. You were funny once—and not really funny at that—but you're singing on my last nerve."

"Yep!" Curly squawked, and Mac regretted—for the umpteenth time today—teaching the bird to agree with everything he said.

There was only one thing for it. Maybe the sheer repetition of the aria had stomped out his neurons, but Mac was relatively certain the only way to stop this bird from singing the same thing over and over was to give him something new to sing. And while the Kentucky Fight Song might have been a masculine choice, Mac also knew that would wear even worse than the opera.

He felt like a complete idiot walking up the stairs to Mary Thorpe's apartment with Curly doing the bird equivalent of humming—a sort of half whistling noise accompanied by a comical head bob—on his shoulder. He didn't, however, have Mary's phone number, and he was sure in another hour he'd be incapable of putting a sentence together. "Behave yourself for both our sakes," he told Curly as he knocked on the door.

She opened the door cautiously, trying not to broadcast her alarm at seeing Curly. "Hi there," she said too kindly, forcing her smile.

"Do you think," Mac spoke, finding the words more idiotic by the second, "we could teach Curly something else? I'm living with a broken record here and it's driving me nuts." On a whim he looked at the bird and stated, "You need a bigger repertoire, don't you, boy?"

"Yep!" Curly squawked, nodding.

"No offense to your opera," Mac confessed, "but I don't think I could take even my favorite song nonstop like he's been doing."

She opened the door a bit more. He could see she'd gotten much farther in her unpacking, and the small apartment was starting to look like a home. "Haven't you taught…" she inclined her head toward the feathered occupant of Mac's right shoulder.

"Curly."

"Curly any other songs?"

Curly bobbed a bit at the mention of his name. "No, actually. I didn't know he could sing until you moved in. Seems bluegrass doesn't interest him, but whatever it was…"

"Mozart," she reminded, a hint of a smile finally making its way across her features.

"…catches his fancy. So," Mac continued, daring to bring Curly off his shoulder to sit on his forearm, "you got any more Mozart for Curly to learn? A CD of something quiet and background-ish to get me through these last two days?"

Mary opened the door wide, raising one eyebrow. "Mozart didn't write elevator music."

"There's got to be something. As long as it's not the 1812 Overture, it'll be an improvement."

"I'm not in the habit of giving singing lessons. Not even to humans."

Curly started in on the aria again.

"I'll pay you. Another ten minutes of this and you can name your price."

Mary looked at the bird. "Hush up, Curly." She had a teacher's voice—gentle, but you knew she meant business.

Wonder of wonders, Curly hushed. *Now* Curly gets cooperative? Where was all that avian obedience ten minutes ago? "Whoa," Mac reflected, turning Curly so he could look him in one traitorous black eye. "Teach me *that* first."

Mary shrugged, as if she didn't have an answer to that, and motioned Mac and Curly into her apartment. Mac was right—she had settled in. The place looked more lived-in than the months Cameron Rollings had laughingly called it his "bachelor pad." She went to her bookcases, traveling through her CD collection with dainty flicks of her finger. "I'm thinking he needs voices, so none of the chamber music will do—that's all mostly instrumental. Oh," she noted and plucked a CD from the shelf, "this might work."

She inserted the disc into her player and a soft, high, female voice lilted out of the speakers. Curly cocked his head to one side. Mary looked at Curly and sang along, conducting with her forefinger. Curly began inspecting Mac's watch.

"I'm thinking that's a 'no.'"

Mary pulled another selection and popped it into her sound system.

The same tenor voice as Curly's previous obsession came over the speakers, but this time Pavarotti was singing Italian songs. The kind guys in striped shirts sang as they pushed boats through Venice. Not very hip, but still better than opera. Mary walked up to Curly and began singing along, conducting with her fingers again. This time Curly took notice, swooping his head around to match the movement of her hand. She caught Mac's eye, and they both nodded. "I suppose technically I have you to thank for my job, since part of my job description is to take everyone's mind off the mayoral conflict. This lesson will be on the house." She sang a few more bars as the chorus came around again, and Curly began making noises. "Future lessons from the tonic for Middleburg's mayoral malaise might cost you."

"Very catchy, but I don't think it's the civic disaster they're making it out to be."

"For what it's worth," Mary said over the swelling music, "neither do I."

"There will be no more lessons. The floor guys will be done with my house by Friday. After that, Mr. Music here stays home." Pavarotti launched into another song, a Dean Martin number Mac recognized from his ma's record collection. "Who knew my bird has such questionable taste in music?"

"Curly has very good taste, actually."

When she looked at him, he realized he'd just insulted her CD collection. Just hitting them out of the ballpark here, MacCarthy, aren't we? She didn't say so, but it glared out of her eyes just the same; better taste than you, evidently.

"Could I make a copy of that CD?" he said sheepishly.

"Music is copyrighted material, Mr. MacCarthy. I'm sure you wouldn't take kindly to my Xeroxing your latest blueprints and passing them around, would you?"

"Okay," Mac conceded slowly, feeling like this conversation had started off badly and was slipping further downhill fast.

She softened her tone as she handed him the CD. "But you may borrow this one for the moment. If Curly needs further…inspiration… I'm sure you can find your way to a copy. An original copy, bought and paid for."

"Absolutely. You got it." Mac took the slim plastic box from her, and Curly put his head up to it, rubbing against the corner in a disturbingly lovesick gesture. "And, well, I'm sorry you got hired to fix whatever it is people think I broke."

"I'm not sorry," she commented, opening the door for them to go, "but if I get sorry, I'll make sure you're the first to know. I think it's sort of sweet, actually, how much people care about getting along here."

"If people cared about getting along here, you could have fooled me," Mac observed. "There's a town hall meeting tomorrow night—come see how much *getting along* we actually do."

"Pastor Anderson," Mary began.

"Dave," the older man corrected.

"Dave," she said, still not entirely comfortable with the concept of calling a member of the clergy by his first name. Up until this summer, she'd seen people like Dave Anderson as almost a different species. High, lofty souls who didn't bother with the likes of "sinners" like herself. Not that she thought of herself as a sinner. She was pretty proud of all her accomplishments then. Back before she'd realized "achievement" didn't always translate into "happiness."

It was, in fact, happiness she was speaking of—at least to Dave. "You know, Dave," she continued carefully, "I'm worried about how much people are expecting out of this Christmas drama."

He smiled. "You'll do fine. Actually, when you think about it, you can't help but do fine. You're our first drama coordinator, so folks don't have anyone to compare you to. You can't help but improve us. And they like you already—I can tell."

How to say this? "It's not the drama I'm worried about. It's the...well, the result you're looking for. Don't you think town unity's kind of a high expectation for a little church drama?"

Pastor Dave sat back in his chair. "That's because you're expecting it to be a little church drama. It will be church, it will be drama, but I guarantee it won't be little. Complications might be just what the doctor ordered in this case." His eyebrows lowered in concern. "I want you to pour your creative energies into making this as all-consuming as possible."

"Aren't there more direct ways to resolve the town's conflict?"

"I suppose there would be—if the town was willing to admit they *had* a conflict. Most of them want a big Christmas extravaganza to make them feel good. Just you and I and a few other wise folk realize they need something to agree on to take their minds off the many disagreements."

"What about Mac and Howard?"

The pastor chuckled. "I think Mac knows he stirred up a hornet's nest. He enjoys it—always has been one to whip things up a bit. I think Howard feels the conflict, but he's likely to read it all wrong. He feels attacked because I think he'd much rather change on his own terms, not on those of someone like Mac."

"But Howard was bound to retire someday." Mary leaned one elbow on the corner of Dave's desk. She was still sorting out the complexities of "simple little Middleburg."

"I'm not so sure Howard's caught on to that truth yet. He's been mayor for so long he may not remember how to be anything else. We've got sixth-graders who've never known Howard as anything but mayor. You have to respect that."

"All things considered, I'm not so sure a Christmas pageant is the way to cope. We're sticking a tiny bandage on a great big wound here."

"Miss Thorpe, you ever been a parent?" He got up from his chair and walked over to his office windows overlooking the preschool. "Ever given a toddler a bandage?"

"I'm sure I have at some point." Mary didn't really see where he was heading.

"They *believe* it makes things better. A child may get stitches for a nasty gash, but they won't calm down until somebody puts on a bandage. It's the stitches that do the real healing, but they still need the bandage. You and I know it's an illusion, but that doesn't mean it doesn't work." He grinned and pointed at her. "Some of my best work is done with Band-Aids."

Mary blinked. "I'm a diversionary tactic?"

He walked toward her. "Would it make it easier if I said you were a coping mechanism?"

This had started out as a simple job. A calmer life serving an undiluted purpose, a chance for Mary to get away from the agenda-laden world of professional music and advertising. Suddenly she had more agendas than a diplomat and a goal so complex and obscure she could no longer say what it truly was. "I've got a headache just trying to make sense of this." She looked up at him. "Can I have a Band-Aid?" It was supposed to be a joke, but Mary couldn't quite muster the confidence to pull it off.

"Take two rehearsals and call me in the morning," Pastor Dave joked.

Mary sat in her living room that afternoon, trying to make sense of it all. How many people thought of the drama as just a nice holiday event? How many of them were aware of its secondary goal of unifying the community? How to balance the two? *Lord, I prayed for hours over this job. I asked You to take me someplace where I could figure out all this faith stuff. Someplace easier than Chicago. This isn't looking easier.*

Mary smiled as the faint strains of Pavarotti's tenor voice singing "Ave Maria" reached her ears. She wondered if Mac found it an improvement over the Mozart aria. It was hard to think of that bird crooning a ballad. Too bad it wasn't summertime; she'd have been able to hear Curly through the open window.

Then again, maybe it was better all the windows were shut. She wasn't entirely sure Curly the cockatoo was up to the high note at the end of the song.

Laughing at the thought of the bird straining to hit the note, his creamy neck extended and his feathers fluttering, Mary reached for the mail that had been forwarded from her old Chicago apartment. She sorted through the envelopes until she spotted the familiar gray stationery of Maxwell Advertising. She'd forgotten, until now, that she had one more bonus coming. She opened the envelope and slid out a substantial check. How ironic that her "swan song" had been her most lucrative project ever. God had given her enough resources to take whatever job she wanted, wherever she wanted. And He had brought her here. Maybe, for now, she could trust that, despite the growing complexities.

Mac shut the door to his office with a fierce *thunk* and walked briskly toward Deacon's Grill. A piece of pie couldn't really do anything about the storm of aggravation he carried around, but it couldn't hurt, either. At least a warm cup of coffee might soothe his annoyance. "Peace on earth, goodwill toward men?" Today felt more like "profits on earth, bad will toward any consumer." No wonder Ma had asked him to handle the procurement of one of those idiotic Bippo Bears for his nephew, Robby. Finding the fuzzy blue singing bear proved to be more like warfare than Christmas shopping. Not counting the two trips to two separate malls yesterday, Mac had just spent three hours on the phone and Internet in search of a Bippo Bear. He sat down on his counter stool at the Grill with such force that the thing rocked under his weight.

Gina, no stranger to diner psychology, read his body language and immediately swapped out the ordinary sized stoneware mug at the island for a much larger one she produced from under the counter. Gina was smart. "Regulars" who obviously had a bad day were quickly given what she called a "comfort cup." That was Gina's entirely-too-female term for "the really big mug of coffee." He accepted it gladly, needing the hot beverage too much to care that it announced his disgruntled mood to the rest of the diner. He was pretty sure his entrance had already done that, anyway.

"And a Merry Christmas to you, too, sugar," Gina said as she slid the sugar container in front of Mac withholding the cream pitcher. Apart from baking the best pies around, Gina also had a great memory for customer preferences. "Rough going on the campaign trail?"

Campaign? Who had time for a campaign when Christmas shopping was sucking half his day into the trash can?

Gina's reference to the mayoral campaign halted Howard Epson in his conversation. Mac hadn't even noticed Howard as he came in, he was so annoyed. Epson and his wife were sitting in their favorite corner booth with Mary Thorpe of all people, probably advising her on the mayor's expected role in all holiday ceremonies. Divine drama aside, he was sure Howard took pains to stay a highly visible mayor during the MCC's Christmas season.

Mac swallowed a gulp of coffee, telling himself to back down off his soapbox. Howard could get to him so easily these days. They'd chalked up a lot of reasons to dislike each other over the years, some of which everyone knew—Mac had a long, checkered history of behavior Howard disapproved of—and some that were more private.

Years ago, when Mac was a senior in high school, he'd

pulled a prank of sorts that ended up with Howard in the crosshairs. Actually, to call it a prank was making it too deliberate—it was more of an impulsive reaction. A stupid, angry gesture that ended up damaging church property and Howard's car one night. The whole town had seen the wreckage, but no one had ever discovered Mac was behind it. When God and the passing years finally granted Mac some maturity, he'd still never found it in himself to fess up to the deed. Howard would surely blow it way out of proportion, and Mac had convinced himself it was one of those secrets best left buried. Not that it hadn't nagged at him over time, but lots of stuff about Howard bothered Mac—civic and personal. It was one of the reasons he felt God had asked him to run for mayor; to prove he was better than the angry kid he once was.

Mac caught sight of one of Howard's campaign brochures on the place setting next to Mary. She was surely getting a suggestion or two about the proper way to vote. At Gina's mention of the campaign, Howard inclined his balding head slightly toward Mac and stopped his words midsentence. Even the French fry on the way to his mouth had been stilled halfway. Mary Thorpe caught Mac's glance for a split second before looking down into her pie.

"No," Mac answered Gina's earlier question clearly enough for Howard to hear. "The campaign's going *fine.*" He tried not to emphasize the word too much. "As a matter of fact, it's a pathetic stuffed animal that has me riled up. I've just wasted half the morning trying to find something called a Bippo Bear for my nephew. Evidently even the secret service couldn't get their hands on one of these if they wanted to—and don't you know, it's the one and only thing Robby wants for Christmas."

"A what?" Gina asked, flipping open her order pad and pulling a pen out of from behind her ear.

"A Bippo Bear. It's blue and sings to you and can't be found for love or money. Already. And it's still early December. What is it with these toy people? Don't they realize they have to make enough of these things to go around? Do they enjoy disappointing kids and making parents crazy?"

Drew Downing looked up from his sandwich a few seats to Mac's left. "Bippo Bear? I saw something on the news last night about those." Drew used to host a church renovation television show until an episode had brought him to Middleburg and introduced him to the love of his life, hardware store owner Janet Bishop. The man knew a thing or two about the power of advertising. "I saw one go for a hundred dollars yesterday on an Internet auction site. This year's must-have toy, it seems."

"Why does there have to be a 'must-have' toy, anyway?" Mac complained in a cranky voice. "My nephew doesn't even like stuffed animals. I'll spend two weeks tracking down one of those things and he'll play with it for two hours before he tires of it."

"Oh, yeah," remembered Gina, "it's that commercial that's on eleven hundred times a day. How could I forget?" She began to hum a few bars of the annoying little Bippo Bear song.

The one Mac had been forced to listen to for forty minutes while on hold with the toy company in a misguided attempt to locate a Canadian retailer. While he thought going foreign to be a smart alternative, the cheerful customer service representative at the Bakley Toy Factory informed him that he was her sixtieth such call of the day.

"Mary," came Howard's voice over his angry thoughts, "are you all right? Your pie okay? You look like you swallowed your fork all of a sudden."

Mac glanced over and Gina raised her head from her order pad. Middleburg's newest resident did indeed appear a bit ill, but Mac doubted it was anything Gina fed her. Howard had probably just said something insensitive, as he was known to do when he became overly focused on impressing someone new.

"Oh, no," Mary protested loudly. "It's wonderful pie." Mac recognized the forced cheerfulness she'd used when telling him it was "okay" that a maniac bird attacked her in her living room.

"Hi, Mary." Mac waved and she waved back, but it was a weak, wobbly gesture. "Hello, Howard," Mac said more formally.

Howard had become extremely formal with Mac since he'd announced his candidacy. "Good afternoon, MacCarthy." Howard had begun calling him Mr. Mac-Carthy or just MacCarthy whenever they met now. He didn't even turn around, just twisted his head half a turn in Mac's direction and puffed up as though they were on podiums debating issues instead of just eating in the same diner.

"Apple as usual, Mac?" Gina interjected. Her tone of voice seemed to imply that all conflicts could easily be solved with the right slice of pie. "I'll even heat it up for you, how's that?"

"Perfect." He settled more peaceably onto his stool and inhaled the rich aroma rising out of his wonderfully enormous coffee mug. "I refuse to let a stuffed blue bear steal my holiday."

"Good plan," Drew Downing offered. "But I know

what you mean. My sister e-mailed me yesterday, and she wasn't too subtle about asking me what strings I could pull to get my hands on one of those for her daughter. The old 'Can't you do this 'cause you're famous?' ploy."

Mac smiled. While Drew still made occasional appearances for his former *Missionnovation* television show, Mac had taken to ribbing him about his "has been" status. And really, Downing had just walked head-on into another teasing with that remark. "You're just not famous enough anymore, sport," he taunted, digging into the pie Gina had just placed in front of him.

Drew caught onto the game and cracked a wide grin. "Hey, I still rate. I still have fans. My Web site got six hits last week."

"Wow. Maybe I should ask you to endorse my candidacy." Mac thought he'd said it quietly enough to escape Howard's hearing, but the man seemed to have radar for that sort of thing, and Mac saw his head incline slightly in his direction again.

Drew caught the exchange. "I've stayed a star as long as I have because I know which battles *not* to get into."

"You're a Middleburg resident now, you'll have to vote soon enough."

"A gratefully private matter, Mr. MacCarthy." Drew poured more cream into his own coffee. "God bless democracy."

Mac leaned in on one elbow. "Why do I get the feeling if Howard wins, you'll tell him you voted for him, but if I win you'll say I had your vote?"

Howard wasn't even pretending not to listen now. He'd turned halfway around to face Mac and Drew, his attention openly on the conversation.

"Eat your pie, gentlemen," Gina cut in, brandishing the pie-cutter knife she was holding. She tilted the spatula in Howard's direction. "All of you."

Drew straightened in his chair. "Don't anger the pie lady," he declared as if he and Mac had been caught passing notes in class.

"Good policy," Mac whispered back loudly, glad to have enough humor to still make a joke. Honestly, his short fuse was way too short lately. He needed to remember to get out more. The combination of year-end workload and campaign tasks on top of his new commission as Bippo Bear procurement agent had gotten to him fast. *I'm going to need an easy nature and a mile-long fuse to be mayor,* he told himself. *That's a tall order for the likes of me. Are You listening, Lord?*

Chapter Four

It couldn't be. I mean, yes, it was Kentucky, and it wasn't like they didn't have snakes in Illinois, but they didn't take up residence under the kitchen sink. That was the beauty of living five stories up in a city. The wildlife stayed *in the wild*. Mary stood very still, both hands vise-locked onto the broomstick she now pushed against the cabinet door. Nothing, no one could get her to stop holding that cabinet door shut and keeping that lethal creature inside. Mary heard something shuffle behind the door and swallowed a scream.

Think. You're a smart girl, think.

No coherent thought came to mind.

If she screamed, surely someone in the building would hear her. Did birds have good hearing? Would Curly be able to hear her even if Dinah or Mac couldn't? The scene of Curly getting Mac's attention, *"Lassie, what do you mean Timmy's stuck down the well?"*-style, flashed absurdly through her head. Town newcomer saved by vigilant cockatoo. It'd be out over the Internet in seconds, along with a photo of herself being loaded, pale and shaking, into a Woodford County ambulance. Sunflower seed reward for snake-killing bird.

Not helpful, Mary. Think. Think rationally.

I can't think rationally, there's a python under my sink.

You don't even know if it's venomous. There are perfectly harmless snakes, her rational side argued.

It will eat you in one gulp, her terrified side rebutted, very successfully.

"Mac!" she yelled, trying for some ridiculous reason to sound calm. When no reply came, she tried "Dinah!" After half a minute and another sinister sub-sink shuffle, Mary cried, "Curly!"

Nothing.

Well of course he can't hear you, it's winter and the windows are shut. A building as old as this must have thick walls. *Lord Jesus! I haven't even had a year as a Christian, I can't be ready for Heaven yet! Save me!*

The floor. She could use the floor. Forcing in a deep breath, Mary tried to mentally compare the floor plan of her apartment with Mac's office below. She'd only seen it once, but it was enough to be reasonably sure that his office was directly below where she was standing. If she just thumped, it would only sound like she was moving things. It had to sound deliberate. Somewhere, out of the dark trivia-hoarding recesses of her brain, Mary retrieved the Morse code for SOS. Three short beeps, followed by three long beeps, followed by three short ones again. While the concept of long beeps didn't directly translate into foot-stomping, Mary guessed she could come close enough. If that didn't work, she could still reach the toaster and begin throwing it on the ground until Mac was convinced the walls were caving in up here.

Tap-tap-tap. STOMP. STOMP. STOMP. Tap-tap-tap. Mary dug her heel into the floor to produce the loudest possible staccato taps. *Lord Jesus, please let Mac know Morse code and not let him think I'm an amateur flamenco dancer.* She repeated the sequence again.

Curly noticed first. Mac looked up from his papers, only barely noticing an unusual noise. Mary sure was doing a lot of banging around up there. Rhythmic, too. Exercise?

Tap-tap-tap. BANG-BANG-BANG. Tap-tap-tap. Curly came down off his perch in the window to stand on Mac's desk lamp. "Your new friend is a bit odd," Mac remarked, raising his eyes to the ceiling. "Even for city folk."

The succession of noises repeated again, louder. Folk dancing? Some jumpy new Chicago fitness fad? Morse code? Mac reached for his calculator, chuckling.

Until the bangs repeated.

Morse code? He knew Morse code. He knew the signal she was banging out, or knew it once. Mac stared at Curly, trying to pull the information out of the back recesses of his memory until...

Tap-tap-tap. BANG-BANG-BANG. Tap-tap-tap. SOS. That was Morse code for SOS.

No way. That was absurd.

The series of bangs came faster and louder now. Quite clearly three short taps followed by three more big bangs followed by three more short taps. SOS. Or something too close to it to ignore. But really, how many people knew Morse code, much less stomped it on their floors? Still, he'd never forgive himself if something really had been wrong and he'd dismissed it. Dashing up there would make him look like a complete idiot—if she was fine. "You think?" Mac said to Curly, pushing back his desk chair.

Curly was already flying toward the door. "Yep!"

He stood at the door, hands poised to knock, and listened for another set of stomps. He'd almost talked himself out of knocking, sure she would find his visit an example of overdone small-town meddling, when he heard the moan. It was not, by any stretch of the imagination, a calm sound. At that point, knocking was no longer needed. Mac flung Curly off his forearm and twisted Mary's door handle, pushing the door wide open and sprinting inside.

"Oh, Lord Jesus, save me from that thing! Who's there?"

Mac followed her voice into the kitchen to find Mary Thorpe impaling her cabinet with a broomstick. Throwing all her slight weight against that door as if an 800-pound gorilla were hiding under her sink. It was comic—in an alarming kind of way—until whatever it was behind there made a considerable racket. Then it wasn't so funny.

Mary shifted her weight, pressing harder against the broom handle, and squeaked "Mac! It's in there!"

"*What's* in there?" Mac said as calmly as he could while scanning her kitchen for heavy objects. He strode to her and took the broomstick, keeping pressure against the door.

She bolted away from him the minute he had a grip, backing into a corner on the other side of the kitchen, her chest heaving. "I don't know. I only heard it. I sure wasn't going to open the door and introduce myself."

Mac worked himself closer to the cabinet, hand-over-hand down the broom handle until he held the door shut with his boot. Nothing pushed back against him, but things were definitely moving around in there. A constant, steady rustle rather than an irregular scurrying. Mary Thorpe had a snake in her kitchen. Not exactly the warmest of Kentucky welcomes. "It sounds like you've got a snake in there," he confirmed, trying to keep his tone conversational, as if kitchen snake visits were commonplace. They weren't rare, but it was unusual to get one on the second floor in December.

"Ooo," she winced, hunching up her shoulders and squinting her eyes shut. "I knew it. Snakes. I hate snakes. I mean I really hate snakes."

Mac started searching for something forklike to trap the head. Somehow he didn't think Mary Thorpe would take kindly to having her carving fork used to skewer a snake. "It's probably a harmless milk snake. They like buildings."

"*Probably* harmless?" Unconvinced didn't do her tone of voice justice.

"There just aren't that many that can hurt you around here. Be thankful it's not a skunk in there." Mac looked at the cabinet again. Don't let it be a skunk in there. "Is your phone hooked up?"

"Yes."

"Is it cordless?"

"Uh-huh." Her shoulders softened the smallest amount.

He looked her straight in the eye, giving her his best *remain calm, things are under control* voice. "Okay, here's what we're going to do. Go get your phone, and we'll call Janet at the hardware store to bring over a snake catcher. She's thirty seconds away, so we'll have whatever it is out of your kitchen in ten minutes flat."

Mary nodded.

"So now you need to go get the phone."

That snapped her out of her shock. She came back with the phone and a roll of duct tape. When he raised his eyebrow at the second item, she explained "Maybe we can seal him in there until Jane gets here."

Mac allowed himself a small chuckle. "It's *Janet,* and I don't think the duct tape will be necessary." He gave her the phone number, and she put the handset in speaker mode while she dialed.

"Bishop Hardware."

"Hey there, Vern, it's Mac. Is Janet around?" he conversed in a friendly voice. Vern would have a field day with a situation like this, especially given his flair for the dramatic. He'd probably play it up, making Mary think a Komodo dragon was gnawing away the woodwork under her sink, hatching little ones who would feast on Mary in her sleep. No, this was definitely a situation that called for Janet's calm female touch. His call was right on the money, and Janet promised to be there within three minutes with the necessary equipment.

"Got a flashlight?" Mac asked, thinking Mary needed a bit of distraction while they waited.

"Um… I think so." Her voice was still a good octave higher than normal. "Why?" she inquired from the other room.

He thought that was obvious. "We need to see who we're dealing with here."

She shot back into the room, flashlight in hand. "Don't you open that door." Just then she noticed Curly perched on the back of her kitchen chair—she'd been oblivious to his presence until then. "Hi, Curly." She said it calmly, as if Curly's intruder status had been stripped—he was a friend now compared to the new invader in her home.

"Hello," Curly responded amiably.

"Mary," Mac began, "we can't get him out without opening the door. It could just be a tiny little mouse making all that noise." He didn't really think that, but it sounded better than "It will go more smoothly if I can see how many feet long the big nasty snake is before we kill it." Said villainous creature chose that moment to push a little against the cabinet door, making Mac gulp and Mary shriek.

"Don't you dare open that door."

"Okay, the door stays shut until Janet gets here. No peeking." After a tense moment, he added, "You know, you could just take Curly down to the bakery and both get a cracker or something while we take care of your little guest here." Mac doubted the vision of a snake twitching on the end of a stick would do much for her nerves, even if he was transporting the harmless creature downstairs to release him outside unharmed as Janet would insist he do.

"I'm staying," she countered, the bravado in her voice was a good, if unconvincing, attempt. "But *over here*." She kept the kitchen table between herself and the sink.

"You know Morse code?" Mac noted, hitting on a diversionary topic while the door thumped against his shin again. Okay, maybe it was a slightly large animal in there.

"Just the important words," she indicated, staring directly at the cabinet door. "You know, yes, no, help, SOS, pizza.'"

"Pizza?"

"Sergeant Sam's gave you four dollars off your pizza if you ordered in Morse code. College."

Mac laughed. She didn't look like the kind to inhale pizza—definitely more the Brie-and-salad type. "And they say our educational system is in crisis."

"Well, before today, I thought that was a piece of useless trivia."

"Hello?" came Janet's voice from the still-open front door of Mary's apartment. "Animal rescue here!"

Mac bought Mary a second cup of coffee as they sat at the little table in Dinah's bakery. "The snake wasn't *that* big."

Mary shot him a look. "*Any* snake is too big in my book. Any snake in my kitchen, that is. I'm not against them in general. God's creatures and all. I'm sure they serve a very important link in the food chain. Just as long as that food chain stays out of my apartment."

Mac hoisted his coffee and swallowed a laugh. "You were very brave. Even Janet was twitching a bit when we finally got that thing out of there—he was a feisty one. But totally harmless. Really. He posed more danger to Curly than to you or me."

She doubted that. All snakes had teeth, venomous or not. She wasn't in any hurry to add "snakebite" to her list of thrilling new experiences. "How is Curly, by the way?" she asked as she changed the subject to a different species. "Expanding his playlist?"

Mac made a face. This was obviously not an improvement in topics. "Not by a long shot." He ran a hand through his head full of unruly sandy-colored hair. "He likes whatever it is you gave him—I have a copy on

order, by the way, so you can have yours back soon—
and I suppose that means he may take up something
from it one of these days, but…"

"But…" she prompted as if she didn't know what
was coming.

His bottle-green eyes took on a teasing expression.
"Let's just say the Three Tenors haven't made it to a
quartet."

"Still drowning in *The Marriage of Figaro?*" Mary
laughed at the thought of that odd bird's fascination with
operatic tenors. "Maybe we can teach him a Christmas
carol and put him in the play."

"Only if you include one of Howard's horses, too.
He'll want equal time."

Mary put down her cup. "Have you always been a
thorn in Howard's side?"

Mac sat back in the chair. He wasn't an enormous
man, more of a strong, lean build, but he looked too big
for the bakery's delicate chairs. He legs refused to fit
under the small round table. He flexed his fingers, putting his answer together in his head. Mac's broad, tawny
hands looked as though they divided their time between
paperwork and oil changes. The kind of man who could
tinker with a spreadsheet just as easily as he could an
engine. Evidently she'd asked a delicate question.

"'Spose I have. We go back a bit, you could say. And
yeah, Howard and I clash on a regular basis. We see
things differently. But I'm not out to get him, if that's
what you're asking."

"Does he think you are? Out to get him, I mean?"

Mac kicked his legs out, and Mary felt like they extended into the center of the room. The man took up
space—literally and figuratively—and he was com-

fortable with it. "I quit trying to figure out what Howard's thinking a long time ago. Still, I reckon Howard would've gotten his dander up at *anyone* who took him on, even if it wasn't someone like me. That's one of the reasons I felt I ought to be the one to run. That kind of heat don't bother me much."

That kind of heat. Meaning all that attention. Mary had learned a while back that men who liked attention didn't much care if it was positive or negative attention. Her former boss, Thornton Maxwell, didn't care if the business columns praised him or bashed him, as long as they discussed him. What was that old saying? "All press is good press." Still, Mary wasn't sure it was right to paint all extroverts with the same sinister brush as Thornton. Just because a guy took the lead didn't mean he was ready to squash everyone in his path. And it needed saying that not one of Mary's artsy advertising colleagues or cerebral music composition classmates could have dispatched that snake so calmly. Mac looked like an alligator would have posed an amusing challenge, or maybe some antlered forest beast would have ended up mounted to the hood of his truck.

If he owned one. Mary had never seen him drive anything but the shiny orange sports car that pulled into the spot in front of MacCarthy Engineering every morning. She still couldn't quite see how that tall man folded into that zippy little car.

"So why'd you do it?" Mary prodded.

"Run?"

"Yeah. Why not just wait until he retired?"

"Howard? Retire? Doubt he would. Not that you shouldn't like your job, but Howard loves his a bit too much. I'm not even sure he consciously knows he projects the 'mayor for life' thing, but I don't think he can see himself *not* in charge. He doesn't know how to follow. The man's in charge of stuff he's not even in charge of." Mac finished off his coffee and pointed at her. "And you ought to keep that in mind. Your newcomer status may be the only thing keeping him from taking over the Christmas drama. And he still might. I saw him in the diner earlier—he's just warming up on you. I give it two weeks before you're knee-deep in Howard."

Mary raised an eyebrow. Mac wasn't looking humble himself at the moment, either. "'Knee-deep in Howard'?"

"Okay, that sounded a bit ridiculous. But you know what I mean."

She shot him a look.

"For what it's worth, I don't think Howard's all bad. His motives are good. He believes he's got the town's best interests at heart." Mac wiped his hands down his face, as if he still hadn't found the words to explain what he was trying to say. "I love it here, but I get so annoyed with people for being so…predictable. People here fall into life by default. No one's run against Howard because everybody is so used to Howard as mayor. But Howard's so stuck in how everything's always been that he can't see the possibilities. I don't want Middleburg to die off just because it's the path of least resistance. Life should never be the path of least resistance, the expected thing."

"And you're the new possibility?" She hoped her skepticism for his speech didn't show.

"Sounds corny, doesn't it? But, well, yeah. I prayed about it for weeks when I first got the idea. Even *I* don't tilt the world sideways without thinking it through. But the honest truth is that I believe this is what God wants me to do. Run, at least. I'll leave the part about whether or not I win up to Him."

She'd seen him at church, heard him lead prayers during services, but it was different to hear him talking about how God affected his everyday life. She was just getting used to this praying-over-decisions thing. Part of it was wonderful; she could bring the Lord of the universe in on even her smallest decisions. Another part of it was frightening, because she'd given up having the final say. God hadn't said no to anything she'd asked Him yet, and she wasn't sure how she'd handle it when He did.

She looked at Mac again. Most of the people she knew in Chicago had so many layers, so many overlapping hidden agendas that a simple conversation gave her a headache. Mac was just the opposite—living, walking "what you see is what you get." It was as unsettling as it was refreshing.

Chapter Five

"I memorized a line today," Gil bragged to Mac as they brought more wood in from the pile in Mac's backyard. He puffed up and bellowed, "Spare not one!" into the night air. Mac had to agree with the casting; Herod was a very good use of Gil's commanding baritone.

"I'm shaking in my boots, your majesty. And you have all of what, six lines?"

"Seven."

"Ain't that useful. I, on the other hand, have no less than forty-two lines to occupy my whopping load of free time."

"Star." It wasn't a compliment.

"I got 'em typed out onto index cards and stacked up on my dashboard. I go over them at stop lights and while I'm waiting at the train crossing. Because *that's* how much free time I have."

Gil dumped his armload of wood into the wrought iron holder beside the enormous stone fireplace that was the centerpiece of Mac's living room. "Rots to be you, don't it?"

Mac dropped his own wood, then bent down to arrange a fire. "Pastor Dave was dead-on casting you as the villain. You're just plain mean. You'll probably scare the little kids or something."

"Emily's delighted," Gil said as he settled into one of the large leather chairs that stood in front of the fire-place. Emily had wound up being Mary, and was over-the-top happy about her starring role, not to mention Gil's. "For all I know, she put Dave up to it."

Mac struck a match to a pile of kindling. "Who knew you had an artistic side? It's almost unnatural." He cast a sideways look back at Gil as he opened the pizza box that sat on the coffee table between them. "I can't quite see you in a crown and flowing robes. This ought to be fun."

"Speaking of unnatural, I heard you got to play hero to Mary Thorpe earlier this week. Peter Epson was telling Emily about it—said he wanted to do an article, but he was afraid his dad would throw a fit." Peter Epson was Howard's son and a reporter for the local paper.

"You see," Mac elaborated as he pointed the tip of his pizza slice at Gil, "that's exactly why I'm running. People do things—or don't do things—way too much based on what Howard will think. Okay, Peter may be a bit of an exception, but you know what I mean. The guy's got too much influence. And I don't even think he goes after half of it. You might be surprised to hear I don't actually hate Howard. Not at all."

Gil raised an eyebrow as he bit into his own slice. "Could have fooled me."

"Granted, he's overblown, self-centered, backward-looking, but this 'mayor for life' thing has gotten so out of proportion that Howard doesn't have to look at something before people *decide* how he feels about it.

Okay, maybe he's grabbed at power with both hands, but we've been handing him more and more over the years without even thinking about it."

"And you're just the guy to turn us around," Gil guessed with his mouthful.

"I'm just the guy God asked to do the job," Mac clarified, meaning it. It bugged him that people thought he had it out for Howard personally, when he just wanted to change people's mind about the inescapability of Howard being mayor.

"Howard might say the same thing."

"Enter the blessings of democracy."

"Man, you really are starting to sound like a politician." Gil took a swig of his soda. "But a snake charmer? Did you and Curly really pull a milk snake out of that lady's sink?"

"The press *should* have been there. I was heroic. An epic battle. The thing was six feet long."

Gil shot Mac a dark look. "Janet Bishop said it was a foot and a half at most and it took you four minutes."

"Four very dramatic minutes. You should have heard Mary Thorpe shriek."

"She's from *Chicago*," Gil said as if it explained everything.

"Cut the woman a little slack."

Gil grinned. "Sounds like you already did. Dinah told me you bought her a nice soothing beverage afterward in the bakery. Charmer, like I said."

"She was afraid to go back into her kitchen just yet. What was I supposed to do? Just leave her standing in the hallway? After all, Curly likes her."

"Just Curly?"

"We're not in the same place, Gil. She's just barely

getting her feet underneath her where her faith is concerned. I admit, she shows some spine, and…maybe under different circumstances…but not now." She wasn't Mac's type, even with those eyes.

"Circumstances change all the time. Maybe she's just what you need." Gil raised an eyebrow.

"What I need," Mac declared narrowing his eyes, "is for people to stop planning my life for me, thinking I need what everyone else *thinks* I need. God and I can tackle my own path just fine, so leave it, okay?"

"Yeah," uttered Gil, drawing out the word with a sarcastic flourish, "we'll just leave it. For the moment."

"We'll just leave it, period."

Stop it, Mary scolded herself as she felt her pace slowing. There was no reason to be afraid of opening her apartment door. Nice people were behind it. Nice people who'd asked her to a local party, to be friendly. Why is it, Mary asked herself as she caught her scowling reflection in the hallway mirror, that "nice" is so hard for you to get used to? Very pleasant people live in Chicago. You just never seemed to meet any of them. Pausing for a second to apply a friendly smile to her face, Mary put her hand on the door handle. She was about to check through the peephole when she heard Emily's voice call out "Mary, it's us!"

As if Emily suspected she had checked the peephole. Suddenly, instead of feeling like a smart, keep-yourself-safe city girl, Mary felt like a suspicious, overly cautious wimpy girl. It played in her head like an advertising slogan or a 1950s B-movie trailer: "She Came from Planet Mean."

These people have been nothing but wonderful to

you. You should be thanking God every second for bringing you here. She squared her shoulders and tugged the heavy wooden door open.

And saw a wall of pine needles.

Two seconds later, that wall of needles tilted off to one side to reveal Emily Sorrent, dressed fit for a Christmas card in a fuzzy white beret, scarf and mittens. Beaming. "Surprise! I told you we'd get a tree in here! Up the stairs and everything."

The tree tilted farther to reveal a sadly resigned Gil and Mac, looking like they'd put up every inch of resistance they had to this little holiday stunt. Emily evidently was as stubborn as Dinah said. Mary didn't think too many people in Middleburg got away with bossing Gil Sorrent and Mac MacCarthy around. Especially when it meant hauling a cumbersome Christmas tree up a narrow stairway.

Mac blew a lock of hair out of his face and craned his neck around a branch. "Can we get this thing settled before the sap starts to run?"

Gil angled the trunk he was holding in through the door while Mac wrestled the top through the arched doorway. "A five-foot tree would have done, Emily," he noted, working to coax the tip under the lintel as pine needles showered everywhere.

"This apartment has lovely high ceilings," Emily defended, tugging off her mittens. "A shorter tree would have looked silly."

Gil set the trunk down onto the floor and straightened up with a groan. "A shorter tree would have weighed less, not that it mattered or anything." His voice said it mattered a great deal, but there was still a hint of humor in his eyes as he looked at his wife.

Mary was still standing there, holding the door open, probably holding her mouth open, as well. When Emily said she would fix her up with a tree, Mary didn't think she really meant it. It was just a nice thought, a pleasant thing to say. They weren't friends or anything; they'd barely met, and already Emily had given her the beautiful blue glass ornament. "I can't remember the last time I had a tree," Mary reminisced, wishing there wasn't quite so much astonishment in her voice. "Actually, I don't think I've ever had a tree of my own."

Emily looked genuinely shocked, which made sense. The woman probably started planning her Christmas decorations in July if the store's holiday abundance was any indication.

"That's horrible. Next thing you'll be telling me is that you don't have a stocking to hang over that lovely fireplace."

Mary started to say something, but Gil gave her a look and a barely perceptible head shake that silently warned, don't get her started.

"Oh, no," Mary lied. "My mom sent my stocking from home just yesterday." Note to self: get stocking from Mom ASAP.

"Well," said Mac, brushing the last of the pine needles off his jacket, "where do you want to put this thing?"

How should I know? Mary was grateful for an on-the-spot brainstorm. "Emily, where do you think?"

It took Emily about four seconds to decide that in the corner by the front windows was the best place for Mary's first-ever tree. "That way people from the street can see your lights and decorations."

"Uh…sure," Mary agreed. Second note to self: ask

Janet to secretly deliver some lights, look up Christmas decorations for beginners on the Internet tomorrow morning. Where was this simple country life everyone kept talking about? Life in Middleburg kept getting more complicated by the minute.

As the men maneuvered the tree into place, Mary stood beside Emily and whispered, "You didn't tell me Mac was coming." She didn't like the evening's sudden "double date" atmosphere.

"Well, Gil couldn't get the tree up here by himself, and I didn't think you'd mind."

Gil looked plenty big enough to bring the tree up on his own, and she wouldn't have minded a three-foot tree if it would have gotten her out of this.

Her reluctance must have shown, for Emily furrowed her brows and said, "Mac was going to be there anyway. We just asked him to make a detour to help us out. He's in his own car and everything—he won't even be riding with us to the high school." The corner of her mouth turned up in a wry smile. "I'm not fixing you up." She looked back at the pair as they planted the trunk into the tree stand Emily had handed off to Gil. "Yet." With a wink, she stepped toward the tree. "Gil, it's not straight. About half a foot to the left."

Mary watched, dumbfounded yet she was moved, as Emily gave orders adjusting the tree this way and that. Someone had gone far out of their way to do something nice, completely unsolicited and certainly unexpected, for her. It did something to the pit of her stomach that she couldn't quite keep under control. She was spending her first Christmas on her own, as a believer, in her new home, and it was starting to actually *feel* like a home. The sight of the bare tree looked glorious to her, even though she was sure it looked sadly incomplete to Emily. "It's beautiful," Mary claimed resolutely. "Really." She shook Gil's hand. "Thank you so much."

"Don't thank me," he countered gruffly. "Thank Madame Holiday over there. She's got three up at the farm already, and she was threatening me with a fourth until she remembered you didn't have one yet. I ought to be thanking you."

Mary felt a laugh bubble up inside her. "Enthusiastic, hmm?"

"That don't even begin to cover it." He leaned in. "Just let her run it out, okay? If she comes back tomorrow with doodads and fake snow, just let her. I'd consider it a personal favor. The guys on the farm are pretty much at their limit."

"I'll take one for the team," Mary joked, liking how it felt. Based on what she'd heard about Sorrent's burly farmhands, she could barely imagine them choking on cinnamon potpourri and tangling in miles of red velvet ribbon.

"Much appreciated." It was the first time she saw Gil Sorrent smile.

"What are you two all whispering about?" Emily asked, returning from the kitchen with the ornament Mary had hung in the window. She'd come with one of those fancy ornament hooks Mary had seen in her shop, which she now held out to Mary with great ceremony.

"I was just giving her tree care instructions," Gil informed. "When to water and all."

"Good idea," Emily concurred. "Okay now, Mary, you do the honors."

The size of the lump in Mary's throat was just plain insane as she selected a bough and hung the single blue ornament on the tree. It was the most ridiculous thing ever. She wasn't about to let on to anyone that she'd just hung her one and only ornament on her first-ever Christmas tree. "Perfect," Mary gulped out, trying to sound ordinary even though she felt foolish and exposed.

Everyone took a second to admire the single ornament, even though it wasn't much of an admirable display. Mary was reminded that nothing in the world smelled like a fresh Christmas tree. A dozen classic carols rang through her memory, and she thought she'd gobble up the first candy cane she could get her hands on. Would Dinah teach her to bake Christmas cookies? If not, there were sure to be plenty within easy reach with the bakery only steps away.

"We should get going," announced Mac, checking his watch. "You know how that place fills up."

Gil and Emily had offered to take Mary to the high school choral Christmas program. It sounded like one of those classic student music programs, where the freshman band struggled their way through various arrangements of holiday music, the choirs and soloists showed their young talent, and parents stood in crowds of camera flashes and video-cam tripods. Where she came from, those types of things were a relatives-only kind of affair, but here in Middleburg it seemed the whole town turned out. That may have had something to do with the "cookie walk" afterward—an event she'd never seen before but everyone seemed to find very ordinary. Hordes of people baked their best Christmas cookies, patrons paid $10 for a box to fill to the brim with whatever goodies caught their eye, and the profits bought things like band uniforms and new sheet music. With a degree in classical music, Mary found the whole thing very intriguing—even before frosting was involved. Did high school choirs still do the "Halleluiah Chorus" at the end of every Christmas concert?

Well, she thought as she wound her scarf around her neck and took a last happy look at the new tree in her living room, there's only one way to find out.

Chapter Six

Mary was just wedging a final almond snowball cookie into the corner of her box when she heard Mac's voice over her shoulder. "Excellent use of space. You've done this before."

She laughed. Not a centimeter of cookie box had gone to waste, and she'd had fun plotting just how to get as many cookies as she could for her $10 box. When Sandy Burnside had mentioned most cookies froze quite well—supposedly explaining why she was holding no less than three full boxes—Mary seriously considered investing in a second box. A tug at her tight waistband, however, lent her the necessary restraint. "I did make the most of my box, didn't I?"

Mac's box looked rather scientifically stuffed, as well. "Hey, it's for a good cause."

Mary took a sip of her punch. "I don't think my sweet tooth qualifies as a noble effort."

"Oh, no," Mac replied, "we do our ethical sugar-binge-ing very well here in Middleburg. Cookies for charity have a long and delicious history in this town. I could tell you stories that could put you off peanut butter forever."

Mary sat back on one hip, selecting half a candy-cane cookie from the platter of broken "freebies" that was at the center of the cookie tables. "I'm still getting used to lots of things about Middleburg."

They moved to the cash register while Gil and Emily were still stuffing the eight boxes it took to feed Home-stretch Farm's many mouths. "Look," Mac explained, "I feel weird about the tree thing. That was sort of pushy. I thought we should have asked first, but, well, you know Emily. You looked a little taken aback about it. I feel bad."

"It was a surprise," Mary admitted, "I guess I'm just not used to people going to trouble like that for me. I feel… I don't know, indebted? I don't even know if Christmas trees are expensive."

Mac looked at her. "You don't have an ornament to your name, do you? No decorations, none of that stuff?"

Mary actually felt her eyes shift side to side, as if she were letting a secret slip. "I could pull off a string of popcorn given an hour or two." She suddenly remembered. "I've got six Christmas CDs—do they count?"

"Emily's gonna have a field day with you. You should let her. She needs a place to put her imagination these days, and I'm pretty sure their living room can't hold another nativity scene. You were smart to give her the role of Mary in the play."

"I don't need to be Middleburg's Christmas charity case." She meant it as a joke, but it wasn't that far from the truth. Even though everyone was treating her like some great answer to prayer, she felt like a fraud—like Middleburg hadn't realized what they were getting in the bargain.

Mac fished money out of his wallet as the Junior

Class Glee Club tied up his purchases. "Don't think of it that way. To put it in engineering terms, Emily's like a great big pressure valve. All that holiday stuff builds up, and it needs somewhere safe to go. She got a jump start on it this year, and both the shop and the farm are all decked out. We still have weeks to go, and she needs a new target. The Christmas play and your empty apartment are just great targets. Gil'd probably thank you if you just let her run wild on your place."

"Actually," commented Mary, pulling out her own money, "he already did. Said he'd consider it 'a personal favor' if I'd let her 'snow all over me.'"

Mac grinned. "You should. That way everyone wins. You get a winter wonderland, MCC gets your full attention on the drama and Gil gets one square inch without mistletoe all over it. Emily can get obsessive. I'd sic her on my own personal holiday dilemma if I could, but I don't think it's her style."

"Holiday dilemma? Your decorations not up to snuff?"

"No, it's actually a bit more complicated than that. Or maybe just expensive. The deal is, I'll be the biggest Grinch in history if I don't get my hands on one of those ridiculous blue bears for my nephew. Pressure's on, and Uncle Mac had better come through."

"You mean a Bippo Bear?"

Mac's grin all but faded. "Man, what I wouldn't do with five minutes alone with those idiots who do this to kids at Christmas. Deliberate shortages. A gazillion ads but no product. Setting little kids up for disappointment at Christmas. It ought to be a felony. I reckon this may end up costing me $500, and that's wrong on so many levels."

"Advertising people are just doing their job. The people who make Bippo Bears need jobs, too. And the people who ship them and work in the stores that sell them. Christmas hasn't gotten so out of whack just because of Bippo Bears. That's not a fair thing to say."

"You know what's not fair? Sitting watching some harmless cartoon with my nephew when the eleventh commercial with that mind-numbing Bippo Bear song comes on, and he knows it by heart. And he looks at me with those enormous blue eyes of his and says 'Uncle Mac, I just gotta have a Bippo Bear for Christmas.' And I already know that every store within a hundred miles of here is long out and can't get more, but they're still running that ad. He's still singing that song. *That's* not fair."

"Life isn't always fair." It sounded like a tired retort—the kind of thing best left to T-shirts.

"No one should have to learn that at *five*." Somehow, he'd realized how worked up he'd gotten, and Mary could see him force calm back into his voice, pressing his shoulders down from where they'd gotten hunched up. "Twenty-five, maybe. Fifteen if girls are involved. But not five."

Mary couldn't think of too many single men who'd get so worked up over a nephew's Christmas list. Most of the men she'd known had Olympic medals in self-absorption, whose holiday or birthday present expeditions never went farther than the gift-card stand at the mall. The thought of Mac hunting down a Bippo Bear in the darkest recesses of Internet commerce was an oddly compelling picture. He'd be genuinely mad if he failed. It showed in his eyes.

Mac took a step back and wiped his hands down his

face. "I'm sorry. It's not your fault, I didn't need to blast you with my frustration. I just want Christmas to be about the baby Jesus for Robby, not about Bippo Bears." He shifted his weight, making an effort to change topics. "On the other hand, I do have an issue that might actually *be* your problem."

Mary wasn't sure she wanted to know what that was. "My problem?"

"Tell me Joseph doesn't really have to wear a dress?"

Mary had to laugh. "It's a *tunic*. And while it's technically not pants, I wouldn't call it a dress, either. No knees involved whatsoever."

"I know Joseph was a carpenter, but you always see him holding a shepherd's crook. I get to hold a big stick, right? I need something to keep up with Gil's armor. And you're giving the guy minions. That's not safe."

"Gil comes with his own minions, though, so it was smart casting. And this isn't about who carries the biggest stick."

"Honey," drawled Mac, grinning and taking the twang in his accent up a few notches, "in this town it's always about who carries the biggest stick. Y'all better figure that out right now." He leaned in as they made their way back to where Gil and Emily were finishing up their purchases. "Howard doesn't get a stick as narrator, but does he get one as God?"

Mary laughed harder. "You really have brought this down to a highly personal level, haven't you?"

He didn't answer, just stood there, smiling.

"God gets a very big book, but no stick. The narrator has no props at all. I guess I'd better think long and hard before I decide which props you get. Wouldn't want it going to your head or anything."

Gil came in on the last of the conversation. "Mac? Something going to his head? Can't be done. This fella's big head is already at capacity." He adjusted the six boxes in his arms. "Matter of fact, I've been thinking if he becomes mayor, his head just might explode."

Mac narrowed his eyes at Gil. "You'd like that, wouldn't you?"

"Nah." For a minute it looked like Gil might cuff Mac—they were like brawling brothers, those two. "Then I'd probably be the one stuck cleaning it up."

Emily came holding two more boxes of cookies. "We're done here, aren't we, boys? I've got a big day at the shop tomorrow and I'm sure Mary could do without the 'Gil and Mac Parade of Manliness.'"

In the five seconds it took them to get their dander up, Emily was practically out the door with Mary close behind. "Sorry you had to see that," Emily apologized, nodding her head back toward the pair of men. "Usually they save it for the barn." She parked the boxes on the hood of the big green Homestretch Farm truck and fished in her pocket for her car keys. "Gil said you might need help decking out your apartment for the holidays now that you've got a tree. I've got a few extra ideas if you'd like…"

"Sure," Mary conceded, wondering if she'd regret it. "I need all the help I can get."

Later that night, Mary picked out a holiday CD, heated up a mug of instant cocoa and sat a big pillar candle in the fireplace. Wrapping herself in a large fuzzy throw, she turned off all the lights and sat on the floor leaning up against the sofa. It was starting to feel like a real Christmas.

Her first Christmas away from the retail version of Christmas. Away from the professional caroling of her musical training, away from the check-the-sales-records competition of the ad career, away even from the old Mary for whom church was something people just did on Easter and Christmas. She began to hum "Away in a Manger," thinking of the baby Jesus with new poignancy. Mac was right, nothing could be further from Bippo Bears than that starlit night. "A night," as Pastor Dave had said in a recent sermon, "that split history in two. That split the universe into 'before and after' and made the impossible possible."

You have, haven't You? I'd have thought it impossible to be here. To be gone from that world and into this one. You've changed my life, and You'll always be changing it, won't You?

So why am I still so afraid? I'm glad to be using my talents for You now, here, but what do I do about all that stuff from my past? Do I throw it away, erase it like I want to? What if my past is coming after me, Lord? I'm so new at this.

You've got to show me what to do, Lord.

Mac wasn't really sure why he needed a special rehearsal in Pastor Dave's office, but when he got the e-mail, he showed up. Script in hand, Mac knocked on the office door and entered.

To find Mary Thorpe and Howard. No Pastor Dave.

"I don't have any scenes with him," Howard objected. He'd noticed, too, evidently.

Mary stood up. "That's right. You don't. Because you two don't seem to be able to get along lately. And, you know, we need to change that." Her voice was unsteady, but determined.

Mac took a step farther into the room, realizing he'd just been ambushed. Maybe he should have left the snake under the sink. "We get along just fine."

"We disagree on several issues," Howard stated formally, "but that's all."

Mary motioned to the chair at the meeting table across from Howard. "What will it take for you two to come out in favor of a community Christmas Eve potluck dinner?"

"A what?" Howard asked at the same moment Mac was thinking it.

"A community Christmas Eve dinner. A potluck. After the drama. Instead of everyone heading off to their own homes, I'm proposing we have a town-wide potluck."

"On Christmas Eve?" Mac had a long tradition of spending Christmas Eve in the privacy of his own quiet home, not surrounded by Jell-O salad and casseroles. "Don't you think it's a bit much?"

"I have to say, I'm siding with MacCarthy on this one. I admire your commitment and creativity, but I think the drama will be more than enough."

"The drama only provides limited interaction," she declared firmly. "And, only for those in the cast and crew at that. While I've made the production as big as possible, that hardly includes the whole town. Pastor Dave and I have talked it over, and we think this is just the ticket."

"Dave thought this was a good idea?" Howard's scowl matched the one Mac was trying to hide.

"He did." Mary stood her ground. "But he also said we'd get nowhere if you weren't behind it, Howard."

Howard always looked like he found that surprising, which was funny, because Mac knew Howard expected to be consulted. On everything.

"That may be true," Howard consented, "but I doubt people are going to want to spend their Christmas Eve dinners in the church basement. Folks have family. Traditions. I'm not keen to mess with that."

Normally, "messing with tradition" would be just the kind of argument to get Mac in favor of something, but not in this case. "Maybe after the dress rehearsal? You know, the night before?"

"That's not the night for it," Mary replied. "The old saying 'bad dress rehearsal, good performance' didn't come out of nowhere. This needs to be a celebration, 'job well done' and such in order to help the community come together." She spread her hands on the table. "You hired me to achieve a goal, and I think this is the way to achieve that goal. You two play a very big part in what this town is going through, that's why we cast you in such visible roles. Think of this as an extension of that."

"No offense, Mary," said Mac, "but I just don't think it's a good idea. Folks will want to be home. *I* want to be home. I have plans already, and I imagine most other people do, too."

Howard crossed his arms over his chest. "I'm just not ready to say yes to this, Miss Thorpe. And that's the truth of it."

If Mary Thorpe had done nothing else for Middleburg, she'd just come up with the one thing he and Howard could agree on.

"Will you think it over?" Mary persisted.

"I doubt I'll change my mind," Howard offered, leaning back in his chair.

"But you will think it over?" Mary definitely wasn't backing down. Where was *this* woman when the snake was in her kitchen? Mac felt a twinge of guilt for pegging her as a "fraidy cat."

"If you insist."

"I insist." Mary held Howard's eye for a moment before turning to Mac. "And you?"

"I'm with Howard. I'm no fan, but I'll give it a day or two."

"I suppose I can't ask for more than that now, can I?"

Mary shut the door behind her two targets, letting out the breath she'd been holding half of the meeting. While she hadn't gotten yes, she hadn't gotten no, either—yet.

Shaking the jitters out of her shoulders, Mary saw Pastor Dave peering around the corner. "So," he prompted, one eyebrow raised but a glint in his eye, "what happened?"

"They don't like it." Mary wasn't quite sure how she came to be disappointed in this, but maybe it was that she just hated friction between people—it was one of the reasons she'd always freelanced in her music and advertising; she just couldn't stand the "creative tension" that seemed to be the necessary evil of those kind of workplaces.

"Well, we knew that would happen. Were you able to keep them from saying an outright no? That's really as far as I reckon we were going to get, anyway."

"They said they'd think about it." That hardly qualified as a success in her book. It just barely edged its way out of the realm of failure.

"That's great!" He clasped a friendly hand on her shoulder, and broke into a wide smile. Well, at least "the boss" was pleased. "That's a victory, Mary. We'll bring 'em around, just you wait. Besides," he leaned in and whispered, "I've got our secret weapon all lined up. It's time to bring in the big guns."

Mary gulped. "Big guns?"

"Have you met Sandy Burnside?"

It was hard for anyone within six miles of Middleburg *not* to meet Sandy Burnside? "Yes."

"I got Sandy on board last night. Sandy is pretty much a force of nature around here. Between Sandy and her buddies, Mac and Howard don't stand a chance. We'll have our potluck up and running by the end of the week."

"They didn't look especially fond of the idea, Dave."

"Of course not. But that's the beauty of a small town like Middleburg." He practically winked. "There's nowhere to hide."

Chapter Seven

Mac was answering an e-mail full of campaign-issue questions from Peter Epson when Sandy Burnside burst into his office. If the woman had anything close to "downtime," Mac never saw it. He'd often wondered why Sandy had never run for mayor—she had locked horns with Howard more than anyone. She plunked down her enormous handbag on Mac's desk, nearly scattering the papers. "Why are you raising such a stink about something as sweet as Christmas Eve dinner?"

Pushing his keyboard away, Mac crossed a foot over one knee and resigned himself to whatever venting was about to come his way. "Sandy, I don't like the idea. But I'm guessing you already know that."

Sandy blew out a breath, shaking her head. "You'd think we had moved Christmas to February the way you two are hollering. Howard was breaking out the hundred-dollar phrases like 'disruption of family traditions.' 'Casualizing of an important night.'" She leaned in. "I ask you, is 'casualizing' even a word?"

"Listen, Sandy…" How he spent Christmas Eve was

his business. He didn't like that it had now become a campaign issue.

Sandy was on a roll. "And wasn't it Howard's idea in the first place to create a holiday drama that would bring the town together? I mean it wasn't actually his idea… I think it was Pastor Dave's to be exact…but doesn't Howard think every good idea was his idea?"

"Howard does like the drama thing. But we both think the dinner's too much. Howard thinks we all ought to go home and be with our families."

"Be with your family with everybody's families," Sandy countered. "All together. That's the whole point."

"Howard thinks the play will be enough and believe it or not, Sandy, I agree with him."

She shot him a *Why do you think I'm here?* glare.

"People have Christmas Eve traditions." He tried another tactic, since her expression wasn't softening one bit. "What about your schedule—aren't your stores open late on Christmas Eve?"

Sandy narrowed her eyes. "Burnside employees," she said gravely, "go home to their families at four o'clock on Christmas Eve."

"See? It's the same thing. People might want to be home. *I* want to be home."

"Getting out of work is different than saying you won't celebrate Christmas Eve with your friends and neighbors." Sandy planted her hands on Mac's desk. "We need unity."

Mac tried to keep his sigh from becoming a grunt. "I'm doing the drama thing, Sandy. I spend Christmas Day surrounded by family and kids and presents and ham and eggnog. Has it ever occurred to you that Christmas Eve is a time I like to be on my own? Quiet?

In prayer even? You're saying I'm a poor citizen—a poor Christian—because I don't want to spend that time over ground beef with people I see every other day of the year?"

Sandy's face took on a look that was far too close to pity. "You prefer to spend Christmas Eve alone?" Her tone was that of *What kind of a sick soul are you, anyway?*

There it was; that annoying *you can't possibly be happy* attitude. That look Ma got that declared a single man couldn't really be happy, only deluded or a very good liar. As if solitude or freedom were things real men outgrew. The kind of look that made Mac want to move to Montana with only cows for company. "Yes," he responded, his voice low and authoritative, "I do."

"Well," Sandy interjected, snatching up her bag. "I think that's the saddest thing I've heard this week."

"Sandy," Mac continued, even though he knew better than to get into this with her, "I've spent Christmas Eve alone for the past four years, and you never thought of me as sad before. I was a fine, upstanding citizen until ten minutes ago. A man needs his solitude."

She jutted out her chin as if the thought was selfish, unpatriotic even. "A town needs unity. Especially now. And if it needs to happen by Jell-O salad, then I'll be the first to whip up a bowl. I expect you to do the same." She turned on her heels and left his office.

Mac sat back in his chair, raked his fingers through his hair in aggravation and stared at the ceiling between him and Mary Thorpe. You did this, he thought. We're in such different places. Faith doesn't boil down to potlucks and the way anyone spends Christmas Eve, Mary. Mary was still in the realm of spiritual blacks and whites, and he'd spent enough years on the road of faith to know the detours numbered in the thousands. There might be things she could teach him, but when a woman challenged him, Mac wanted it to be about more than a Christmas Eve potluck.

The fact that Mac was walking into a costume fitting didn't do much for his sour mood. Big blue rectangle with sleeves—those Bible-era robes didn't need tailoring. Beyond how tall he was or how long his arms were, what else did they need to know?

Everything, evidently. Mac was just about at the end of his patience by the time Audrey Lupine took enough measurements to fit him for a tuxedo. Audrey was efficient and detail-oriented, which was a big plus in librarians, but he wasn't sure tunics demanded that much attention to detail. Between that, and the four times he'd been stabbed with a pin, Mac was practically stomping his way to Mary Thorpe's office to complain about the way it had invaded his life when he heard it.

Walking by the sanctuary, Mac was startled by a clear, sweet melody overhead. A violin in the choir loft, as near as he could tell. An amazingly pure, almost ethereal tune he recognized as one of those old, classical English carols. The kind he'd heard on Christmas albums, but almost no one knew the lyrics. Something that sounded as if it should be echoing in an Italian cathedral rather than through the rafters of MCC.

It was almost a minute before he realized it must be Mary—he didn't know anyone else in Middleburg who could play the violin that well, and he remembered her orchestral background from Pastor Dave's introduction. He'd forgotten that she'd been a professional musician before coming to Middleburg. The quality of her playing stunned him, making him want to hear more. He pushed through the back doors of the sanctuary so that he was standing underneath her in the choir loft.

She finished the one song, but he heard her move to the piano and begin to play. Something jazzy and contemporary, surprising him when he recognized it as "I'll Be Home for Christmas." She began to sing, and her musicality lost its precise rigid quality, the notes dipping and sliding free in a way he felt down the back of his neck.

There was such emotion in her voice and her playing. Sadness pulled at the edges of her notes. Why wouldn't Mary Thorpe be homesick? It had to be tough to inject yourself into a completely new town at Christmas. And one not dealing well with the season at that. She'd probably expected to come into a Norman Rockwell painting, not an episode of bluegrass Jerry Springer. His first impulse was to simply slip back out the door, but that would be the cowardly thing to do. So, even as her voice took on a greater sadness, Mac made his way up the choir loft stairs until he saw her seated with her back to him at the piano. He let her finish the song, but only because something told him that she needed to get all the way through the music.

"Mary," he said quietly when the last chord had died down.

Despite his effort to be unintrusive, she practically jumped off the piano bench. "Mac!"

"I'm sorry to sneak up on you. That was beautiful." He winced inwardly, thinking that sounded dumb. "Both songs. You sing so well." Again, he thought he sounded bumbling.

She blushed. "Music major. Comes with the territory I suppose."

"You okay?" He regretted asking the minute it left his mouth. What would he do if she said no? She sounded so emotional when she sang, so sad, and he definitely wasn't ready to get into that with her.

"Fine." She said it quickly and defiantly. In a way that broadcast she was anything but fine. They both looked down for a moment, uncomfortable. "Did you need something?"

"I was here for a costume fitting. We've finally found Curly's new song, by the way."

"Really? Who'd he take a liking to?"

"You'd get a kick out of who he likes now." He rolled his eyes. "*Someone* ought to get some enjoyment out of it."

She swung her legs around the piano bench to face him. "Who'd he choose?"

"Well," Mac began to say as he took a few steps into the choir loft and sat down in one of the chairs. "I wasn't getting anywhere with any of the other CDs you gave me, so I put the radio on to one of those stations playing all Christmas music. One song came on, and he went nuts, just like he did for the tenor guy you were playing."

"Another tenor?"

"Well, I suppose you could say that. Three of them, actually."

"Oh, the *Three Tenors?* He has good taste."

"Not exactly. More like the three rodents. Curly's taken a shine to Alvin and the Chipmunks. Believe me, the only thing worse than the chipmunks' version of that 'Christmas Time is Here' song is Curly's version.

It's like cats dying." He frowned at the sheer memory of Curly's yuletide caterwauling. "I never thought I'd say this, but I prefer opera to that noise."

"Oh, my!" She was trying not to laugh. "I think that would be awful."

"No thinking about it. It *is* awful. You ought to be downright grateful Curly isn't in the office this week. It'd turn your ears black."

"Part of me wants to hear it, and the other part of me is glad I missed it."

Mac cracked a smile. "Listen to the part that happily missed it. No one but Curly's closest kin should be subjected to that racket."

Mary saw he was about to go, and she didn't want to let him leave without asking one question. "Speaking of kin," she added, catching him with her voice when he shifted his weight to rise, "Why don't you think the potluck Christmas Eve supper is a good idea? I mean, no offense, but it's not like you have a family to worry about or anything." That came out all wrong. Of course Mac had family—she'd met his parents and he'd talked about siblings and nieces and nephews. But he didn't have a family of his own. "That didn't quite come out right. I'm sorry."

"No," he admitted, "but I think I know what you mean." He settled back into his seat. "And I suppose it's a fair question, seeing as I don't have a wife or children, you might reckon I'd spend Christmas Eve with my folks. The truth of the matter is that I have a very important Christmas Eve tradition. One I'm not thrilled to give up, if you don't mind my saying." He relaxed in his chair, crossing one long booted leg over the other in the manner of someone about to tell a story.

"Five years ago my sister Nancy got real sick around Christmas time. Just after she had my nephew, Robby, to be exact. Anyways, we'd had plans for a big Christmas Eve thing, with the first grandbaby and all. Ma was pulling out all the stops. Except it came to a screeching halt when Nancy and the baby got sick and had to go back into the hospital. I'd come down with a bit of a cold, so I couldn't go see her or Robby, but Ma and Pa and my other sisters spent every minute there. So, instead of a big celebration, I ended up spending Christmas Eve alone. By myself."

"I'm sorry," she offered.

"Don't be," he replied. "I mean, it started out as a first-class Mac pity party, with me feeling all sorry for myself. I did feel bad at the beginning—and plenty worried about my new little nephew and all. But that's just it— that worry and feeling sorry forced me to turn to God. It turned out to be one of the most amazing nights of my life. I reckon I'd have never spent that night in front of my fire praying and reading my Bible like I did if things hadn't been as bad as they were. I'd never have remembered what an amazing gift a baby can be. Up until that night, I'd been so busy, I'd forgotten all the real stuff behind Christmas. Not that I don't love the noise and chaos of Christmas Day with my family. But I need both parts— what Ma calls my 'Silent Night' and the craziness of the next day." He looked up and caught her eyes. His eyes were straightforward and transparent; they made it easy to believe what he was saying. "So now maybe you can see why I'm in no hurry to trade that in—even for Middleburg's sake. They're *both* part of Christmas for me."

It wasn't what she was expecting. She thought she was about to be lectured about horning in on traditions or how everyone should get to celebrate in their own way—something less personal than this story. The thought of a man deliberately spending such a festive evening alone with God came as a shock of sorts. The men she'd known didn't behave that way—they just didn't run that deep.

In the music and retail advertising circles she had traveled, work went full tilt right up until Christmas Eve. Which meant everyone who worked together spent Christmas Eve together as sort of a finish-line extravaganza. After concerts or the final stretch of retail ad campaigns, Mary had spent the last two Christmas Eves at parties that started at the office or the concert hall and went on through the night. Parties that mostly seemed about consumption—running through as much food, alcohol and money as possible. Mad dashes to find the holiday cheer that always seemed just out of reach, or the thing everyone *else* had. After all, Christmas concerts were just another workday for musicians. This past year had been particularly surreal; Thornton had gone through so much champagne that he'd tried to corner her in the coatroom of the restaurant where they were all having dinner. As a matter of fact, it had been the frantic excesses of that evening—and the emptiness of that following holiday morning—that had begun her journey back to the church. She'd been so disillusioned by the experience that on Christmas morning, she had wandered the city until she found a church service and stepped into a sanctuary for the first time since elementary school. It was one of the reasons another Christmas in the advertising business had become too much to bear.

"Too many people spend Christmas Eve alone, Mac, and not because they want it that way."

"That's probably true in a city like Chicago, but not so much here."

She couldn't let that go. "Are you so sure?"

"What do you mean by that?"

"Aside from the point about getting everyone together to celebrate the drama, don't you think there ought to be a place where people can come if they don't have somewhere else to go for Christmas Eve?" She made a point to keep the emotion out of her voice. Truth was, she suspected that without the potluck, she'd be spending Christmas Eve cleaning up after the drama so that the sanctuary was ready for Christmas morning services. Part of her knew that she'd probably get an invitation from someone in Middleburg, if not several, but another part of her worried she was too new to end up anywhere but amid boxes in the church basement.

He crossed his arms over his chest. "Well, sure I think it'd be fine to invite people to get together if they need somewhere to go. But to *make* everyone?"

"Oh, so you mean it should be some kind of last resort? A lonely hearts club for the poor souls with nowhere else to go?" He'd hit a nerve, making her feel inferior to him because she resisted a night alone during the holidays when he'd mastered his solitude.

"I didn't say that."

"Didn't you?"

"No."

"So the folks who need to get together, who haven't achieved your level of spirituality, can band together to get each other through the holiday as long as they leave you alone?"

Mac's eyes darkened into the color of stormy seas. "Hey, wait a minute. You're blowing this way out of proportion. I didn't say anything like that. I'm trying to be nice."

"Nice? By making anyone without significant holiday plans feel shallow?

"What's up with you? I came here to explain myself, and you stomp all over me."

"You came here after eavesdropping on my music. Thanks for that, by the way. How long were you down there listening? 'Both songs,' you said, right?"

He stood up fuming. "Now look here. I'm not stalking you. I was on my way to look for you when I heard you singing. I thought you sounded nice, but I didn't realize what a crime it was to compliment you. And you're way out of line on the Christmas Eve thing, if you ask me. If you want to know who's passing judgments, it's you, expecting me to ditch something important to me just because you've decided something else is more important to you. Turning Christmas Eve from a holiday into some kind of civic test I've got to pass or fail." He stormed toward the door. "You haven't lived in Middleburg long enough to know how much I don't take to being backed into a corner, ma'am. I don't. Not at all. I'll do the play, and do it gladly. But you've got me at my limit, so don't push me beyond it." He added "Please," almost as an afterthought before he ducked down the stairs.

Mary heard his heavy footsteps stomp out of the choir loft and balled her fists. How had that conversation gone from complimentary to confrontational in so short a time? She heard the sanctuary doors bang shut and decided she was glad she couldn't make out whatever it was that Mac was mumbling. She was sure it wasn't "Merry Christmas."

What happened, Lord? He'd startled her, but that wasn't grounds for jumping down his throat. He'd offered personal information, gone out of his way to explain himself. The uncomfortable truth was that he'd simply hit a nerve—the exact wrong nerve—and she'd overreacted. He couldn't know how much personal meaning Christmas Eve held for her, or that his own personal connection with the night was at odds with hers. *Oh, Lord, this is all wrong. Couldn't we be dealing with Easter? Why'd You give me the idea to host a community Christmas Eve?*

Chapter Eight

Dinah Rollings came up to Mary after the next rehearsal, putting a hand on her shoulder. "Nicely done. You handled those two well. Even the best horse trainers would have been breaking a sweat over Howard and Mac tonight."

Mary sighed, pushing the stress out of her shoulders with the breath. "They were prickly, weren't they?"

"Well, pricklier than usual." She walked with Mary through the sanctuary as they began shutting off the banks of lights. "This mayor thing is turning out a whole lot more complicated than anyone thought it'd be. I give Mac credit, though, for doing it at all. Most of us wouldn't have had the nerve."

"It's my fault," Mary conceded. "It's asking a lot of him to spend Christmas Eve at the church."

Dinah stopped and turned to look at Mary. "You are not. You're asking him to rethink ideas and take hold of a better one. I think the Christmas Eve thing is a fabulous idea—course, you already know that. But the way I see it, you're not asking anything different than he's asking of the town to think about voting him in as mayor." She furrowed her brow for a moment, considering. "Come to think of it, that may be why it bugs him so much. Cuts a little too close to home."

"No one wants to get stressed out at Christmas."

"And no one wants to be alone—okay, maybe except for Mac, but we already know he's odd. I mean, look at that bird. The guy needs a normal pet, don't you think?"

Mary laughed. "Well, that may have had something to do with it, too. I don't think it's done wonders for Mac's stress level to have Curly belting out nonstop opera. And now…"

"Culture's good for guys." She hesitated for a moment. "And what do you mean by 'and now'?"

Mary shut off the last of the lights. "He hasn't told you?"

"I haven't talked to him much this week. Come on, what's behind the 'and now,' Mary?"

"Mac's been playing the radio to try and find Curly something new to sing. Well, Curly found something, but even Mac'd consider it worse than the first."

"Curly's got a new song, hm?"

"The Chipmunks' 'Christmas Song.'" It really was hysterical when you thought about it. Every time Mary tried to imagine Curly's screeching tenor rendering the squeaky, cheesy tune, she burst out laughing. If she didn't think he'd find it so offensive, Mary would have asked for a command performance.

Dinah's eyes grew wide. "No. You're kidding!"

"That's what he said."

Dinah erupted into giggles alongside Mary. "That's rich. That's just priceless. Oh, I think I'd pay to hear that. I might even pay to watch Mac listen to that."

"Don't ask him. Please. It'd just make things worse."

"Oh, I don't know. This is just so delicious. Curly. Singing chipmunks. I couldn't make this stuff up. Oh, Mary, you just made my day. And don't worry about Mac. He and Howard will get over themselves in time to get everyone on board for Christmas. And you've got me—and Janet, and Emily—on your side. That's got to be worth *three* grumpy mayors at least."

They'd reached Mary's office and she locked up for the night. "Thanks. I hope you're right."

"I am. You just stick to your guns."

Mary looked up from the box of props she was sorting when she heard the knock on the church storage room door. The last person Mary expected to see in the open doorway when she looked up was Howard Epson. "Hard at work, I see?" he said a little stiffly.

"Lots to do," she proclaimed, pushing the box back into its place on the shelves. "Nice to see you, Howard."

"Do you have a moment, Miss Thorpe?" he asked formally, officially. As if he'd prefer to have this conversation somewhere more conventional than a storage room.

"Please, you can call me Mary. I was just on my way to the kitchen for some coffee. May I pour you a cup? We can talk in my office." She still loved being able to say that phrase "in my office." Freelancers and musicians just didn't have offices. Most of her work got done on her kitchen table, in ad agency conference rooms and in rehearsal halls. It felt marvelously homey to have even the tiniest of offices.

"That'd be fine."

They collected their coffees and settled into Mary's small office. "Mary," Howard spoke, setting his mug down on her desk carefully, "I've come to talk about the Christmas Eve potluck." His manner had become, if possible, even more official. She wondered, at that moment, if she'd ever seen him laugh. Smile, yes, but she couldn't recall hearing the big old man laugh.

"I figured you had," she offered, trying to sound as encouraging as possible. His formality was more than a bit intimidating. Did he know that and wield it, or was it just an unavoidable by-product of his take-charge personality?

He adjusted the buttons on the cardigan sweater—standard grandfather issue to go along with his white hair, round build and silver glasses. "I've been giving a lot of thought to this."

"I'm glad," she commented, remembering she'd asked both him and Mac to consider the idea carefully before rejecting it outright as they seemed ready to do. "Please, go ahead."

"I feel a certain obligation," Howard began, folding his hands across his lap, "toward your success here. It was my idea to bring you on board because I felt this town was in grave danger of a deep division. One of the reasons we're investing in this little drama is to help renew the town's community spirit. I take this town's best interests to heart every day. I take my mayoral calling very seriously."

That was obvious. "I'm sure you do. I think that says a lot about you, Howard. And a lot about Middleburg."

"So I've decided that a higher level of civil service is required. I've prayed about this, long and hard, and I've decided that if I'm serious about my commitment to town unity, if I started this by bringing you here and if you believe this potluck is going to achieve that goal…well then, I'd be a hypocrite if I didn't sacrifice my family's private celebrations for the greater good."

He pronounced the words as if she'd asked him to undertake a suicide mission. He looked down and folded his hands across his lap with grave resignation. Howard was so tremendously, deeply serious that she didn't dare smile, even though she found his attitude a bit absurd. It was, after all, just a holiday potluck supper.

But Howard—and half of Middleburg, for that matter—didn't see it that simply.

"Howard, I admire your willingness to give this a try." She tried to make her voice as formal as Howard's even though it felt foolish. "I think that's very…civic of you. I appreciate it more than you know. I'm sure you won't regret it."

"It's my prayer that you're right, Miss Thorpe. The last thing this town needs is another reason to argue. Especially at Christmas."

"I appreciate that, sir." Mary didn't know where the urge to call him sir came from, but he seemed to like it. "I'll do my best to make good on the trust that you've given me."

His declaration made, Howard rose and took his coat from where he'd folded it across the back of his chair. "Middleburg is an astounding place, Miss Thorpe. A rare, wonderful place." She could see that he meant every dramatic word. The man really loved his hometown.

Mary extended her hand warmly. "I hope I come to love it as much as you do, Howard. I'm sure I will."

"See you at rehearsal." He shook her hand with a public official's firm grip. "I've all my lines memorized already, ahead of schedule."

As God/Narrator, Howard had no need to memorize his lines as he would "read" his part out of a giant prop Bible. She'd told him that, twice, but she swallowed her point and smiled. "That's wonderful."

"Good day."

It wasn't until he'd left the room that Mary realized he'd never touched a drop of his coffee. What an odd, surprising fellow Howard Epson was.

Mac hit Enter, thinking there was something supremely wrong with the world when a grown man paid that much money for a blue singing teddy bear. He knew Bippo Bears were just the fad of the hour, and that if he went over to his sister's house in January and asked Robby to show him his Bippo Bear, the boy might not even remember where he put it. Mac knew all this. He knew the evils of consumerism, he knew the craving was purely a profit-seeking game the toy retailers played every year. None of that stopped him from doing whatever it took to make Robby happy. Maybe it was that they'd come so close to losing him on his first Christmas. Mac could just never stomach the thought of disappointing that boy at the holidays. His role was indulgent Uncle Mac, and maybe that was best. *Mac, you have no spine. You'd make a lousy parent.*

He shut down his computer and closed up the office for the day. After an errand or two, he'd settle down for a relaxing night memorizing the last of his lines for the play. Curly had fallen off his passion for chipmunk tunes, and things were feeling almost normal around his house. As a matter of fact, Ma had only harped on him once this week about his approaching thirtieth birthday.

His birthday. Only weeks away now. It did bug him

that he was turning thirty, but not in the way others seemed to think it did. He wasn't having some sort of benchmark-year crisis, but he didn't want to enter his fourth decade on earth just sliding into some bland expected path. He'd always felt wired differently than everyone else—as if doing things differently were part of his nature. And while other folks might think of that as odd, Mac thought of it as being equipped for God's more unique tasks. He could take more heat, swim upstream, go against the grain and be creative better than anyone he knew. Someone like that just doesn't do the "settle down with a spouse and kids and an Irish setter" lifestyle that his sister had done. He loved Robby, but always thought he was more suited for the adventurous bachelor uncle than any kind of stable homestead.

He walked down the street toward Bishop Hardware, admiring the Christmas tree in the park along Ballad Road as he went. The town really was at its best for the holiday season. The season's first snowfall was forecast, and it would just dust everything with a painting-worthy coat of white. The place would look like a Christmas card scene over the weekend. Not only was that nice to look at, it brought the tourists out in droves, and tourists spent money. Charming weather meant chiming cash registers, and Mac knew many of the retailers in town were counting on a good holiday season this year.

He was just finishing his purchase when he caught sight of Mary Thorpe in the aisle where Janet kept her small selection of Christmas lights. They hadn't left things well at their last encounter, and he couldn't decide whether or not to get back on better terms. She'd jumped down his throat. Then again, he'd done whatever the musical version of eavesdropping could be called.

She walked up to him. "Hey, Mac." She had a "Can we start over?" expression on her face.

"Hi. Adding to the decorations on your tree?"

She managed a smile. "No, the tree's actually pretty full. Emily's been busy. I think I've only paid for about one tenth of the stuff on my tree. She's calling it overstock, but I don't believe her."

"She loves that stuff. And she loves doing things for other people. She went a little nuts when I first moved into my house. I thought she was going to throw me one of those shower things women do, she kept bringing me so many household gadgets. I'm here to tell you, men do not need a garlic press. We smash garlic with knives." He was running on at the mouth, nervous about how they'd gotten down each other's throats so quickly at their last meeting. She made him antsy, and he wasn't used to that.

"Look," she offered, "I wasn't very nice to you the other day. I guess I'm a little wired up about this holiday and you hit a nerve or something."

"I wasn't too friendly, either. Seems there are a lot of people on their last nerve." He thought about the last customer service rep he'd talked to earlier this morning in his endless search to score a Bippo Bear for something less than three times the manufacturer's price. That poor employee sounded like she wasn't going to make it through the day, much less the remainder of the holiday shopping frenzy. "That was unfair, listening in on you like that. But really, I wasn't snooping or anything. Your voice just caught me by surprise."

"Violin, I do in public. My singing is more personal. But you couldn't have known that." She drew in a deep breath. "I'd like to make a peace offering. Pie at Deacon's? That is, if you're not busy. I'd understand if you had work to do and all. But seeing as you're already out…"

His first impulse was to decline. They seemed to be able to rile up each other too easily. Not only that, but small-town eyes would catch the two of them together, one-on-one, and might start small-town tongues to wagging. He definitely wasn't ready to give anyone reason to pair them off. Still, for all his thought of being the more "mature" in his faith, it was her extending the olive branch when he'd hesitated to do so.

She was putting in an effort, and they really did need to clear the air between them. You'd be a louse to say no, he told himself. No one in their right mind said no to pie at Deacon's, anyway—she'd picked up on the local habits right quick. "I think that'd be fine. Nothin' waiting for me back at the office but more reports, anyway. A little pie might be just the ticket to get me over what I just forked out for the nephew's Christmas present."

"Do you have any little people you have to buy for this Christmas?" Mac started the conversation as they slid into a booth at Deacon's Grill.

"My brother is married, but they're not the family type. He and his wife travel all over the world for his exporting business. No kids, no plans for kids. I don't think I'll get the chance to be an aunt anytime soon."

"Well, this year, count yourself in good standing. I just paid an unnatural sum for one of those Bippo Bears, even though I knew better. Those advertising people should have their heads examined."

She got that odd look on her face again, growing quiet. Finally, he saw her make a mental decision of sorts.

"Yeah, about that…."

"About what?"

He couldn't quite place her expression. It was a trapped, end-of-my-rope kind of look in her eyes, but then again not. A half nervousness, half ashamed, cornered look that seemed completely out of place for their circumstances.

"About the Bippo Bears. I…um…well, there's something you should know about me and Bippo Bears."

He didn't think she'd asked him out to pie to talk about Bippo Bears. What did this year's toy fad have to do with anything? Why did she have such an odd, pained look on her face?

"You're a closet Bippo Bear fan and you wanted to know where I scored mine?" He tried to lighten the mood, unsettled by how tense she was.

Mary laughed casually, but it came out a bit choked and forced. "No, not at all. It's more the other end of that."

"You're morally opposed to Bippo Bears? Or uncles splurging for unwary five-year-olds?"

At that point Gina arrived to take their order. Mac ordered his usual, with ice cream, and Mary went for the triple berry. Once Gina left, Mary spread her hands on the table. "I'm trying to figure out how to explain this. I suppose you don't even have to know, but, well, I suppose someone should know. The whole Bippo Bear thing," she went on, looking supremely uncomfortable, "well, I'm partially responsible. Actually, I feel like I'm a lot responsible. I suppose that's debatable, but not really to me."

She wasn't making sense. "Mary, what are you trying to say?"

"It's what I used to do before I came here, Mac. I wrote…" she winced on the word "…I used to write jingles, and I wrote the Bippo Bear song. The reason all those kids can sing that song endlessly to their parents? That's me. The reason you felt like you had to shell out whatever it took to buy one of those? It's me. I wrote the song, I created the frenzy."

She wasn't explaining, she was confessing. She squinted her eyes shut, as if some force would come out of the blue and knock her over for her crimes. "You? You're the evil Bippo Bear mastermind? No offense, but you just don't look the type." Sitting endlessly on hold, he had imagined the guy behind Bippo Bears as a cross between Ebenezer Scrooge and the Grinch. A slimy guy in a shiny suit punching triple-digit profits into his laptop. Not a soft-spoken blonde who barely topped five and a half feet tall.

"I'm just the mastermind behind the Bippo Bear *song*." She said it as if it would brand a scarlet *B* onto her chest.

"That silly song? That incredibly annoyingly silly song? That's yours? You wrote that?" He stared at her, still trying to put the information into some kind of context that made sense. "Well, if you're working on commission, I can see how you can afford to live on what MCC can afford to pay you." He regretted that remark the minute it left his mouth. That was a lousy thing to say. No one held a gun to your head to make you plunk down that money for that bear, Mac. You're to blame for how much you spent, not her. He'd said something wounding at a vulnerable moment. He'd done that more than once now, hadn't he? What is it with this woman that brings out the worst in me?

"I'm not particularly proud of myself, if it makes you feel any better." Her voice sounded definitely hurt. "Yes, I seem to be able to write tunes that stick in people's heads. I'm very good at it. And before...before I woke up to faith, as I like to put it...it didn't bother me at all, because I made a lot of money in music, which was something I loved. I had the kind of job other people dreamed about. I could do as much or as little work for the ad agency as I wanted, depending on my schedule with the orchestra. I could support myself as a musician, and not a lot of people can say that."

"I suppose that is an accomplishment. Sounds like a pretty sweet deal."

"Like most sweet deals, it tends to get to you after a while." The pie arrived, providing irony and a bit of a break in the serious nature of the conversation. Mac was having a serious conversation about Bippo Bears. It was just too odd. "Well, at least it got to me," she went on. "The funny thing is, once I realized how big Bippo Bears were going to be, once I realized what was going on and what I was helping to create, I couldn't stomach it anymore. Now that I've learned what Christmas is supposed to be about, I couldn't be part of the *buy this, buy that, put yourself in debt to give your kids ten seconds of hollow bliss* machine. That sounds simplistic, but it was like I was choking on my own work. I was getting physically ill. I couldn't sleep at night. I'd cringe anytime I heard the commercial—I still do. And so while it wasn't exactly a brilliant plan, the best thing I could do was just leave."

Mac felt like whacking his forehead. "And since you've met me, I've spent a good chunk of time railing against the sinister fiends who made little kids want

Bippo Bears. Mighty hospitable of me. Look, I'm sorry. If I'd have known…"

"You'd what?"

She had him there. "Well, I might have kept my mouth shut for starters."

She eyed him, a little bit of that spine he saw over the potluck coming back. "You don't strike me as the kind of guy who holds back an opinion on anything."

"Still, I might have used nicer adjectives than 'idiotic.' You were just doing your job. You were hired to sell bears, and believe me, you're selling bears. Your little song just duped me out of a hundred and fifty dollars plus shipping and handling."

She pointed at him with her fork. "See? That's *just* why I left. Yes, I was doing my job, and people pay lip service to the idea at first, but then there comes some remark about how my song took their money. You did it yourself." Mary speared her pie with a little too much emphasis. "Most people draw a very thin line between advertising and manipulation, and I'll tell you, it's no fun living on the dark side of that line. That's why I don't tell people. That's why I had to get away." She shook her head. "The funniest thing of all is that I came to Middleburg to find someplace where all the commercialism and fighting over Christmas *didn't* reach. And I found you forking more than one hundred dollars for a Bippo Bear and a town fighting over mayors. Where's this simple life I keep reading about?"

Mac felt stung by the lecture, mostly because she was dead on. He could have easily said no to Robby's nonstop requests for the bear. Probably should have. And yet he had attached *her* talent to *his* weakness— personally—the moment he'd found out. Suddenly, her former employment didn't seem such a dumb secret to keep after all. "Simple life? Here in Middleburg? No such thing. We like to make everything complicated." He looked at her. "Why tell me? Couldn't have been my overwhelming sensitivity. I know I wouldn't have told me if I were in your shoes."

She seemed stumped by the question. "Actually, I'm not sure. Probably just to get you to stop complaining about it, I suppose. You and I do seem to have a talent for stomping on each other's last nerve." She dragged her fork through the huge dollop of whipped cream Gina had doused onto her pie. "You paid *how much* for that bear?"

"A hundred and fifty plus shipping and handling." He'd felt pained but victorious when he'd secured the bear. Now he just felt conned and stupid.

She managed a smile. "Thornton lives for people like you."

"Thornton?"

"My boss. My *ex*-boss, that is. Thornton hired me out of grad school, thinking he could get a few catchy tunes out of a music major. I can blame him for discovering my dark talent for earworms."

"Earworms? Sounds gross."

"Earworms are those tunes you can't get out of your head. Jingles, television show themes, that sort of thing. They're an incredibly powerful marketing tool because you can't get rid of them even when you want to." She pointed to herself. "And that, sir, is what I seem to be able to do better than anyone in the Midwest." Her hands dropped, and her shoulders with them. This really did bug her. She definitely classified this as a curse rather than a talent.

Suddenly he had to know. "What else have you done? Are there others I would know?"

She blushed. Actually turned crimson right there in front of him. And he realized what a mean question that was. "I mean, you don't actually have to tell me," he backpedaled. "It's your business."

She looked down at her pie for a moment, then said quietly, "Jones Bars."

"The ice cream bar?" That song had been so effective ice cream trucks had taken it up as the tune they played as they came down the street. "The ice cream truck song? Whoa, I know parents who would do you bodily harm."

She grimaced. "I got a double Christmas bonus for that one. And a weekend in Bermuda. And then there's Paulie's Pizza."

Even his nephew could sing the Paulie's Pizza song. And yes, it was annoying. But, like she said, almost anyone could dial the Paulie's Pizza 1-800 number from memory.

"See?" she said with a lopsided, bittersweet grin, "I've got a résumé that would make your ears burn."

Chapter Nine

She'd told him. She'd actually told someone and she hadn't spontaneously combusted. Nor, evidently, had he. He was a long way from impressed, and he definitely looked at her a bit sideways, but he hadn't up and left the room. And he had a one-hundred-and-fifty-dollar reason to hate her now that he knew. While Mary could argue with herself that this didn't rank very high on the scale of possible human secrets, she still felt like a thousand pounds had just flown off her shoulders. "I'm not proud of what I did," she admitted. "Actually, I was proud of it back then, but now it just feels, well, hollow. A lousy use of whatever talent God chose to give me." She dared to look him in the eye. "I won three awards for the pizza song, you know. And, according to Thornton, the Bippo Bear jingle has already been nominated twice. I could write my own ticket with Thornton if I wanted to go back. *If*."

"But you don't, do you?" Mac leaned back in the booth. "Mary Thorpe, jingle star. Man, I'm not sure I could walk away from all that money and attention. I've been trying to figure out how someone like you landed someplace like this, but it sort of makes sense now." He shook his head. "Bippo Bears aren't cute, you know. They're all bug-eyed and smiley-faced." He made a disturbingly accurate impersonation of the distinctive Bippo Bear face. "No offense."

She managed a laugh. She hadn't yet been able to laugh about her former job. The last day had been so horrible with Thornton. You'd have thought he'd never lost an employee before, the way he had ranted and raved. Granted, she hadn't exactly given two weeks' notice, but this wasn't a situation that fell within the confines of normal personnel policies. Those final days, when the store orders came flooding in for Bippo Bears and the manufacturer's rep had taken her and Thornton to lunch at a very ritzy restaurant and crowed about how much money they were going to make, how desperate kids would be to get their hands on Bippo Bears, Mary had been unable to eat. From that lunch until the moment she typed up her résumé, she'd barely been able to keep anything down. And here she was, laughing about it over pie. If that wasn't God's grace showing up in her life, then she didn't know what was. "I can't believe I actually told you. I told myself I wouldn't tell...."

At that moment, as if by horrible design, the television behind Gina's counter kicked into a commercial for Bippo Bears. Mary felt the tune and lyrics as if they were physical blows. She closed her eyes and gripped the table. And waited. For the excruciating moment she knew would follow.

"See that?" a tiny voice from across the room said. She didn't even have to turn. She could picture the tiny, chubby hand pointing to the television while the other hand tugged insistently on Mommy's sleeve. "I want that. I really want that. I gotta have one, Mommy! I gotta!"

"You and every other little guy on the planet, sweetie," came Gina's voice. "Rare as hen's teeth, those are."

Mary felt the collar of her turtleneck sweater tighten around her throat.

"We'll see," warned whoever's Mommy, in that parental tone of voice everyone knows really means *No, but I'm not going to say no right now.*

She opened her eyes to find Mac staring at her. "Wow," he noted quietly, "that really gets to you, doesn't it?"

"I can't wait to have success in something less dastardly." Mary gulped down some coffee, feeling the warmth ease the ice-cold viselike grip that song had on her neck. "I used to love hearing my stuff on the television. Now it's just awful." She put down her mug, feeling the old anger rise up. "Did you know the company actually scans the Internet to find the highest current going price and sends out a press release? If they spent as much time and money on making more bears as they do on feeding the frenzy…" she didn't even finish the thought.

The child at the diner counter had now dissolved into a nonstop, earsplitting "I wanna Bippo Bear" whine. "Okay," he relented. "I can see why you might want to keep this under wraps."

"I did that," Mary confessed, inclining her head toward the drama playing out behind them.

"You did your job. And now you don't do that job anymore. You got a fresh start, and maybe that was the best choice to make if it bothers you so much."

* * *

Despite earlier frustrations, Mac had to consider it a pleasant evening. He'd scored his Bippo Bear—even if it had made him crazy and broke to do it—and patched things up with Mary Thorpe. Mac decided he couldn't complain.

Until his phone rang within thirty minutes of getting home.

"Hello, Ma," Mac greeted as he answered. "I got Robby his bear, so we're all set."

"Are we?" Ma asked in sugary-sweet tones. "Audrey Lupine just called to say she saw you and Mary Thorpe having a very serious conversation in quiet tones over at the diner. She's a pretty girl, Mary is. Anything you want to tell me?"

I love Middleburg, Mac thought to himself, *but then there are days where I just hate it.*

There wasn't a single empty branch on that Christmas tree. It was starting to look like a holiday catalog exploded in her living room. So when she opened her apartment door to find Emily Sorrent with three large boxes in her arms, Mary gulped. She'd thought Gil was exaggerating about Emily, but she no longer doubted the man. If she didn't think of a new target for Emily's decorating urges, she'd have trouble finding her furniture under all this.

"Emily," she began congenially as the woman deposited the boxes on her dining room table. "You've done enough. Really. More than enough."

"Oh, no, it's nothing," Emily countered, pulling the top off the first box. "Just a bit more extra stuff I've got."

"I don't think my apartment can hold much more. Look around. I think I've got more decorations than furniture."

Emily actually looked around. Mary willed her to see the abundance that was bordering on ostentation. Would it be rude to call for a yuletide intervention? "Well, I suppose there's a lot in here already, isn't there?"

Mary offered the warmest smile she could produce. "How about we have a cup of tea instead of breaking out more mistletoe? I don't need another decoration, Emily, but I'd love your company." She pulled Emily toward the kitchen.

"I decorated the church yesterday, and I had this left over. I just hated to see it go to waste."

"I'm sure you'll find a place for it. And the church looks better than most of the department stores I've seen in Chicago. I'd say you've done more than your share."

Emily settled herself into one of Mary's chairs. "I guess you're right. Gil says I should rest more than I do. But this Christmas, I just seem to be in constant decorating mode. Listen," she said, shifting a bit in her chair. "Can you tell me how you cast the drama?"

"How?"

"You know, how you decided which person should get which part."

There wasn't much to say. In fact, Mary was a bit embarrassed by her casting method. "Well, actually, I just laid the script out on my table and said a prayer each time I looked over the list. I started with the smaller parts first, and then divvied the larger parts up from a list of people Pastor Dave thought would do a good job." She'd gotten a weird feeling when she'd cast Emily as Mary, but she didn't think that was the sort of thing

302	*Bluegrass Christmas*

she ought to share. "I just made it up as I went along, I suppose."

Emily was paying very close attention to her process. "That's how you did it? You prayed?"

Now Mary felt embarrassed. It felt important to pray over her decisions when she'd made them, but now, saying it out loud, it felt rather foolish. "Well, I tried to think things through from a practical standpoint, too. I knew Mac and Howard would need big roles based on the whole reason we were doing the drama."

"But me, you prayed before you cast me?" There was something behind Emily's questions, and Mary couldn't decipher if it was a good something or a bad something. "Really?"

"Emily, are you uncomfortable with being Mary? It's not too late to change it if you feel like you'd rather not." It was a lie—it'd be a huge problem, but the look in Emily's eyes was making her panic. Emily had looked ecstatic when she'd first found out she'd be playing Mary, which made the woman's current questioning all the more baffling.

"No, I'm really glad to be Mary."

"Is something wrong?"

"No, not at all. I just wanted to be sure before I told you."

"Told me what?"

"Why it means so much to me that you cast me as Mary. And especially if prayer was involved in your casting, because that just confirms it." Emily wasn't making a whole lot of sense, until Mary watched her hand steal protectively across her abdomen, when it suddenly made a whole lot of sense. Within seconds,

Mary could easily guess what news was coming next. "I'm pregnant," Emily confided.

"That's wonderful news," Mary offered. She couldn't help but smile—the expression on Emily's face rivaled any of the twinkling lights she'd loaded onto Mary's tree.

"It's been a bit tricky, and we weren't sure when to tell everyone. I've been bursting with the news, but the doctors told us to be cautious for another couple of weeks. And then, when I could barely stand it a moment longer, you told me I'd be playing the part of Mary. I knew it was God's way of telling me everything would be okay."

It was a disorienting combination of wonderful and awful. While it felt amazing to be used by God in such an extraordinary way, Mary felt like far too much was now riding on a very minor decision. Based on Dave's information, there hadn't been that many women to play Mary—many of the other women who were suited for the role were being used in other aspects of the drama. Emily could easily be reading far too much into a decision that wasn't intended to be the portent of anything. *Oh, Lord, is this right?* "Do you think God really works that way? I mean, I know I'm new to this faith business, but…"

"I'm not saying that this makes everything fine— there's still a lot Gil and I will have to face. But yes, I do think God answers prayers for comfort, and that's what I was praying for. What I was most upset about, funny enough, was not being able to be publicly pregnant, if that makes any sense. I've waited so long to be a mom. Gil is my second husband. My first husband died before we could start a family. So when we found out, I was just exploding with the need to tell everyone, even though the doctors told us to take it slow. I wasn't coping very well. If you can believe it, I was actually more…enthusiastic…about the holiday decorating at the farm."

"Oh," said Mary, "I can believe it."

"I prayed that God would send me a way to cope with not being able to shout it from the rooftops. This is just what I needed." She looked up sheepishly. "My goodness, that sounds crazy when I hear myself say it. You must think I'm insane."

Mary could only smile. "I think you're a woman who is just very, very happy to be pregnant. And I suppose if I believe God can work through anybody, then I'd better believe God can choose to work through me. Although I'm a bit freaked out, if you really want to know. It explains a lot. I mean, in a good way. I mean…"

"It's okay. Gil's hinted that I went a bit overboard in the holiday cheer department." She paused, looking around the apartment. "I suppose I did, didn't I?"

"It's kind of nice. I feel so welcomed. I was worried I'd feel sad, that my apartment would feel empty."

Emily broke into a chuckle. "No chance of that with me around. I promise I'll take it down a notch from here on in, okay?"

He'd found her.

Mary suspected—knew down deep somewhere—that Thornton wouldn't take her exit lying down. He was a controlling sort of man, incensed when he didn't get the last word, and she'd certainly set her resignation to be just that. Despite the P.O. box and forwarding addresses she'd arranged with her parents, someone as skilled and determined as Thornton Maxwell would find a way. The fact that he'd contacted her, without her parents knowing he'd located her, just proved his ability to deceive.

And, just like Thornton would do, he'd been anything but direct. The final paycheck had arrived in an ordinary fashion, like any number of Christmas cards or electric bills mailed daily around the country.

It was her final paycheck. Hand-signed by Thornton, and mailed here, even though she'd not given the agency her Middleburg address. She'd purposely, carefully made sure the agency only had her parents' address in Illinois, and her parents forwarded her mail to a P.O. box, but Thornton had her *actual* street address. The envelope held only a check—no written message. Then again, it didn't need to. Without a word, without anything, Thornton's delivered check broadcast, "I found you."

Mary sank down on the step, too stunned to finish the flight of stairs to her apartment. He'd gone looking for her, which meant he still wanted her back, and Thornton was a man used to getting what he wanted. A man who'd built an empire on his persuasive abilities. She could imagine the lengths Thornton would go to, the incentives he would dangle, the pressure he'd apply. It was why she'd made the drastic step of running away—she wasn't sure she could withstand the full-force of the former power and money.

She set the letter down while her head sank back against the wall.

Jesus, stay beside me. You gave me the strength to walk away from all that once. Am I strong enough to keep away? Especially if it's Thornton doing the chas-

ing? Her mind produced the verses of "O Come, O Come, Emmanuel" as if pulling them out of the fog of her memory. Emmanuel. God with us.

"Hey, are you okay?" Mary opened her eyes to find Mac staring at her from the bottom of the stairs. After a second, he dropped his briefcase at the landing and walked up the half a dozen stairs to where she lay slumped against the wall. "You are definitely not okay. Not even close." He noticed the pile of mail on the step below her. "Nasty Christmas card or something?"

"Sort of." She couldn't manage much more than that.

He looked at her. She felt like a good half of the time they'd ever spent together had been comprised of him looking baffled at her. "Should I check to see if something's ticking?"

"A bomb? Too blunt for Thornton. He's a hunter. A stalker. Explosions would be too quick and easy."

"Thornton. Your ex-boss sent you something?" He found the envelope on the top of the pile and inspected it. "Looks like an ordinary check to me."

"Exactly. That's how I know it's from Thornton. He'd know I'd know."

"I'm not getting it. Why *shouldn't* you get your final paychecks from your previous job?"

"I should, just not *here*. They don't have this address. I made *sure* they didn't have this address. All my mail from the agency is supposed to go to my parents in Illinois." Mary grimaced. "He found me."

"This guy sounds truly creepy."

"Thornton goes beyond creepy."

Mac set the envelope back down. "Look, I don't know much about the whole situation other than the little bit you've told me, but do you think you might be reading too much into this?"

A huge part of her wanted to believe him. To give Thornton the benefit of the doubt and to believe she'd really made the clean getaway she planned. "That'd be nice, wouldn't it?"

"Has this guy threatened you, Mary?" His voice was low and sharp. Mac's eyes darkened to an intense glare as he sat back against the wall, his long legs extended across the narrow stairway. He'd formed a barrier between her and the door, protective, even though she was sure he hadn't consciously done so.

"Thornton threatens everybody. He's one of those people who's a powerful friend but a more powerful enemy. But if you mean has he threatened me personally, physically, no. Again, that'd be too blunt for Thornton. That," she said, pointing to the check, "is his way of letting me know that he knows where I am." She tried to say it calmly, but it came out as the menace it was.

Mac was surprised at the worry in her eyes. She had an unsteady quality to her voice she probably thought she was hiding, but her body language was bordering on fear. "I think I get it now. You'd hoped to hide from this guy. Escape from the old Mary and her job out here in the middle of nowhere. Well, it explains a lot." He paused for a moment. "I'm not sure it's any of my business, but you look anything but calm. Are things more… personal than that between you and your old boss?"

"No. Well, he took my leaving very personally, but it's not like you think. It's just that no one walks out on Thornton Maxwell. He'd fire anyone in a heartbeat, but you don't quit until he tells you to. He doesn't want me back because he wants me, he wants me back because that way he wins." She poked at the offending check with a cautious finger. "And Thornton will do just about anything to win."

"If this guy worries you so much, don't you think maybe you need to talk to the police?"

She forced out a tight laugh. "Oh, that'd do wonders for my entrance into the community, don't you think? 'New drama director reveals own stalker.' Harbinger of the Bippo Bear boogeyman—that's just the first impression I'd want to make."

"You didn't choose this. People here wouldn't hold that against you." He tried to crack a joke to ease the tension. "As for the bear song, I can't make promises, but no one in Middleburg would hold a jerk like Thornton against you."

"He'd never come here." It was the most unconvincing statement Mac had ever heard. She didn't believe that— not for a second—and it came through in every word.

He moved a few inches closer to her on the stairs. "Mary," he said, making his voice as gentle as he knew how, "would he hurt you?"

"No," she replied far too quickly. When his gaze held her eyes for a moment, she said "Not really." She broke away from his gaze and looked down. "I don't know."

That made Mac's stomach ignite. "Over a job? Over stuffed bears? What kind of a monster is this guy?"

"His job is his life. The Bippo Bear account was his personal coup, and he thinks he needs me to keep it. I just figured he'd move onto his next protégé when he got tired of me. But then the campaigns became successful, and Thornton likes success enough to make very sure he stays successful. He told me I could never leave, never work for anyone else but him, and like I said, you don't 'just say no' to Thornton Maxwell."

Watch me, Mac thought. It struck him, as she pulled her knees up to hug them to her chest, that it made perfect sense now why she'd want to surround herself with people on Christmas Eve. If Thornton hadn't actually threatened her physically, he'd come mighty close. And maybe it wasn't even a conscious thought to her, maybe she really did think the potluck was a path to town unity and her fears just made the idea that more appealing. "Has he sent you anything threatening? A bear full of razor blades or something?"

"No."

"That's your money, right? You earned it?"

"Yes."

"Then cash the check. There have to be ways to get yourself over this." She needed to get into the community, get a jump start on this new life she seemed eager to build. "Like coming to Gil and Emily's on Friday night. It's going to be the Christmas party to end all Christmas parties, and you'll be surrounded by people."

"Emily's already invited me, but…"

"But nothing. You need to go. I'll even take you out there myself. Seems to me, the best defense you have against your old life is to get on with your new life and be happy."

She looked unconvinced. "I don't know." She stood up and gathered the pile of mail.

"You don't have to know," he declared, deciding not to take no for an answer. "I know. I'll pick you up at 6:30. If you own a Christmas sweater, this is the place to trot it out. You have to wear red or green or you don't get in. *Really.*"

Chapter Ten

At the sound of Mac's engine, Gil came out of the barn coiling a length of rope and grinning. "Mr. Mayor. Nice of you to drop on by. I had something to ask you after rehearsal tonight, but you beat me to the punch. What's up?"

Mac cut the engine and walked toward the barn. "A few developments you ought to know about."

"Sounds intriguing." He nodded toward the tack room in the barn, where a pair of wooden chairs sat propped up against the wall. He flicked on the lights and the little space heater, then hung the rope up on a peg, and sat down. "Let's hear it."

"Well, you know Mary Thorpe used to live in Chicago," Mac began as he sat down. "It seems her previous boss wasn't too keen on seeing her go and might be applying a lot of pressure. She's a bit of a surprise, our Mary."

"Good thing you can be there for her." Gil grinned. A wide teasing grin.

"Hey, cut that out."

"I'm just saying you always seem to be around at the

right moment. You might think God set it up or something." Gil sat back in his chair and folded his hands
behind his head in frustrating confidence. "So you like
her and you want to make sure she's okay. That's a good
thing. Civic, even." He brought his hands back down
and looked at Mac. "You do like her, don't you?"

"Depends on who you ask. If you talk to Ma, we're
all but ring shopping." Mac threw his hands up in exasperation. "Come on, Gil, you live here, you know the
rumor mill. It's impossible to see someone 'casually'
in this town. Middleburg makes a couple go from zero
to serious in under six seconds. And I'm not ready for
serious. Not with her."

"You just told me all the reasons why you *shouldn't*
like her, but that ain't answering my question, is it?"

"She's nice." Mac wanted to whack his forehead for
not being able to come up with anything more convincing than that. Gil's expression told him "nice" had
definitely not been convincing. "But that's all." Like
that helped.

Truth was, he found her more than nice. But that was
the trouble with small towns, there was no way to stay at
"nice." If he was found "out" with her alone again, the
snowball of predictions and gossip would begin rolling
and there'd be more drama than any campaign could
ever generate. Mac knew all these reasonable objec-
tions, he could recite them on command, but it hadn't
stopped him from looking up at his office ceiling instead of working for many days now.

He'd bought a jazz violin CD when he was in a
bookstore in Lexington the other day—a jazz violin
CD—just because they'd been playing it over the store
sound system and it sounded like her. Worse yet, he'd

opened it and popped it into the car stereo before he even got home.

"Forget the rumor mill," Gil advised. "You think I haven't known you long enough to pick up on it? Do you realize you've talked about her every time we've seen each other? You stare at her. It's kind of like the way you stare at a bridge that isn't working right, and that's kinda weird when you think about it, but you definitely stare. She gets to you. I think that's the only way you'd ever parade onstage in a blue bathrobe. Take a chance and bring her to the party Friday."

"Um… I already asked her." Talk about the worst idea ever. Why had he gone and asked her?

"She seems *very* nice," Gil conceded, still grinning. "A little more delicate that I would have picked for you, but it seems to bring out your hero tendencies. Snake-hunter. Actor. A regular renaissance mayor."

Mac launched off his chair to pace the small room. "You can be a real jerk sometimes, you know that, Sorrent?"

"Emily says so, especially when I'm right." He motioned for Mac\to sit back down. "So she got to you. It was bound to happen sometime—why not now? You said you were feeling restless. Maybe it was more than just political unrest."

"*Why not now?* Because this is the worst time ever. She's not in the same place as me, faith-wise. And in the middle of this mayor thing? If I do bring Mary on Friday, it'll just encourage Ma. She's already more than a bit nutty about the thought of having a thirty-year-old still-bachelor son. She'd be all over this, knitting for grandbabies by Saturday morning."

"It's not like you've never dated before, Mac. You

can handle your Ma and anyone else who jumps to conclusions. Bring her Friday." His grin made Mac want to throw him in a horse stall. Headfirst.

"I have to, now. That was the stupidest thing to do. Seriously."

Gil pulled a clipboard off the tack room wall and headed for the door. "Maybe not. You're always talking about how no one in Middleburg is willing to explore the possibilities."

Mac followed, glad to know this ridiculous conversation was coming to a close. "You *want* me to date her?"

"I want you to be happy. My baby deserves a happy godfather."

"Like you've ever really cared about..." Mac stopped. "*What* did you just say?"

Gil turned with the strangest look Mac had ever seen on his face. "I said my baby deserves a happy godfather. Mayor or not, no miserable man gets to godfather my baby."

Mac picked up his jaw off the floor. "Emily's *pregnant?*"

"She is indeed."

Gil was going to be a father. The guy he'd thrown into mud puddles in second grade was going to be a father. "You're gonna be a dad."

"It generally works that way, yes."

Mac grabbed his friend and pulled him into a quick hug. Gil and Emily were going to start a family. It was one of the best shocks he'd ever had. "Congratulations. Wow. When?"

"Sometime in June. We haven't told too many people yet. Emily's had a few complications and we thought it better to keep it private for a little while longer. The

Mary role is a big deal for her, and now you know why. But you need to keep this under your hat for a while, especially on Friday. Consider it your first duty as godfather. You will, won't you?"

"Godfather? Of course. And sure, I'll keep quiet. But man, that's amazing news. Are you excited?"

Gil actually looked jittery, which was saying something on his usually stoic features. "Excited, freaked out, worried, amazed, running out of ways to cope with that herd of hormones putting up a Christmas tree in my kitchen... I'm all sorts of things. Just not sane."

His kitchen? Gil'd been married for how long and still thought of it as "his kitchen"? He could just imagine how well that was going. Gil had been surrounded by men—farmers, foremen, the teenagers and twenty-something men whose lives he had helped rebuild—just a little bit too long. Mac slapped Gil on the shoulder. "You've been raising great big kids for five years. How much harder can one tiny guy be?"

"*If* it's a guy." Gil practically gulped the sentiment.

The thought of what Gil's frilly, vintage-loving wife would do with a baby girl made Mac break into an amused grin. He imagined Gil holding a frothy bundle of pink lace in those great big farmer hands, and broke out laughing. "Now who's in more trouble? You or me?"

Pastor Dave came to Mary's office door early in the afternoon, as she was marking lighting cues on a script. The high school had lent the church two spotlights, both of which had a selection of color choices, so she had the chance to add a few small-scale special effects to her production. Now, when Mary and Joseph walked through the Bethlehem night, it could actually *look* like night onstage. Progress in inches, she thought. "Mary?" Pastor said as he knocked on the open door. He'd brought her a cup of coffee. People were always bringing each other coffee in this town.

"Oh, I could sure use that. Thanks." She rose and took the steaming mug, coming around her desk so they could sit on the pair of chairs in front. She had an office, with actual chairs, instead of her cubicle at the ad agency and her locker at the symphony hall. That felt so good.

"You're doing a great job. They can be an unruly bunch, even on their best days." He sighed. "Tonight, they may be at their worst."

Evidently the coffee was for fortification. "What's up?"

"I just got off the phone with Sandy Burnside. Evidently Mac and Howard got in a bit of a row at the dime store this afternoon. The store started offering a ten percent discount to Epson supporters. Which made the car wash across the street offer a ten percent discount to MacCarthy voters. Mac and Howard ended up shouting at each other with the store owners in the middle of the street until a policeman had to ask everyone to leave. Quite a row, evidently. They've been civil so far, but things are clearly getting out of hand." He shook his head. "I don't know what's gotten into folks."

Mary had visions of a cowboy saloon fight, with dusty buckaroos being thrown out swinging shutter doors by a star-studded sheriff. "Voting discounts? That's ridiculous."

"Once people start taking sides, it doesn't take much to get things out of hand." He set his coffee down. "They'll show up tonight, but they'll be prickly, that's for sure. You have your work cut out for you."

"Oh, boy," she murmured over a gulp of her coffee.

"It's tough." Dave nodded. "But this is *exactly* why you're here. Folks need a place to put aside their differences for a common goal." He rose from the chair. "You just hang onto the reins tonight, and don't let 'em start up again. Forewarned is forearmed."

"Well, tonight's the night they all have to have their lines memorized. Fortunately, that tends to put people in their place very quickly."

"You want me to come? Watch over things?"

While it was an attractive idea, Mary thought it best to hold onto what little ground she had. "Well, keep your cell phone on and I'll have you on my speed dial."

Pastor Dave laughed. "Pastoral 9-1-1? Good enough. Sandy'll be there, too, and Gil, and those two could wrangle just about anyone if you need backup."

"Sounds like I'll need every heavenly host I can get my hands on."

Mary did keep them in line, but only barely. The tension in the church hall was thick enough to cut with a hatchet, much less a knife. Howard said nothing all evening—except his lines of course, and bristled with annoyance and discomfort. Mostly he just frowned and made a point of sitting as physically far from Mac as possible.

Mac, on the other hand, was openly prickly. More than once she'd had to "shush" him from a cutting comment or other whispered comeback to something someone else said. She'd spent half the rehearsal wondering whether or not to follow the policeman's lead and just dismiss the two, but it was equally clear that dozens of other people would take up the argument in their absence. She pretended she hadn't heard about the fiasco, hoping a feigned ignorance would save her from having to take sides.

More spiritually mature, hm? Who'd say that based on how you just behaved tonight?

Mac hung back after rehearsal, recognizing how he'd behaved and wanting to apologize for the jerk he'd been this evening. Actually, he'd been a jerk most of the day. With the discount stunt, Mac felt like Howard's supporters were out to get him, and it was pretty clear Howard felt equally threatened. How had it eroded into this bickering? Mac didn't run to create scenes like this, and he doubted Howard found them useful, either. He did his best to put it behind him for the rehearsal, but he hadn't done a very good job.

Mary wasn't exactly scowling when she gathered up her coat, but she was close. "Are you two going to be able to get this under control?" she asked in a tone that was way too teacher-ish.

"I'm sorry," Mac said in a tone that was way too much like a third-grade ruffian. "Things got out of hand today."

"You can say that again. I'm glad Pastor Dave warned me, or I'd have been blindsided."

Great. Pastor Dave had found it necessary to warn her. It was the grown-up version of having the principal send a note home to your mother. He pushed the wave of annoyance back down into his gut and deliberately unclenched his fists as he pulled open the church door for her. "You didn't deserve to get pulled into this."

She looked at him. "Actually, when you think about it, maybe I did. I'm supposed to be the distraction from all that. It'd be foolish to think it wouldn't find its way into rehearsal now and then. It's actually kind of amusing, from where I sit anyway. Discounts. You all are acting like children. Stomping and snorting around each other like angry bulls."

"No cow metaphors, please, this is horse country."

She laughed. "Actually, when Pastor Dave told me the police broke up your fighting in the street, that's just what I pictured. The whole cowboy-burst-through-the-swinging-doors-of-the-saloon thing. So is that a cow metaphor, or a horse metaphor?"

That made him laugh. "That question doesn't even merit an answer." The western-movie vision hit him anyway: him standing in a dusty alley, hand twitching over his holster, ready to shoot it out with Howard at the O.K. Corral. He laughed harder.

"That's better." She pulled on her gloves and they walked in silence past the huge lit Christmas tree in the park. After a pause, she asked "Is it worth it? All this bickering?"

"You mean am I sorry I ran? No." He tucked his own hands into his pockets; the evening had turned cold and damp. "I'm sorry it gets messy like that, but this is a small town and people are all up in each other's business all the time here. If we cut out just because we argued, we'd never do anything. Howard and I will be fine after this is over." He turned to look at her. "Maybe not *right* after all this is over, but fine eventually."

"I find that hard to believe. Isn't this the part of the country where families feud for generations? Hatfields and McCoys and all that?"

"Oh, please. A woman as smart as you should know better than to buy into a stereotype like that. Short of the occasional 'y'all,' have you seen anything that would make you believe that?"

A wry grin crept across her face. "Were you in the same church I was tonight?"

"Okay, above and beyond the normal human bickering factor."

The grin didn't let up. She was sparring with him, and he was enjoying it. "Is there a normal human bickering factor?"

Mac shrugged deeper into his coat, pretending at an annoyance he no longer felt. "I thought we were discussing my call to civil service."

She mimicked his formality, the grin now a full-fledged smile. "Oh, yes, of course. Expound, please."

That made him raise an eyebrow. "Expound? Quite a 'hundred-dollar word' as Sandy would say."

"I do have an advanced education. I'm only two years and a eighty-page thesis away from a doctorate."

He chuckled. "And you write jingles. *Wrote* jingles. Or will you continue to sell blue bears on the side? I doubt the Christmas Drama Coordinator pays much of a living wage."

Now she played at annoyance. It satisfied him, on some level, that they'd reached the ability to joke—even lightly—about Bippo Bears. His dad always said you never really conquered something until you could laugh at it. "I believe we were discussing your call to civil service."

He nodded. "And I can't miss my chance to expound now, can I?" They stopped to admire a shop window done up for the holiday, all full of snow globes and an elegant crèche.

"Howard's missing the point on too many things.

Things that are going to be crucial for Middleburg in the next couple of years. We need more compromises if we're going to survive. Howard thinks the way to stay charming and quaint is to make sure nothing changes. I think Middleburg can keep what makes it Middleburg and still walk into the future. It's 'change or die' these days, and I don't want to see my town die. A change of mayor, or even just the *idea* of a choice of mayor, is a good place to start." He shrugged his shoulders, aware that he'd given her quite a speech. "I'll get off my soapbox now," he said, motioning for them to continue walking. "But I've got a question for you first."

Chapter Eleven

Mary wasn't sure what question Mac had in mind. "Okay," she said a bit warily. She made herself promise to answer, even if it felt like tiptoeing out onto thin ice.

"Why are you alone at Christmas? I know you have parents and a brother and his wife, you must have had other places you could have gone for the holidays than to come here where you didn't know anyone."

She felt her spine straighten, her defenses rise. "What makes you think I'll be alone at Christmas?"

"I don't think you'd be pushing so hard for the pot-luck if you had somewhere else to be."

Her first thought was that he was shooting holes in her reasoning, knocking down her plan to get the town together on Christmas Eve. When she looked at him, however, she realized it was a genuine question.

Tell him, she told herself. It's no secret. Still, it felt like she was letting out private information she wasn't quite ready to share. "My parents were planning to come at first. But my brother hasn't been well. They called just after I took this job and asked if it would be okay with me if they spent the holidays with my brother since he needs the help. They invited me to come out, offered to pay my plane ticket to fly in on Christmas Day even though I can afford my own airfare. I almost did, but then it just seemed to me that maybe here was the best place for me to be after all."

"Why?"

Mary wasn't sure she was ready to get into this with him. He wasn't prying, he just didn't realize how personal a question that was. "It's complicated," she answered, just to buy herself a moment to think. "I haven't been a Christian for very long. I mean I always believed, my parents took me to church every once in a while, but it was never anything real. Anything personal or meaningful. When you work in retail advertising and in music, Christmas is crunch season. You're working long hours, and almost every working musician I know has a job on Christmas Eve or Christmas Day if not both. 'Christmas is a music holiday, but it's not a holiday for musicians,' my college professor would say."

"I suppose you're right," Mac said thoughtfully. "Never thought about it that way before, but it's true."

"Last Christmas, it just struck me how empty it all was. The sales figures, the concerts, the drinking and hard partying. It was like we were all going out of our way to have fun just to convince ourselves we weren't missing out on anything. Thornton used to proclaim 'We make Christmas.' Last year I realized I didn't want to make Christmas, I wanted to *have* Christmas. Or what was *behind* Christmas."

"Meaning Christ?"

"Yeah, although I didn't know it at first. It was like I was gravitating toward church, being pulled in to places and people who seemed to have whatever it was that was supposed to be behind Christmas. And when it all finally clicked, when it fell into place and I realized that I needed Christ, needed that faith, then everything I did before seemed so...pointless. Hollow." She allowed herself to look at him, to gauge whether or not her poor explanation was making any sense. "I'm not very good at explaining it."

"No," he responded more warmly than she would have expected. Certainly more warmly than her parents had reacted. "I get it," he agreed. "You didn't need just a minor alteration, you needed a clean break, a major overhaul. To go somewhere completely new and different. I get that."

"I'm glad somebody does." She tried to laugh, but it didn't quite work.

"I take it your mom and dad aren't exactly thrilled with your choice?"

"They paid a lot of money for my education. This feels like a huge step backward for them, and they don't understand why I'm leaving a lucrative career for a 'Podunk part-time job.'"

They'd reached his office and her apartment, and she found herself sorry this conversation had to end just when it had gotten started. It felt enormously satisfying to find someone else who understood why she'd turned her life upside down.

He stood in the doorway while she got out her keys. "Faith rarely makes sense to folks who don't have it. If you haven't figured that out yet, you will. God asks us to do things that don't follow logic."

"Like an unheard-of campaign for mayor?"

"Yeah." He laughed. "Just like that." He stuffed his hands in his pockets and took a step back as her key turned the lock. "You keep at it, Mary Thorpe. Middleburg's a good place to launch a fresh start. You might do okay here."

"You think?"

There was a look in his eye, a split second of carefully guarded affection, that tripped up her pulse before she could reason it away.

"Yeah," he said. "I think. Don't let that fool Thornton take that away."

The mention of Thornton's name sucked the warmth out of the air. It struck her that she was going upstairs to an empty apartment, and for a moment she felt the urge to ask Mac to stay and talk awhile. Which was a really bad idea. Before she could stop herself, she heard herself ask, "We're going Friday to Gil and Emily's, right?"

"Sure." Mac smiled, nodded and hit some button on his key chain that turned on his zippy orange sports car without him even being inside the thing. He smirked as behind him in the parking space outside his office, the coupe's lights and engine roared to life.

"You're a show-off," she teased him.

"Guilty," he said as he turned and opened the car door. "Curly had to learn it somewhere."

Friday night, Mac was nervous. Actually nervous. He couldn't remember the last time he'd felt nervous about a woman, which made it worse. He felt an attraction to her, true, but also wanted to protect her from the small-town talk that would surely be the result of their appearance tonight. Even though the threat of gossip wouldn't have bugged him before, he felt differently about subjecting Mary to any of it. He wanted tonight to be about all the good things a small town could be.

To give her a shred of that old-fashioned Christmas she seemed to want so badly. After all, she was new to her faith and this Christmas would be special for her. Mac had to tread carefully, though. If she was so drawn to old-fashioned charm, she was probably the kind of woman eager to settle down—and he was not that kind of man. And this was feeling a little too much like that kind of date.

She was buttoning up her jacket as she came down the stairs, and he caught a glimpse of her pale neck above a mint-green sweater. The sweater was the fuzzy kind, with little silver sparkles woven into it. It looked elegant, but festive, and it made the creamy-white-blonde of her hair nearly glow. She'd put on lipstick and wore little sparkly snowflake earrings that kept absconding with his attention even when he tried to look elsewhere.

She caught him looking at her and blushed. "You said we had to wear red or green. This was the closest thing to Christmas green I had."

"It's fine," he said earnestly. She did look fine, very fine. He opened the car door and let her step in.

"What do you think?" he asked as he slid into the driver's seat. Even parked, a Nissan 350Z was an impressive little roadster, and he knew it.

She grinned. "Very snazzy. It suits you. You don't strike me as the truck type, anyway."

"Oh, I own one, back at the house. For yard stuff and all." He patted the dash of the two-seater convertible with admiration. "You'd never catch me loading bags of mulch into this baby."

She laughed and looked around. "They wouldn't fit anyway."

"It's more fun with the top down, but we'd freeze."

"I'll wait till spring, thanks."

They made small talk for the short drive out to Gil's farm, commenting on the blanket of Christmas lights Emily had set up outside. He'd seen the inside yesterday, and it rivaled a department store window. Emily had claimed she wasn't half done, and it already had twice the decorations he'd seen on any other home. It was going to be fun watching Mary take it all in.

It was. "Wow," she noted, accepting a cup of spiced cider after they'd done a quick tour of the house. "Gil wasn't kidding."

Mac could barely contain his laughter when Gil, man of the daily flannel shirt, appeared in a red striped sweater. Sure he couldn't say anything without cracking up, Mac just gave Gil a sharp look and a nod, to which Gil raised an eyebrow that broadcast, "You wanna make something of it?" The image of Gil making goo-goo faces at an infant invaded his brain with a shock. Gil's going to be a father. *The world is shifting, Lord.*

"Emily's gone bananas," Gil muttered. "Each horse has its own wreath up on the stalls. She gave the guys Santa hats to wear, but they refused. The horses have their own tree, for crying out loud."

"This I gotta see," Mac declared, nodding in the direction of the barn behind the house. "Want to come?"

"You two go," Gil declined. "I'd best stay with Emily before she starts hanging mistletoe everywhere. That woman's dangerous in her condition."

Mary laughed and without thinking, Mac took her hand and led her to the back door, where he grabbed a thick red blanket off a bench and wrapped it around her as they dashed across the yard to the horse barn.

"Oh, my," Mary observed, pulling the blanket closer as they walked down the aisle separating the horse stalls in Gil's barn. Sure enough, each stall had its own wreath, and each wreath had the horse's name spelled out in glitter on a red velvet bow. "He wasn't kidding."

Mac couldn't help but laugh. Gil must be reaching the edge of his endurance with all of Emily's decorations. "That woman takes 'deck the halls' a bit too seriously."

Mary touched one of the wreaths. "Romeo. Lady Macbeth. All the horses have names from Shakespeare."

"Yep. For all his rough exterior, Gil's a well-educated guy. Both book smarts and the school of hard knocks. I'm glad to see him so happy."

"They are, aren't they? Emily's so excited to be expecting."

"I'm the godfather, you know. Gil asked me the other day." He was busting-his-buttons proud but since they hadn't revealed the pregnancy to anyone, he'd had to keep it to himself. She knew, though, so he was glad to be able to talk about it to someone.

"In deference to your humble spirit, no doubt," she teased, her blue eyes glinting under that fringe of bangs. "Or is it to curry political favor with the next mayor of Middleburg?"

"'Curry favor'?" He gave her a challenging look. "Let's put those hundred-dollar city words of yours on a horse for ten minutes and see how well you ride." He broadened his Kentucky twang and swaggered over to her. "Don't pick a fight with a horseman in a barn unlessen you can hold your own."

"It just so happens that I can ride horses. Just the kind that go up and down on poles, that's all. I have also ridden lions and unicorns, for that matter."

There it was again. A glimpse of that amazing spunk. What had beaten the fight out of her in Chicago? He looked at her, his engineering mind trying to solve the logical puzzle of her but getting lost in the definitely illogical allure of her eyes. The way she tucked her hair behind her ears. He wondered if that freshness, that sense of newness in her expression, was there for him when he first came to faith. It seemed almost too long ago to remember, even though it had been just under a decade. She struck him as both jaded and innocent— another illogical impression. She was a paradox, which is a very dangerous and irresistible thing to throw at an engineer.

Suddenly—and then again, maybe not so suddenly— alone in the barn seemed a dangerous and irresistible place to be with her. Mac felt them teetering on the edge of a place where they shouldn't go.

She must have felt it, too, for Mary shivered and declared, "We should get back. It's freezing out here."

They wandered in and out of the party, sometimes moving through the large farmhouse's many rooms together, other times being swept into different conversational groups. He kept "half an eye" on her as Pa always said, half listening for her voice or occasionally glancing her way to see where she was when they weren't together. Just as he expected, people were welcoming Mary warmly; she got the stuffing hugged out of her from Sandy Burnside, and Emily pulled her all around the room making introductions to any Middleburgian she hadn't yet met. He caught Mary laughing uproariously in the kitchen with Dinah and Janet one minute, and getting a demonstration of Gil's monstrous flat-screen television from one of the farm's teenage boys the next. She was fitting in just fine, looking more comfortable as the evening went on. As he took to the piano the way he always did at parties, even Howard pulled her into a song or two with no hint of the tension everyone had seen at rehearsal. For a split second, he thought he should have asked Mary to bring her violin, remembering the jazzy number he'd heard in the choir loft. She could probably pick up a bit of bluegrass twang with little or no effort and be a hit in no time.

Things seemed to be going wonderfully until the same teen burst into the living room with the television remote still in his hand. "Mr. Gil," he interrupted far too loudly, "you gotta see this. These people are nuts!"

Like everyone else within earshot, Mac followed Gil and the crowd into the den. And gulped.

There, in high-definition clarity, was a live news shot of a knockdown, drag-out fight taking place at a nearby mall. Something close to a riot had broken out at a discount chain store, and the cameras were getting spectacular shots of one man throwing punches at another man. A man who protected a Bippo Bear box behind his back. "Bippo Bear Brawl" flashed under the shot as the camera cut to a disgusted-looking newswoman. "'Tis the season," she began singing in the Bippo Bear melody, "to misbehave, even if Santa is watching." Mac silently berated the television as he scanned the crowd for Mary. "The mad craze to get Bippo Bears took a turn for the worse today," the newswoman went on, "as two men let the stress of the holiday and the craving for those stuffed blue bears get the better of them...."

She continued, but Mac didn't hear the rest of it. He

darted through the crowd gathering in Gil's den, hoping to head off Mary before she caught a glimpse of this. The brawl might serve as conversation, entertainment even, for the rest of the partygoers, but it would hurt Mary to the core.

He was too late. Just as he cleared the edge of the crowd, he saw her, standing in the hallway with a clear shot at the television, her face a mix of horror and guilt. Speeding up his steps, he caught her elbow and tried to drag her out of the den as the camera showed a close-up of the two grown men hurling insults and actual punches at each other. It was like one of those ridiculous tabloid talk shows, only it was happening less than twenty miles from where they stood. "C'mon, Mary, you don't need to see this."

"See this?" she whispered harshly, "I *did* this. Did you hear her? She was singing my song."

"There's no point in watching this." This was the excruciating moment when the crowd in the den began talking among themselves about the evils of Christmas toy marketing. He had to get her out of here—which wouldn't be hard, because she looked like she was going to bolt any minute.

"It's an abomination," Howard asserted as his voice rose above the rest while Mac pulled Mary through the hall toward the other end of the house. "Don't those toy people know better?"

"Don't those grown men know better?" came Sandy's voice in reply. "What fools put this nonsense on the television anyway?"

"Mary..." Mac began, not even sure what to say.

"Don't!" She objected sharply, putting her forehead against the hallway wall. "Don't even try to make this better. I knew I couldn't run from this. I knew I'd have to pay for what I'd done."

Mac started to say something about taking the drama a bit too far, but he bit back his comment. "You didn't do that," he argued, even though he doubted it would have any effect.

"Didn't I? My directives were to create a song kids could bug their parents with. To drive parents to the kind of shopping frenzy we just saw." She glared at him. "How can you say I didn't do that? I did *just* that."

Months of worry, and stress she hadn't even realized had built up, boiled over into an unreasonable panic that grabbed hold of Mary and wouldn't let go. "I'm sorry I ever did any of it," Mary blurted out for the hundredth time.

Mac shifted his weight. "Don't you think you're taking this a bit far?"

Easy for him to say. Mary flung one hand in the direction of the talking behind them. "People—parents—are behaving like animals and I started the feeding frenzy. They'll hate me once they know." The world worked the same everywhere. You were only as good—or as bad—as your latest accomplishment. This news would overshadow whatever brief history she'd had with these people, and parents were likely to run her out of town once they knew.

"I know. I don't hate you. The question is, do *you* hate you?"

What a pointless question. She simply scowled at him. This was not the kind of situation that could be placated by a simple "Jesus loves you." Actions—*consequences*—mattered.

"Did you tell them to behave like that? Does it say 'hit each other' anywhere in that song?"

"Don't oversimplify this. It was my job to 'create the craving' as Thornton always put it. I did my job exceptionally well, don't you think? I really should get an award for this one."

"I've got a thing for Dinah's snickerdoodles. She intentionally leaves the bakery door open when she bakes them because the smell is so good. And I get it full force, right next door. When I smell those cookies, I want 'em. Bad. But it wouldn't be Dinah's fault if I held up the bakery to get them."

"It's not the same." Why was he trying to reason with her?

"Of course it's the same. You just won't see it that way. Look, Howard's a good fifty pounds overweight, mostly thanks to Gina Deacon's pies. He knows it, Gina knows it. Howard doesn't hate Gina. As a matter of fact, he's mighty fond of her. They've been friends for twenty-five years." Mac leaned up along the wall beside her. "I know you feel bad about what you did, but feeling bad isn't the same thing as being guilty. You're not guilty of anything. In fact, you did something most people wouldn't have had the nerve to do—you walked away from all that. You've got this blown way out of proportion in your head. The only person who thinks Bippo Bears are your crime is *you*."

"You don't know that."

That got his dander up. "No, I *do* know that. You think this is such a black mark on you. Haven't you figured it out yet, Mary? Every one of us has got a black mark." Now it was his turn to glare at her. "It's the whole point of Christmas. Bippo Bears weren't the first Christmas craze, and they won't be the last. So how about you use all your talents—the ones you think have been so bad—to focus people on the real point of Christmas. You're doing it. You're proving to be just as good at this job as you were at the other one. People won't stop liking you if they know. Why can't you see that?"

He was Middleburg's favorite son, running for mayor, for crying out loud. A model citizen even if he did have a touch of the renegade in him. "And how on earth would you know?"

Chapter Twelve

He didn't know. Mary was right. He wouldn't know
if Middleburg was as forgiving as he said because he
hadn't given them the chance to forgive his big black
mark, either. That's why he couldn't sleep. He'd figured
out why Mary's predicament seemed to bother him so
much. Some part of him had known for months that his
"senior prank" had to come to light, he just kept convincing himself it no longer mattered.

It mattered. Now that he was running for mayor,
against Howard, it mattered more than ever.

And it mattered because he couldn't tell Mary one
thing while he was doing just the opposite. She'd asked
that he take her home almost immediately after the fiasco, saying she didn't feel well. It didn't help that everyone seemed to think they were just trying to steal a
moment alone. Every time he dismissed her fear as illogical and out of proportion, his own came barreling
back to him. God's final blow came when he opened
his Bible for guidance and found himself smack at the
verse about "the log in your own eye."

How dare he judge her for thinking her secret loomed

so gigantic and harmful that she couldn't bear the thought of telling people? Hadn't he done just the same? He'd managed to dismiss it over the years as the unfortunate centerpiece of a large collection of high school pranks—some less harmless than others, dismissing it as a "small sin." But it wasn't small, it wasn't harmless, and if he really was the kind of man who could lead Middleburg, he needed to be the kind of man who could own up to this.

And not just for him. Mac couldn't sit there and assure Mary that Middleburg wouldn't lynch her for writing the Bippo Bear song if he believed Middleburg wouldn't forgive him for what he'd done.

God had made it abundantly clear that Mary Thorpe needed to hear his secret. From him. And it couldn't stop there: Howard and all of Middleburg would have to hear it from him, as well.

I hate this character-building business, Lord, Mac complained as he wandered the church looking for her the next afternoon. *You ask such hard things.* He had to walk past the manger setting, bearing the quiet message of all the hard things God had asked of His Son, and felt his throat constrict.

He found her in the back of the sanctuary, fumbling with a very industrial-looking key chain. "Just the guy I need," she said, trying to sound natural even though there was tension between them. "I need to see if there's a prop stored upstairs. Pastor Dave said there was a huge star used in a Christmas concert a couple of years back, and he thinks it's still all the way up in the steeple."

The steeple. God had cornered him, and he knew

it. For the first time since high school, Mac felt his palms sweat.

"I've never been up in a steeple before," she continued as they started up the church stairs toward the choir loft where the hatchway to the steeple was.

"It's not very exciting," Mac stated, thinking his voice had gone up six notes from the tension. "It's not like it has windows and you can see out over the town or anything."

"You've been up there before?"

He didn't want to answer that. "I've been all over every corner of this church. When I was in the seventh grade, our youth pastor's favorite game was something called 'Sardines.'"

"Oh, I've played that. Sort of like Hide and Seek, isn't it?"

"Yeah, only more troublesome." He gestured for her to go first up the steep narrow stairway to the choir loft. He noticed, as she passed him, that her hair smelled good. He felt the hair on the back of his neck stand on end, and tried to casually wipe his palms on his pant legs as he started up the stairs behind her.

His memory of that night in the steeple loomed like a grown-up monster in the closet. As much as he didn't want to tell her about it, he knew that if he didn't, this feeling would only get worse. When she wrestled the padlock off the small hatch door, he went first, like diving into a cold lake to get the shock over with fast.

He thought it would be cold. It was December after all, and this corner of the church wasn't heated. But as an engineer, he also knew heat rose, and as one of the highest points of the church, it had collected sufficient heat to feel comfortable if not cozy. The sharp angles of the steeple formed a little cone-shaped room, dusty and dark until he reached for the cord that he knew turned on the single bare light bulb hung from the ceiling. She came up behind him, wide-eyed, turning in a small circle to take in the room. "I used to imagine secret rooms like this," she revealed in a hushed tone that tickled down his spine. "Chicago apartments are just white-walled boxes. I always wanted a top-of-the-tower secret room like this in my building."

He found the space unattractive at the moment, but hearing her voice, Mac could remember his own fascination with it when he was younger. He'd been caught up here dozens of times—sometimes getting into trouble, sometimes just being alone when everyone else was in choir practice or church banquets or whatever.

Mary begin rummaging through bins and boxes. "It's a pretty big star, it shouldn't be too hard to find."

In truth, the thing was right behind her, she just hadn't seen it. "Like that?" Managing a grin, he pointed, and she spun around to see a large silver star shape covered in shiny tin.

"That's it." She moved aside a few rolls of what looked like old wallpaper and pulled out the star. While the top was intact, the bottom point was in fact completely snapped off. It looked more like an awkward silver crown than any kind of celestial beacon. "Oh, I suppose this won't do after all." She gave a little sigh. "We can build a new one." She put the leftover star back down and then turned to sit on a wooden box. "It was still fun to discover this place."

God had pretty much handed Mac his opening. He sat down on a box across from her—although with nowhere near as much grace. The roof's sharp angles made it difficult for someone of his height to move easily. Had he really been that much shorter in high school? "Yeah," he concurred, pulling up his knees to rest his elbows on them. "I had a little too much fun up here in high school."

That brought out a scandalous look from her. "Little Joey MacCarthy stealing kisses in the church steeple?"

For a split second he thought that the perfect lie. He could just say yes, they'd laugh about the recklessness of youth and it'd be over. But it wouldn't be over. "I got into a bit more trouble than that," he began. "Mary… um… God's made it clear to me that there's something I should tell you." He shook his head, rolling his eyes. "Man, that sounds so incredibly stupid."

She looked puzzled, but she didn't say anything.

"I told you the folks in Middleburg will be all fine with your Bippo Bear thing. And they will, really. Even if twelve more fights break out in malls between now and Christmas."

She wasn't getting the connection, but then again why should she until he told her the story? "Believe it or not, I understand why you couldn't get out of Friday's party fast enough. I get it about having something you think makes you awful. Having a secret, something you're sure will brand you as the bad guy. I know yours. God seems to think you need to know mine."

"'God seems to think'?" she echoed, "What do you mean?"

"I sat there Friday night and told you that you were unreasonable about the Bippo Bear thing. And I realized—or actually, God hounded it into me—that it's not fair to tell you that, if I can't pull that off myself. Truth is, you didn't bring me up here by accident." He ran his hands through his hair, feeling unbelievably awkward. A minute ago this felt important and painful, now it just felt ugly and ridiculous. "I'm not making a good start at this, am I?"

"Keep going… I'm confused, but I'll hang on. Although, I have to say, I didn't hear God making any commands to get you in the steeple."

"God doesn't always do the burning bush thing. Sometimes, like you said, He just lines up events in a way that you know He was working. So, even when it feels dumb…which would be now, by the way…you learn to go with it." Did he really just say that? His tongue was tangled worse than his brain.

She looked around, shrugged her shoulders and offered a small smile. "So, we're here in the steeple. Go with it."

"I've lived here my whole life, you know that. And kids do stupid things in high school, even if they grow up to run for mayor." He picked up an old, dusty candlestick and began fiddling with it. "I, well, I was a high-achiever in the stupid-kid stuff. If a prank happened at Middleburg High, it was a good guess that I was involved. Mostly dumb, harmless things. Toilet papering people's houses, letting animals out of barns, flying things from flagpoles, the kind of thing Pastor Dave would call 'shenanigans.'"

"I have heard a story or two," she offered. "Mostly from your mother."

"Yeah, well, like most mothers, she only knows the half of it." He put the candlestick down. "There was one thing I did—one pretty bad thing—that no one knows about. I mean everyone knows it happened, but no one knows I did it. I think it's part of why I ran for mayor, because I needed to prove that I was better than that stupid kid now."

She brushed a blond lock off her forehead. "I guess I follow you. You're saying that telling me to stop feeling guilty about the Bippo Bear song showed you that you've never come clean about…whatever it is you did?"

It sounded so logical the way she explained it. It had mostly just bumped around in his conscience until he couldn't stand it anymore. "Yeah, I suppose that's a good way to put it."

"That doesn't make a whole lot of sense."

"I know that. Believe me, I've talked myself out of this half a dozen times, but God doesn't seem to think I get to rest until I do this." He shot her a miserable look. He was used to having the witty remark, the perfect one-liner to gloss over the tense situation, and at the moment he was a babbling fool.

"Does it have to do with this steeple?" she guessed, reaching out and touching one of the dusty beams. She was trying to help, and that only made it worse.

"Actually, it does." He was mature enough in his faith that he should not be choking on this. He should understand the concept of forgiveness, should be man enough to own up to his own mistakes. But, like her irrational fear of what folks would think of Bippo Bears, sense never did seem to enter the picture on these things. Just start, he told himself. Just tell the story. "They were building the steeple, well, building this *new* one, back when I was a senior. The old church had a small steeple, and a few years back—before they built the preschool wing and all that stuff that got hurt in the storm that brought Drew here." He was digressing, avoiding the subject. He grunted, pulling his hands down across his face, frustrated with his own ridiculous weakness when it came to this. "I'd had a huge fight with a teacher. A math teacher that told me I'd never be an engineer if I couldn't get my Algebra grade up. I knew I wanted to be an engineer then, and it just seemed to me like this guy had it out for me, that he was purposely failing me. You know the way teenagers think, all doom and drama."

"I remember high school," she said, encouraging him with her eyes.

"I didn't exactly have the longest fuse back then, and I stormed out of school. I came here to watch the construction, to prove to myself I could understand all of what they were doing. I tried to get them to let me help, but I was just a kid, and all the construction workers naturally wouldn't let me lend a hand, which just made me more angry. So I came back that night and climbed up the scaffolding into the steeple. It was May, and pretty warm, so I could sit up in the studs of it and look out over the town because the walls hadn't gone up yet."

He'd never told another living soul the next part. It felt like he had to drag the words out from somewhere deep in his gut. "I wanted to show everyone. And I got an idea. A horrible, mean, destructive idea. I'd never done anything like it before then or since. I wouldn't have even thought myself capable of something like it. But I found a hacksaw lying on the floor, and something came over me." Mac looked down, preferring not to meet her eyes. "I sawed through the studs, leaving just a bit of the wood, so that the first good wind would topple the steeple over. I didn't think about the people who could have gotten hurt or the damage that could have been done. I didn't think at all. It was a streak of mean. Pure mean. You know, I actually remember laughing when I did it. It was the worst thing. I can't even believe I was that kid. But I was."

He stopped for a moment, feeling the sensation of the secret leaving him. It was an odd combination—the lightness of release, the press of panic. He felt raw, almost wanting to wince from the feeling of being exposed, even to *one person*. How could she not be frightened of exposing herself to a *whole* town? "I hid the saw and snuck away, proud of my 'senior prank.' I went home and sat smugly in my bed, thinking I'd shown them all. I had great visions of the steeple smashing down into the church parking lot, sort of like my own private disaster movie playing in my head."

"What happened then?"

"Well, I was no idiot, and it turns out I may have botched Algebra but I knew my engineering geometry. I'd sawed in all the right places. I think I'd convinced myself that it couldn't really happen. That I'd just make the builders mad, slow them down, make them do the steeple over. But a storm did come in early the next morning. I'd picked all the right places to weaken, and the steeple came clear down off the roof. Howard had carpooled with the pastor to some weekend church function so his car was in the parking lot overnight. A large part of the steeple landed right on top of his car. The wood had smashed into enough pieces—and I'd sawed at enough odd angles—that no one ever saw the cuts I'd made. The congregation all assumed God had saved them from some horrible accident by showing them a weakness in the steeple before it was finished."

He stopped, letting the words evaporate into the air. It was out. Mac felt an excruciating tangle of emotions. "No one ever knew it was me. And I've never told anyone." For an awful second, some part of him panicked; a gut instinct of "she knows; she can expose me" that for all its irrationality felt chokingly real. He stole a glance at her, suddenly needing to know what she'd do now. She knows. It was thumping through his head like a pounding pulse. She knows. He knew that all his platitudes back at the farmhouse about how she shouldn't worry about people knowing were just that— useless phrases that belonged to logical thinking. And fear wasn't ever about logical thinking. Why doesn't she say something? The seconds seemed to stretch out endlessly.

"You've never told anyone you did this?"

It made him sound like such a moral weakling the way she said it. And that was half of the torment—not only was he owning up to the deed, but his weak inability to come forward. This was the crown jewel of "you should know better." If this was bad, what would it feel like to tell the whole town?

"You?" she said with the most awful look on her face. "You don't strike me as the kind. At least not now."

"Yeah, well, we all grow up, don't we?" The excuse he'd told himself for years now sounded worse than hollow.

"Don't you think…" she mentioned as she furrowed her eyebrows, calculating the time that had passed "… twelve years is enough time to let it all blow over? You're not fool enough to think people will hold this against you—now?" She realized her own words, echoing her fears that people would hold the Bippo Bear fiasco "against her," and an odd smile turned up one corner of her lips.

She had this enigmatic, Mona Lisa kind of smile.

He felt the primal panic in his gut go down a notch or two. Some part of him knew she wouldn't brand him as a monster, but it was one of those things he had to actually see to believe. "I don't know," he responded, exhaling. "I'm dumb enough to run for mayor against Howard Epson."

Mary hugged her knees. "What do you think Howard will do when he finds out?" She didn't even have to say, "Because you are going to tell everyone now, aren't you?"

Mac had the sensation of being bound to her in an odd unspoken way, stuck together by their mutual secrets. *Is this what You were after, Lord? Putting us together like this? She frightens me. There, I said it. She makes me feel things I'm not ready for.*

"That dumb kid—the frustrated high school boy with the mean streak—are you still him inside?"

"Of course not," he shot back. Surprised at his harsh tone, he tried to crack a joke. "I'm still dumb and frustrated, but I've grown out of my mean streak." It fell short of humor, and a long awkward silence filled the steeple. The light bulb fizzled as if it only had a few more minutes left in it. "Look," he spoke up to fill the quiet, "I have no right to tell you what to do or how to feel. But maybe this will help you figure out that your bear thing is pretty small in comparison to some of the secrets people lug around."

They sat there for a long, raw moment. Then, her whole face changed. He was sure even the light bulb flickered with the flash of her eyes. "So, tell," she said with something he could only describe as quiet certainty. "I will if you will."

It was both the best and the worst dare he'd ever had.

Chapter Thirteen

December twentieth. Christmas Eve was four days away. Mary let the glorious tones of Handel's "Messiah" seep into her spirit as she sat on her couch and watched the flames on the trio of candles she had lit. The aroma of spiced cider filled out the sensory splendor of her Sunday evening.

It was the kind of night she'd have never sought in Chicago. For a woman who'd lived alone since grad school, Mary hadn't realized how much she'd avoided being alone. She was always filling time with things—arranging events, working late, playing in ensembles or participating in work-related social events. After all, it was much easier to avoid the emptiness with such a full schedule.

You did this, Mary said within her spirit. Communication with God on such a natural, conversational level had been such a surprise to her at first. Prayers were once elaborate verbiage to be recited, now prayer had become the sharing of thoughts and feelings with her Creator. *Alone is different for me now.* She'd read somewhere about the difference between "aloneness" and "solitude," thinking it only semantics then. She understood—or was coming to understand—the blessings of solitude. *I'd still like a cat,* she mused, wondering what God would think of something so close to a joke.

What would Curly think of that? It was an amusing question, but it brought her thoughts to a far more serious topic. What about Mac? A week of solitude wouldn't untangle her thoughts on the subject of that man and what he'd revealed to her yesterday. She'd had the feeling their lives had collided since the day they met, but she was powerless to say what sense it all made. Some days it made lots of sense and she could see things they held in common. Other days it seemed like they had no business even living on the same planet, much less taking up space in the same building. *Why'd he tell me those things?* She knew way too much about him now—things no one else knew. Yet.

Is that what You planned? That bargain that jumped out of my mouth after he told me? That didn't even feel like me. That was some other woman, some braver, stronger woman. Since that moment, Mary felt as if she'd set some terrifying sequence in motion. A part of her could grasp the good that would come out of it, but most of her just couldn't get past the process that would have to come first. *I don't know how I'm going to do this, Lord. No idea at all. Is this one of those things I just have to trust to You?* "Your move, Lord," she said out loud as she blew out the candles and got ready for bed. "I know I'm stumped."

Monday was supposed to be her day off, but with the drama only days away, today would have to be a workday. Even so, she'd planned to go in at noon and work clear through the "loading in" of the set into the sanctuary space tonight. Costumes, sets, lighting and the other myriad technical aspects of a small production had to come together in the next hour. *"Well, Lord,"* Mary thought as she pulled her thick hair into a practical braid down her back, *"thank goodness it's not a musical."* She stared at the mirror, amazed at the woman of her reflection casually conversing with God. The Lord Almighty who used to be carefully contained in Sunday services now seeped effortlessly—and wonderfully—into all her days and hours. Does it ever get old? Is it always this wondrous?

Her thoughts were interrupted by a knock on the door. Evidently the sets weren't going to wait until noon—surely something had gone wrong already, even though her phone hadn't rung yet. She stood on tiptoe to peer through the peephole, expecting Pastor Dave or Janet or Emily with a list of problems.

Instead, she saw Mac, smiling sheepishly with both hands in his pockets as she opened her door. "Do you have a minute to come to my office? I think we ought to talk."

Mary had been thinking the same thing. It seemed odd and uncomfortable to leave things where they had. "Sure," she said, tucking her keys into her pocket as they walked downstairs into the foyer that joined her stairway with the cut-through entrances to both Mac's office and Dinah's bakery.

Mac opened the door to his office, and she noticed a bakery box and two cups of coffee on the small conference table in his front window. Mac motioned to a seat and walked over to pull the string on the white bakery box. "I don't like to think on an empty stomach, so I got us something Dinah called 'Yuletide Blend' and a generous supply of gingerbread beings."

"Beings?"

"Dinah doesn't do just gingerbread men. Diversity, you know." He tilted the box toward her. "There's a whole gingerbread population in there—boys, girls, cats, dogs, horses, cows, you name it."

He wasn't kidding. It was as if the woman used every cookie cutter in the bluegrass region. She picked up a gingerbread pig sporting a red and green frosting bow and couldn't help but laugh. "Only Dinah."

"She's something, that's for sure. Nothing's ever ordinary with her." Mac's phone rang, and he glanced over to its display. "Rats, I have to answer this, but it'll only take a second. Have at that pig while you're waiting. Middleburg's the only place in America where you can munch on a Christmas gingerbread pig, so enjoy it while you can."

She scanned his office while he spoke briefly on the phone and hovered over his fax machine. A collection of certificates and awards took up one wall, along with a few requisite photos of Mac and probably officials holding shovels at groundbreaking ceremonies of one sort or another. A bookshelf hosted a collection of car books—coffee table photograph books about sports cars, a row of tiny toy cars and a pair of parts catalogs. She could picture him zipping down the road in that little convertible on summer days, even though it had hardly been warm enough for a ragtop since she'd moved here.

Thornton drove a fierce-looking black Italian sports car. It would stand out on Ballad Road twice as much as

Mac's orange one, because while Mac's car looked fast and fun, Thornton's car looked like a predator.

There was another photo—several of them, actually—of Mac on a high mountaintop. The kind taken with a camera timer, showing him tanned and grinning in the middle of vast wildernesses. They'd not really talked about it, but she could easily guess that the reason Mac could be "on" so much—be so public, so talkative, so engaged—was because of the reservoir of private time and space he guarded so closely.

Thornton, on the other hand, had no wells to tend and didn't care about depth anyway. While the energy looked similar to Mac's on the outside, Thornton's vitality was a get-all-you-can-before-you-die hoarding, a frantic consumption of things and people. *Lord,* she wondered silently, *could I have seen that before You? Does faith give me new wisdom? Will You help me know what to do now?*

Mac scanned the paper, signed it and then fed it back into the machine. As the page hummed its way through the fax, Mac took a deep drink of his own cup. "Dinah says with enough sugar and caffeine you can save the world." He settled into the chair and pulled a black leather notepad in front of him. "I'm a bit weirded out after last night. I thought maybe we should talk some more. How are you? Okay?"

"Yes. And no. I mean, I'm calmer than I thought I'd be at the thought of telling people. But I'm still, well, 'weirded out' like you said."

"Look," he explained, "I meant what I said. I have no right to tell you what to do. But I do think you're underestimating Middleburg. No one's going to slam you for giving their kids a case of Bippo Bear fever."

He was awfully sure of her reception for a man in his position. "Well, I'm not as sure as you," she countered, "after all, your reaction wasn't exactly rosy."

"I'm an idiot. And that was before I knew it was you. I made fun of Drew Downing's TV show before he moved to Middleburg, too, so don't take it personally." He opened the notepad. "I wanted to show you something. A little crisis management tool I invented called the Mac Five. I think this is definitely time to fire it up."

"The Mac Five?" It sounded like a music group.

"Silly name, sound thinking. Watch." He grabbed a pen and began drawing a diagram of sorts, a circle with five circles around it. "This is the MacCarthy crisis management protocol, affectionately known as the Mac Five. Any situation has a first step to the solution, and most times it involves finding the five people who need to know first. Then, you can get them all together to figure out what to do next. Never thought I'd be using it on such a personal level...." He started to say something else, but bit his tongue.

Mary didn't know what to think. This didn't seem like the kind of situation that boiled itself down to a diagram. She didn't remember asking him for advice on how to reveal her past. Then again, she couldn't remember Mac asking before doing anything.

He raised one tawny eyebrow at her suspicious expression. "No really, hear me out. It applies. Lots of bad news gets delivered in my line of work. Things go wrong all the time. I realized last night—actually about two this morning—that this isn't much different." He wrote "Mary" in the center circle, then pushed the pen and pad across to her. "Humor me. Pick five people you think you might be able to tell. Just five."

The first person was obvious; Pastor Dave should be told. He knew a little bit about her former job, but certainly not about her particular bear-related achievements. Emily was one of the few people she'd classify as her friend in Middleburg, so she wrote her down. Drew and Janet fell easily into that group as well, especially since Drew's past as a public figure might give him particular insight into handling her problem. There, she'd filled in more than half the circles. Mac's crazy method seemed to have some value, for a thin layer of calm really was working its way into her as she wrote down names. Each circle she filled in helped her brain come up with a new idea. "Dinah and Cameron have been so nice to me, I think they'd react okay." Somehow she'd convinced herself that she didn't have friends in Middleburg yet, but that was wrong. And while it felt horrible and vulnerable to tell the whole world about her connection with Bippo Bears, she could handle these people knowing. *Maybe I could,* she realized, sitting up straighter and even reaching for another cookie. *Maybe I could tell them and it'd be all right.*

"There's something about getting it down on paper, isn't there?" He confirmed, taking the pad from her and tearing off the sheet. "I learned that from my dad my first week in business."

Mary looked at the diagram. "I don't know about the last circle. Sandy maybe?"

"Could be. I always try to think, 'Who's a stakeholder?' You know, who is or just considers themselves to have a stake in the problem."

She cringed at the thought; that reasoning led straight to Howard. He'd considered himself the catalyst that brought her here. And he was not the kind of man who cared to hear news secondhand. As judgmental as she feared he would be, she feared his reaction would be far worse if he wasn't told. With a heavy sigh, she filled in the last circle with Howard's name.

Mac let out a sigh, as well. "I had the same thought, I just didn't want to tell you what to do."

She gave him a doubtful look. "That one feels the worst."

"He might surprise you," Mac theorized, attempting a smile. "He's a man who appreciates results, and no one can argue you haven't seen spectacular results with that song."

"Spectacular?" That wasn't the word she'd have chosen.

"Well, maybe just 'big.' Plus, Howard's been known to play the indulgent grandfather a time or two. He may have even been a customer."

Mary shut her eyes against the vision of Howard glaring down a young mother over a store's last Bippo Bear. She found it disturbing to think of people she knew buying the toy. That was one of the things that had let her know it was time to leave. She used to love the idea of friends eating Jones Bars or Paulie's Pizza. She was proud of that work. She could never find it in herself to be proud of the Bippo Bear campaign. Mac, however, had not only succumbed to the campaign, he'd been a prime result—indulgent uncle shelling out far above the retail price to score a Bippo Bear. "What about you?" she asked, her pen hovering over the paper. "Since you already know, where do you go?"

He paused for a long, cumbersome moment, then slid Mary's page in front of him. Pulling another pen out of his shirt pocket, he drew a little line, sectioning off a bottom slice of the circle that held her name, so that it was sitting on the line. Under the line he wrote "Mac" in large, wide letters. "Right underneath you." He looked up at the ceiling. "Same as always."

He held her gaze for a moment, and she felt something deep down inside slide into place. Sure, his design was a useful crisis management tool, but that wasn't why she felt stronger. A quintet of circles didn't suddenly undergird her confidence. It was this man, this baffling, full-of-surprises man who dared to stick his neck out right alongside her. And, truth be told, had a far bigger secret with far darker consequences than the one she hid. "I still don't get why you're doing this," she remarked softly.

"Maybe it's just time I really *be* a leader instead of just acting like one." He kept his eyes on her. "But sometimes, God shows you something you don't want to see and somehow you know down deep what it is you need to do. It's the whole point of faith."

"It's terrifying," she confessed, wishing she could borrow some of the confidence in his eyes.

"It never stops being terrifying, you just get a little more used to it."

"You look so calm."

"I fake it well. I'm petrified on the inside."

Mary didn't think he looked it. Unnerved, maybe, just by the way he fidgeted with the pen or the way his easy smile wasn't quite as easy. But not the deer-in-headlights panic she was fighting. "Who's on your chart?" she asked before she realized what a personal question that was.

Mac leaned over and pulled out a folded piece of paper from his jeans pocket. "Funny that. It might look a bit familiar.…" He unfolded the paper to reveal five circles around his name.

With the exact same names as hers.

Without a word, Mary took the paper from him and drew a line over the top bit of the circle with his name on it. She wrote "Mary" above the line, so that his center circle matched hers. "I got your back, Mac," she volunteered, managing a small laugh.

"Technically," he corrected and chuckled, "you've got my head."

She threw him a teasing look. "Don't get technical."

Chapter Fourteen

Mary made an "appointment" to talk with Pastor Dave for the following morning, and he met her with a cup of coffee as she returned the baby Jesus doll to the manger on the set. She'd stayed up late to sew the right arm back onto the doll. Last night Tommy Lee Lockwood, determined to buck his angel-role status when it didn't entail as much high flying as he'd hoped, had flung the poor Savior clear across the sanctuary in a fit of anger. It was one of those moments where the entire room fell silent, aghast that anyone—even an angry eight-year-old—would consider catapulting the baby Jesus into the choir loft. Mac tried to lighten the moment with a joke about next year's softball team. Howard pinned Tommy Lee's already-embarrassed mother with a disgusted stare. Emily gave out an exasperated sigh loud enough to be heard in Louisville.

While surprised, Mary tried to remember all the appalling things soprano divas had done during her musical career and calmly sent Tommy Lee up into the choir loft to fetch back the Christ child. Things deteriorated when "fetching back" simply meant flinging the doll back down from the choir loft, resulting in a physical separation that gave new meaning to "the right hand of God." Even though they still had two more scenes to get through, Mary had declared the rehearsal over. It didn't exactly do wonders for her confidence regarding this meeting.

"Tough crowd last night," Pastor Dave said as he eased himself down on the edge of the stage. "You're not here to tell me you're quitting, are you?"

It hadn't even occurred to her that he might interpret her request to meet that way. "Oh, no. We might not open on Broadway, but things'll pull together in the next two nights. Although, I'd be lying if I said I wasn't really looking forward to the potluck."

"Because it means your job will be over? Well, the harder part of your job?"

"A bit," she admitted. "But I also don't think I can skip town without tasting Howard's award-winning yuletide chili."

Pastor Dave leaned in. "His wife makes it, but we'll keep that little secret between ourselves, shall we?"

Secret between ourselves? God had handed her a blatant opening for the conversation she had in mind. "Funny you should mention secrets." She took a sip of coffee, shooting up a prayer for courage. This was so ridiculously hard. It didn't help that this morning's television news had broadcast a story of some poor Texas family putting their son's Bippo Bear up for sale on the Internet because the dad had been laid off this week. She was ready to turn off the television until New Year's—facing another Bippo Bear news story felt beyond her strength. "I... I have something to tell you," she began weakly.

"I gathered that," he said without a hint of judgment or worry in his voice.

Mary tried to take courage in his gentle demeanor. If the man hadn't excommunicated Tommy Lee for dismembering baby Jesus, maybe he'd take it better than she feared. "You need to know some things about my job before I came here." Mary took a deep, shaky breath. "And the man I used to work for."

"You already told me you worked for an advertising agency. I've never met anyone before you who made television commercials. Sounds rather exciting."

Thornton Maxwell wasn't exciting, he was frightening. "Well, yes, but it's more complicated than that."

"Why don't you tell me how?" She was hedging and he knew it.

"Well, Thornton Maxwell—my former boss—is a powerful man."

Pastor Dave gave an encouraging smile and glanced upward. "My boss is powerful, too. I think we can handle Mr. Maxwell. Has he done something to you?"

He looked so kind, so calm, Mary told herself to spit it out. Just say it. It's not as bad as you think, just blurt it out. Her mouth felt like it was full of cotton; words refused to form.

Dave put down his own mug. "Mary, would it help if I told you last night isn't the worst behavior I've seen out of this feisty little flock? I'm hard to shock anymore. But by the look on your face, you're about to admit to me that you're a government spy or a jewel thief."

He was trying humor, trying to make her comfortable. It made it all the worse. This looked so easy on Mac's diagram. She rolled her eyes, disgusted with her own ridiculous fear. "I wish."

Pastor Dave stared at her. "You *wish?*"

"Those sound less embarrassing. I think you'll find this crime a bit more...well...odd."

"Crime? What's going on, Mary? Just tell me."

"I did very particular work for Maxwell. It's musical. Sort of."

"So it's a...a musical crime?"

"Yes, and no. Well, you might find a few parents looking to lynch me—especially this week."

He shot her a look that let her know she wasn't making any sense. Of course she wasn't making any sense. All of this defied any sense whatsoever. Mary wiped her hands down her jeans and took a deep breath. "You see, I'm really, really good at writing advertising music." She had to say the *J* word. This should be like a bandage—just rip it off fast and get the worst pain over. "Jingles." She blurted it out. "I write ad jingles for kids. I... I wrote the Bippo Bear jingle. Those brawling parents? I did that. Those black-market Bippo Bears going for hundreds of dollars? I did that. It's me."

There was an enormous, awful silence. "You're telling me," Pastor Dave restated slowly, "that your crime against humanity is the Bippo Bear jingle?"

"Yep. Everything bad about Christmas wrapped up into one highly effective forty-second ditty. Mine. Miserable parents and disappointed kids everywhere? My doing. They'll be flinging *me* headfirst into the choir loft when people find out."

"You think people will blame you for what's going on over these bears?"

"I *am* responsible. I created the craze." Once the admission was out, Mary felt words tumble from her mouth in a nervous gush. "Just because it was my job doesn't mean it was right. My job was to fire up a frenzy with an annoying song kids could instantly memorize and endlessly sing to their parents. Get it? My job description was to give kids the tools to make their parents miserable and desperate. And I did it really well. So well I'll probably never live it down."

Pastor Dave took a long drink of coffee. "So, you're public enemy number one this week, hm? Hated by parents around the globe? A virtual catalyst for bad behavior and everything that's wrong about Christmas?"

Weren't pastors supposed to make people feel better? She hadn't expected him to welcome the news with open arms, but Mary expected something a little more understanding than this. "Um, yeah." A lump rose up in the back of her throat. She couldn't even look him in the eye.

He's going to fire me right here, Mary realized. Two days before Christmas and I'm going to get the boot.

"You can't have this job."

Oh, Lord, You can't let him fire me. "I know. I'm sorry about everything."

"The job of taking on the sins of the world is already filled. You can't have it."

She looked at him.

"I can't vouch for how well everyone in Middleburg will take the news—I did hear someone griping at Gina Deacon's diner just the other day—but I don't think your life is in danger. And I think you've let yourself whip up a whole lot of worry over something that doesn't warrant it."

Okay, maybe it wasn't the torment she had imagined. But he was a pastor, he was bound by certain codes of loving-kindness, wasn't he? "I don't think everyone will see it your way. I heard one of those women on the television. She was calling 'those advertising lowlifes' a couple of names I won't repeat in this sanctuary."

Pastor Dave sighed. "You won't be everyone's favorite. But no one is. You opened the door to a lot of bad behavior in your former job, but it's not that different. Part of my job is to hold up a mirror to folks' bad behavior. And while I admit I get an occasional dose of 'shoot the messenger,' it happens less than you think." He leaned back against a set wall. "Would you say that Bippo Bear campaign was a wake-up call for you?"

"Definitely. That campaign—and how delighted Thornton was with it—showed me things about my job I couldn't stand anymore. Not after I came to faith. Now, I can't understand how I found it so attractive. It feels so empty…even the money. Thornton used to say 'we breed greed' and we all smirked like that was a great thing. I'm ashamed." There. She'd said it.

"You're right. You're ashamed. Shame can be one of God's most effective weapons—when only He gets to wield it. It's we down here who tend to do harm with it. Me? I'm not so sure you're the criminal you make yourself out to be." He stood up. "I, for example, am simply giving thanks to God that He's refocused your fine talents in a better direction." He extended a hand to her, winking. "Of course, I ain't shelled out big bucks for a bug-eyed blue bear, neither. Matt Lockwood might have a thing or two to say to you."

"Tommy Lee wants a Bippo Bear?"

"Tommy Lee has a little sister. One who learns fast."

"Oh." Mary almost managed a chuckle. It was as if life had loosened its choke hold on her neck. Someone knew. Two people knew, actually, and neither one of them hated her. Maybe it wasn't really as dark a secret as she had thought.

They began walking to the church offices. "Am I the only one who knows?"

"No," she admitted. "Mac found me one day after Thornton sent me a warning of sorts."

Pastor Dave stopped walking. "A warning? What do you mean?"

In all her worry over the jingle, she'd not even mentioned her former boss's nastier tendencies. "Well, as you can imagine, Thornton wasn't thrilled to lose me. People generally don't walk away from his agency— until he fires them, that is. I didn't tell him where I am now because I didn't want him to come looking for me. But my last paycheck arrived at the apartment. So he knows."

"How do you reckon he found you?"

"This is an ad exec we're talking about. The man has ways."

Pastor Dave pinched the bridge of his nose. "Mary, you should have come to me earlier with this. I don't take to the idea of you dealing with this all by yourself."

"But I haven't been. Mac's been helping…." She realized that for the admission it was as soon as it left her mouth.

"Yes," Pastor Dave said with a knowing smile, "then there is Mac."

"No," she countered quickly, "it's not…"

"…anything I need to know at the moment," interjected Pastor Dave. "What I do need to know is what you think this Thornton fellow's intending. Is he just rattling your cage or does he have real harm on his mind?"

That really was the question, wasn't it? Was Thornton toying with her like the predator he was, dangling her a bit while he licked his chops, just to show he could crush her if he wanted to? Despite all his meanness, Thornton did have a very keen sense of just how cruel he could be and still fall within legal bounds. He'd only crossed that line once while she'd known him, and paid a whopping harassment fine as a result—crime doesn't pay especially when a senator's daughter is involved. "I'd feel a lot better if I could be sure," Mary admitted, "but I don't think he means harm. I think he just wants me to be miserable because I'm not working for him anymore."

Pastor Dave looked at her over the top of his circular gold glasses. "And are you miserable?"

"Only a bit." She smiled. "But only two people know so far. And there's two more days until Christmas."

He actually winked. "Miracles don't take long."

Mary should have settled down to work on some paperwork, but she couldn't. She had told Pastor Dave, and survived. Pastor Dave wasn't necessarily a barometer of how shorter-fused Middleburgians might take the news, but he hadn't fired her on the spot, either. As a matter of fact, he seemed to be fine with it. Thankful for the strength of her talents. She'd never thought to see it that way. *This is a good sign, Lord. One that ought to be shared.* She put her coat back on after fifteen minutes at her desk and told the church secretary she was going out to run last-minute errands.

That was true—she did have several things to pick up at the hardware store—but this trip was mostly about giving Mac a dose of good news. Humming to herself, she walked briskly down Ballad Road, turning to wave at Dinah as she pushed through Mac's office door…

…and right into a nasty argument in full-blown process between Mac and Howard. Mac's diagram hadn't worked out nearly as well for him.

"How many years are we talking about, MacCarthy?" Howard was bellowing. "Takes you over ten years to find your nerve?"

Mac was pacing the back of his office. "And I suppose you've never done anything but sheer upstanding conduct your whole life. C'mon, Howard, I was all of eighteen. I'm not having fun here, but I'm owning up to my stupidity. When's the last time you admitted you were wrong?" It was at this point that Mac even realized she'd entered the room. "Oh, no," he said, clearly unhappy to see her. He and Howard exchanged a series of warning looks. "Howard, don't," Mac said almost under his breath in a way that made Mary wonder how low the conversation had sunk before her arrival.

"And you, young lady," Howard spat as he turned to her. "Are you proud of your résumé? Tell me, do you find your job here sufficient penance for your part in the Christmas-profit machine? I hear Bippo Bears are going for upwards of $300 in Louisville."

All the glow of her conversation with Pastor Dave left the room in a wave of ice. "Mac?" she asked.

"I lost my cool," he explained, looking angry and miserable. "I'm sorry. Howard's infuriating."

As if that were an excuse. And how on earth had arguing with Howard over his teenage actions drawn him to spill her secret? The two topics weren't even mildly related.

"I stuck my neck out on your behalf," Howard said sharply. "I had a right to know."

"Bippo Bears have nothing to do with what Mary does at MCC," Mac shot back before she had a chance to say anything, which annoyed Mary further.

"Haven't you said enough already?" she snapped at him. "I'm not proud of what's happened with Bippo Bears, Howard. I agree it's the worst side of advertising. It's why I left. But I *did* leave."

"This reflects terribly." Howard scowled. "The whole church looks foolish. Have you seen the news lately?"

That was a ridiculous question. She felt like she'd been living the news with all the Bippo Bear frenzy coverage. Thornton probably had four full-time public relations people fielding press releases to every major news network, considering the coverage they were getting. "I'm miserable about it, Howard."

Howard glared at her. "At Gil and Emily's party, you didn't leave because you were tired, you left because all that Bippo business was on Gil's television. Grown people hitting each other over your toy. How can you sleep at night?"

"Cut it out, Howard, it's not her fault," Mac ordered, coming around the desk.

"You," Mary started, her own anger rising at Mac, "you had *no right*." She then turned to Howard, who was putting on his coat to go. Most likely to call an emergency meeting of the church council, if she knew him. Thank God she'd had the wisdom to go to Pastor Dave first. Maybe. Howard looked mighty sore at being caught unaware of what he considered a vital church issue. "Howard…" she began.

"Mary," said Mac.

"Mac!" She glared at Mac, letting her full fury show.

"I'm going to need to discuss this with Pastor Anderson," Howard announced. "And as for you, Mr. MacCarthy, I think perhaps we should take a good look at the legal fallout of what you've just told me."

"I've already talked to a lawyer, Howard. I'm not going to pretend this isn't serious. But I'd prefer to talk to Dave personally."

"I'll bet you would," Howard fired back. He glanced from Mac to Mary, obviously painting them with the same guilty brush. "The two of you."

"Don't go off half-cocked, Howard. It won't do anyone any good. Come back in here and let's try and have a reasonable conversation."

Mary could just imagine how "reasonable" the conversation would had gone. She wasn't feeling one bit reasonable and she'd been in the room for about thirty seconds. At the moment she wanted to beg Howard to keep quiet and to throttle Mac for not being able to keep quiet. She didn't need Thornton's help to have a miserable Christmas—misery was thriving just fine. Howard said some mumbling form of goodbye and nearly slammed Mac's office door shut behind him, leaving her to glare furiously at the man she'd come to encourage. Sufficient words just wouldn't come.

Mac was an unbearable combustion of frustration, anger and regret. He knew he'd lose his cool with Howard, he'd planned for what to do when Howard pushed his buttons—and he'd failed on all counts. He couldn't even remember how the conversation had bent itself in such a way that he revealed Mary's connection with Bippo Bears. He'd wanted to slam his head against the desk once the words slipped from his mouth, knowing full well the betrayal he'd committed. God had been especially cruel to see to it that she walked in at the moment she had—the ultimate in bad timing.

"How could you?"

He deserved every bit of the ice in her eyes.

"With all you knew, how could you tell him? Him!"

"I don't have an excuse, Mary. He got to me and suddenly I told him and I'm sorry." He'd never felt like such a lowlife.

"He'll tell everyone. He's probably on his way to Pastor Dave right now."

Which meant that Pastor Dave would hear what Mac had done to MCC from Howard. Worst possible scenario. Mac thought it served him right; whatever Dave thought of him based on Howard's revelation was nothing less than what he deserved. But Mary didn't deserve what he'd done to her, and his top priority now had to be to put things right with her if at all possible. Her current expression left little possibility. "Have you talked to him yet?"

"You know," she said, hugging her arms across her chest, "I was just coming in here to tell you how well it went. He was wonderful. Supportive." She leveled him with a hurt, furious look. "I was coming to tell you how right you were, coming to encourage you. Imagine that."

"Mistakes compound mistakes," Pa used to say, and Mac was feeling that in every bone in his body right now. His original mistake had been bad enough. Keeping it under wraps for a decade had made it worse. Now his attempt at confession had not only hurt him, but seriously hurt the person he was most trying to help. Not even a Mac-*Fifty*-five diagram could fix this. "I'm sorry," he apologized again, feeling the words woefully inadequate. "That was beyond stupid of me, and I'm so sorry." A crush of self-loathing pushed against his chest and made it painful to breathe.

"We have rehearsal tonight," she said in an unsteady, trying-not-to-cry voice that let him know he could actually feel worse than he already did. "I don't know how I'm…we're going to do this. I'm going to go upstairs and figure out what to do next."

"I…"

"Don't!" she snapped back at him, fisting her hands. "Don't talk to me."

He felt the slam of his office door as if it had busted every one of his ribs. Worst of all, as he gathered up his coat and keys, he could just make out the sound of her crying as it came through the floorboards between them. Mac had seen buildings fall, timber splinter, dynamite explode through solid rock, but the sound of Mary Thorpe crying did the most damage of all.

Chapter Fifteen

Mac barreled down the pike in his car, taking turns too fast and downshifting the car so hard it shuddered. He slammed the coupe through its gears, not caring what road he took or where it led him. The stereo was up so loud it thumped in his chest. Taking his anger out on the road ahead of him, he drove recklessly, half hoping someone would pull him over and arrest him like the jerk he was. It wasn't until he missed a turn and sent the car skidding into a gravel-spitting spin that he pulled his temper back into check. He sat there, turned the wrong way of a deserted intersection, panting from the effort of holding the car through its spin, and let his head fall sharply against the steering wheel. It had all gone horribly wrong. Somewhere in the beginning of this mess he'd had good intentions. He'd run for mayor not only to push Middleburg toward its future, but to make up for his past. To prove to himself—and, he now realized, to Howard—that he wasn't that angry teenager anymore.

But he was.

Everything had been lost in the never-ending sin of

his short temper. Even the morning after the steeple fell, he'd never felt so utterly worthless. He banged the stereo knob with the heel of his hand, silencing the music to hear the echo of his own misery. He'd been so full of pride. So convinced of his ability to make the world a better place. And now look at you. At what you've done. *Lord, I wouldn't be half surprised if You washed Your hands of me right this minute.*

His cell phone rang. He ignored it.

It rang again. On the third time, he fished it out of his coat pocket to see Gil Sorrent's name on the screen. Here we go.

Gil didn't bother with a greeting. "Where are you?" He knew. Mac could hear it in his voice.

Mac didn't even know. He looked up, squinting at the route signs. "About a dozen miles out of town, I suppose."

"Did you do it?" There was no need for any clarification of details. Mac knew exactly what Gil was asking and why.

"Yes." Mac wiped one hand down his face and groaned. "I've messed this up something fierce. I don't know what to do."

"Come to the farm."

Gil was right. The office was no place to go now. "Sure, in twenty minutes, tops. But I think I'd better drive a little slower than I have been." In some sick desire to feel as bad as possible, he asked, "Who knows?"

"By the time you get here, probably everyone. Howard ain't much for being subtle when he's mad."

Mary's imagined lynch mob had come to life. Her overblown fear about people's conceptions of her Bippo Bear involvement would get mixed in with their justified anger over his secret, and the whole thing would get tumbled together in a Christmas nightmare. "Mary…"

"Emily's on the phone with Dinah now, sending her up to Mary's apartment to stay with her until we all figure out what to do next."

What to do next? That didn't really need a lot of planning. Mac had to stand and face the music, that's what happened next. There was an odd, almost hysterical freedom to having the whole process ripped from his hands. Mac was smart enough to realize he had very little control over how things played out from here. It could be everything from a touching reconciliation to a lawsuit to being run out of town—Mac resigned himself to whatever God handed him as a consequence for his actions.

Mary, however, was another story. She'd brought none of this on herself. She was working through a highly emotional issue in the best way she knew how. God was clearly at work within her, and he'd made it all worse instead of offering the help he'd intended. Faith was still a new underpinning for her life—it had caught some tender part of him to watch her reliance on God grow. He'd barely realized how much he'd come to care for her.

That is, of course, until he hurt her in the worst possible way. He'd always been able to smooth over his outbursts with a clever remark, a funny story, or even a prank to bring people back onto common ground. A hundred clever comebacks would never save him from this betrayal. He'd known that God had trusted him with the precious secret of Mary's situation. Known the delicate nature of her new faith and her new place in this community. And he'd done it terrible harm.

The fact that Howard goaded him into it wasn't even close to an excuse.

* * *

Mac wasn't surprised to see Pastor Dave's car in the drive in front of Gil's house. Nor was he surprised to see the look of supreme disappointment on Gil's face when he opened the door. Gil said nothing, just nodded and ushered Mac into the huge den. Before its massive fireplace, Mac remembered, was where Homestretch Farm conducted all of its most serious business. Well, thought Mac, this qualifies.

Pastor Dave looked tired. "This isn't fair to you," Mac offered as he took one of the large leather chairs that circled the hearth. "I'm sorry."

Pastor Dave took off his glasses and ran a hand across his eyes. "I'd much rather have heard this from you." Mac could only imagine Howard's rendition. He started to give his version of the story, then thought better of it. Whatever evils Howard had ascribed to him, he probably deserved them.

"I had planned to tell you…next." It sounded so weak, even if it was true. "I thought Howard needed to hear it first. It was his car that was damaged, after all. It was a terrible decision to keep this to myself all these years."

Emily entered the room, carrying mugs of coffee for the group. "Why now? What made you bring this up two days before Christmas?"

"It was Mary, actually."

Gil looked up as he took a mug from Emily. "Mary?"

"She was so terrified about what you all would think of her when you knew about the Bippo Bears. The secret was making her crazy. At first I just wanted to help, to let her know everyone has things they hope no one finds out. Then I realized I wasn't much better. It was like God used her as a mirror to hold up against my own secret—if that makes any sense. I thought if she could see me survive mine, she'd know she'd survive hers."

"What's Mary got to do with Bippo Bears?"

Mac was not going to open his mouth. He was not going to heap more onto his whopping pile of betrayal, useless as it was now. He looked at Pastor Dave, silently asking him how much should be said.

"Mary's job before she came to Middleburg was with an advertising agency. Mary is the person who wrote the Bippo Bear jingle. She feels personally responsible for all this nonsense going on over these bears. And she's pretty sure you all won't think too highly of her when you find out."

Gil and Emily exchanged surprised glances. News of Mary's supposed "sins" hadn't reached them yet evidently. "That silly Bippo Bear song? The one in the commercials? That's Mary's?" Emily asked, taking a mug for herself and sinking into a chair.

"It's a dumb song and I'm sick of it, but how is it her fault?" Gil inquired.

"Her job," Mac explained, "was to write a song kids could sing to their parents that would get stuck in their heads. To create that kind of 'I want it' fever so parents would do whatever it took to get their kids a Bippo Bear for Christmas."

"It worked," Gil replied. "I hate that song and I don't even have kids." He paused a moment before adding, "yet."

Emily looked between Mac and Pastor Dave. "He knows. Actually, except for Dinah, we're the only four who do. Oh, and Mary—I told her when she cast me as Mary."

"Her boss basically charged her with writing a song that would incite parents to riot," Pastor Dave described before taking a sip of his coffee. "She did her job. Actually, it's part of why she left advertising altogether. Once she came to faith, that sort of thing stuck in her craw. I admire her—she took a big risk to act on her convictions."

One I failed to take for years. Mac chided himself silently. "She's miserable. She saw the way we've been trashing the Bippo Bear people—come on, everyone's been harping on them, even me. I mean, I paid big bucks for one of those things for my nephew and I told folks I was steamed they were in such short supply. You couldn't find one anywhere, and that made them easy scalping. And then when the fights were shown on television, what was she supposed to think? That we'd all compliment her on a job well done?"

"She's supposed to think that we're smart grown-ups who know the difference between an advertising campaign and a toddler tantrum." Emily replied sharply. "I'm embarrassed. Do we come off that judgmental? Does she really think we'd hang her over Bippo Bears?"

"Maybe not hang her," Pastor Dave clarified, "just fire her off the church staff. And, I'm afraid, she's not too far off the mark. Howard ain't exactly a bundle of mercy at the moment."

"Why on earth did you tell Howard about Mary and the Bippo Bears?" Emily asked, making Mac feel even lower than he already did.

"I wasn't supposed to. Howard just…was Howard." Mac relayed the whole argument, how Howard called him a coward, a "poor reflection of the community's fine character" that should "never be allowed to run for office," which goaded Mac into a few choice remarks about Middleburg's character, which led to how they'd made Mary afraid for her secret, and so on. "He pushed my buttons and I got stupid," he said as he concluded his account of their argument and how Mary walked in at the worst possible moment. "I ought to know better than to let Howard get to me like that. I hurt her and I have no excuse for what I did."

"Howard," Pastor Dave said while he sighed, "feels the church had a right to know before we hired her. He feels betrayed, and worries all this bear ridiculousness will reflect badly on the church."

"I'll tell you what will reflect badly on MCC," Emily replied. "If we treat her like some kind of criminal just because she used to do what she used to do—that'll reflect badly on the church. I can't believe people think like that!"

"I can," Gil admitted sadly. "I overheard folks in Deacon's Grill the other day. People are steamed about all the press these bears are getting. They keep running ads even though no one's got any more to sell. Can't say I haven't thought the same thing, but I wouldn't take it out on Mary personally."

"She doesn't know that," Mac revealed. "She has no way of knowing that."

"I think," offered Pastor Dave gently, "that we're getting off the topic of what to do about you, Mac. You've got a serious issue on your hands. If anything, you may be a blessing to Mary, taking the focus off her." Mac hadn't thought about it that way, but it didn't help much.

"Stuffed animals aren't exactly the same level of seriousness as deliberate vandalism to a church," Pastor Dave continued. "And a car."

"*Howard's* car," Gil reminded the room, although Mac surely didn't need reminding. "He could press charges, I suppose, but I would think the statute of limitations has run out by now."

"Are you ready, Mac, to stand up and deal with this?" Pastor Dave asked Mac with seriousness in his eyes. "To everyone? Tonight?"

"I have to. I don't really see how this can wait until after Christmas." This'll go down as my worst Christmas ever, Mac thought to himself. "We need to deal with this now. Tonight's a good as any, although I think it'll blow any chance of rehearsal clear out the window."

"Well, then," Pastor Dave continued, standing up, "I think it's time for God to show up in big and mighty ways." He set down his mug with a nod of thanks to Emily and reached for his coat. "I think it's high time I go check on Mary."

"Tell her I'm sorry," Mac relayed, catching the pastor's elbow.

"I think you ought to do that yourself. You two have a fair amount to work out before either one of you come to rehearsal, I'd say." Dave checked his watch. "It's two now, so why don't I tell Mary you'll come by at around four?"

Mac nodded, just as his cell phone went off. "I have a feeling that's Ma," he guessed, reaching into his pocket. It was. These days, the only thing that could outpace his car was the speed of small-town gossip. "I'd better get over there." He extended a grim hand to Gil. "Start praying. I think God's about to take me down a peg—or six." He leaned down and gave petite Emily a peck on the cheek. "Congratulations," he spoke softly. "I haven't had a chance to say that yet. I'll try to straighten out my act by the time the little fella gets here. If you'll still have me." It stuck in his throat with an unexpected lump.

"Nonsense," Gil objected, leveling a serious look right in Mac's eyes. "God's just gettin' started on you—I expect big things on the other end of this mess."

"See you tonight," Emily vowed, squeezing Mac's hand. "We'll be there. Promise."

"Mary, talk to me. We've got to talk about this." Mac had been outside her door for ten minutes now. A more mature woman, someone with years of solid faith under her belt, might have been able to open up that door to the man who'd betrayed her worst secret, but Mary was not there yet. She looked at her dining room table, where the envelope from her parents' house lay open. Thornton had sent hard copies of four different e-mails. Four different media outlets asking for interviews with "the creator of the Bippo Bear jingle." He'd mailed them, along with a Christmas bonus and a personal note asking for her return to Maxwell Advertising, to her in care of her parents even though she knew he now had her Middleburg address. It was a masterful manipulation—wrapped in loyal employer language that would coddle her parents, but letting *her* know he could go public at any moment. Mary knew the only reason he *hadn't* was that the mystery somehow served his purpose. The duplicity of it all made it worse than the outright blackmail she'd suspected from him.

Which made Mac just like Thornton. She'd allowed herself to believe she could expect loyalty from Mac, and instead he'd done the one thing he knew would hurt her most. No, she couldn't open the door and face that man. He'd hurt her worse than anything Howard could have said, because she'd allowed herself to care about Mac. She looked at the paper with the circle diagram as it sat next to Thornton's clever note, remembering the tenderness of Mac's voice as he said, "Right underneath you, same as always," and she wanted to crumple the thing and send it into the fireplace to burn. "Go away," she said to the door with as much strength as she could muster, then she walked into her living room and turned up the stereo loud enough to drown out any persuasion he might try next.

Chapter Sixteen

Mac felt like the very air in the church sanctuary was on the verge of combustion. The whole building had a surreal dissonance to it—the joyful decorations at odds with his miserable spirit. The sanctuary looked amazing. Each of the stained glass windows were framed in fragrant pine boughs frosted with dozens of tiny white lights, and each window sill hosted a trio of hurricane candles circled in holly and red ribbon. The set, while nothing that would turn heads on Broadway, was brilliantly colored and made the church look, well, happy. *Everything* looked happy. The trouble was nothing *felt* happy.

After all that preparation, Mac felt as if he was standing on the brink of the worst Christmas ever. It was ten minutes past the hour, and no one had seen Mary all afternoon. *Take care of her, Lord—I sure can't. You know how much I wanted to go into this with things settled between me and her.* Still, it wasn't as if he had the right to have things the way he wanted. This mess—large or small—was his own doing.

Mac stood up. There was no chance he could feel

worse, and it was time to take this mistake into his own hands anyway. Howard stood up seconds after Mac rose off his chair, and for a moment there was a silent challenge as to who would take command of the room. Mac cleared his throat loud enough to make everyone in the room turn to look at him. Everyone, that is, who wasn't staring at him already. "I think," he announced as steadily as he could, "that we might as well tackle this here and now. It looks like rehearsal isn't going to happen, and I doubt anyone here is in the dark as to why."

Howard made some sort of gruff sound, but said nothing as Mac walked to the front of the room.

"Just in case you've been hiding under a rock for the last few hours, I did, in fact, admit to Howard that I was behind the steeple falling down during its construction twelve years ago. I was an angry kid who did something stupid. I reckon it will go down as one of my life's biggest mistakes—both then and now—but somehow I'd fooled myself into thinking it didn't really matter."

Howard coughed loudly, transmitting his disagreement.

"Well," Mac went on while looking Howard straight in the eye, "it matters a whole lot. I get that now. And it's up to me to put things right as much as I can. And I figure there are some parts of this that I can't put right, and I'll have to take that as it comes." He took a deep breath and thrust his hands into his pockets to stop the urge to fidget that suddenly overtook him. He shifted his eyes to several people around the room, catching some supportive expressions and others that were condemning. The duality of it matched his current emotions; this was at once both easy and horrible. Easy in that he hadn't even realized how the weight of this secret had pressed on him over the years and had now been released, and yet horrible in that it made him feel disliked and vulnerable and at the town's collective mercy. "First off, I'm sorry. I'm sorry I did it, I'm sorry I lied about it then and that I didn't come clean before now. I damaged Howard's car, the church and put people in danger. I didn't handle my anger well and I allowed it to let me do something wrong. And dangerous."

"Every one of us has done things we regret," Sandy Burnside acknowledged, looking around the room.

"Every one of us," repeated Matt Lockwood—father of the less-than-angelic Tommy Lee, "didn't hide it and then run for mayor. What else we gonna find out about you?"

"Hopefully, that I set things right when I can. Howard, I looked up the value of your car that was hit by the falling steeple, and I'm prepared to write you a check to cover those damages. Even the ones covered by your auto insurance." He'd planned to tell Howard this when he confessed to the deed earlier this afternoon, but the argument had spiraled out of control before he'd had the chance. "And I want to say I'm sorry, to you personally, here in front of everyone."

He paused briefly, hoping Howard might say something along the lines of "apology accepted," but Howard remained silently standing. Howard would probably accept the apology in the long run, but he wasn't the kind of man to do something like that quickly.

"Now I'd apologize to our former Pastor Donalds if I could, but I don't know where he moved to. I'm going to try to find him." Mac scanned the back of the room until he found Pastor Anderson. "But in the meantime, I'll apologize to Pastor Anderson for damaging the church the way I did, and I'm trying to work up some figures so I can pay MCC back in some way. You don't need a new steeple anymore, but I'm sure he'll find some use for the money."

"I accept your offer of restitution," Pastor Anderson responded with a formal tone. "On behalf of the congregation back then and the congregation now."

A few folks in the room looked like they weren't so ready to let it go at that, but no one actually said anything. The tension in the room changed to awkward mumbling that wasn't a riot, but wasn't quite silence, either.

"And then there's the other thing," Mac continued. Howard began moving toward the front of the room. "I think we need to get that out on the table now, too."

"There's more?" The alarm in town librarian Audrey Lupine's voice wasn't helping matters.

"It seems Mac was privy to some important information about Miss Thorpe," Howard interjected. "Information we should have known before we hired her."

"Information," Pastor Anderson added, "Mary was under no legal obligation to provide us. She gave us her employment history in all the detail we asked for."

"Matters of church staff go beyond legal obligations," Howard declared. "She had a moral obligation to tell us."

"Tell us what?" a woman who worked on the costumes asked.

"Haven't you heard?" said another woman in a less than kind voice. "About the Bippo Bears."

"Yes, Mary Thorpe is part of the Bippo Bear atrocity." Howard's tone was grave. "She worked to make those crazy blue bears into something every child wants. Into something that's starting fights at stores and turning Christmas into nothing more than a profit machine for some soulless toy manufacturer. That's the person we hired to run our Christmas drama. Someone who not only had that in her background, but purposely hid that from us because she knew the response we'd have to it."

Atrocity? Howard made it sound like she was out knocking small children down with a baseball bat. "See? This is exactly why she chose not to mention it. The woman was just doing her job for the advertising agency where she used to work. The one she left when her faith called her to do something else. The same faith that called her here," Mac informed.

"You're defending her?" said the first woman. "You?" As if he were the last person in the world who should stand up for Mary.

"He knew about it. He'd discovered her deception and didn't come forward. This is why I'm so angry. All of this shows an alarming lack of integrity. We've got to have people who look out for the public good running for office in Middleburg. I've said it before and I'll say it again, I'm not against someone running for mayor. I'm against the *wrong* person running for mayor. I'd say you've shown yourself to be the wrong person, MacCarthy."

Mac felt his blood begin to rise. "Back off, Howard. We're talking about Mary."

"You're both equally guilty."

"Y'all hang on a minute, the two of you." Sandy Burnside stretched out her hands between them like a referee. "Calm down. The way I see it, Mary wrote an advertising jingle. One she was paid to write. I can't see the crime in that."

"Have you heard that thing? I reckon it really could fix folks to riot," Vern from the hardware store chimed into the discussion. "Gets stuck in your head like a bad cold. My daughter spent her whole Christmas budget getting one of those things for my grandson just 'cuz he whined so much to get one. Crazy if you ask me."

Emily stood up. "But that's not Mary's fault. She's embarrassed about what's happened with the bears, and that's why she didn't tell us. She was afraid of what we'd think. And we've proved her right, haven't we?"

Gina Deacon spoke up. "I'm sick of hearing about it in the diner. Obviously, y'all find enough to fight about without adding some Christmas bear nonsense to the mix. I know for a fact she heard folks going on about how bad the ads were right in front of her face. I don't know that I blame her for keeping it quiet."

"We should have known. In advance," Howard countered. "She should have known it would become an issue, especially over the holidays. She showed poor judgment. Poor character. A person of integrity would have come forward immediately, knowing the nature of the situation." About one-third of the room nodded along with Howard. "It reflects poorly on the church and what it stands for this time of year."

"And what *does* the church stand for, Howard?" demanded Dinah Rollings, standing up and squaring off at Howard. "Where's the 'peace on earth, goodwill to men' in all of this?" She swept her hand around the room. "I doubt Jesus would be too pleased with what's gone on today. Lost tempers. Fights. People not being able to forgive each other or not owning up to things they've done. Folks afraid of other folks for no good reason. Calling each other's character into question and telling things that ought not to be told. This sure ain't the kind of Christmas I hoped for when I moved to Middleburg." Another third of the room nodded in agreement to Dinah. "How we're gonna pull off tomorrow night now, Lord only knows. I sure don't." With a dramatic huff, Dinah moved to the back of the room where she paced with annoyance.

Things were about to spiral out of control. "Look," said Mac determined to pull out whatever stops it took to keep this from dissolving into disaster, "let's put everything on the table here. This play was a small bandage on a big wound and we all know it. I'm sorry I've upset you all, but if you want me to be sorry I ran—am running—for mayor, I won't. Maybe I'm not perfect. Maybe I messed this up on a global scale and some of you can't get past that. I can live with that. But what I can't live with is what we've done to Mary. We hired her for all the wrong reasons, Howard. We thought we could all distract ourselves from the real stuff by putting on this ideal Christmas drama—as if Middleburg would heal itself like one of those old movie musicals where the kids put on a show in Grandpa's barn and save the world. We put her in such an impossible situation that she was afraid to be part of our community. Afraid to let us know this tiny little detail—this ridiculous bear thing—that has her so frightened. She's ashamed of something she has no reason to be ashamed of. You know why I found the spine to tell Howard after all these years? Because I wanted to show her that Middleburg wouldn't hang her for a mistake. I figured if I 'fessed up to my actual criminal act and survived, that she'd realize she could let people know about the jingle and be fine. I was trying to help her let her secret loose, but I let Howard get under my skin and I told her secret instead. And that's low. Me, I deserve what I get. But Mary's done nothing but try and pull this thing together under impossible circumstances and she's deserved none of it. She's an amazing, talented woman who deserves to be welcomed into Middleburg as part of our community. Which, if you ask me, is what she needed most and why God sent her here." Suddenly realizing he'd made a very long speech, Mac shut up and sat down on the edge of the stage.

"Where is she anyway?" asked Sandy Burnside. "She's supposed to be here. Has anyone checked on her?"

"I just did," Dinah answered, pulling open the sanctuary's back doors. He hadn't even noticed her leaving the room—he was so busy speechifying. Dinah stepped aside to reveal Mary standing behind her. "She was coming in as I went out. Just in time to hear someone's big speech. And for once, I don't mean Howard's."

Every single eye in the room was on Mary. Her entrance into the room was as painful as she had expected—she couldn't for the life of her tell if the crowd was ready to welcome her or what. Some man in one corner looked down and shook his head. Pastor Anderson stood up slowly, as did Emily. Howard looked like he'd have crossed his arms over his chest again if they weren't already there. The sanctuary was excruciatingly silent.

"Well," acknowledged Sandy Burnside, "you're here. 'Bout time, too. So I suppose there's only one question worth asking now. Are you really the gal behind that troublesome little song?"

Mary caught Mac's eyes staring right at her. His eyes were a storm of fear, worry, regret, embarrassment— it surprised her that she could read his expression so clearly under such dire circumstances. Quite simply, he looked awful. Mary took a deep breath and stood up straighter. Some odd little part of her recognized she was about to finish off all the remaining circles in her Mac Five in one fell swoop. "Yes, I wrote the Bippo Bear jingle. I'm not proud of it, but there it is."

Tommy Lee Lockwood looked at her with an awed expression. "Cool."

She couldn't help but smile. "Not really."

One older woman Mary recognized from the choir shook a finger at her. "Aren't you ashamed of yourself?"

Mary thought it would be horrible the first time she faced someone like that. It wasn't as bad as she'd feared. "As a matter of fact, I am," she replied, amazed at the steadiness of her voice. After all, there really wasn't anything left to lose at this point. "I'm ashamed of whom I used to be. At what I used to think was important. But that's the point of faith, I think."

"I could go into a big speech of that being the whole point behind the coming of the Christ child," said Pastor Anderson, walking to the center of the room, "but I think we've heard enough speeches already." He turned to Mac. "Do you admit that you've made a mistake and you're willing to make up for it?"

Mac nodded. "Already have admitted it, and I've already offered to do whatever I need to do to set things right."

"Mary," continued Pastor Anderson, "do you admit

it might have been wise to let us know what was going on in your professional life beforehand and that your fears and our alarm might have been avoided if we'd just talked about this earlier?"

"I suppose I've come to realize that's true, yes."

Pastor Anderson turned to Howard. "Do you admit to having an understandable reaction to some news but that you would be able to get past it, given a little time?"

Howard unfolded his arms and shifted his weight a bit before admitting, "That's a possibility."

Pastor Anderson swept his hands around the room. "Do all of you agree that maybe we've gotten our spirits out of joint here for any number of reasons? And that the only true solution to all of this is the Christ we're supposed to be welcoming?"

Janet stood up and crossed her hands over her chest. "It's Christmas," she declared in the take-charge voice of a stage manager. In fact, Janet had made an outstanding stage manager, and it didn't look like she was going to stop now. "If we can't find a way to get along at Christmas, then we should be ashamed of ourselves. Mary, I want us to rehearse. I've put too much into this to have it all go to pieces now. As far as I'm concerned, scene one starts in five minutes. Anybody else want to give it a try?"

As awful as everything was, Mary felt a surge of blessing to have Dinah and Janet in her corner. Emily, too. She'd been wrong thinking everyone would reject her.

She caught Mac's gaze over the crowd, and felt her own emotions tangle up with the tumult in his eyes. Everyone had made so many mistakes. Mac had hurt her, but he'd made that mistake in the process of trying to help her. There was a powerful pull in that. If she could feel that pull, even now after what he'd done, then wasn't there something important under all that human imperfection? Mary gave him the slightest of smiles, an "I'll try" slip of a smile, and she watched that tiny piece of encouragement light a spark in the green of his eyes.

Dress rehearsal went as well as could be expected under the circumstances: namely, a complete disaster. Cues were missed, baby Jesus, although now in possession of all his limbs, never made it onstage for the final scene so that Emily cradled a limp roll of cloth instead of the Almighty Savior. No one knew the Magi's bottle of frankincense was real glass until the actor dropped it and it shattered, sending Audrey Lupine running for the church first aid kit to bandage Shepherd Number Three's left hand. Howard and Mac were barely above useless, repeatedly forgetting lines in between mutual onstage "stare-downs" and a smattering of curt remarks. Mary found herself praying with all her might that the old adage "bad dress rehearsal, good opening night" was true.

She closed up the costume closet with an exhausted sigh, happy to find Pastor Dave just behind her with a mug of hot chocolate—the man seemed to specialize in "comfort muggings" as he jokingly called them. "Think we'll survive?" he asked, his tone a mix of humor and genuine concern.

"I've never felt less in control of anything in my entire life," Mary stated and leaned back against the wall, clutching the mug with both hands. "I've told God eleven times in the past thirty minutes alone that this is way beyond me. That only He can pull this off tomorrow night." She looked at the older pastor, amazed that he could be so calm when the world seemed to be spinning out of control. "I should be panicked out of my skin, but you know, I'm not. Maybe I'm just too tired to know I ought to be panicking."

Pastor Anderson chuckled and leaned back against the wall opposite her in the hallway. "Maybe God's getting through to you that it was His job to pull it off all along. We're stubborn folk this side of heaven. Sometimes I find God has to rip the control out of our hands to make us recognize we never had control in the first place. That place where you are? The place where it feels like, unless God shows up, you're sunk? Well, I find that's the place where God usually shows up. In big ways. Doing things no one expected."

"Oh," Mary said and sighed, "that would definitely be now."

"How do you feel now," Pastor Dave continued as they started walking back up the stairs toward the sanctuary, "now that everyone knows?"

"Okay. Not okay. It's nice to know not everyone blames me. But I've gotten my share of dirty looks today—some people really do blame me. Except for Tommy Lee Lockwood. He's asked me four times if I can get him a bear."

"For his sister?"

"No, actually," Mary replied with an amused whisper. "He told me he could get twice what they're worth through some Internet site."

"Tommy Lee Lockwood's too young to think Kentucky has a black market," Pastor Dave observed and then laughed.

"Tommy Lee's too young for lots of the things he thinks and does if you ask me."

Pastor Dave stopped at the top of the stairs. "Vern Murphy tells me folks used to say that about young Joseph MacCarthy. Mac had a talent for trouble, but I think he turned out okay. He'll turn out okay when all this is over, too. It's the man who *doesn't* learn from his mistakes that you need to watch out for."

Mary didn't have a reply. She just nodded and sipped her cocoa again as they pushed open the sanctuary doors where her coat and script still lay along with a box of props that needed mending.

The sanctuary was dark except for a handful of small lights and the moonlight coming in through the stained glass windows, but it wasn't empty. A single figure sat at the front of the pews, head resting on one hand, shoulders hunched. Mac.

"Like I said," Pastor Dave whispered, turning back toward the hallway that led to the parking lot, "God shows up."

Chapter Seventeen

Mary felt a dozen different emotions as she walked up the aisle toward Mac. He turned and looked at her calmly, as if he'd been waiting. The expression in his eyes unwound something deep in her chest. Did she really have the capacity to forgive him? Or was she just too exhausted to be angry anymore? She sat down in the same pew, and for a moment they both looked at the rebuilt silver star that now hung in the top of the sanctuary. She remembered the time in the steeple, when they went to look for that star.

"I've been thinking," Mac said in a hoarse voice, "how to apologize to you, but everything I come up with falls short. What I did was awful. I should be able to say something meaningful, you know, eloquent, to make up for it. But all I keep thinking is that my run-on mouth is what got me into this to begin with." He looked up at her, his green eyes piercing the darkness. "I never meant to hurt you. Not in a million years. But I did, and I'm beyond sorry."

"Did you mean what you said earlier? That you first thought about telling your story to help me?"

"Yeah," he conceded. "Twisted as it was." He managed a weak laugh. "It didn't quite turn out the way I planned."

"Thanks. For trying to help, I mean." She surveyed the sanctuary, imagining the crowd of people who'd been in here earlier. "Everybody knows now and I'm still alive. I suppose in some respects you were right—it's not as bad as I thought it would be. I'd turned it into some kind of horrible thing in my mind."

"We can do that, you know. Twist things up in our minds. God can give us a good idea and we can foul it up something fierce." He paused for a moment before he leaned back in the pew and looked up at the ceiling. "Like running for mayor," he said softly. "I know God wanted me to run, but I thought it was so that I could be a big shot, the guy who could take on Howard."

"And now?"

"Now I know God wanted me to run so I could clean up my own house."

Mary wasn't quite sure what he meant by that. She leaned over to try and decipher the feelings exposed on his face, but the shadows hid his features. "How so?"

He turned toward her, and Mary felt her heart jolt at the sight of his expression. The man before her had been stripped of his bravado, of his clever words and fancy plans. This is what it felt like to look into someone's soul—unedited, unprotected, exposed. "I'm *not* ready to run for mayor. Maybe someday, but I've got a load of work to do on the inside before I try and change the world. I'll be thirty in seven days and I've never felt less grown up. I let one guy goad me into hurting someone I…someone I've come to care a whole lot about. That's not a guy who should be mayor."

Mary thought it would be a long, hard process, but it wasn't. It was a single, clear moment that swept across her like a breeze. "I forgive you," she said, amazed how the words felt both large and effortless at the same time.

He looked at her with a startled amazement. "I wouldn't blame you if you didn't. I'm such a jerk—I think God allowed me to believe I was helping you because I'd have never 'fessed up on my own."

"Maybe God fixed it so you told because I'd have chickened out of telling on my own. I don't suppose that really matters at this point." She sighed. "Now what? The town's in worse shape than when I started."

"Oh, I don't know. Maybe this wasn't one of those things you could fix creatively. We had to tackle it up front, out in the open, ugly and all." Mac let his head fall back against the pew. "I think down deep we all still like each other. We've just got to find our way back to that."

That was it, wasn't it? Could she find her way back to the affection she felt for Mac after what he'd done? He'd said it himself, that his original intent had been to help. His failings had gotten in the way of his intent. Could she say much differently? Hadn't her original intent to do a good job been hampered by her own faults?

"I want to find a way back," she proclaimed, turning to him. A way back for Middleburg, and maybe even a way back for the two of them.

"Hanged if I know how," he admitted, more to the empty room than to her.

"Actually," Mary revealed, sitting up, "I think maybe I do."

"Oh," groaned Mac, "you're not talking about the potluck, are you?"

"Oh, I am. Besides," she concluded, amazed she could find it within herself to smile, "now you *have* to come."

This is my Christmas gift to myself. Mary took a deep breath, grabbed her phone and dialed the number the following morning.

"Mary, darling!" Thornton's overly dramatic greeting was too loud and too cavalier. He was almost shouting; she could hear the noises of a city bar in full swing behind him. "I just knew I'd be hearing from you today. How are you out in the middle of nowhere, wherever you are?"

It would be hard to pack more untruths into three short sentences: Mary was by no means his "darling," he had no right whatsoever to expect to hear from her ever again—much less on Christmas Eve—she doubted he cared one bit how she was doing and he knew exactly where she was. It surprised her, at just that moment, how she'd allowed this man to hold such power over her. The time for that was over, and she was ready to end it.

"I'm great actually. Very happy."

"No kidding." Thornton's voice dripped with doubt. "And here I was sure you were calling to ask for your old job back for Christmas. You can have it, you know." His tone implied that he'd be the big man and forgive her the terrible sin of leaving him.

"No thanks, Thornton. I just wanted to call and say Merry Christmas. This will be our last phone conversation. And there will be no more mail. No more communication. I'm done, and I just wanted to tell you myself."

He didn't speak for a moment; Mary heard only the

yelling and revelry from wherever he was. People trying too hard to be happy. It sounded so empty.

"Come on now…" he finally said in the fumbling way of someone who can't think of anything better to say.

"No, really. You can tell whoever asks that I wrote the song, but you ought to also tell them that I'm not inclined to give interviews. And if I catch you giving out this number to anyone, I won't be nice about it. I mean it, Thornton."

She heard glasses clinking, as if he'd just taken a swig of a drink. "No, you don't."

"Oh, I do."

Thornton let out a string of the colorful adjectives for which he was famous. Actually, she'd expected to be called far worse—Thornton wasn't at all used to people cutting him off. The language fell sharp and repulsive on her ears. "Be that way," he snapped at the end of the off-color diatribe.

"I'm happy where I am, Thornton. Leave me alone now."

"No problem," he practically shouted in her ear. "You just dropped off the radar, sweetheart."

"I really do wish you a Merry Christmas, Thornton. The Bippo Bear campaign looks like it was everything you wanted it to be. Enjoy your success."

"What's with the holier-than-thou attitude?"

She could just imagine him, pacing the hallway of some posh Chicago bar, tie loosened, drink spilling out of one hand.

"You know what, doll? I'm glad you're gone. Everyone's replaceable. I got people lining up for your job, and none of them will spout sermons at me. You're *gone*."

With that pronouncement, Thornton hung up on her.
And she didn't mind.

She *was* gone. Long gone, and glad of it. Mary wondered, as she hit the disconnect button on her phone,
how she'd ever been so afraid of that man. With a flourish, she deleted his contact information from her cell
phone. It didn't matter who knew what she'd been, because she knew now who she was. And *Whose* she was.

Emily's shop smelled fabulous when Mary pushed
open the door half an hour later. The cinnamon-pine-
berry scent of whatever potpourri she had set out—and
Emily always had something fragrant and wonderful
set out—filled Mary's head with visions of a Dick-
ens Christmas. She could almost imagine a pie baking
somewhere behind Emily's counter. Music-box ver-
sions of Christmas carols filled the air. Mary placed a
small wrapped gift on the counter just as Emily came
out from the stock room in the back of her shop. "Oh,"
Emily said with a bright smile, coming around the counter in a welcoming rush, "it's you. I'm so glad to see
you this morning." She wrapped Mary in an enormous
hug. "Merry Christmas Eve. How are you? I mean really, after yesterday and all, how are you? I've been
sending up prayers for you all night."

"Well, I'm not as bad as I thought. I decided to stay
away from the TV news today—if Bippo Bear brawls
are breaking out in cities across the country, I'd just as
soon not know about it." She could actually joke about
Bippo Bears. Mary wasn't sure that day would ever
come, much less come on Christmas Eve.

"I think that's a great idea. I'm sure I won't have a
free moment to turn one on today, either. I used to stay

open late on Christmas Eve, back before Gil." Mary had since learned the long and painful story of Emily and Gil's courtship. It was part of the reason she was here this morning, actually. "Now I close at the regular time—even a bit early this year." She struck a theatrical pose. "I have a performance to prepare for."

Emily's transformation from shy reluctance to a wonderful performance was one of the most rewarding things about Mary's new life in Middleburg. It was so satisfying to watch someone discover a strength or talent. So much more satisfying than even her largest bonus checks at Maxwell Advertising. Mary discovered she could actually thank God for all He'd done in her life this year, even now. She had struggled, no doubt, but the struggles God sent could be trusted as good things. "You'll be great tonight," Mary said to Emily, meaning it. "I know last night was shaky, but I feel good about tonight. So I brought you this." She pointed toward the box. "To say thanks for all your kindness, and decorations, and support, and a little advice I'm about to ask for."

Emily pulled off the wrapping paper to find a box of exotic Chinese tea. "It smells divine." She looked up at Mary with a narrowed eye. "Advice, hm? How about we brew some of this up and have a chat over some tea?"

Mary smiled. "That's exactly what I had in mind."

When the pair had been settled in the little chintz-covered table by Emily's window, and the fragrance of jasmine mixed with the holiday scents around the room, Emily wrapped her hands around her mug and said, "So, what's on your mind?"

"Well," Mary began, "first of all, I wanted to ask you what people think. I know a few people are upset about the Bippo Bear thing, and I understand that, but

I don't know how many people are upset with me because I don't think they know me well enough to come to me personally. Yet."

"Are you that worried about what people think?"

"Well, that's just the thing of it. I'm not sure how worried a Christian ought to be about what other people think. I mean look at Mac. He needed to worry, and I'm not sure he did. Should I worry?"

Emily sat back in the little wrought iron chair. "Well, that's a tricky point. One, actually, that Gil has to deal with all the time, especially with all the guys. When you reform young criminals on your farm, you can't ignore what people think, but you can't let it dictate what you do, either. I think the best thing is to ask yourself if what you're doing honors God, and honors what you believe God's will for you is at the time. And you have to be ready for His answers. God likes to shake up our idea of what's a good idea."

"Yeah, I'm coming to understand that part. I thought it was a good idea to hide my former life at first, but I think I would have avoided a lot of problems if I'd told a few people earlier. I needed the Mac Five about a week before I got it, if you ask me."

Emily raised an eyebrow. "The 'Mac Five'?"

"Mac's trademark crisis management plan. Sort of a 'pick five people you can trust and let them help you solve the problem' thing. Involving circles and diagrams and all that engineering stuff Mac loves. You were in my Mac Five, by the way, I just never got around to talking to anyone but Mac and Pastor Dave before it all…well, you know."

"Oh, boy, do I know." She gave Mary an inquisitive look. "But why do I think I don't know all of it?"

Dinah had talked about Emily's canny intuition. It seemed like Middleburg was filled with women who knew what anyone *really* wanted to talk about before they could get the words out of their mouths. "Well, I wanted to ask you, actually, about Gil. About you and Gil."

Emily smiled. "No, you didn't. You wanted to ask me if it's okay to fall for someone like Mac even though he hurt you."

Mary tried not to knock over her tea. It was a full minute of choking before she could say, "Wow, you're good."

"No, just observant. You two couldn't take your eyes off each other at the party. And he talks about you a lot. And I could see how miserable you both were last night. And, yes, I have a little experience with a wounded heart." The tender way Emily put a hand on Mary's arm, Mary thought her feelings of shock and exposure must be flooding her face.

"I don't know what to do," Mary admitted finally, surprised to find tears gathering behind her eyes. "I don't know what to feel or think. I shouldn't care for him. Not now, not so soon. The timing's all wrong."

"Maybe only to you," Emily replied. "The two of you have been through a lot in a short time, it's true. But sometimes that's just God's way of getting our attention."

Mary watched the steam from the tea make graceful curves in the air. "I forgave him last night. I didn't think I had it in me, but when he explained how he felt, it was like I suddenly had the ability to do it when I never thought I would. And it was both very hard and not hard at all, which makes no sense."

"It makes a whole lot of sense to me," Emily asserted. "That's what faith does. It gives us the ability to do things that should feel impossible. Mercy is always undeserved. It can never be earned, only given." Her smile was warm and understanding. "I'm a big believer in mercy. It took me a while to get there, but that's a story for another time. Do you think there's something worthwhile between you and Mac?"

"I do." Mary couldn't believe a tear was finding its way down her cheek. This all seemed to be ridiculously melodramatic, but she couldn't seem to stop the flood of emotions. "I know it's crazy, but I do."

"Then you should know I had a particular customer this morning. A man—oh, I'd say just a few days shy of thirty—looking for the perfect gift for someone. He drove an orange sports car, by the way. He wanted a star for the top of a young lady's tree. The absolute best star I had, because he said they had a history of trouble with stars, and that he had a lot to make up to her, but that she meant a lot to him." Emily smiled. "You have any idea who that might be?"

Mary's pulse started racing. She'd noticed Mac wasn't in the office this morning. Mary felt something electric run down her spine. A giddy energy that made her unable to hide the blushing grin she felt break out on her face. "Mac was here?"

"Good thing you've got it for that man something fierce, because from where I sit, he's got it something fierce for you. Go on home. We can finish our tea another time, and I believe you have someone waiting for you there."

I could be sitting at my desk. I could be getting work done. Well, I could be pretending to get work done. Mac sat on the steps leading up to Mary's apartment and fiddled with the yellow gift bag from Emily's shop. He'd once kidded Gil for holding one of those bags—Emily always stuffed her bags so full of frilly tissue that no man could hold his head upright while carrying the thing. Gil's face had looked exactly like he now felt. Ridiculous but unable to help himself.

It can wait.

No, it can't.

He had to know things were set right between himself and Mary. He had to declare his…his what? He didn't really know. He mostly just had to know if she felt what he felt. If that thing that wouldn't let him alone—the thing that wouldn't let him think or sleep and drove him to do things like 'fess up decades-old secrets—if that thing wouldn't let her alone, either. He'd seen it, well, glimpses of it for weeks and even last night in spite of all the pain. What was that old saying about "you only hurt the ones you love?"

Did he love her? Maybe. She sure affected him as no other woman ever did. She was beautiful—she'd practically knocked the breath out of him when she came down the stairs in that soft green sweater for Gil's Christmas party—but it was more than that. He'd always been an ambitious man, but Mary somehow pulled inner aspirations out of him. Urges to be a different *kind* of man, to reach for a different, deeper faith. Mostly he knew that if she ever looked at him again with the hurt and betrayal she had yesterday afternoon in his office, he wouldn't live through it. And so he was willing to do anything and everything—including sitting on some steps bearing a frilly yellow bag—to win her favor.

Oh, Jesus, I won't last another half hour. Have mercy

on me, I'm dying here. Mac tunneled one hand through his hair and pushed out a breath. *If it's all going to go sour, just get it over with. But please, please don't let it go sour. I don't know how You did all this, but I'm willing to see it through to the end if You'll just cut me a little slack here.*

He looked up and saw Mary through the window in the door at the bottom of the stairway. She was standing in the foyer that joined her door, his office door, and Dinah's bakery; peering into his office window. Looking for him. *Oh, Lord, please let her be looking for me and not looking to avoid me.*

She stepped to the door and fumbled for her keys, and Mac felt his blood go still. He'd know the second she looked at him. It would all be there in her eyes—it was always there in her eyes—and he'd know if he stood any chance at all. He'd never deserved mercy less or craved it more.

She looked up, held his eyes for a moment that seemed to last all day, and let a tender smile steal across her face. She pushed open the door and stood at the bottom of the stairs, gazing up at him. She was, at that moment, the most welcome sight in all of history. She tucked a strand of hair behind her ear, and feelings scattered across his chest like shock waves. "Hi," she said softly, putting one foot on the first step.

"Are you okay this morning?" He felt as inelegant as a sixth grade boy, about to break out in sweat any minute.

"Yeah, actually I am. I think it's going to be okay tonight. How'd it go with Howard?"

Mac swallowed. "Harder than I thought, but better than I thought. He made no bones about agreeing I should pull out of the race. I wouldn't exactly call him gracious. He could have put it better than 'you've got some growing up to do.'"

Mary came up a step. "Even I know Howard doesn't do subtle. To him, you're still in your twenties, which means you're a young'un. Just a smart-aleck kid."

"'Young'un'? Aren't you from Chicago? Besides, I like to think I'm becoming a wise man."

"No, the wise men don't show up until scene four tonight. But you do have a history of seeking stars, so there's hope for you yet."

Taking a deep breath, Mac held up the bag. "Merry Christmas," he said, his voice feeling foreign in his own throat. "It's not a bear, I promise." He realized, with an absurd relief, that she was as flustered as he was. He chose to believe that meant he stood a chance. "I'm coming tonight."

"Breaking with MacCarthy tradition?" Her smile broadened and she came up more steps.

Time to go for broke. "Because you asked me to." He saw her pull in a breath. She was two steps below him, her face even with him as he sat on the pair of steps above her. He thought if he stood up now, the way the oxygen seemed to be thinning right out of the room, he'd fall clean down the stairs in a stunned heap of nerves. He placed the bag in her hands. "I need you to have this."

She blushed, then pulled at the tissue paper until it revealed the spun glass star with silver and gold strands spiraling around each other in the glass. It was an exquisite, exorbitant piece of artwork, a stunning sculpture, and he'd have gladly paid three times what Emily charged him just to put it in Mary's hands this morning.

They'd shared that first moment of secrets in the steeple beside the broken star. She'd forgiven him under the big star in the sanctuary. He wanted to—*had* to be the one to give her a star for her tree today, Christmas Eve.

"Oh, Mac, it's beautiful." She ran her hand across the delicate angles and Mac felt it down the back of his neck. "You didn't have to…."

"Yes," he interrupted, "I did. I… I need to know we can get past all this. I need to know I haven't thrown away what…" the rest of the words tangled up in his throat.

"You want to help me get this on top of the tree?"

Her voice was warm and soft and charmingly nervous. He hadn't lost his chance with her. The realization sent relief pouring through him.

"More than anything." That sounded dorky, but he was past caring.

She let him into her apartment, the morning sun streaming through the big front windows. It was a blue-skied Kentucky winter's day, and her bedecked tree shimmered in the splashes of sunlight. It was a huge tree—probably twice the size she'd have chosen for herself—and he'd nearly thrown his back out getting that behemoth up her stairs and through her front door. Still, he was glad to notice there was still a foot or two between the top of the tree and her apartment's high ceilings. "You'll need a chair to get up there," he remarked, walking into the kitchen. He carried a kitchen chair into the living room and planted it next to the tree while she put down the bag and slipped the final tags off the star.

"I wasn't sure there'd be room," she joked as she brought the star over to the tree.

Mac held out his hand to help her up onto the chair. It felt small and perfect in his palm, and he was sure she sucked her breath in the way he did when they touched. With one hand holding hers and the other gripping the chair to keep her safe, he helped her step up. Then, to his reluctant joy, he found it necessary to hold her waist while she used both hands to settle the star on top of the tree. So much for his original intentions to keep a restrained distance from her.

"Oops…wait a minute…there, I got it. Yep, it just fits." She made a delightful sighing sound. "Oh, Mac, it's perfect."

She turned in the chair so that Mac was holding her waist as she stood above him, and it struck him again how absolutely beautiful she was. She placed her hands on his shoulders, and any shreds of control he had left evaporated into the sunlight that gilt her hair. He hoisted her down from the chair and stood dumbstruck by the color of her eyes. "I'm so glad," he said in a wobbly voice that didn't even seem to belong to him.

After a moment—or maybe it was an hour, he couldn't be sure—she lay her fingers against his jaw. Her face bore a pleased but puzzled expression, as if she was trying to work out a very happy riddle.

"How'd we get here?"

Even though it was a vague question, he knew exactly what she meant. He'd asked it of himself—of God—repeatedly over the last day. How had they managed this rocky path to the brink of such an implausible relationship? "I reckon that's one of the things God does best," he said, settling his hands around her, astounded by how perfectly she fit in his arms. "He knows what we need better than we do, and just how to get us to sit up and take notice. I'm pretty sure I'd have never figured this out on my own."

She let her full hand settle against his jaw. "It's harder than I thought. But it's better than I thought, too."

"Ain't it?" Mac couldn't stand it anymore. He leaned down and kissed her. Carefully, tenderly at first, until she brought both arms up to circle his neck and shot his restraint to pieces. They kissed with surprise and wonder and freedom until Mac pulled away, nearly gasping from the power of it. "*That* was better than I thought. And I thought about that way too much."

Mary laughed and settled herself into the perfect spot under his chin. Mac let his head touch her hair and decided the world had achieved perfection. Middleburg's first-ever Christmas Eve Drama and Potluck could implode to ashes and he'd still call this the Best Christmas Ever.

"Dave was right," Mary said as she twisted her head up to meet his gaze.

"Pastor Dave? How so?"

"He said that even when it looks awful, you can count on God's plan because His end is always better than anything we could dream up for ourselves."

"Yep," Mac agreed, kissing the top of her forehead just because it felt so wonderful to do so. "I think Dave's right on the money." He kissed another perfect spot, this one above her right eye. "Merry Christmas, Mary Thorpe."

"Merry Christmas…hey, your first name's Joe, isn't it?"

Mac applied a teasingly sour face. "We try not to mention that around these parts."

She snuggled against him with a sigh he felt to the soles of his feet. "Mary and Joseph. It's just too funny."

"No it's not. It's absurd."

"This from the man with the operatic cockatoo."

Mac let out a breath. He'd forgotten all about that. "Yeah, about Curly…"

"Oh, no," Mary said, "I really like him, I was just kidding you."

Mac pulled away. "No, I mean there's something about Curly." In the intensity of the morning, Mac hadn't yet had the chance to bring up his current dilemma. "I learned something about Curly while I was gone last night."

"What?"

Mac picked up the chair and returned it to the kitchen table. "It seems my feathered friend doesn't care for your little blue buddies. I left my nephew's Bippo Bear out on the dining room table while we were at rehearsal last night so I could wrap it this morning, and well, Curly had at it." He threw his hands up in the air. "That mangy bird shredded it. I came home to a very expensive fuzzy blue blizzard."

Mary gasped, wide-eyed. "Curly ate your Bippo Bear?"

"Not exactly. He just demolished it. I found one ear on top of my refrigerator and an eye in my bathtub. The only way I can give Robby his Bippo Bear now is in a plastic bag. I'm done for."

"Good thing you know someone on the inside," she smiled. Now it was her turn to pretend at annoyance. "I happen to have a spare Bippo Bear or two in my own personal collection. I've kept them hidden in the bottom of my closet. But it'll cost you something fierce."

"You have no idea how much I was hoping you'd say that. Name your price. I'm prepared to pay anything."

Those creamy arms wrapped around his neck again,

and Mac thought there wasn't a single thing she couldn't ask of him. "A potluck dish, one perfect performance and maybe a few more of those kisses."

Mac leaned in, delighted to oblige. "Wow. Best bargain ever."

Chapter Eighteen

It was after midnight, and very few people showed any signs of wanting to leave the MCC basement where the Christmas Eve potluck was still going in full swing. As a matter of fact, cries of "Merry Christmas" rung out at midnight, and only those with young children had gone home. Everyone else stayed eating and chatting and singing every verse of every Christmas carol until voices were hoarse. The whole evening had the happy charm of an old Bing Crosby movie, and Mary soaked in every minute of it as if life had started all over again this morning. Then again, perhaps it had. Was everyone's first Christmas as a new believer like this? Or had she been given some special gift?

Pastor Dave came up and gave her a big hug. "Howard asked me this morning if I regretted hiring you. I told him 'not one bit' then, and I feel doubly glad now. Well done, Mary. Well done."

"Thanks," she responded and hugged him right back. "For everything."

"You know," Pastor Dave said as he saw Howard making his way across the room toward Mary, "I think you succeeded on all fronts. We may have taken the long road to unity, but I have a feeling we got there all the same. Course there's really only one man who can tell you if that's true...." The pastor stepped back to allow Howard his say. He didn't look as cheery as some of the other guests, but he didn't look ready to run her out of town, either.

"I'm not known for keeping my opinions to myself, Miss Thorpe," he began. "And I still wish you'd have been upfront about your résumé."

"I think I agree with you, Howard, for what it's worth. It was a mistake not to bring it up."

"Speaking of mistakes, you'll be surprised to know I don't mind them much." He tucked his hands in his pockets and rocked back on his heels. "Mistakes are life's best teachers, if you ask me. It's folks who don't own up to their mistakes that get under my skin. But I reckon you already knew that."

It wasn't hard to know what got under Howard's skin. He made no efforts to hide it, ever. "I figured it out pretty quick."

"So I'm going to own up to mine and say you did a good job here. This potluck thing was a good idea, and I was wrong about it at first."

He was going out of his way to say she'd done well, and that made her feel good. "Thanks for the vote of confidence, Howard. It means a lot."

"Ah, yes, votes," Howard said with an odd tone of voice. "Tricky things."

"Mac pulling out of the race pretty much hands you another term as mayor, doesn't it?"

"It does." His comment was carefully neutral, but not all together comfortable. "Unfortunate business, all of it. I actually think MacCarthy has promise." He smiled and offered her a cookie from the table they were standing near—one of Dinah's gingerbread menagerie. "He was running for *half* the right reasons." He raised a suspicious eyebrow at Dinah's gingerbread hippopotamus before taking a healthy bite. "Besides," he went on, "that fellow had better find a longer fuse to his temper if he's going to last ten minutes in my shoes."

Mary stared across the room where Mac was having a warm conversation with his parents. It had been a tough evening—not everyone was ready to give Mac a second chance, or quick to forgive him for his youthful faults. The room still contained its fair share of cold shoulders, despite the holiday glow. "Mac says he's still sure God wanted him to run, but now it wasn't to be mayor, it was to learn a lesson."

"And do you think he has?" Howard asked, following her stare and giving out a sigh. "Learned the lesson, that is?"

"I do." She gave Howard a grin. "He may actually be less trouble to you now." She pointed at the last bit of yuletide hippo as Howard popped it into his mouth. "Maybe we should talk Dinah into running for mayor. *She* still loves to give you the business."

"Young lady, that is an absolutely hideous idea. Keep it to yourself." His speech was dark and formal, but his eyes twinkled. "Merry Christmas, Mary."

"Merry Christmas, Howard."

Epilogue

Mary was staring into the roaring fire at the Mac-Carthy house when Mac caught her by the elbow from behind. "Come here, quick," he whispered. "You need to see this."

Mac's parents' house was brimming with MacCarthys of all shapes and sizes, from infants to grandparents. From the moment they'd arrived, the house was bursting with enough noise and chaos that Mary could understand Mac's need for peace and quiet before weathering this familial storm.

"What?" she asked, only to be "shushed" by Mac as he led her through the house down to what Mrs. MacCarthy called "the rumpus room," which was basically a finished den currently overrun with grandchildren.

Grandchildren who were singing.

As Mac and Mary hid at the top of the stairs, Mary saw a gaggle of children gathered around Mac's nephew, many of them reaching out to touch the Bippo Bear she'd supplied. Uncle Mac had indeed "come through" with the gotta-have Bippo Bear by raiding Mary's private stash. As such, Robby was the envy of his peers.

As they stroked and pawed and fussed with the bear, tiny voices broke out repeatedly in the jingle. *Her* jingle. Only it wasn't that whining, pleading version the news stories ran or the sugary, chirpy version on the commercial. It was sweet children's voices singing out of sheer Christmas happiness. She'd never heard anything like it in her life. Mary felt like her heart had, as Dr. Seuss so aptly put it, "grown three sizes that day."

"Wow."

"Yeah," said Mac softly into her ear. "I thought you needed to see this. You did this."

She looked back at him, affection for him flooding her triple-sized heart. "I did, didn't I?" She listened for another wondrous moment. "I've never heard kids singing it before. I mean really singing it, not whining it."

Mac looked at her. "You weren't there when they had the kids singing it for the commercial?"

She laughed. "Oh, Mac, kids don't sing on commercials. We hire actors who can sound like kids." She remembered the days when things like that sounded perfectly normal to her.

Mac's expression told her it sounded ridiculous to him. "You gotta be kidding me."

"No," she said, allowing herself the delightful luxury of setting into this arms as they slipped around her waist. "It's true."

"I'll never trust another television commercial as long as I live," he teased into the back of her neck, making tingles run down her spine. "Now I know the ugly truth about you ad people."

"We're not all bad. Just some. Same as people who do anything for a living. Like engineers. Or mayors."

"Or former mayoral candidates/engineers?"

"No," Mary objected. "Those are looking pretty good right now." She reached up and let one hand wander through his sandy hair. His eyes fell shut and his head swayed involuntarily toward her touch.

"When are we going to let people know?" Mac asked.

"When I'm ready, and not a moment before. Got that?" Mary gave him as serious a look as she could manage under the circumstances. There would be no more breaches of confidence between them. She was strong enough to demand that now. She also was pretty sure she wouldn't be able to hold it in for long. "Like when you're thirty."

Mac rolled his eyes and groaned. "I'll never last five days." The playfulness left his eyes, replaced by a promise that he'd never betray her again. "But I'll find a way." Mac's voice was low and alluring. "How about five *minutes?* I'm an impatient guy."

She laughed softly, enjoying the sway she held over him. And that it didn't feel anything like manipulation. It felt more like a gift from God. "Maybe four. You know us advertising types. We're always open to negotiation." She leaned in and gave him a gentle kiss in the shadowed privacy of the den stairway, serenaded by the Bippo Bear song, which had just become her favorite piece of music, ever.

* * * * *

Get 4 FREE REWARDS!

We'll send you 2 FREE Books plus 2 FREE Mystery Gifts.

FREE Value Over **$20**

Both the **Love Inspired®** and **Love Inspired® Suspense** series feature compelling novels filled with inspirational romance, faith, forgiveness and hope.

HARLEQUIN
PLUS

Announcing a **BRAND-NEW** multimedia subscription service for romance fans like you!

Read, Watch and Play.

Experience the easiest way to get the romance content you crave.

Start your **FREE 7 DAY TRIAL** at
<u>www.harlequinplus.com/freetrial</u>.